ALL'S WELL

ALL'S WELL

MONA AWAD

THORNDIKE PRESS
A part of Gale, a Cengage Company

GALE
A Cengage Company

Thorndike Press® Large Print Core.
The text of this Large Print edition is unabridged.
Other aspects of the book may vary from the original edition.
Set in 16 pt. Plantin.

LIBRARY OF CONGRESS CIP DATA ON FILE.
CATALOGUING IN PUBLICATION FOR THIS BOOK
IS AVAILABLE FROM THE LIBRARY OF CONGRESS.

ISBN-13: 978-1-4328-9224-1 (hardcover alk. paper)

Published in 2021 by arrangement with Simon & Schuster, Inc.

Printed in Mexico
Print Number: 01   Print Year: 2022

For Ken

■ ■ ■ ■

PART ONE

■ ■ ■ ■

CHAPTER 1

I'm lying on the floor watching, against my will, a bad actress in a drug commercial tell me about her fake pain.

"Just because my pain is invisible," she pleads to the camera, "doesn't mean it isn't real." And then she attempts a face of what I presume to be her invisible suffering. Her brow furrows as though she's about to take a difficult shit or else have a furious but forgettable orgasm. Her mouth is a thin grimace. Her dim eyes attempt to accuse something vague in the distance, a god perhaps. Her bloodless complexion is convincing, though they probably achieved this with makeup and lighting. You can do a lot with makeup and lighting, I have learned.

Now I watch her rub her shoulder where this invisible pain supposedly lives. Her face says that clearly her rubbing has done nothing. Her pain is still there, of course, deep, deep inside her. And then I am shown how

9

deep, I am shown her supposed insides. A see-through human body appears on my laptop screen showcasing a central nervous system that looks like a network of angry red webs. The webs blink on and off like Christmas lights because the nerves are overactive, apparently. This is why she suffers so. Now the camera cuts back to the woman. Gray-faced. Hunched in the front yard of her suburban home. Her blond children clamber around her like little jumping demons.

They are oblivious to her suffering, to the red webs inside of her. She looks imploringly at the camera, at me really, for this is a targeted ad based on all of my web searches, based on my keywords, the ones I typed into Google in the days when I was still diagnosing myself. She looks withered but desperate, pleading. She wants something from me. She is asking me to believe her about her pain.

I don't, of course.

I lie here on my back on the roughly carpeted floor with my legs in the air at a right angle from my body. My calves rest on my office chair seat, feet dangling over the edge. One hand on my heart, the other on my diaphragm. Cigarette in my mouth. Snow blows onto my face from an open window above me that I'm unable to close. Lying like this will supposedly help decompress my spine and let the muscles in my right leg unclench. Help the fist behind my knee to go slack so that when I stand up I'll be able to straighten my leg and not hobble around like Richard III. This is a position that, according to Mark, I can supposedly go into for relief, self-care, *a time-out from life.* I think of Mark. Mark of the dry needles, Mark of the scraping silver tools, his handsome bro face a wall of certainty framed by a crew cut. Ever nodding at my various complaints as though they are all part of a grand upward journey that we are taking together, Mark and I.

I lie like this, and I do not feel relief. Left hip down to the knee still on vague fire. A fist in my mid-back that won't unclench. Right leg is concrete all the way to my foot, which, even though it's in the air, is still screaming as if crushed by some terrible weight. I picture the leg of a chair pressing onto my foot. A chair being sat on by a very fat man. The fat man is a sadist. He is smiling at me. His smile says, *I shall sit here forever. Here with you on the third floor of this dubious college where you are dubiously employed. Theater Studies, aka one of two*

sad concrete rooms in the English depart-
ment. Your "office," I presume? Rather shabby.
Downstairs, in the sorry excuse for a
theater, they're waiting for me.
Where is Ms. Fitch already?
She should be here by now, shouldn't she?
Rehearsals begin, well, now.
Maybe she's sick or something.
Maybe she's drunk or on drugs or some-
thing.
Maybe she went insane.
I picture them, my students, sitting on the
stage. Swinging long, pliant legs over the
edge. Young faces glowing with health as
though they were spawned by the sun itself.
Waiting for my misshapen body to hobble
through the double doors. Quietly cursing
my name as we speak. About to declare
mutiny, any minute now. But not so long as
I lie here, staring at this drug-commercial
woman's believe-me-about-my-pain face. A
face I myself have made before a number of
people. Men in white lab coats with fat,
dead-eyed nurses hovering silently behind
them. Men in blue polo shirts who are ever
ready to play me the cartoon again about
pain being in the brain. Men in blue scrubs
who have injected shots into my spine and
who have access to Valium. Bambi-ish medical assistants who have diligently taken my

case history with ballpoint pens but then eventually dropped their pens as I kept talking and talking, their big eyes going blank as they got lost in the dark woods of my story.

"For a long time, I had no hope," the woman in the drug commercial says now. "But then my doctor prescribed me Eradica."

And then on the screen, there appears a cylindrical pill backlit by a wondrous white light. The pill is half the yellow of fast-food America, half the institutional blue of a physical therapist's polo shirt. *I believe it would help you,* my physiatrist once said of this very drug, his student/scribe typing our conversation into a laptop in a corner, looking up at me now and then with fear. I was standing up because I couldn't physically sit at the time, hovering over both of them like a wind-warped tree. I still have a sample pack of the drug somewhere in my underwear drawer amid the thongs and lacy tights I don't wear anymore because I am dead on the inside.

Now I attempt to hit the play button in the bottom left corner of the YouTube screen, to skip past this hideous ad to the video I actually want to watch. Act One, Scene One of *All's Well That Ends Well,* the

13

play we are staging this term. Helen's crucial soliloquy.

Nothing. Still the image of the blue-and-yellow pill suspended in midair, spinning. *Your video will play after ad,* it reads in a small box in the bottom corner of the screen. No choice. No choice then but to lie here and listen to how there is hope thanks to Eradica. The one pill I didn't try, because the side effects scared me more than the pain. No choice but to watch the bad actress bicycle in the idyllic afternoon of the drug commercial with a blandly handsome man who I presume is her fake husband. He is dressed in a reassuring plaid. He reminds me of the male torso on the Brawny paper towels I buy out of wilted lust. Also of my ex-husband, Paul. Except that this man is smiling at his fake wife. Not shaking his head. Not saying, *Miranda, I'm at a loss.*

Knock, knock at my door. "Miranda?"

I take a drag of my cigarette. Date night now, apparently, in the drug commercial. The actress and fake hubby are having dinner at a candlelit restaurant. Oysters on the half shell to celebrate her return from the land of the dead. Toasting her new wellness with flutes of champagne, even though alcohol is absolutely forbidden on this drug.

14

He gets up from the table, holds out his hand, appearing to ask her to dance. She is overcome with emotion. Tears glint in her eyes as she accepts. And then this woman is dancing, actually dancing with her husband at some sort of discotheque that only exists in the world of the drug commercial. We don't hear the sound of the music at the discotheque. The viewer (me) is invited to insert their own music while "some blood cancers" and "kidney failure" are enumerated as side effects by an invisible, white-washed voice that is godly, lulling, beyond good and evil, stripped of any moral compunction, that simply is.

"Miranda, are you there? Time for rehearsal."

Watching the actress's merriment in the discotheque is embarrassing for me. As a drama teacher, as a director. And yet, watching her rock around with her fake husband, wearing her fake smile, her fake pain supposedly gone now, I ask myself, *When was the last time you danced?*

Knock, knock. "Miranda, we really should get going downstairs."

A pause, a huff. And then I hear the footsteps fall mercifully away.

Now it is evening in the world of the drug commercial. Another evening, not date

15

night. Sunday evening, it looks like, a family day. The bad actress is sitting in a nylon tent with the fake children she has somehow been able to bear despite her maligned nervous system, her cobwebby womb. Hubby is there too with his Brawny torso and his Colgate grin. He was always there, his smile says. Waiting for her to come back to life. Waiting for her to resume a more human shape. What a hero of a man, the drug commercial seems to suggest with lighting. And their offspring scamper around them wearing pajamas patterned with little monsters, and there are Christmas lights strung all across the ceiling of the tent like an early-modern idea of heaven. She smiles wanly at the children, at the lights. Her skin is no longer gray and crepey. It is dewy and almost human-colored. Her brow is unfurrowed. She is no longer trying to take a shit, she took it. She wears eye shadow now. There's a rose gloss on her lips, a glowing peach on her cheeks (bronzer?) that seems to come from the inside. Even her fashion sense has mildly improved. She cares about what she wears now. For she is supposedly pain-free. *LESS PAIN* is actually written in glowing white script beside her face.

But I don't believe it. It's a lie. And I say it to the screen, I say, *Liar.* And yet I cry a little. Even though I do not believe her joy any more than I believed her pain. A thin, ridiculous tear spills from my eyelid corner down to my ear, where it pools hotly. The wanly smiling woman, the bad actress, has moved me in spite of myself. The fires on the left side of my lower body rage quietly on. The fist in my mid-back clenches. The fat man settles into the chair that crushes my foot. He picks up a newspaper. Checks his stock.

But at least my video, the one I've been waiting for — where Helen gives her soliloquy, the one where she says yes, the cosmos appears fixed but she can reverse it — is about to play.

And then just like that, my laptop screen freezes, goes black. Dead. A battery icon appears and then fades.

I picture the power cord, coiled in the black satchel sitting on top of my desk, the cord gray and worn like the snipped hair of a Fury. I contemplate the socket in the wall that is absurdly low to the floor, behind my desk. I picture getting up and hunting for the power cord, then bending down and plugging it into the socket.

I lie there. I stare at the dead laptop screen smudged by my own fingerprints.

Snow from the open window I cannot

close because I cannot bend keeps falling on my face. I let it fall. I close my eyes. I smoke. I've learned to smoke with my eyes closed, that's something.

I feel the wind on my face. I think: *I'm dying. Death at thirty-seven.*

The fat man on the chair whose leg is crushing my foot raises his glass to me. Drinking sherry, it looks like. *Cheers,* says his face. He is pleased. He settles deeper in. Returns to his newspaper.

I shake my head in protest. *No,* I whisper to the fat man, to the back of my eyelids. *I want my life back. I want my life back.*

"Miranda, hello? Miranda?"

A soft knock on the half-open door. And then that voice again from which I instantly recoil. The fires rise, the fists clench, the fat man looks up from his newspaper. I can hear the new age chimes in that voice twinkling. It is the voice of false comfort, affected concern, deep strategy, it is a voice I often hear in my nightmares. It is the voice of Fauve. Self-appointed musical director. Adjunct. Mine enemy.

"Miranda?" says the voice.

I don't answer.

I feel her consider this. Perhaps she can see my feet poking out from behind the desk.

18

"Miranda, is that you?" she tries again.

I remain silent. So I am hiding. So what?

At last I hear her retreat. Soft footsteps pattering down the hall, away from my door. I breathe a sigh of relief.

Then another voice follows. Decisive. Brisk. But there is love in there somewhere, or so I tell myself.

"Miranda?"

"Yes?"

Grace. My colleague. My assistant director. My . . . I hesitate to say *friend* these days. Both of us the only faculty left in the once flourishing, now decrepit Theater Studies program. Both of us forced to be the bitches of the English department. All of our courses cross-listed. Offering only a minor now. Grace and I share this pain; except, of course, Grace has tenure. As an assistant professor, four years into the job, I am more precariously employed.

"Where are you?" she asks me now.

"Just here," I say.

I feel her suddenly see me. Firm footsteps approaching. Timberlands, even though we are nowhere near mountains. She's wearing a hunting vest too, I'm certain. Camouflage, possibly flotational. Grace is always dressed like she is about to shoot prey with a sharp eye and a clear conscience. Or else hike a long and perilously ascending trail. And on this journey, her foot will not stumble, though the terrain will be uneven, treacherous. She will whistle to herself. Her footfall will frighten all predators in the dark woods. Her footfall is the sure stride of health coming my way, and I feel my soul cower slightly at the sound. I keep my eyes closed. I will her away. Can I will her away?

No.

Her boot tips rest at my head, stopping just short of my temple. She could raise her boot and stomp on my face if she wanted to. Probably a small part of her does. Because that's what you do with the weak, and Grace comes from Puritan stock, a witch-burning ancestry. Women who never get colds. Women who carry on. Women with thick thighs who do not understand the snivelers, the wafflers, people who burn sage. I picture those women in my daymares, the great-great-great-grandmothers of Grace, standing on Plymouth Rock or else a loveless field, donning potato-sack dresses patterned with small faded flowers, holding pitchforks perhaps, their bark-colored hair tied in buns, loose tendrils blowing in an end-of-the-world wind, which they alone will survive.

Now I feel Grace's small bright eyes assess the situation as surely as I feel her glowing with actual health beside me, a health that is unbronzed, unblushed. Grace does not ask what I am doing lying here with snow on my face beside a dead laptop. This is not the first time she has encountered me in a strange configuration on the floor. Nor does she comment on the absolutely prohibited cigarette.

Instead she walks over to the window. Begins to close it.

"Unless you wanted it open?" she asks, but it isn't really a question.

"No," I say.

She closes it easily — I feel how easy, as I lie here, staring at the ceiling — and for a brief, brief moment, I hate her. I hate Grace. I long to slide into Grace's pockmarked skin and live there instead of here. How easy. How lovely. How lightly I would live.

She takes the dead cigarette from my fingers, the column of ash sprinkling over me like so much fairy dust, and tosses it into the garbage. She hops onto my desk. Pulls a cigarette from my pack and lights it. This is a bond, a small defiance Grace and I silently share, illicit smoking in the office, in the theater. Basically, wherever we can get away with it. I watch her booted foot swing to and fro over my face.

"Well, they're waiting for you, Miranda."

"Okay," I say. "Just trying to give my back a break before rehearsal. Just need a few minutes here."

Long pause. Should she ask or shouldn't she? Dare she open that can of worms?

"Are you all right?"

"Fine," I lie. "Just you know. The usual." I try to smile, to put an eye roll in my voice, but I fail miserably. I hate the crack in my tone, the whining simper. If I were Grace, I'd crush my own face.

"Right." She takes a sip from her water canister and looks down at me, lying on the floor, with my legs on the chair seat and my feet dangling in their holey tights, my bare, unclipped toenails there for her to examine.

"Well, whenever you're ready," she says.

"I'm ready," I say. But I don't move.

"All right. Well. I'll leave you to it, then." She's about to get up. Panic flutters in me, briefly.

"Grace?"

"Yes?"

"How are they tonight?"

"What do you mean?"

"Do they seem . . . how do they seem?"

"How do they seem?" she repeats.

"Well . . . are they . . . mutinous?"

22

Grace considers this. "Maybe. They're down there, at any rate."

"Miranda, do you want one of us to do the talking today? We can, you know. There is that option. You can give yourself . . . a break." This from Fauve, who has apparently been standing silently in the doorway all this time. I look over at Grace. *Why didn't you tell me she was there?* Grace merely looks down at me lying on the floor. I can't help but feel like a deer she has just shot. She's looking at me to see if I am a clean kill or if she needs to put one more bullet in me for good measure.

"Is it your hip?" she asks.

"Yes."

"Oh. I thought it was your back?" Fauve ventures. She is invisible to my eye, but I can feel her hovering in the doorway, the chimes and feathers of her. Clutching that silvery-blue notebook in which I imagine she records all my inconsistencies, my transgressions, with an ornamental pen that dangles from her pendant-choked neck. All false concern that is also taking literal note in shimmering ink. Sharing her findings with Grace.

She told me it was her back.
She told me it was her hip.

"It is," I tell them. "It's both."

23

Silence.

"I'll be right down, all right?" I say.

"Do you need help up?" Grace asks.

It's like she doesn't even ask for help.

It's like she's always asking for help.

Well, nothing helps Miranda.

"No. Thank you though."

"Well," Grace says, mashing her cigarette into my teacup, "I better get down there."

Fauve says nothing about Grace's cigarette. If she just found me in here smoking, as she often does, she'd cough and cough. Wave her hand violently in the air as though attempting to swat at a swarm of flies. Scribble scribble in her notebook. But Fauve just smiles at Grace through the smoke.

"I'll go with you," Fauve offers. "I have to photocopy something."

"Great."

What sort of a name is Fauve, *anyway?* I once asked Grace at a bar after rehearsal. *Sounds like an alias to me.* Grace looked at my nearly empty wineglass and said nothing.

They leave together. Hand in hand, I imagine. Surely Grace's ancestors would have burned Fauve's ancestors at the stake, wouldn't they? Pale women who cast wispy shadows. All feathered hair and cryptic

24

smiles. Reeking of duplicity and mugwort. How Fauve and Grace became friends is a true mystery to me. Not a mystery exactly, I know when it happened. It happened, I suspect, after my falling-out with Grace. Fauve insinuated herself then, of course she did. Stepped right in on her soundless sandals.

I am so glad when their footsteps fade away. The fires within actually quiet a little. The fat man might abandon his post to make tea.

I get up, and for a moment I fill with hideous hope. But no. The entire left side of my body is still ablaze. The right side is in painful spasm. All the muscles in my right leg still concrete. The fists in my back have multiplied. The fist behind my knee is so tight that I can't straighten my leg at all, can only limp. My foot is still being crushed by an invisible weight. I think of telling Mark this at our next session. But would he believe me through the wall of his certitude?

Our ultimate goal, Mark will say during a session, often while stabbing needles into my lower back and thigh, *is centralization. To move the awareness* (he means my pain) *from the distal places* (he means my leg) *and return it to its original source* (he means my back).

The distal places, I murmur. *Sounds poetic.*

Mark appears confused by this word, *poetic.*

You could think of it like that, I guess. He shrugs but looks suspicious. As though this way of thinking is part of my problem.

From the bottle marked *Take one as needed for pain,* I take two. From the bottle marked *Take one as needed for muscle stiffness,* I take three. I look down into the dusty bowels of the plastic orange pill jar, and I briefly consider taking all of them. Throwing the window back open. Falling to the floor. Lying there and letting the snow fall and fall on my face. Pressing my hand to my chest until the pounding of my heart slows and then stops. Joe, the custodian, possibly finding me in the morning. I'll be beautifully blue. He will grieve. Will he grieve? I picture him weeping into his broomstick. Didn't a fairy-tale heroine die this way?

I take a well-squeezed tube of gel that contains some dubious mountain herb that one of the polo-shirted, one of the lab-coated, one of the blue-scrubbed, said I might try, that is useless. *You could try it,* they all say with a shrug and a Cheshire cat grin. I rub it all over my back and thigh and I tell myself it does something. I can feel it doing something. Can't I?

Yes.

Surely it's doing something.

CHAPTER 2

When I get to the theater, they're already
sitting on the stage as they were in my day-
mare. Legs swinging over the edge. Faces
shining but unreadable. Mutinous? Maybe.
Hard to tell. Still, they're here. They each
appear to be holding a copy of *All's Well*
(my director's cut) — that's something.
They haven't torched them in a communal
burning. Yet. That's something too. Third
rehearsal. They have already formed vague
alliances in accordance with the social
hierarchy and are sitting in their respective
clumps. Not smiling. Not frowning. Waiting. Just staring with their young eyes that
think they see. Briana sits in the center, my
soulless leading actress, my Helen, who
doesn't deserve at all to play Helen. Beside
her is Trevor, her boyfriend, who is playing
Bertram. And of course there's Ellie in the
corner. My gray-fleshed, gray-eyed favorite.
My dark mouse of a soul. Last year she

played the nurse in *Romeo and Juliet*. This year, she plays the ailing King, though she would be the perfect Helen. The rest of the students to me are a sea, a dull and untalented sea, and have been cast accordingly. They stare at me, their glazed eyes registering my decrepitude, their open mouths yawning in my face.

My leg stiffens. I smile. "Hello, all," I say.

They murmur hello back. Their smallness, their radiant faces, their youth, usually move me a little. So adorable, really. Today though, I only feel fear.

Have you ever directed a play before? the dean asked in the interview.

Oh, yes, I lied, nodding. *Shakespeare. Brecht. Chekhov. Beckett, obviously. Lots of Beckett.*

They look at me now. Waiting, I realize, for me to speak. Because there are things I say, apparently, aren't there things I say? That light them up? That sway them? I have forgotten these things that I say. Tonight even more is required, I can tell. A stirring up of morale. They've read the play a few times now, the play I have chosen over the play they wanted. And there are hurt feelings. There is incomprehension. *Ms. Fitch, we don't understand. Why? Why are you making us do this play?*

I feel cold sweat down my back, and my right leg seizes up even more. I become terribly aware of my limp, my hunched hobble. I lean against the table. I try to smile more warmly. I'm their friend, yes? Remember? I imagine the student evaluation: *It's clear that Ms. Fitch is trying her best, but she's really disorganized and loses control of group discussion a lot. I feel we would get more out of the experience if she were more like a real director.*

"And how is everyone?" I ask. Trying for a soft voice, for brightness. This fails. I am met with only dead-eyed faces. So I switch gears. I try for a certain mysteriousness. I make a fog machine of my expression, a hard line of my mouth. But I'm a bad actress these days. Even they can see that. I don't convince.

"Good," they murmur. Or else they say nothing. Or else they just blink. Briana, my lead, doesn't even blink. Briana keeps her leaf-green eyes wide open. They stare with wondrous bitchiness at my entire body. She looks at my teal tea dress, its sad pattern of orange flowers, which is the dress I'm just realizing I also wore to class and to rehearsal last week. Ditto the oversize, worn black cardigan with its gaping-open pockets rattling with pills.

She is judging me, her eyes say this.
Don't judge me, you little bitch.
"What was that, Miranda?" Grace says.
"What?"
"You mumbled something."
"No. No, I didn't."
Silence from Grace. Silence from the students.

Not only is Ms. Fitch late for rehearsals these days but she is also insane.

Ms. Fitch talks to herself. I totally heard her.

"Well," I say to them. My tone is so pleasant. My tone is daisies swaying in a field, the field of the drug commercial. "Why don't we just dive in, yes? Act One, Scene One? Helen's soliloquy?"

They don't move.

"Shall we begin? Please?"

Nothing. I'm actually pleading with them, has it really come to this? I have no vision; that's clear. They still hate this play; that's obvious. All of them are staring at me now, all limply holding the scripts in their half-open hands like they could let go at any time.

I recall the disastrous table reading, held a month ago on this very stage. The questions, no, the accusations.

All's Well That Ends Well, *Ms. Fitch? I mean, is it even a Shakespeare play?*

31

Why are we doing this play, Ms. Fitch?

Weren't we supposed to do the Scottish Play this year?

I don't get this play, Ms. Fitch. I mean, a girl is so into this guy who doesn't even want her? It's kind of lame, honestly.

Also, Ms. Fitch, weren't we supposed to do the Scottish Play this year?

Yes, Ms. Fitch, my understanding was that we were doing the Scottish Play this year.

And I failed to win them over to it with my Valium-laced vision, which I delivered with my voice faltering. They did not nod. They did not smile. They did not blink. They exchanged contemptuous glances, and they did not care if I saw this or not. If I hadn't stumbled so much through my director's speech perhaps they would all be on board. Long pauses there were, during my speech, where I admit I just zoned out completely. Every now and then Grace would cough, clear her throat, call my name. *Miranda? Miranda. Miranda!*

What?

You were saying?

Oh, yes. I was saying . . . . what was I saying? And I actually asked them.

They stared at me then as they are staring at me now.

Look, it's not like any of these kids are

going to go on to be professional actors. We have no real legitimate theater department anymore, just a burgeoning minor thanks to me and Grace. The annual Shakespeare production is purely extracurricular. A club, basically. I have no real credentials to be directing them. Not really. I'm faking it mostly. I want to tell them this now. *I'm faking it and you're faking it and we're all fucked, basically.* And yet. And yet look how far we have come. Two regional Shakespeare competitions. In which we placed ninth both times.

A cough. I turn to see a tall man in paint-splattered jeans and a Black Sabbath T-shirt standing in the side entrance of the theater. Long golden hair in his face. Smiling apologetically. My set designer and builder, Hugo. At the sight of him, my chest tightens, catches useless fire. Oh god, what is he doing here? He can't see me like this, he — but Hugo's not looking at me, never looking at me. He's looking past me at the planks of wood stacked against the back wall of the stage.

"Sorry to disturb," he says to the students. He points to the wood. "I'll be gone in a flash."

"Of course," I say, and I actually run a hand through my hair like a fool. But

Hugo's already headed upstage. I catch a scent of wood as he passes me and almost close my eyes.

"We were just getting started," I say to the students. "Weren't we?"

They still just stare at me. Briana smirks now.

"Ms. Fitch?" Trevor says at last, raising his hand as though we are in class. Trevor. Long, layered brown hair. Terribly tall. Not quite in control of his body or his charms. Before he opens his mouth, you think Byron. You think George Emerson in *A Room with a View* climbing a tree and screaming about beauty and truth. But Trevor will deeply disappoint you. Last year he played a lukewarm Romeo who touched his sword too much. Trevor has his moments though, mainly because of his hair. Trevor's hair is very expressive.

"Yes?"

"I had a question about the play."

Oh god no. "Yes?"

"Well. I was reading through it again." He flips the pages around as if to demonstrate to me the act of reading. "And I'm not really connecting with it?"

Not a question. I close my eyes. Smile at the black space.

"What is it that you're not connecting

with exactly?"

"Honestly? Just the whole thing?"

Inner red webs blinking more quickly. Concrete leg crumbling. I open my eyes. I stare at Trevor in all his handsome, breath-taking idiocy.

"Can you be more specific?"

"Well, like the premise?" Trevor says. "And the story line? And the characters seem, I don't know. I can't relate to them at all?"

I gaze at his hands in their fingerless gloves, mildly clenched at his sides. His poetic hair that too often compensates for his lack of a soul. Beautifully, ludicrously tanned in January. Cowrie-shell necklace around his young throat. Though he has no real innate charisma, he's tall enough that if he declares mutiny, they will all follow.

"I see. Well, Trevor —"

"Like that main woman?" Trevor continues.

"Helen."

"Right. Yeah, *her* I really don't get."

"What don't you *get*?" Careful, Miranda. Careful.

"I don't know." He shrugs. "She's just not a very compelling heroine to me. She's just . . . sort of pathetic, isn't she?"

He gazes right at me now. How I'm leaning wildly to the left because all the concrete on the right has crumbled. Beside him, Briana appears neutral, merely interested in this confrontation, not at all complicit. Not at all the stirrer of the pot. Just an innocent spectator of the show.

I look over at Hugo, who's still busying himself with the planks of wood. Not looking over, not paying attention at all. For once, I'm grateful.

I try to smile at them. I try not to accuse them, even with my face. I try not to say, *You don't fucking understand anything.* My face says, *I'm indulging your candid youth, the brute stupidity that you are trying to pass off as charm.* I play the romantic soul, the misty-eyed art teacher.

"She's in *love,* Trevor. Aren't we all a little *pathetic* when we're in love? Have we not *all* been there before? Aren't some of us there now?" *Like you? Who is so obviously Briana's puppet?*

Trevor looks at me like he doesn't compute my words. He shrugs again.

"Honestly? I don't get that guy she loves either."

"By 'that guy' you mean *Bertram.* You mean *your* character."

"I mean I *get* why he doesn't like her back," he continues. "Because she's lame, obviously. But he's an asshole about it. And

36

then he suddenly likes her in the end? In one line at the end?"

He shakes his princely head as if this were impossible. As if such impossibility wasn't the whole point. Wasn't the magic of the play itself.

You're a fool, I think.

"Sorry?"

"I said that will be your great challenge, won't it, Trevor? As an actor," I lie. I almost laugh out loud when I say *as an actor.* Trevor an actor. The idea is suddenly hysterical to me. Yet I remain straight-faced. Perhaps I'm not as bad an actor as I thought.

"I think you're absolutely ready for it," I tell him.

"I guess I just still don't get the whole thing," Trevor insists.

Beside him, Briana now openly beams. Perhaps she'll give him a hand job later, in his Saab, as a reward.

"Well, it's January. Plenty of time for you to *get it.* In fact, that will be the work of rehearsal. We will *all* be discovering the play in rehearsal, including me," I say. "Now —"

"Actually, Ms. Fitch —" Trevor interjects.

"What?" I say, but I'm still smiling. Or trying to. Am I smiling? The pills make it hard

37

to feel my face. I'm gripping the back of the chair.

"Well, I was wondering . . ." He looks over at Briana, who continues to stare at my body, eyes sweeping up and down, observing my hands clenched on the chair. "We were all wondering, actually, if it wouldn't be too late to change?"

Dumb. Play dumb. "Change?"

"Well, we all talked about doing the Scottish Play this year. Instead. I don't know if you remember?"

Hugo's turned to look at me. He's actually looking right at me for once. With pity, I see. I feel my face catch fire now. I can feel my face after all, it seems. I look around at the other students. All turned toward Trevor as though he were some sort of god, even the boys.

Shut it down. Shut it down now.

"I remember we had a discussion," I say. "I remember we *conversed*. And then I remember I determined" — I put the emphasis on *determined,* leaving the phrase *as director* implied but unsaid — "based on a *number* of factors, that we would be doing *All's Well* this year, an equally wonderful but far more compelling play."

I look over at Grace now for support. She's looking at me like, *Really? "Far more* compelling"? *Come on, Miranda.*

"This is a problem play," I continue. "Neither a tragedy nor a comedy, something in between. Something far more interesting."

I attempt to smile at them, but no one, not Hugo, not even Ellie, will meet my eye. I look back over at Grace, seated in the audience, staring at her laptop, her non-expression glowing by the light of the screen.

I thought you said no mutiny! I try to hiss with my face.

But Grace just looks at her laptop with still greater concentration. Pretending to assess the schedule, perhaps, but I know she's just shopping for camping gear. Or perhaps cage accessories for her bearded dragon. I believe Grace is having some sort of affair with her bearded dragon. She has an absurdly intimate relationship with it. Named him Ernest from Oscar Wilde's *The Importance of Being Earnest*. It makes me deeply uncomfortable to watch them in close proximity to each other, which they have been each time I've gone over to her apartment. She'll take Ernest out of his terrarium at night and let him climb her shoulder. Let his tongue dart in and out just by her cheek. She'll very nearly close her eyes. Tilt her head back. It's upsetting to watch. It's —

"Professor Fitch?"

This from Ellie. Her moon face beautifully miserable, her long hair a nondescript dark that is neither brown nor black. That reminds me of the sky in Scotland on November afternoons, when the light that has just receded is all the the light there will be for the day. And yet Ellie is my light.

"Yes, Ellie? What can I do for you?"

Probably Ellie is a virgin, poor thing. The product of an absent father and some suffocating mother whom she has quietly contemplated murdering. She loves Trevor, of course. Even as she hates him and hates herself for it. When he speaks, it's the only time I've ever seen her gray flesh go pink at the cheeks.

"Are we competing in the Shakespeare competition this year?"

"Yes, Ellie. Absolutely."

I can already picture the inebriated rich people clapping. The smell of the well-manicured gardens in Rhode Island making me drunk and vaguely horny. The afternoon light on my face. The sight of all those young bodies moving so easily in the June sunshine. Making me ache for some kind of life other than this. The judges smiling flatly at Briana's impassioned attempts to have a soul. Trevor's handsome face fiercely scrunched in the throes of his shallow performance. Ellie's quiet molten core revealing itself unevenly, only in unexpected moments. For a brief moment, she can take your breath away.

"Well, I think *All's Well* could be an interesting choice for that. Because no one else would be doing it."

My sweet Ellie. If I were to have a child, it would be Ellie. Of course, what with my irredeemably broken body, that ship has long sailed. Ellie has aspirations for the stage, which I've encouraged, I've fed. *Think big, Ellie,* I've told her many an afternoon in my office, the door closed. *One day you will leave all these plebeians behind. And it will be a wondrous moment for you. To no longer be among communications and English majors who do not appreciate your nuance, your dark grace.*

"But if we're *competing,* shouldn't we choose a more *substantial* play?" This from one of Briana's girl underlings. Some boring name I always forget. Like Ashley or Michelle.

"*All's Well* hardly ever gets staged because it's so *problematic,*" she adds. Clearly so pleased with her Wikipedia knowledge.

Briana, I note, still has yet to speak.

41

"Well, then it will be a challenge for us, won't it?" I say. "And I love a challenge. I'm certainly ready for it. Are you?" I'm gripping the back of my chair fiercely now lest I fall down.

Grace has now been joined by Fauve in the audience. Grace is still looking at her laptop, but Fauve just stares at me. Eyes wide. The picture of the innocent bystander. Expression inscrutable. But I can feel her willing me to fail. Her blue notebook sits open on her lap. Her ornamental pen, uncapped, poised in her painted talons. *Mon. 01/21, 5:55 p.m. Mutiny met with directorial pigheadedness. Evidence of drug abuse. Prevarication. Steamrolling.*

Hugo's gone, I see. Left without saying goodbye. Though why would he say goodbye? I feel my heart sink in spite of myself.

Now, at last, Briana raises her hand. Briana of the burnished hair. Briana of the B-minus mind who yet believes she deserves an A for breathing. Reading an essay of Briana's will make you fear for the future of America, will make you hiss *What the fuck are you talking about?* aloud at the bar where you have to go and get loaded on pinot grigio in order to grade Briana's paper, so that the bartender will say to you, *Miss, are you all right?* He will even put his hand on your

42

shoulder, he is that concerned. And you will say, *I'm fine, I'm so sorry.* And you will look up into his face, and his eyes will be so blue and kind. You will recall when such a face and torso stirred something deep inside you, in a place where there are now only dead leaves skittering. You will look back at Briana's paper. You will observe that she chose the Garamond font. You will proceed to write *B−* in the top left-hand corner even though it is a C tops. But you will hesitate, your pen suspended over the page. You will mentally fast-forward to the moment when you hand Briana her essay back, branded with this B−. She will receive it and immediately look as though she has been stung by a thousand wasps, and you will wish that she had brought this to her performance of Juliet. You will watch her face redden first with embarrassment, then with outrage, her chin tilt up, up, up in defiance. She will assume you have given her this grade because you are an idiot and/or jealous of her beauty and youth. You are not the former, but you are most certainly the latter, and so it is not without some fear, some guilt, that you will watch Briana march toward your desk after class, watch her flip her shining hair around in an attempt to blind you as she complains. Watch her eyes grow big and wet and desperate. Watch her outrage bloom like an out-of-control flower. For this is not the way of the universe, the universe of Briana in which you are merely a cog in the great machinery of her ultimate success. The universe wishes for Briana to succeed, to win. Hearing Briana protest like this, knowing your own inner failings, you might bow down to her will. You might hand over the A. Because you are so tired. Because Briana's voice not only hurts your hip and spinal cord, it also lights up your inner red webs, flashing more quickly under her gaze. You might spare yourself all of this and give her the damned A to start with. And Briana won't even thank you for this. She'll just feel like you were an unfortunate spider creeping around her dollhouse but you were kind enough to die on your own. After all, her parents are donors to this school's decrepit theater program, hence the fact that Briana is Helen this year, hence the fact that Briana was Juliet last year, hence the fact that Briana was Rosalind the year before. Hence the fact that you have heard the soliloquies of Shakespeare's most complex and formidable heroines die in her unworthy throat. And yet. She is also the reason you have the ghost of a program at all, and she knows this.

I hate that I want Briana to like me even though I hate Briana and I hate that I hate Briana because what is Briana's future going to be, really? A few years in the big city pursuing her acting passion to no end because there will be no mother or father to open the doors to those gilded places. She'll be forced at last to stare her own mediocrity in the face. She'll marry a stock broker, start a vegan mommy blog. Enlist her future spawn in ballet.

Grow up, I tell myself. Be the adult. Be the teacher. Lie to this long-haired child and tell her the reason we are doing this play is because it will stretch her and her fellow cast members to take on a play that is disturbing but not in an obvious bloodbath/orgy way; that is witchy without the cackling hags; that is funny-sad rather than simply sad; that is dark-light, rather than just dark, just light; that is problematic, provocative, complex, and mysterious; a hidden mountain flower growing in the shade of Shakespeare's canon that hasn't been put on by a million fucking schools already. And is timely too. Socially relevant.

"Miranda," Briana says.

Briana always calls me Miranda, never Ms. Fitch, let alone *Professor.* She looks at me now, and I cower, can you believe this? I

45

brace myself. Brace myself for —

"Couldn't we warm up first?" She already begins to stretch her body in anticipation. Stretches her arms high above her head. *See how much my body needs and loves this?*

I have a vision of killing her. It's not the first time.

"We really need to get a move on today, I'm afraid," I tell her.

I always forget their warm-ups. I can't help it. I hate the warm-ups. Leading them through that. It pains me to watch them. How their movements are so easy, so quick, how their movements lubricate their already lubricated bones. Give oxygen to their already oxygenated musculature. Make their faces grow flushed. Really, it's like watching them all fuck. But Briana warming up is the worst. The sight of Briana's lithe body moving beneath the stage lights actually hurts my eyes. Causes them to water. It's like staring directly right at the sun. It's like willing yourself to go blind.

"I'll do a quick one for them, Miranda," Grace says quietly into my ear.

I turn to her, standing beside me now.

"Fine," I say. "Fine."

I dissolve into the dark wing. There, I watch their bodies bend and sway. I grab a

bottle from my pocket and pop another pill.
I don't even bother to check which bottle.

CHAPTER 3

The Canny Man with Grace. A Scottish pub in our neighborhood where we go after class or rehearsals to discuss the production or if neither of us can face going home. Grace is eating a burger and fries with a vigorous appetite. As if no rebellion has occurred. Just another post-rehearsal night. All's well. I watch her drink a monolith of dark beer with a thick, creamy head that would slaughter me to imbibe. Beside the beer is a tumbler, which she's nearly drained, of Scotch. Healthy as a horse. Utterly unkillable. I'm sitting hunched over a white wine spritzer and a green salad. My entire body a throbbing, low-grade ache. Hip to knee in full-on spasm. Back full of fists. On vague fire in various places, all over, all over. Burning too with humiliation and rage.

"You okay?" Grace says.

Okay? How can she even ask me that? Was she not there? Did she not see? I want to protest. To rage at Grace.

"Fine," I say.

Grace looks at me hunched crookedly over my food. "Haven't touched your . . . what is that anyway?"

"Salad."

Grace wrinkles her nose. Returns to her burger, which appears to have cheese, even bacon, it looks like. Possibly a fried egg. Why isn't Grace dead? But I know this meal won't kill Grace.

Grace will belch once, quietly, about an hour from now in her living room while watching Netflix. She'll pat her obediently digesting stomach lightly as though it has been a good dog. She will retreat to her bedroom, which is uncharacteristically feminine in decor, every surface cluttered with tiny, ornate jewelry boxes, each fit for only one ring, each wall foaming pale rose drapery, and there on a cushion-bedecked bed, she will sleep the sleep of angels. Her heart will not drum perilously into her ear. She will not lie awake plagued with visions of her own imminent demise. She will sleep and then wake at a decent hour, and go for a run in the morning. Reinvigorated. Ready to take on life.

She made a face when I ordered my white wine spritzer and salad, then ordered her rich meal and drink, as if to atone for my lameness.

I really shouldn't drink with these pills, I explained to her.

Grace nodded. *Sure. Whatever.*

But it's true that I shouldn't drink with these pills. I shouldn't even be taking these pills together, let alone washing them down with wine. Got them from two different physiatrists who, unlike my golf-shirted physiotherapists, have the power to dispense drugs. One was suspicious of me, the other unusually merciful, smiling with the whimsical benevolence of a trickster god I'd happened to catch on a good day — *Now why don't we give these a try, Ms. Fitch, hmm?*

Yes, I cried. *Yes, let's!*

Now, you don't want to take anything else with these, Ms. Fitch.

Oh, of course not, I told the good doctor, shaking my head again and again. *No, no, I would never.* His white coat shone before me like the robes of God. The white so bright I shed tears.

Now I sip my spritzer and stare at Grace, guzzling her beer contentedly as she watches the hockey game on the small TV screen above my head. Oblivious, completely, to this evening's disaster. Well, she can afford to be.

"Well, that went terribly," I say at last.

Grace looks at me, unfazed. "What?"

"The rehearsal?"

She shrugs. "It wasn't that bad."

"Not that bad? Weren't you there? Didn't you see?"

She stares at the TV screen. "I saw."

"So then you know. They hate me," I whisper.

Grace rolls her eyes. "Miranda, don't be stupid."

"They do. They hate me, and they hate this play."

"Well, of course they hate the play, Miranda. *All's Well That Ends Well?* Come on."

"It's a great play," I mumble.

"I don't know about *great*. I mean, it's fine. But it's not exactly going to compete with murder, madness, and witches."

"It's got a witch in it," I say.

"Who?"

"Helen. She heals a king."

Grace shakes her head as if to say, *Don't get me started on fucking Helen.* Whenever Grace shakes her head about Helen, fucking Helen, I think she's really passive-aggressively expressing her feelings about me. *Helen is so delusional,* she says. *Helen is sick,* she says. *Helen is so entitled,* she says, *so self-centered. Helen's always* whining, she

51

says. *Helen's pain is really her own fault. And Helen doesn't even really know what pain is. If only Helen would get over herself. Stop obsessing.*

"She's in love," I say. "It's a love story."

Grace snorts. She chugs her beer. "A totally fucked-up one."

"I think Helen's love is beautiful," I say to the table.

"Helen is delusional."

"Well," I say, "we're all entitled to our own readings."

"Well, that's my reading," she says, looking at me.

I gaze down at my spritzer. Is she thinking about my weeping phone calls to my ex-husband, Paul, which I often made drunk in the pub bathroom or post-rehearsal in the theater when I thought I was alone?

Everything okay, Miranda? she'd call from the door.

Fine, just on the phone.

Has she sensed my unreciprocated lust for Hugo? Caught me drugged out and staring fixedly, helplessly, uselessly at his back muscles rippling through his T-shirt as he paints scenery onto a large wooden frame, transforming the blank canvas into the interior of a French court? A paintbrush

52

held tenderly between his white teeth like a rose.

Doesn't he look just like a Norse god, Grace? Thor maybe?

No, Grace will say.

Hugo will feel that he's being watched and eventually turn and see my crooked figure lurking in the shadows. *Hey, Miranda,* he'll say kindly enough. *Didn't see you there.*

Of course you didn't, I think. *You still don't. You never will.* But all I always say is *Oh.*

Anything I can do for you? he might ask.

See me as I once was. See me at the very least as fuckable. But my lust is a sad, withered thing. The truth is, if Hugo were to turn to me and say, *Miranda, I'd love to be intimate with you,* I would limp away. My fantasies only involve Hugo being nearby, in vaguely erotic proximity. Smiling at me suggestively, perhaps over candlelight. But Hugo's usually looking past me at the clock on the wall. I'm taking him away from his work. Or he's looking at me with pity, like he did tonight.

"Miranda, are you listening to me?" Grace asks me now.

"Yes."

"Look, you know I'm on board for anything. I love making theater. The students are just pissed that you didn't go with

53

Mackers is all."

I picture it. Briana as Lady Macbeth. Covered in fake blood. Flipping her hair onstage. Her white dress showing pale, freckled cleavage. Her shrill wailing about a spot. Drawing from what particular misery and anguish? None. All of it ringing false.

"I have enough pain in my life right now, all right?" I tell Grace.

"Didn't want to see Briana playing Lady M?"

"Don't be ridiculous," I say.

"She'd be terrible, I'll give you that. And she's a Helen if there was ever one. Insisting the universe operate as she wishes."

I close my eyes. I want to tell Grace, *You have no idea about Helen.* That it takes a depth of soul to understand her. It takes a life of pain. A kind of wisdom only won by time spent in the shadows. Grace is an Oscar Wilde specialist; she really should understand more about these things.

"It has nothing to do with Briana," I lie. "I actually don't happen to think she's a good fit for Helen."

Grace just looks at me.

"I honestly just thought we'd do something different for a change, that's all. I really don't see what's wrong with that."

"Nothing at all."

"It'll be a change of *pace.* I mean, aren't you tired of seeing them destroy *Hamlet*? Or *Romeo and Juliet*?"

"They *are* students, Miranda."

"Exactly."

"Look, you're the director. You had your *reasons.*"

My reasons. I know Grace is very suspicious of my reasons.

How many times has she found me lying on the floor of my office, my laptop by my head, watching my Helen on YouTube? Brilliant production. Poorly taped. The camera being shakily held by some anonymous tweaker in the audience. But I'm so grateful to the tweaker for capturing my performance, the audience, that night. I can even see who I think is Paul in the crowd. The back of his shoulder, a sliver of his spellbound face turned toward me on the stage.

Grace has watched me watch myself with tears in my eyes, mesmerized by my own face, still dumb to its dark future, unlined with sorrow. My ability to walk across the stage like a human person.

What are you doing, Miranda? she'll ask from the door.

Nothing, I'll say. *Research.*

"You had your reasons," she repeats now. "So you'll make them come around."

I recall their dead-eyed faces gazing at me. The defiance in the air so palpable it made a crackling sound. "And what if they don't come around?"

"You'll make them. You're the *director.*"

"I'm the director," I whisper.

My legs have grown dead beneath me. I know that when I eventually stand up I'll have to pay. I shouldn't sit in a chair for longer than twenty minutes, according to Mark. Of course, therapists will disagree. It's thirty minutes according to John. *So long as you get up every hour or so and walk around you should be fine,* said Matt the sadist. *Does it really matter, in the end?* Luke said. Luke, the fatalistic philosopher. *Honestly, just let your pain be your guide,* said Dr. Harper, my hip surgeon, giving me a wan smile, a shrug of his sculpted shoulders. He treated my hip surgery like it was a one-night stand he wanted to forget. Every time I sat in his office telling him how I still had pain, reading off my symptoms from the Notes app on my phone, then my list of questions, he'd just mumble about Advil and Mother Nature and not make eye contact. And then there was Dr. Rainier, who didn't believe I needed to take any such measures at all. I recall his helmet of silver hair glowing dully beneath the fluorescent lights as he gazed at me with such smug certitude. Certain that my pain was not the result of a hip injury followed by an unsuccessful surgery followed by a bad recovery that caused a back injury that then compressed multiple nerves running down my legs. No, no. My pain was my dead mother, my divorce, my failed aspirations for the stage.

Ms. Fitch, I want to perform surgery on everyone in New England. But you? He smiled. Shook his head. *You I don't want to cut. Why would I?* he said softly, looking at me. *Nothing to cut.*

And I suddenly felt like a loose woman who sat with her legs spread wide before him while he politely but firmly refused to fuck me.

To continue to insist like this, Ms. Fitch, would really be undignified, embarrassing for both of us, really.

But I can't walk, I pleaded. *Or sit or stand.*

Ms. Fitch, he said, leaning in. *If you can't walk, then tell me: How did you get here?*

"I don't know."

"What?" Grace says now. "Miranda, did you hear what I just said?"

"You said I'm the director," I whisper.

"That's right."

"It doesn't matter. They'll never get off

57

book." I observe this fact as though it is a bonfire I'm watching from a great distance.

"It's still early." She points at the snow outside the window, heavily falling, then signals to the waiter.

"It always goes fast, you know that. Before you know it, it'll be here."

"What?" she says, rifling through her handbag.

"Spring." I shudder. I never hated spring until I began directing the play. Never dreaded the melting of snow. Never shivered at the sight of green buds on a branch. The smell of plants having sex, the chirping of birds, the scent of wet grass. Briana probably loves it. Welcomes it. Performs some sort of ritual to make it all quicken.

I look at Grace. Her face is suddenly surrounded by a cloudy haze.

"Are you sure you're okay, Miranda? You seem . . ."

"What?"

"I don't know. Not here, or something."

"It's just" — I rub my leg — "it's been a lot. All of this." I try to smile weakly as though I'm smiling through something. A veil of pain. But even though it's true, I am, it rings false, it's a bad performance. I'm the woman in the drug commercial. I'm pleading.

She can see through it. She lowers her eyes. Picks at her fries.

"Look, you can always ask for help, you know, Miranda? You do know that, right? I mean, I'm literally just right down the block from you. I can do laundry. Get groceries. Close windows."

It's like she doesn't even ask for help.

It's like she's always asking for help.

"I know. Thank you."

Grace and I used to be closer. Friends? Maybe friends. There was a time, not so long ago, when I'd stop at her place for a drink before I went home most nights. I'd lie on my back on her living room floor while she sat curled on her flowery couch letting her dragon crawl all over her. We'd bitch about the English faculty. Commiserate about the theater program hanging by a thread. She'd ask me to tell her about my stage days. Or I'd just tell her about my stage days. If she was drunk, she'd ask me to tell her again about my summer playing Snow White at Disney World, a job that seemed to fascinate her far more than any of my Shakespeare gigs. Or we might do her rose-petal face mask and watch one of her murder shows. *Mask + mystery tonight?* she'd text. I'd always text even though I thought the shows were formulaic and her petal mask gave me hives. I was just happy to be with Grace. She always had white wine in her fridge for me. And I always had beer in my fridge for her when she came by. She was sympathetic about my pain in her brisk, efficient way.

That's hard, she might offer.

Yes, I might say. *But,* I'd add, always meaning to end on something positive, to lighten the mood. But I'd just trail off into a silence neither of us filled.

She'd fill it by pouring me more wine.

Then last year, just before opening night of *Romeo and Juliet,* she told me my pain was all in my head. Not looking at me when she said it. Hands on the steering wheel of her SUV. Staring at the streaked windshield, the gray New England spring. I'd just had another round of useless steroid shots in my back. She was driving me home from the hospital.

I could take you, she'd said.

I really don't want to trouble you, I'd said. I always said this.

It's fine, she'd said. Both of us knowing there was no one else who could take me.

I'm happy to do it, she'd said. But she hadn't looked happy at all.

Better now? she asked me when I hobbled out of outpatient surgery.

I won't know for a few days, I told her.

Silence. On we drove.

Probably won't work, I added. *Nothing does,* I said, and sort of half laughed, mainly for Grace's sake, but the laugh came out dark and hollow. Then I felt the tears come. Spilling ridiculously, hotly down my face. And then, just like that, Grace pulled over to the shoulder of the road. *Miranda, look,* she said, though she wouldn't look at me. *I'm saying this for your own good. Have you ever considered that maybe . . .*

And as she spoke, we both stared straight ahead at the gravelly shoulder of the road.

Since then? Since then, not so close. We're still friendly, professional. We still get drinks after rehearsal out of habit, but things have shifted. She stares at me now from a distance. I want to tell her, *You don't have to do this anymore. Pretend to be interested like this. Pretend to care.*

But I just say, "I appreciate it, I do. And you're right, it'll be fine in the end."

"What'll be fine?"

"The play."

"Of course it'll be fine. It's just a play after all, Miranda."

"Right. Of course it is. Just a play," I lie.

"All right," she says. "I'd better head out. You coming?"

61

I picture the limping walk back to my joke of a car. A black bug. Paul got it for me as a thirtieth birthday present. I still remember him smiling at me through the windshield as he pulled it into our driveway. He'd even filled the tiny plastic vase with daisies. That was back when I could climb into and out of a small, low-to-the-ground vehicle with grace. Back when getting out of a car, any car, wouldn't fill me with dread. I can already feel the pain of lowering myself into the bug. The pain of driving. The pain of getting out of the bug. The pain of hobbling to the front door with a dead leg. My stoned super sitting on the icy front steps, drinking tequila straight from the bottle. Having to stand there with my body on the brink of collapse while she talks to me inanely about the weather. She was not expecting such snow! How I'll force myself to respond. Force the joviality into my voice, the smile onto my face. I used to be such a good actress, trust me.

"No, you go on ahead. Think I'll stay here for a bit. Have another drink. Listen to the bagpipe player."

Grace looks at my empty glass. Then at me. A third drink? The bagpipe player? Am I fucking kidding? Also, what bagpipe player?

"The music?" I insist.

But there is no music. Only the drunk murmuring of drunk men at the bar. Only silent hockey.

"Karaoke is going to start soon," I tell her. Suddenly I'm weirdly eager for her to leave. The sound of Grace's voice, the sight of Grace's face, Grace wanting answers for my unusual behavior, all of it hurts. Hurts my body, my head most of all. I will her away. Can't I will her away? No, she's still sitting there. Looking worriedly at me.

"Miranda, you sure you're okay?"

"I'm fine." My voice is a pair of hands pushing her out the door.

"All right. Well, maybe we could do something this weekend. Go for a coffee or something?"

"Maybe. Sure. Yeah. I'll see you." I try to smile.

"I'll Never Smile Again" swelling on the jukebox. How appropriate. Makes me misty. Makes me dreamy. Maybe just the pills, the alcohol. Wasn't supposed to mix. Mixed anyway. *Too late now, Miranda. Enjoy the ride in this misty, misty room with its dark red walls.* Room suddenly seems redder somehow, is that possible? Lots of animal heads on the walls, I notice now. Stags. Black goats.

Regarding me with their glassy black eyes that glint. Never noticed that before.

"Do you think someone actually shot those?" I ask Grace, and then I remember Grace is gone. I pushed her away with the hands of my voice. It's just me here now. At this high table for two by the bar. My hands cupped around my empty drink like it's a flame about to go out.

Lights dimming, are the lights dimming? Maybe they're closing already. I look around the bar. I didn't realize how huge this place is until now. The space just goes on and on and on. And I'm the only one in it, it seems. Except for a few lone men at the bar, it's just me. Alone here. How did that happen? Where did everyone go? Hello? The song seems to have melted, shifted into a different tune. Just violin. I've heard this before. Haven't I heard it before? Yes. A tune Paul used to play. Not on the violin, on the piano. He played the piano each night after work and for hours on the weekend, that was his release, his bliss. *Like theater is for you.* Whatever this particular tune is, it was one of my favorites. Sounds like soft rain, moonlight on moving water. I'd listen from wherever I was in the house. Sometimes I'd stand in the doorway of the living room, gazing at him bent at the piano, the back of his head. I could call Paul on the phone now. Not now. Don't fuck him over with one of your pill-addled alcoholic phone calls. Don't cry into the crackling vat of his phone silence. Don't simper-hiss, *I miss you; do you miss me?* Probably having dinner with his new girlfriend in our old house, the one I hobbled away from like it was on actual fire. *You were the one who hobbled away, remember?*

I need a drink, but all the waiters seem to have disappeared. How did that happen? Are you guys closed or open? Hello? The lights are still on, though they're dimming, dimming. "Stardust" on the jukebox now. Nat King Cole and his bewitching voice. Louder than it should be. Is this a trick? How the light keeps dimming? How the light's gone out everywhere except at the bar. Just one bartender behind the bar now, a man, pale-faced and wearing a pirate shirt. There are a lot like him in this town. Probably reads tarot cards to tourists in his spare time, though I can tell he's not the sort to predict that all will be well. He's the sort that tells them terrible, thrilling fates. And they actually tip him more for this, I've seen it.

I think you're in great pain, I hear this sort of man say to his dupes with such feigned gravitas.

I am, I am! replies the dupe behind the curtain. Desperate.

Sometimes that voice belongs to me. Sometimes it's me behind the curtain. Allowing myself to be fooled. Tears in my eyes. *It's true,* I whisper. *It's all true. How did you know?*

Now he's wiping a tumbler that will remain dirty. The glass, I know, is for me.

I rise from the table, limp over to the bar.

The bartender, seeing me approach, pours Scotch into the spotted glass caked with another woman's lipstick.

Instead of telling him, I just wipe it off with my thumb.

I take a very long sip. The sort of sip I never take anymore. Always small sips these days. Always so careful. Not tonight. Fuck being careful. Fuck walking gingerly. Fuck being mindful of drug interactions. Fuck how long I sit or stand. Forget it all. Just let go, isn't that what the meditation recording tells me to do? I tried it for a while, dutifully. Even lit a candle, can you believe it? For ambiance. To set the mood. Turned on my rock-salt lamp. Lavender oil billowing into my face from a nearby diffuser. Lying on my back on the floor, my arms splayed like a corpse. It's funny now, to think of my former faith in these rituals. How earnestly I believed that one day they would all make me well.

I allow myself a stroll further down memory lane. It's quite like the dirt lane of the drug commercial. Flanked here and there by strange flowers. There's a tilted wooden fence to the right, a field of swaying grass to the left. I stare down the lane with my misty vision, all cloudy around the edges, like looking at a dream. Thinking about the time when I could stroll freely. One foot in front of the other. A hop to my step. A hope to my step. I wore swishing French dresses as casual wear back then. Little cardigans with bows for buttons. I was so fucking adorable, you wouldn't believe it. You might have wanted to kill me. Maybe you did. Maybe you cursed me quietly as you watched me pass. I didn't even see you. My mind was blissfully blank. I was climbing crags in my heart-shaped leather heels. Digging my hearts into the earth. Velvet purse full of plays and makeup and a journal slung across my body and knocking against my thigh, where it might leave a bruise. But I didn't care. I was invincible then. Silk stockings I wore, can you believe this? When I climbed hills! Fishnets that would rip and I'd let the run go right down the leg to the ankle, get bigger. I didn't care about that either. I'd walk until my heels were scuffed and caked in mud. I'm doing this now. Walking up up up in my old heels on the dirt lane, which has become a trail in Edinburgh that I climbed when I came for the Fringe, came to play Helen. My twenty-four-year-old legs so pliant and strong on the trail. There's a lookout point coming up where I'll be able to see the whole city. I can feel Paul behind me on the path. His golden-red hair hanging in his face. Flushed and huffing. Trying to keep up. We only just met two weeks ago, after he saw me onstage. A fellow New Englander, a Mainer, just in Edinburgh for a few days, on his way to do a summer walking tour of the Highlands. But Paul never ended up going to the Highlands. Instead he comes to see my Helen each night, waits for me outside the theater. It sounds stalkery, but it isn't. Maybe it only isn't because he's young and hot. I'm turned on by his aggressive attention, his confident pursuit. I spend my nights at his hotel on Princes Street instead of sleeping on the floor with my fellow cast members in a dank, one-bedroom apartment in Leith. Each night I leave the theater, the sky still a bright blue, and there he is, smiling, strapping, bewitched, waiting to

take me away, to follow me anywhere —
down the closes, up the crags. I'm high from
the performance; I'm high from the attention of this beautiful fan, this stranger who
doesn't feel like a stranger at all, whose
quiet voice and kind eyes feel like home. If
I turn now on the trail, I'll find him looking
up at me. How he would look up at me with
such a strange expression on his face.
Admiration? Not quite. Fear? Awe.

Maybe it was awe.

You're unstoppable, he would say to me,
and I'd smile.

But when I turn around now, all I see is
nothing. Black.

The clouds around my field of vision are
closing in. Closing in on my future husband's face saying these words to me.

I'm alone on memory lane in my grim
cardigan, my orthopedic shoes, my gaping-
open pockets rattling with pills. It's grown
dark on the lane. The sun is gone. The
strange bright flowers have vanished. Nothing now. Nothing but black, starry black as
far as I can see.

"You're back," says a voice. A male voice.
Soft. Low. Almost a whisper.

I open my eyes. Three men. Three men
sitting with me at the bar. One to my right.
Two to my left. One tall, one fat, one mid-

dling. All wearing dark suits. All holding drinks. How did I not see them before?

The middling one is looking at me like I'm a mirage he's been waiting for all night. He must have been the one who spoke. Gray face. Red, alcoholic eyes. Hand cupped around a squat glass full of golden liquid.

"Excuse me?" I say.

He smiles sadly at me. Beside him sits the fat man hunched over his Scotch with his head down and his hands over his face as though he can't bear to see. Long, stringy silver hair that is yellowed in places. What I can see of his face through his stubby fingers is terrible — pockmarks, burst veins, a blotchy redness — but familiar. Like a politician I've seen in the news. No way. No way could he be at this bar on a random Monday.

To my right, I feel the third man. Slender. Tall. Handsome, even though I see him only out of the corner of my eye. I don't so much see him as sense him in the back of my neck, the hairs there pricked up. Something tells me not to look directly at him.

The middling man is still smiling at me as though we are both in a tragic dream.

"Where were you?" he asks me.

"Where was I?" I repeat.

He's looking at me hunched over my glass,

how I'm gripping the bar with both hands like it's the railing of a ship.

"You look like you went somewhere far, far away. In your mind."

I look at him. *How the fuck do you know anything about my mind?* But I nod slowly. Yes. "I guess I did."

Why am I telling him this? This stranger with his alcoholic's eyes boring into my soul like he thinks he sees it right there under my skin.

"Not the best trip, I take it?" he says.

I don't know what to say.

"No," I say before I can even think.

"Too bad." He makes a sort of sad face. Sympathetic.

Who the hell are you? I want to ask him. Instead tears fill my eyes. Stupidly. He becomes a suited, smiling blur.

"Let me guess. I used to be good at this." He looks at me with his head cocked to one side.

I gaze at him gazing at me. I should just leave. Tell this man to mind his own business. But I'm pinned there by his watery stare. I take a drink from my glass. Feel him taking me in deeply with his red-rimmed eyes. My hunched frame. My hand gripping the glass. My flushed face, my gaze cloudy with crying and drugs.

"L-four L-five," he says at last. "On the right. On the left, L-two L-three."

I burst into fresh tears.

"Prednisone," he says tenderly, as if it is a word of comfort. "Then steroid shots, am I right? More surgeons than you can count. They have conflicting views about your MRI. Shaking their doctor heads. Playing God. Some say, *Let's cut her open.* Others say, *Cut what? Nothing to cut. Nothing here.* Then what? Physiatrists and their pill solutions. Probably a dozen physical therapists. Some say stretch. Some say don't dare stretch. Some say to bend forward. Some say to bend backward. Some say, *Rest, just rest, sometimes you need to rest.* Some say, *Keep moving, just keep moving. Movement heals. Movement is king.* Some tell you heat. Some tell you ice. Some tell you heat and ice. Some tell you, *Oh, whatever feels good.* But nothing feels good, does it?"

I shake my head. Nothing, nothing.

"Some tell you, *Let pain be your guide.*" He smiles. "Some guide, am I right?"

I nod.

"Then what? Let me guess. You've pursued all the alternative therapies. Acupuncture. Biofeedback. Had hope swell in your heart again and again. There was that Japanese acupuncturist who left the needle tips in you. You almost walked out with a long needle right between your eyes once that you didn't even see. Massage? Probably just makes it worse, am I right?"

"He means well," I whisper.

"Oh, they always mean well, Ms. Fitch. And you like that you can go to him. Talk to him. That someone touches you every Sunday with kindness. You have so few actual friends these days."

Did he just call me Ms. Fitch? "Do I know you, sir?"

He smiles sadly. "So down you are."

"Down, down, down," the man to my right mumbles. Behind his hands, the fat man whines.

"So dead inside."

"Dead, dead, dead."

"So lost and drifting in the benzo sea."

"In the black waves."

"How do you know all this?" I ask. "Are you . . . do you have issues too . . . are you in the field?"

"The *field*," repeats the fat man.

The third man snickers.

Behind his hands, the fat man begins to laugh hysterically. His huge body shakes with it.

The middling man stares at me, dead serious. "I'm a fellow sufferer, Ms. Fitch. I'm

73

just like you." He pulls a handkerchief from the inside of his suit. Dark red. Silky-looking. I didn't even think people had handkerchiefs like that anymore.

He hands it to me. "There, there," he says.

I shake my head, but he insists. Waving it in my face. *Surrender, surrender.* Under his gaze, I take the handkerchief, dab politely at the corners of my eyes. The silk feels cool and watery on my skin.

"Thank you," I say. I look at the fat man sitting beside him. He's now completely slumped over onto the bar. His red, pained face is buried in the crook of his arm, his other hand gripping a drink. "Is he all right?"

"Him? He's wonderful. He's in the prime of his life."

A small chuckle from the third man. Leaning casually with his back against the bar. I still can't see his face.

The middling man raises his glass to me. What's in it looks golden to my eye. Beautiful.

"The golden remedy," he says.

The bartender refills my glass with the same golden drink.

The middling man looks at me so intently, I can't bear it. His murky gaze all over my face. His bemused smile as though I'm a funny dream. He raises his glass higher and mutters something I don't understand. Something that sounds almost like backward English.

We drink with our eyes on each other, while the fat man slumps and the third man glows in the corner of my eye.

Drink it all down. Everything. To the last drop. Drown. Gold fire. Drown in gold fire. Now walk whistling along a golden shore.

"Better?" he asks me.

"Yes," I say. And it's true. The music has switched to "Blue Skies." And I feel as though there is a blue sky inside me. Cerulean. Bones I don't feel. Blood light as air for once. I think I'm going to cry again, but instead I smile.

"Of course, it's just a temporary fix. You know what they say, don't you, Ms. Fitch?"

How the fuck do you know my name? I want to ask. My lips stay closed and curve into their wide smile. I shake my head slowly at the middling man. He's still a fuzzy blur even though I've wiped my eyes. The skin around my eyes is cool. So cool it almost feels like it's dewy, glowing.

"No. I have no idea what they say."

He puts his hand on mine.

" 'Our remedies oft in ourselves do lie which we ascribe to heaven.' "

Act One, Scene One. Lines 218–219 from Helen's soliloquy. The first time she turns toward the audience and bares her soul. The line Briana murders every time she opens her mouth. The line I whisper along with her in the dark wings of the auditorium. Tears in my eyes then as there are now. Thinking of my Helen. I played her as she was meant to be played, as an enigma of a girl. You should have seen me. My voice was low but deep. I was desperate but calm too, as Helen is. Knowing what I had to do in the face of great adversity, my face said so. Knowing I had to take things into my own hands, I had no choice. I looked right into the eyes of the audience when I spoke. They were bewitched. I was bewitching.

I look at the middling man.

How does he know this play of all plays? Why would he quote these lines to me? Am I dreaming him? Am I lying on my back in bed? My eyelids fluttering in the dark?

But instead of asking I say, "Are you in theater?"

First the fat man, who I thought was dead, laughs again. Bangs his fist upon the table. Then the soft, low laughter of the man to my right, the one I can and can't see. Whom I can only see with the eye of my mind.

The middling man just looks at me.
"Aren't we all?"

CHAPTER 4

"I think it's worse," I tell Mark. We're in a treatment room, which is essentially just a white cell with a medical table, a couple of hard chairs, and a diagram of a skinned human on the wall. Mark looks at me, confused. Of course he does. I watch as a furrow creases his brow. He folds his muscled arms defensively.

"Worse?" he repeats.

I nod. I think of the brief relief I felt last night after that drink. How I sailed home from the bar as if on air and slept, then woke up to the familiar pain.

"Much worse." I sound apologetic. Or do I sound challenging? Maybe both.

He gently shuts the door to the treatment room. Lest I infect the other patients in the gym beyond with my lack of faith. My misgivings.

He leans back against the medical table where I will soon be positioned flat on my stomach, my face pressed tightly into the too-small doughnut hole, leaving a crease on each side for the rest of the day. Meanwhile Mark will prod at my back with a surgically gloved finger. He'll roughly scrape the skin with a cold metal instrument. He'll knock on the knobs of my spine like they are doors leading to potentially interesting rooms.

Now he crosses his legs like we have all the time in the world even though we have only thirty minutes. Twenty-three, really, because Mark was late again. He's always late these days.

"Tell me," Mark says. "Talk to me." He says it kindly, gently, as if he actually wants me to tell him the truth of how I feel. Like we're about to have a serious heart-to-heart.

I look at Mark patiently waiting for me to speak. The soul patch under his lower lip. His freshly buzzed crew cut. A yin-yang pendant hanging from his neck on a corded rope, the features of his handsome bro face arranged in an *I'm listening* expression.

But this is a lie. Does he really want me to talk to him? Surely our relationship couldn't bear such honesty. Surely he couldn't.

I open my mouth to tell him the words and phrases that I have been practicing all the way over here. In my car to the streaked windshield, to the empty passenger seat at stoplights. In the waiting room, where I stared at the covers of dated, heavily-thumbed-through fitness magazines until my eyes watered, the pages wavy as though they'd been dragged through water and then dried out, greasy with the fingerprints of a thousand injured wrecks. Enumerating my points on my fingers. Typing notes into my phone so I wouldn't forget. All the parts of my body that had not been improved by our year together. All the exercises that hurt to perform — that felt like I might be doing actual damage to myself. That I felt like we didn't really have a plan anymore, Mark and I. That we were just in a weird rehab limbo now. No destination. No goals.

It was Dr. Rainier who first recommended Mark to me, nearly a year ago. *Fortunately for you,* he said, *there's a nationally renowned spine rehabilitation center right here in Massachusetts.*

Really? I said through my drugged tears.

Oh, yes, Ms. Fitch. Right here in this very building. In the basement, in fact. He smiled. *And I know just the therapist to pair you with. He'd be perfect for you. Mark.*

And I remember I repeated the name as though I were receiving the Eucharist. *Mark.* I held it on my tongue like it was holy sustenance. I closed my eyes. Surely Mark would be better than Luke. Or Matt. Or Todd.

He's going to help you, Ms. Fitch.

He's going to help me, I repeated. And I believed it. When I first took the elevator down to the basement, to SpineWorks, Mark was standing there just beyond the doors. Waiting for me, clipboard in hand. His yin-yang pendant gleamed around his neck.

You must be Miranda, he said.

Wow, he said. *I just love your T-shirt. The koi is my favorite fish, truth be told.*

I gazed at Mark like he was a god.

Tell me, Miranda, he said gently. *I want to know the whole story.*

And I did tell Mark. I told Mark my whole case history — my fall off the stage, followed by the left hip pain, followed by the failed surgery, the bad recovery; the sudden pain down my right leg; the disc herniations; the MRI no doctor could agree upon; the steroid shots to the hip, to the spine; the acupuncture, the biofeedback, the man in the white lab coat who stabbed my breast like he was driving a stake through the heart of a vampire, the Chinese-medicine doctor who needled my peroneal nerve and then I involuntarily kicked him in the face — and

81

Mark listened; he nodded; he made little noises of what I presumed to be sympathy; he pressed his palms together as though he were praying for me; he pressed the tips of his index fingers to his lips.

Tell me more, Mark said. Like he couldn't get enough of my story. Not since my stage days, in fact, had I had such a rapt audience.

It was hard to keep everything straight, of course. Facts and precise descriptions and the order of things kept escaping me. I kept apologizing for this.

Never, Mark said. *Never apologize. You're doing so great. You're doing so well.*

When I was done talking, how thoughtfully Mark nodded. How tenderly he took me through a diagnostic examination. Asking me to bend forward. *Carefully, carefully.* Then bend backward. *Easy now. How does that feel?*

I thought I could tell Mark the truth.

It hurts, I said. *Terribly.*

I expected Mark to roll his eyes, to shake his head at this. I was so used to the cruelty of Luke, to the indifference of Matt. But Mark only nodded. Of course. Of course it did.

I believe I can help you, Mark said at last.

You do?

82

And I remember he took my hands in his. They were in blue surgical gloves, but I could feel their warmth pulsating through the latex.

I'm going to take ownership of your pain, Miranda, Mark said. He put a gloved hand to his chest, like he was making a declaration of love.

But what if you can't help me? I whispered.

Mark smiled. *How about we cross that bridge when we get to it?*

We. My heart soared. Tears swelled behind my eyes though I did not cry. I had been trained by Luke, who told me he didn't do crying.

If you cry, Luke had said, *I'm going to walk out of this room.* He'd said it smiling.

Miranda, Mark said gently, *I'd like to show you something.*

What? I whispered.

It's a video. I'm going to send you a link. Will you watch it, Miranda? I think it would be such a great place for us to start.

Us.

Of course I'll watch it, I said. *I'd love to.*

I watched the video later that evening, standing crookedly by my dining room table, my laptop propped on a stack of theater textbooks. What would it be? A new series of exercises? A new kind of therapy

83

we were going to try? I was so excited when I clicked the link. It was a cartoon. It starred a giant cartoon brain with large unblinking eyes. A spinal cord dangled from its back like a rat's tail. It had a stick for a body. Little stick arms and legs too. I watched the brain wander on its stick legs through a roughly drawn world under a smudgy charcoal sky. It looked sad. Because it believed it was in pain. Because, according to the voice-over narrator, pain lives in the brain. I remember feeling a flicker of rage then. Was this how Mark truly saw me? As a dour cartoon brain trapped in its own gray world? I recalled his wide-open eyes gazing at me in such rapture. His pressed-together palms. The warmth of his hands through his surgical gloves when they held mine. No. No, surely I was mistaken.

That was almost a year ago.

Now? Now after nearly a year of twice-weekly sessions, in which I have not improved, in which I have only gotten worse, things have grown colder between us. Now Mark doesn't meet me at the elevator doors anymore. Now I have to wait for Mark in the waiting room, and he is often late, still with the patient he sees before he sees me. I can hear a woman's hellion laughter ringing from the gym, and I know it is the laughter of a woman who still has faith in Mark's capabilities. Now Mark barks my name from the opposite end of the hall, and he looks away while I rise from my chair and limp toward him, dragging my dead leg, no less stiff for all the needles he has driven into it, all the times he's tugged on my foot attempting to pull my hip from its socket, scraped my thigh with stainless steel, pressed the pads of his fingers so deeply into the flesh that he's left black bruises.

How are we doing? he'll ask as I approach, but he's already walking away from me toward the treatment room down the hall, my ever-fattening file tucked under his arm. Because he already knows how I am. No better, never any better. One of those patients. One of those sad cartoon brains who wants to live under a smudgy sky of her own making. Who refuses to believe in little victories. A fire he's been valiantly trying to put out, but then I constantly, brazenly, insist upon erupting into flames again.

"Talk to me, Miranda," Mark says to me now.

I think of the brain-pain video Mark sent me so long ago. The sad cartoon brain trailing nerves like jellyfish tentacles.

I want to tell Mark that I am capable of following instructions. That before Mark,

85

there was Luke, and Matt. And I did everything they asked of me even though Luke
was cruel and Matt a clueless sadist. How I
followed Luke's draconian program to a tee.
His little hand-drawn illustrations of exercises, I did them, even though they made
my spine and the nerves running down my
leg scream. I also followed Matt's, even
though Matt looked very confused and
afraid of me most of the time. All my questions and fears to which he had no clear
response, no words. *Umm,* Matt would often
say. *Let me think about that.*

And I have followed Mark's program too.

I want to tell Mark that I *can* trust. I *am*
a good patient. I am capable of placing
myself in another person's care for a reasonable period of time, weeks, even months.
I've just been so disappointed in my experi-
ences, and sadly, Mark is no exception.
That's why I started secretly seeing John on
the side. Even though John isn't especially
good either. I have no idea where I am going with either of these relationships.

It's all a journey, Mark says.

Pain is information, Mark says.

What can I even say to a man who says
and believes these things? Believes them
absolutely.

"Miranda," Mark says again now.

"Yes?"

"Tell me."

But the things I want to tell Mark — specific things, important things, I had a list somewhere — have all flown away from my brain or come apart.

"My leg is still stiff," I tell Mark.

Mark nods. *Of course it is.*

"I can't even bend it."

Mark nods. Of course I can't.

"And it hurts," I tell him at last. "A lot."

Mark nods. Of course it does. And that's fine. Absolutely. Pain, after all, is information.

I watch him scratch his soul patch.

"Where does it hurt exactly?"

"Here and here and all down here," I say. "Back here too. Oh, and it sort of wraps around here."

Mark nods again. Sure. This is all part of it. Part of the journey Mark and I are taking together for the next nineteen minutes, hand in surgically gloved hand. Mark always likes to remind me that he has been hurt once too, oh yes. His lower back, in fact: *Just like you, Miranda.* A herniated disc. L4 L5, believe it or not. A common injury. His was so bad he had foot drop. He almost needed surgery. Yes, really. He went to see three different surgeons, Mark did, including one all the way in New York. This last New York surgeon told him, *You're lucky I'm a busy man,* because looking at Mark's MRI, he should've taken him into the OR that very minute. But because he was busy, the surgeon was going to try to let Mark cure himself. And Mark did cure himself, with back extensions. It took a few weeks, sure. But he improved, why? Because he believed he could improve. Little victories. Mind over matter. *The mind is so powerful, Miranda.*

"How does it hurt?" Mark asks now. He's leaning in. So intent, so sincere, that for a moment I almost feel sorry for him. I almost feel like I'm faking.

"Can you describe the pain?" Mark says.

Suddenly I am so tired.

"I don't know how to describe it," I say at last. Shaking my head. I feel close to crying. But I won't. I almost never do.

Mark nods at this too. It's all so interesting. It's all just more information.

"Try," he says.

"I guess . . . sort of like a burning on this side? And a tightness on the other? And around here, a tightness and a burning too? Almost like the area . . . I don't know . . . feels . . . red."

"Red?" Mark repeats.

88

I nod. Yes. Red. "And pulsating."

"Pulsating," Mark says. "Interesting."

"And my foot," I add. "It's like there's a chair on it or something. It feels like it's being crushed."

"A chair."

Yes.

"Hmm," Mark says. He refolds his arms. He looks deeply into the middle distance. A chair. Red. Pulsating. He's really thinking now. I feel hope swell up in spite of my bad faith. Perhaps Mark will have a new idea today.

"All right, why don't we do some tests," he says at last.

"Tests?" I feel the dread in my legs. The nerves already humming. How I used to love tests. *Tests, yes, let's do tests!* I used to cry. That was back when I thought tests led to something. A diagnosis that led to a plan, a cure. But tests, I know now, never lead us anywhere. Tests are dark roads with no destinations, just leading to more dark.

I look at Mark, who looks so pleased that he came up with an activity for us, and I think, *Fucking run. Don't ever look back.* But then I remind myself I can't even walk. I picture myself hobbling away from him in defiance. Mark watching me drag my dead leg, shaking his head. *You'll be back.*

"Okay," I say. "Tests."

He leads me through a number of diagnostic exercises he's led me through a million times before. He makes me bend forward. *That's it.* Then backward. *Good.* He makes me walk on my heels, then my toes. He makes me sit slumped forward on a chair and raise my right leg. Then my left. Nerve flossing, he says it's called. I do it all with great despair, with great fear that we will only agitate things further and to no end. He watches me with an expressionless face, which is Mark's diagnostic face, his look of intense concentration. He takes no notes.

"All right, hop up on the table," he says, patting it. "Lie on your stomach; that's it. Face in the hole. Good. Now bend backward."

Oh no, not these, I think. We already know these agitate me. We've had infinite discussions about how these agitate me. Luke had me do them. Matt had me do them. Mark has had me do them. And each time I do them, all they ever do is make things worse.

"Um, but remember we already —"

"Let's try again," Mark says, cutting me off. "Remember our goal is centralization. We want to get that pain out of your foot. Put it back in your back where it belongs, am I right? Just humor me and try ten, okay?"

I do. And it's just as I predicted. The stiffness in my right leg increases like crazy. The fires rage on my left.

"How does that feel?"

Terrible. It feels fucking terrible. As I knew it would. As I told Mark it would.

"It's stiffer down through here now. And more painful on this side."

I look up at him.

Mark looks at me with a neutral expression that gives no anger away. He nods. Absolutely. What he expected. Of course I think it makes it worse. Because I've already decided, haven't I? Because I insist upon misery. I don't want to be helped. I don't believe in little victories.

"Do that ten more times," Mark says calmly.

"Ten more?"

"I just want to see something," he says. He has his hands pressed together in front of his face, as though he's praying.

I repeat the exercise ten times. With each backward bend, the stiffness and pain increase.

Mark watches me from the doorway with his arms folded, looking bored. He says *good* every now and then, his gaze roving around the gym.

"How was that?" he asks when I'm done.

"I really feel it down my leg now," I tell him. "Like all the way to my foot." *You know, the place you want the pain to leave?*

Mark appears to consider this. "I'm okay with it," he says at last. "In fact, do another ten."

"Another ten? Are you —"

"Yup. I'm just going to go to the restroom."

I do another ten while Mark is gone, my legs screaming.

When I'm finished, I just lie there, my body on fire. Fists blooming in my back. Mark is nowhere to be seen. "Mark?" I call pathetically. "Hello? Are you —"

"Yup," he says, coming around the corner. "You did great. How does it feel?"

"I'm sorry to say this but it really hurts now."

Silence.

"All right. Just rest here for a few breaths on your stomach. Scan your body mindfully."

"But my leg is really —"

"Just keep breathing diaphragmatically," Mark says. I feel his hand pulling up my T-shirt from behind. He's applying some kind of cold gel to the small of my back.

"You know how to breathe like that, don't you? You're an actress, right?" He says this so softly. No more punishment for today.

I feel the scrape of cold steel on my skin.

"An actor," I say. I think of my fiefdom of dead eyes, yawning faces. *Not an actor anymore, a teacher.* But I don't bother to correct Mark. "Right."

"So neat," Mark says. He's said this before. "Any films I might have seen?" He wants to be conversational now. Easy breezy. Light of tone. When all I want to do is ask more questions. *Will I ever be healed? Am I broken? Is it neurological? Structural? Please tell me.*

"I do theater," I tell Mark. *I told you I do theater.* How many times have I told him this? Doesn't he remember that I fell off the stage? Theater is what led me here, to this basement, this treatment room, the gloved hand of Mark scraping my back red with a Graston tool, the end of my acting life and the beginning of my waking death as Briana's servant.

It was Paul who first showed me the teaching job post five years ago. "Assistant Professor in Theater." Some small liberal arts college we'd never heard of, not too far away from where we lived then. "In addition to teaching three courses per semester,

93

the candidate will also be expected to direct the annual Shakespeare production."

But I've never taught or directed, I said to Paul.

You have a theater degree, don't you? Plus, you're an actor. You were onstage for what, ten years?

And I remember I shuddered at his use of the past tense.

I'm just saying teaching might be a good opportunity, that's all, Paul said. *For now,* he added quickly.

Get out of the house, you know? Out of your head. I think it's worth trying, don't you? I remember he looked desperate. By then we were hanging by a thread. For a while, after the accident, I'd tried and failed at playing housewife. I went full kitsch, bought all the requisite props and costumes online. Muffin tins, French rolling pin, a pearl-lined apron that said *Kitchen Witch.* I ordered gardening and cocktail books, imagined I'd become a baker of complex breads, grow my own tulips and tender-leafed lettuces, mix all manner of martinis. When Paul came home from work, I'd be there, limping but smiling in the doorway, ready to lead him out to our lush little garden for happy hour. But I grew nothing, mixed nothing, baked nothing. The apron stayed in its drawer along with the pin. The earth in our front yard remained unturned, untended, while I gazed out at it darkly from the living room window, from my reclined position on our pullout couch of stone.

So I cobbled together a CV. So I got a few of my old directors to put in a good word for me. All of whom had heard of my accident. All of whom felt sorry for me, lied for me.

You come very highly recommended, the dean said approvingly during my interview. *Do I?*

"Theater, right," Mark says. "You know, my fiancée and I went to see *Phantom* just the other day. She just loves musicals."

Of course she does.

"Do you ever do musicals?"

"No. I hate musicals."

Mark laughs, so good-natured. Obviously, I would hate musicals. Musicals have joy. I am the antithesis of joy. I lie there thinking uncharitable thoughts while Mark scrapes me. About the fiancée. About Mark and the fiancée seeing *Phantom.* I feel him breathing close beside me. His clinical hand warm on my back. The only kind of hand that has touched me in four years, since Paul and I split. Of course, Paul didn't touch me much toward the end. Our intimacy had disintegrated from infrequent, wincing sex to me blowing him occasionally, and then, when the drugs and the pain blunted my desire for anything but a hug, to the odd kiss.

I could do something for you? Paul would offer, always. But the endless prodding of PTs and surgeons had made me far too disconnected from my body, which felt medicalized and alien, forever under clinical lights and eyes.

Could you just hug me? I used to ask. Knowing how pathetic and sexless I must have seemed by then. Such a far cry from the creature I was before the fall, when sex and intimacy were as vital to me as air. I couldn't even look at Paul when I asked. He'd sigh and open his arms. Limply, but not unkindly. And I'd hang on to him like a drowning wretch.

"Little pinch," Mark says now. And then I feel the dry needle driving into my back. I scream.

"Good job. Good twitch there," Mark says. "All right. Walk it off a bit."

He has me walk the length of the gym under his observation, my back and legs pulsating from all Mark has done. I pass other patients in the midst of their exercises, kicking and punching the air with their atrophied limbs. A woman with swollen legs is pedaling a taped-up bike. An older man is attempting to situate himself in the leg-press machine to no avail, making little cries of anguish with every shift of his stiff, veiny limbs. Meanwhile, his therapist, a young, scared-looking girl with a ponytail, watches in wonder.

"And how are we now?" Mark says. He looks so fucking hopeful and triumphant it kills me.

Worse. So much worse. You are breaking me, do you hear me? You are fucking breaking me.

"I still feel it," I say apologetically.

Mark looks perturbed. *Still? Couldn't be.* "All the way down to the foot still?"

I nod.

"But less?"

No. Absolutely not fucking less.

"Maybe less," I lie, hating myself. Hating Mark.

"You see?" Mark says. "Little victories."

"I do feel weird though," I insist uselessly.

Mark says I should continue to do the exercise at home, ten to thirty reps each hour.

"Each hour?"

He shrugs. "Or just whenever you're feeling like you need it," Mark says, looking over my shoulder. I feel him detaching

97

himself from my misery, my predicament. No longer his problem.

"Just whenever things get agitated."

"But things are agitated now," I say. *Because of it.*

But his next patient has arrived, I can tell by his eyes, which are looking past me to the waiting room. I turn and see a woman in workout tights waving at him, smiling. She must be new. I can tell by the brightness of her eyes, the palpable quality of her faith. I panic.

"What about my floor workout?" I say, positioning my crooked body between him and his view of the waiting room.

"You can do that, sure."

"And can I walk?" I always ask this.

"Just listen to your body, Miranda." Mark always says this. "Let pain be your guide. Remember pain is information. Use heat if you like."

"Heat? How often, how long?" I hear the desperation in my voice. A remedy!

"Or ice," Mark says. Mark, the great equivocator. "Ice if it feels good. Either/or."

"But which is better?" I plead.

"Whatever feels good."

I think of the three men at the bar last night. That golden drink making my blood brighten and sing. The watery red eyes of the middling man fixed on me in such sympathy. *But nothing feels good, does it?*

"What was that?"

"Nothing."

Mark claps me on the shoulder twice. "Hang in there," he says.

And I can't help it. I picture my dead hanging body for a second. Swinging from a hook on the ceiling. Mark getting the news by phone. Nodding soberly. Perhaps even burying his face in his hands. It puts things in perspective for him. It makes him understand that pain is not just a guide, not just simply information, not just a friendly teacher of lessons I need to learn. And then it's Mark's body hanging from the ceiling I picture.

As I walk out, I pass the new girl, who is happily stretching on a gym mat. Rolling the backs of her legs and butt with a foam roller, the way Mark showed me, the way Mark shows us all. He's walked over to her, and she and Mark are bantering about their running schedules. Probably she has something easy and treatable, like plantar fasciitis. All she needs is for Mark to rub her feet, to demonstrate some targeted stretching. Or maybe she does have something more grave, more elusive. Maybe she is one of the Nerve Women. Women of the invisible pain.

Chapter 5

Hideously long afternoon between classes. White winter light on my face. Snow falling into my open mouth again because someone (probably Fauve) opened the window in my absence. I lie on the floor in my office in my usual configuration, my calves on the chair seat, feet dangling over the edge. Today, this position does nothing. Less than nothing. I gaze up at the underside of my desk, at the punctured plywood, at the spider in its corner. Normally I would scream at the sight of such a spider. This afternoon, I just stare into what I imagine to be its eight eyes, which seem to regard me with a surprising degree of compassion. *Miranda, I'm so sorry you're going through this. Miranda, what can I do?*

I taught my script-analysis class this morning leaning against my desk. I have no idea what I said for seventy-five minutes. Something about witches. Something about

Shakespeare's time. The chain of being perhaps? The students took notes, anyway. Some of them did. Many of them just stared at me or at each other.

Where was I? I kept saying to the dust motes in the air.

Where was I? I asked the clock above their heads.

I recall drawing a spiral on the board at one point. Spiraling and spiraling outward. Out of control. Help. *Visuals help,* I told them.

My leg and spine are still screaming from whatever Mark did yesterday. I could feel it when I hobbled out of SpineWorks, drove myself home in my clown car. Not the usual pain that I always feel when I leave Mark, when I leave any of them, telling myself, *Oh, it will be better in time.* Just give it a night of ice and drugs and a glass or two of wine. This was something new. Something real, definitely. Like my lower back was actually bleeding. Like my leg bones had shifted around in my pelvis. Like my pelvis itself had been twisted. Like my spinal cord was suddenly pressing itself into the skin of my back as if it wanted to burst from my body. Like the bones in my left hip had swelled obscenely under my dress. I swallowed pills all the way home, all the way home. I got out of the car, and both legs protested violently at my attempt to stand up. The right leg remained rigidly bent at the knee, crouched and low to the ground. I could hear it growling beneath me like an angry dog.

As I hobbled toward the door, my super, Sheila, observed me from the apartment steps, where she was sitting and vaping in her pajamas and parka. Sheila lives alone with a feral cat in the unit next to mine. Every time I see her, she's either drunk or stoned, but then so am I. I was stoned right then, in fact. I watched little sparks of light fall from the sky, fizzle around her head.

Miranda, are you okay?

No, I wanted to say. *I'm scared. Panicked. Broken. Sad. Terribly alone. I need to go to an emergency room. Please come with me.*

Doing well, I told her. *How are you?*

You seem to be limping quite a lot there. You sure you're all right?

Fine, fine.

But I'm sure she could hear me crying through the apartment wall later that evening.

I'm broken, Goldfish, I whisper-blubbered to Paul over the phone. Goldfish was my nickname for Paul because of his gold-red hair. I called him after my second glass of chardonnay. Even though I swore to myself I would stop calling. Paul has no desire to talk to me anymore. *I've moved on, Miranda.* How many times has he said that to me? *You were the one who left me, Miranda, remember? You were the one who walked out the door.* I resent so much when Paul tells me this. Because though it's the truth, it isn't the Truth. If our relationship were on a stage, the audience would surely see, surely know. They would say to themselves, *He pushed her out with his coldness. He was sick of her sickness.* They would weep for me, absolutely.

Miranda, Paul said, *you're going to have to speak up. I can hardly understand you.*

I said I'm broken. They broke me. And then I cried for a while into the crackling silence.

Who's they? Paul asked at last.

My physical therapists.

Oh. Are we talking about your knee again? He sounded annoyed.

For a moment, I was startled out of my sadness into outrage. My knee?

Not my knee, Paul. My hip and my back. Remember I had to have hip surgery?

Yes, Miranda, I —

And then I hurt my back in recovery? And now my legs are —

Look, it's just hard for me to keep it all

straight is all. He sighed.

Right, I said. *Of course. That must be very hard for you.*

Silence.

Are you there? I asked him.

I'm here.

You were never there, I thought. Which was unfair of me, I suppose. Paul *had* been there for me at least in those early years, hadn't he? Hadn't he run lines with me in our living room? Sat on the blue couch countless times, patiently watching my auditions? He even read my reviews before I did, shielding me from any potential harshness. *Fuck this prick,* he would always declare, if it was a bad one. *You eclipsed them all.*

And just like that, he'd conjure my mother. She used to say these very words to me all the time drunk. She'd said it first when I was in second grade, after I'd bungled my lines as Father Bear in our school production of *Goldilocks* and all the kids onstage had laughed. *Fuck those idiots,* she'd slurred when she found me crying in a shamefaced ball backstage. Her hands on my furry seven-year-old shoulders, her chardonnay breath in my face. *You'll eclipse them, do you hear me?*

But Paul said it sober, with clear eyes and a face full of warmth and conviction. I

105

remember in those moments, he felt preor-dained.

You're so fucking lucky, my actor friends would say, seeing Paul in the audience yet again, bearing flowers yet again, a look of naked admiration on his handsome face. *You eclipsed them tonight, Princess.* Princess is what he called me then. A nickname teas-ing me for my Snow-White-in-Florida days. Or maybe it had been born on our honey-moon in the Highlands, when I'd made a comment about the toughness of the mat-tress at our inn. *You're like the Princess and the Pea,* he'd said, joking but fascinated. Cruel irony that in a few years, I'd be relegated to the living room floor, to the pullout mattress of stone. Paul hasn't called me Princess in a very long time.

I have to never call him again, I thought, my phone hot in my damp fist. *This has to be the last time.*

Look, Miranda, this isn't a good time, all right? Can I call you back?

No! And my voice was pathetic, desperate. *I'll call you back, 'kay?*

He didn't call me back, of course. Prob-ably his new girlfriend was calling him to dinner. They'd made the meal together, both of them standing at the marble island in our kitchen, chopping and stirring.

Spaghetti with a marinara sauce made from last summer's tomatoes, from the garden they grew together. Both of them out there in the backyard that I let go to shit, bending down easily to the now fertile earth, tilling the soil and smiling at each other in the sun.

Who was that on the phone? she'd ask, sitting easily in the kitchen chair, her legs tucked neatly under her.

Oh, just Miranda, he'd say.

She needs to stop calling you, Goldfish. In my nightmares, she also calls him Goldfish.

Oh, I know, I know. But how can I tell her that? She doesn't have anyone else, you see. She lost her mom when she was in college. Her dad died when she was little. I was kind of like a brother or a father to her, you know?

It makes me well up to imagine Paul saying that. He'd be right about him being like family, but wrong about who in the family. Paul was more like my mother without the alcoholism and the dark desire to live vicariously.

Also, Paul would remind the new girlfriend, *she's not well.*

That's her own fault, the new girlfriend would point out sagely. *That's not your problem anymore, is it? She's the one who left you, remember?*

Probably they had sex afterward, her on

top. He loves that she can fuck without wincing. She's not worried about pissing off a nerve or a joint. She's willing, energetic, experimental even. And fertile, of course. Fertile as the rich, tilled earth in their lushly growing garden. Oh god. Probably they're even trying for a —

I spent the rest of last night weeping. Not grading idiotic essays. Not prepping for the two classes I was to teach today. Not going over my rehearsal plans, which consist of a blank sheet of paper with *All's Well???* scrawled at the top in red ink. Instead I watched hideous television that made me want to kill myself. Ordered Greek delivery, which I ate standing on one leg. I peed standing too, for fear of sitting down and not being able to stand back up. I gazed at my lovely red couch, which I hadn't sat on in a year, like it was a mirage. I looked at my phone and longed impossibly to call my mother, though even if she'd been alive she would have likely offered little comfort. Still, she would have been a voice, a voice I missed terribly even for all its slurred, careening descents into darkness, there was love in there always.

Instead I lay on the living room floor, my laptop suspended in the air above my head thanks to a Korean "lying-down desk" I ordered on eBay, and I donated more money to a sickly black goat in Colorado. I've given the goat money before. He was born with some sort of terrible disease that prevents his legs from working correctly. He even has one prosthetic goat leg. I watched his GoFundMe video again and again. His owner is a young woman bursting with blond health and yet hysterical with love, worry, and deluded hope over a bloated paraplegic goat whom she has insisted on saving.

I watched footage of the goat enduring his many medical trials, his many backslides into near death. I watched his brief moments of recovery, in which he limps along on his prosthetic goat leg in a hand-knitted sweater or gets pulled down a snowy hill on a sled. I watched the goat's ears flop in the wind and my heart shredded. He looked so indescribably happy being pulled in the sled. I cried at what I perceived to be his small smile. So vulnerable. So helpless. His pain bottomless, yet he takes his joy when he can. I watched the video again and again until I passed out on the floor.

Now as I lie here in my office, I hear a knock on the door. Then another. I shiver. Fauve, probably. Definitely. Checking in to see how I'm doing, which is bullshit.

How goes the play, Miranda? she'll say, looking down at me on the floor. Smiling sorrowfully. *Oh dear, performing our misery again, are we?*

Normally I would have nothing but empathy for an adjunct. But Fauve is another animal, you know the kind I mean. She believes that it is she, with her PhD in *Cats* and her spotty career in musical theater, who should be an assistant professor here, not me. That this should be her office. That she should have the privilege of clawing her way to tenure. Because she has the claws, after all. Always freshly painted, always shimmering.

And because I'm a fraud. She can smell it, absolutely.

Where did you get your doctorate, Miranda? she asked when we first met. Like she was only just terribly interested. Didn't already know the facts.

Miranda's a stage actor, Grace said, patting me on the back. Grace still loved me then. Loved that I was an actor and not a scholar. That I didn't have a stick up my ass like the rest of the department.

An actor, Fauve repeated, actually widening her eyes. *Really? Anything I might have seen?*

I was with a company in Massachusetts for a long time. Defunct. *And then Shakespeare festivals, of course. Lots of festivals,* I lied. *Edinburgh, Idaho.*

Idaho, Fauve repeated breathlessly. *Really.*

I try to remind myself that the adjunct life is a shitty life, that it can turn you into an asshole. That you can't help but look at the faculty around you and think, *Why the fuck are you here permanently and not me?* That of course Fauve would turn her gaze on me. Deformed and drugged out of my mind. Forgetting my words mid-speech. CV full of filler and lies. I am easily usurped. She need only bide her time taking note with her neck pen, amassing her case, watching the train wreck that I have become go careening off the rails. And when it does, she will be there, of course, to pick up the pieces.

Anything I can do to help? she'll say. *You seemed like you had your hands full the other day. The students seem so terribly unhappy too.*

Knock, knock again at my door.

Not Fauve, no. This is a soft knock. A kind knock. Something in its softness makes my eyes water as I gaze up at the underside of my desk. The spider is long gone.

"Who is it?" I ask the door. I shudder to

111

think of Briana. Even Grace I don't want to see right now. Oh god, not Hugo either. If it's Hugo, I'll —

"It's Ellie," Ellie says quietly through the door.

Some darkness in me lightens.

"Helen," I whisper.

"What?"

"Just a minute."

I get up, trying not to make huffing sounds. When I rise, I immediately falter and so lean against the desk, casually, coolly. But I can't meet Ellie this way. So I force myself to sit down in my office chair. The pain I feel upon sitting, the slicing sensation behind each knee, makes me cry out.

"Professor, are you okay?"

"Yes. Come in, come in," I call.

Ellie enters hesitantly, as she always does. Wearing her sad-girl clothes. Her no-color hair hangs lank around her bloodless face. Her gray eyes are, as usual, mournful. Her hands tremble at her sides, the fingers twitching uselessly, performing an anxious arithmetic. It gives me such joy to see her.

Ellie says she hopes she's not disturbing me. I assure her she isn't. Of course not. Never. She is welcome here anytime. *Have a seat, my dear.*

112

"Are you sure you're okay, Professor Fitch?"

She looks so genuinely concerned.

"I'm fine, Ellie," I tell her. "All's well." I try for a smile, but it cracks.

Ellie gazes at me with her sad eyes that see all.

"You don't look fine, Professor Fitch."

"Actually, Ellie, I'm not the best. Truth be told."

"Are you in pain?" she asks so gently, as if even the question might hurt.

Ellie is so wise. So intuitive.

"Just an injury from my stage days," I tell her. "I still haven't recovered, I'm afraid."

"Oh. I'm sorry." She looks sorry. Actually lowers her head. I observe the dull blond roots that precede the dull dyed black. "Is there anything I can do?"

She looks at me exactly, exactly the way I would want Helen to look at the ailing King of France when she offers to cure him with her dead father's ointment. Is it an ointment? A remedy. Some might even say a spell. Her desire to help is genuine, but she desires something in return too, something unspeakable.

I want to tell her, *Ellie, I hope you know the only reason I don't cast you in lead roles is because of bitch Briana's parents. How I* wish I could have cast you as Juliet last season. You would have been so perfect with your melancholy fire and your cheeks that burn bright at the sight of Trevor, our Romeo. You would have been in close proximity to Trevor for three months. Three afternoons a week, you would have felt his teenage breath on your face. You would have breathed in his boyish musk. You would have looked up into his empty, beautiful eyes. His dumb, deep voice would have been at your ear, his lips close to your unpierced fuzzy lobe, making all the dark hairs on your pale body stand on end. He would have crushed your cold hands in his sweaty warm ones. He would have given you things to masturbate about for months, perhaps years; you would revisit this material in the dark, after a day of tending to a cruel and ailing mother who fails to see your gifts. How I would love to have given you this experience, as your drama teacher, as a kind of other mother. Rather than see you off to the side, in old woman's makeup and dowdy servant's clothes, playing the nurse. Giving Briana/Juliet pep talks backstage. Watching Briana and Trevor from the wings, smoldering with envy, grief. Ah, but it deepened your soul. It gave you pain. Pain is a great actor's gift, Ellie. It is a burden but it is a gift too. To be mined. If one is in control of one's pain, of course.

I want to tell her, *You are my true Helen.*

But I say none of this. Instead I say, "You understand pain, Ellie. I hope you know that's a gift. As a theater minor."

Ellie doesn't know what to say. I've made her uncomfortable. She looks down at her boring black clothes as if there were a response somewhere in their linty folds. A small, cheap silver pentacle dangles from her neck.

"Thank you," she mumbles to her knees.

I really don't know what you see in that girl, Grace often says.

Everything, I tell Grace. And I cry a little if I'm drunk. And Grace looks away.

She's a little creepy if you ask me, she once said.

Aren't we all a little creepy at that age? I asked Grace. *I certainly was. Weren't you?*

No, Grace said.

I look at Ellie now, her silence containing multitudes. "What can I do for you, Ellie?"

"I wanted to warn you," Ellie says, looking up at me, her pale face grave.

"Warn me?"

She nods. Looks over her shoulder at the hallway. She left my door half-open. Too late to close it now. "There's been some . . . dissatisfaction."

115

"Dissatisfaction?"

"Dissent."

I smile, though it hurts my hip, my spine, my pelvis, my femur bones. "Which is it, Ellie? Dissatisfaction or dissent?"

She looks over her shoulder again, then back at me.

"I think a complaint is going to be made," she whispers.

I burn. Spine seethes. Hip swells. Legs are screaming for me to rise even though I can't stand up any more than I can remain seated. "A complaint?"

She nods.

"About what?" Even though of course I know about what. And I know who is responsible. Can picture her at the helm, flipping her burnished hair in righteous outrage, amassing validation from her Ashley/Michelles, emboldened by Fauve, who no doubt took her aside after rehearsal. *My dear, I just want you to know that I witnessed Miranda's pigheadedness firsthand, and I feel you're absolutely within your rights. It's your theater club, after all. If you need anyone to back you up, you just let me know.* Trevor, her right-hand man, nodding dumbly like First Murderer in *Macbeth*. All of them marching to the dean's office together.

Or.

Perhaps Briana betrayed me to her mon-eyed parents on a weekend home away from campus. I picture a dining room ablaze with golden light. Briana sitting in a gilded chair with clawed armrests, hair gleaming under the chandelier, complaining while stabbing idly at a gold-rimmed plate of poached salmon and braised asparagus. *She cast me as a poor unlearned virgin*! Her parents nod-ding sympathetically as they sip large-lipped glasses of amber wine. Her mother placing the call to her dear friend, the vice president, the stem of glass number two between her manicured fingers. About the insane drama teacher. Her stupid insistence upon a play she and her daughter have never even heard of before. *All's Well That Ends Well?* Is it even a Shakespeare play? Can't something be done? Surely something can be done.

"Some of the students," Ellie begins, look-ing over her shoulder yet again, "are upset about the choice of play this year. And they're going to complain. Formally. I over-heard."

I feel my face go red. I look up at Ellie.

Ellie won't look at me now. Her gaze is for her black pants, her thick thighs alone. Because she is so tender-souled, she's al-lowing me a private moment to process all of this, to gather myself. And yet clearly she burns with rage on my behalf.

"When did you hear this?" My voice is calm. Only curious. Not at all wavering.

"After rehearsal. On my way out."

I can't cry in front of Ellie. I will myself not to. *Don't, don't.*

"Thank you, Ellie. Thank you for letting me know." My voice is definitely wavering now. She needs to go.

"Professor Fitch?"

"Yes, Ellie."

"I just want you to know that I wasn't part of the discussion at all. I would never do that."

"Of course not."

"I just felt you should know."

"Of course you did. Thank you for telling me."

"Professor?"

I try to will Ellie away. So I can weep openly. Drop back down behind the desk. Take more pills before my Playing Shakespeare class.

"Yes?"

"I don't know if you would be up for this. . . ." She clears her throat, and I half expect her to pull out her Lady of Shalott journal and begin reading one of her depression sonnets to me aloud.

I look at Ellie now, gazing at me so fixedly. "I make these baths, Professor," she says. "I'd love to make one for you."

"Baths?"

"It's just dried herbs and essential oils and salt," she says quickly. "Anyway, they're very healing. Relaxing in a way. They might help with your pain. They're supposed to have restorative properties." She blushes, the pentacle pendant around her neck glimmering against her bloodless skin.

"I make them for people," she says. "For myself too sometimes."

"Do you?"

I picture Ellie lying in a bathtub filled with stagnant water, her necklace glowing in the dark. Wet hair slicked back. Wan face floating above the steam, lit weakly by a tealight. Her eyes are closed with palpable intensity.

"Would you be interested in a bath?" she asks me.

I try to smile. "Ellie. I'm sure you have better things to do than make me a bath."

She doesn't smile back. Just stares at me, dead serious. "I'd like to," she says. "It's easy for me."

"Well, I'm a bit beyond baths, I'm afraid. But thank you. Thank you for thinking of me."

My office phone begins to ring. The dean?

Possibly. Ellie and I both look at the phone.

"Maybe I'll make you one anyway," she says, getting up. She slings her canvas bag over her shoulder. Smiles at me with something like love in her eyes.

"See you later in rehearsal, Professor Fitch."

Class is a black hole. Playing Shakespeare, what a joke. I gaze at my students. Already so unemployable. Already doomed. *You're doomed,* I want to tell them. Instead I say, "Good afternoon." I attempt to lean back against the desk, but my sitting time with Ellie has made even this posture unbearable. Grunts inadvertently escape my lips. My face, I know, looks pale and cracked down the middle. My lips hiss with dryness no matter how much I lick them. The good thing is Playing Shakespeare can pretty much teach itself. Get them to read whatever play aloud in class. A play, after all, is meant to be performed. Get them to perform a scene. Two scenes, why not? Get them to discuss the staging of said scenes in groups. Get them to discuss *at length.* Get them to present their findings to one another. Appear to take note of all this from where you lean against a wall, trying not to die. If you have time left over, play a video clip. Play the whole fucking video. Patrick Stewart and Ian McKellen when they were young and beautiful and talking about scansion. A Lifetime network version of a contemporary and utterly implausible *Othello.* A shakily shot YouTube video of *Dream* being staged in a Utah field. It's all instructive. Ignore the ringing of your cell phone. Which is the dean calling again, surely. He's in his office. Likely standing at his window observing the quaint campus green, the dollhouse residence halls and white church-like buildings that make up this toy college. Cell phone to his ear, stupid smile on his face. Perhaps Fauve is in the office with him, bearing witness to my humiliation. She'll often pay him visits, ingratiating herself. Bringing him coffees, baked treats, new animal ties.

I saw this one with little donkeys, and I couldn't help but think of you.

Fauve, he'll say, *how thoughtful.*

She's told him about me, surely. Her fears about my competence as a director, my questionable teaching credentials. *Was she ever even a teacher before this? She isn't a scholar, I know, but she isn't exactly a real professional either, is she? What has she done, a couple of festivals?* He enjoys Fauve's company. It perks up the afternoon hours, which he usually murders by just smiling at the wall. But today there is this annoying phone call to make too.

Pick up, pick up, he is attempting to tell me with his mind. But the dean has no psychic powers over me.

You don't. I won't, I tell him quietly in my mind. *I'm teaching. I'm in the middle of a class, have you forgotten the schedule? Playing Shakespeare M and W 2:30–3:45, hello? There are life lessons being learned in this very room at this very moment.*

"Ms. Fitch?"

This from Skye, sitting in the far corner. Lovely Skye. All in black. With her long hair and shimmering, painted lips both the blue green of the sea. A heavy-metal mermaid.

"Yes, Skye?"

"Kendall," the girl corrects. Auburn bob. Pug face. Frowning at me, confused. "Who is Skye?"

"Skye?" I look around the room, but Skye isn't to be found anywhere. Just regular children looking at me with regular horror.

"Ms. Fitch, are you okay?"

I stare at them all, staring at me. For once, no one looks bored.

I think this is going to be a great new beginning for you, Miranda, Paul said when I got this job. *I really do.* The way he was looking at me, beaming. Like maybe we were going to be okay after all. Maybe this job would save me, save us. I remember he brushed my hair away from my face, kissed me like he hadn't in a long time. *Let's go out and celebrate, all right?*

All right. And I tried to smile, to hide the sinking feeling. That I was in over my head. That I'd soon be drowning.

The students are going to fucking love you, I'll bet. And talk about an easy gig, right? You can do it in your sleep!

"Ms. Fitch? Ms. Fitch, are you —"

"Fine. Why don't we cut out early today, yes? Give yourselves a break. You've all worked so hard." Such a lie. Such lies I tell them. But it works every time.

"Good night," I tell them as they go walking out the door.

"It's still only afternoon, Ms. Fitch."

Before I limp to the theater for rehearsal, I look at myself in the bathroom mirror. *This is it for you,* I tell myself calmly, slowly. It is a truth, that's all. To be swallowed like a pill, how many have I swallowed? To be internalized. *You are no longer a human woman. You are no longer sexually viable.* I observe these truths a long while, and my eyes do not water. I am hypnotized by my

123

own ruin. By this new face that is apparently my face, its static misery lines that I do nothing to disguise. Before, oh before, how I would have. I would have applied a red lipstick to my cracked, pale lips. I would have squeezed and squeezed at my cheeks until I burst blood, or beat the sides of my face with a blush brush. I would have plucked out the gray hairs. A woman attempting to crawl up the crumbling vertical wall of a cliff from which she has already fallen, her hands full of loose dirt and spiders. Desperate creature. Denial, denial, denial. My mother, God bless her, would have approved of this. A memory of her comes to me, from just before she died, one I think of often. She's drunk, as she always was then, straightening face towels in the guest bathroom and singing to herself. Meanwhile downstairs, the kitchen was going up in smoke. A grease fire she'd accidentally started and then forgot about. Instead she was up here in the bathroom, her forehead pressed into the wall tile, straightening tiny useless towels, humming "Que Sera, Sera."

CHAPTER 6

When I get to rehearsal, it's just Ellie sitting alone on the edge of the stage. Her canvas bag strapped over her shoulder, lank dark hair in her moon face. Her heavily lined eyes do not look at me but at the unswept stage floor, at the dust balls fuzzy under the bright stage lights. *I'm so sorry, Professor,* says her silence. *I did warn you.*

I stare at the violently empty theater. Even Grace isn't here. I see Briana's triumph. Her smile. She is gazing at herself in the three-way vanity mirror in her bedroom while her mother stands behind her brushing her daughter's burnished hair with long, slow strokes, a glass of golden wine in her other hand. *All taken care of, my dear.*

A low, broken cry escapes my lips before I can help it.

"Professor Fitch, I'm so sorry," Ellie says.

"It's fine, Ellie," I say. I smile. "I'm sure

everyone will be coming along any minute now."

Ellie looks at me like I'm insane. "Professor, I'm sorry, but I really don't think anyone is coming."

"Of course they are, Ellie," I say. Why am I saying this? "There's a rehearsal."

And then I lean against the lip of the stage as though I'm actually waiting for them to show up. I attempt to phone Grace under Ellie's furtive gaze. No answer. Sometimes Grace will work out at the school gym before rehearsal. Strength day, she calls it. She'll show up at the theater still in her ostentatious workout clothes, clutching a giant sports drink. Or she'll change back into her vest and slacks, showered and shining with health, her still-wet hair gleaming. Looking so recharged and content I can barely stand it. But I'd give anything to see her walking briskly into the theater now. I call again. I text, *Where are you???*

I look up at Ellie and smile as if I expected all of this. As if my body were not an emergency. As if I were not sometimes seeing two of her. As if all were well.

I say to Ellie, "Well, Ellie, since we're still waiting for people to show up, why don't you go ahead and practice Helen's soliloquy?"

Ellie looks at me confused. "But Briana is playing Helen," she says.

"Well, Briana isn't here, is she?"

"No."

"And you're her understudy, yes?"

"Yes."

"So why not rehearse? In case anything should happen. In case anything should befall poor Briana. Accidents. Illness. The flu. Mono. You never know, Helen."

"Helen?"

"I mean Ellie. Ellie, why not practice Helen?"

Ellie looks around her. "But there's no one else here."

"You don't need anyone else here!" I say this shrilly. And then I gather myself. A few deep diaphragmatic breaths as I was instructed to do by Mark, back when Mark still had a plan for me, for us, back when he believed I could be healed.

"You're the only one on the stage in that scene, yes?"

"Yes."

"So go on, then. I'll be back. Everyone should be along soon. I'll just go out into the hall and check."

But the hall outside is violently empty too. No Grace. No students milling around. Just the hum of vending machines. Framed posters and photographs of our past productions on the concrete walls. *The Tempest. As You Like It. Romeo and Juliet.* Me lurking darkly in the far corner of each photo like I spawned them all. As if I actually chose this life. But my face, which looks increasingly pained with each production, gives me away. Eyes more hollow and sunken. My hunched body swallowed by a darker, drabber dress. Meanwhile, Grace looks the same in every photograph. A grave young woman in a flotational vest. Same Joan of Arc cut to her fox-brown hair. Forbidding smile of the hunter posing beside her kill. She will eat the meat, of course. She will tan the hide. Mount the head on her rose foam wall. It used to be that I could do no wrong in her eyes. I used to hold such charms for her. *I saw you onstage in Boston once,* she told me when we first met during my campus visit. *In* A Winter's Tale. *You played Perdita. You were good,* Grace said. And I already sensed that from Grace this was the highest praise. Later, when we went for drinks, she revealed that she'd had acting aspirations at one point in her life. She'd even played Lady Bracknell, the ruthless mother, in a college production of *The Importance of Being Earnest.*

Lady Bracknell? I repeated, and made a face. *Talk about bad casting,* I said. Thinking of the pink ballet slipper key chain I'd noticed poking out of her purse. All of her earnest, bright-eyed questions about my summer as Snow White. *I think you were a born Cecily,* I told Grace. Cecily, the pink rose, emblem of elegant femininity. Grace looked at me over her pint. Her eyes shone.

We should do the play together, she suggested after my first semester.

We should, I agreed.

How far from Grace I've fallen. Still, she wouldn't abandon me like this, would she? I look at my phone. Still no text from Grace.

"What is happening?" I ask the hallway.

Then I notice the workshop room door is half-open, spilling light into the dark corridor. Hugo's lair. I hear faint music coming from inside, the sound of thrashing guitars. My heart drums inside me. He's there. Still working on the play, my play. Making the world of it palpable.

When I enter, the sweet smell of wood hits me like a drug. Suddenly I'm filled with peace. Late-afternoon light shines down on me from the large high windows. All around the room, propped against the walls, are half-painted flats. Some depicting the interior of a French court, others the exterior of pastoral Italy — blue sky, green leaves, climbing vines, all illuminated by the sun. The sky and leaves and vines of *All's Well.*

I look around the room, and my heart lifts. The pain quiets a little. Goes from a shout to a whisper. The chair leg lifts from my foot. The flashing webs dim slightly.

And then I see it. Sitting on a large wooden table in the center of the room. Covered with a drop cloth. The maquette. A mini replica of the set for this production, a micro portrait of the world of the play.

I hobble over to it excitedly. I admit, I'm moving faster than I thought myself capable.

What aspect of my vision will it depict? I wonder. Will it be Act One, Scene One, when Helen's plight is first revealed to the audience — that she worships Bertram and can never have him? Or will it be the moment when she uses her witchy powers to heal the ailing King? Or when Bertram is told by the now cured King that he must marry Helen, and he doesn't want to and we hate him so much? Or when Helen receives Bertram's cold letter that he has fled to Italy to fight a war because he'd rather die than marry her? Or when finally, finally, after moving heaven and earth, Helen makes Bertram love her? And he tells her and the world that at last he does, he sees her, finally, in that single impossible line?

"Miranda?"

And there he stands before me, hair in his eyes, hammer in hand. Wearing a Led Zeppelin T-shirt, his usual paint-splattered jeans. Looking like a stoned Norse god.

"Hugo," I whisper.

"Miranda," he says. "Thought I heard someone back here." He smiles and a light inside me grimly flickers.

What can I tell you about Hugo except that for a while I thought I dreamed him? Conjured him out of air and Valium to give myself a reason to come to work, to go on living. But I didn't conjure Hugo. Hugo is a real human. His real job is plant operations, essentially the school's handyman. But during the winter and spring, he also doubles as my set designer and builder. He is so handsome it feels like a joke God is playing on the women of the English department, a coven of quietly broken creatures with fathomless lusts for Sting. As if to tell us, *You see, crones? This is life. Right in your midst. Smelling of evergreens. Making gorgeous things out of wood with his large, thickly veined hands. Behold him and pine. Observe the tattoo vines and leaves climbing his* muscled arms as if he grew out of the earth itself, my best, most wondrous tree.

He is also an ex-con. What Hugo did to end up in jail, I have no idea, but I love to speculate with Grace. *Attempted murder? Auto theft? Aggravated assault? Who do you think he assaulted? Someone who deserved it, I'm sure.*

Miranda, who cares? He builds great sets.

He does build great sets. He's brilliant.

Prison, Hugo once told me at a cast party, is where he fell in love with Shakespeare and learned set design. Before that he didn't give a fuck about Shakespeare or theater — *Sorry, Miranda.*

Oh, don't apologize, I said. *Please.* Dead leaves stirring in the dark alley of my heart.

Prison is also where Hugo learned how to work with minimal tools, with limited resources, which made him brilliant for working at a college that has no real budget for theater. I told him so at the party. I said to him, *You're brilliant.*

Hugo didn't know how to respond.

Thank you, he said quietly, and sipped his wine cup. Then he excused himself. Drifted toward his maintenance buddies. They began talking loudly about a metal show they'd all seen together. I watched Fauve lurk in the periphery. Widening her eyes and laughing along at whatever Hugo said. Pretending like she cared about that stuff, she could hang, she didn't have a stick up her ass, a Sondheim playlist on infinite repeat in her car, no, no. No, she was into this. She even had thoughts, apparently, because she was speaking. And Hugo seemed to be listening to her, nodding.

I went to go find Grace, who was smoking in a corner, who had seen it all. She didn't say anything to me except, *Light?*

I can never bring myself to look directly into the strangely flecked eyes of Hugo. Their irises serene, slightly stoned, and ever changing in the light. Or the hair of Hugo, the color of sunbaked wheat in a field. I can never bring myself to contemplate his perfect mouth, made even more perfect by the jagged grin-shaped scar on one side of his lip. A prison injury, perhaps? His other smile. That's grinning at me now. My body lightens, brightens.

"Didn't see you there," he says.

Of course you didn't, I think. *How could you possibly?*

There was a time when I would have been able to bring the likes of Hugo to his knees. I picture the young woman I was. Her head-shot beaming brightly at me from my old *All's Well* Playbill. I keep it stuffed in the very bottom of that dead lingerie drawer, though I fish it out some nights to torture myself. Turn the well-worn glossy pages. And there she is. My impossibly luminous young face framed by a tumble of slick, dark waves. Beautiful. Slightly cruel. Blissfully ignorant of all that was to come.

"Sorry to just wander in," I tell Hugo. "I heard the music. . . ."

He grins. "Sabbath lured you in, huh?"

I stare at him with what I hope is a smile.

"Don't apologize," Hugo says. "Always good to see you."

Is it? Really?

"Hey, Miranda, are you all right?"

Don't tell him about your pain. Don't fucking tell him about your pain, you hag, the beautiful young me says. *Shhh. Shhh.* She brings her slender finger to her perfect lips bright as cherries. I press my cracked lips together and nod.

"Yes, just rehearsing," I tell him. "Well, waiting to rehearse. No one's shown up yet."

I look at the floor, the sawdust. I absolutely cannot cry in front of Hugo.

"Oh," Hugo says softly. "I'm sorry."

I flash back to his look of pity at the last rehearsal. How he witnessed my humiliation at the hands of fucking Trevor, silent, smug Briana. I feel myself get hot and red now under his gaze.

"It's fine. I'm sure they'll be along any minute," I say to the floor.

"Sure they will be," he says, not unkindly. I look up to see him pulling a cigarette from behind his perfect ear. A strange urge to bite it rises in me like a weak wave. "Too early for mutiny, right?"

"Never too early," I whisper.

Hugo laughs. He thinks I'm being funny. "Actually, I'm glad you're here, Miranda."

My name in Hugo's mouth. I close my eyes.

"You are?"

He doesn't mean it literally, you idiot. He's talking professionally, hello?

"Yeah, I wanted to show you . . . well" — he laughs — "I guess you already found it." He points at the cloth-covered box. "The maquette."

"Yes. I haven't looked yet. But I'm very excited to see."

In my mind, the beautiful young me shakes her head from the glossy Playbill page. Beyond hope. I'm beyond hope.

"It's just a preliminary idea, mind you. I only just put it together today. I wanted to get your take before I went any further."

"You did?" I'm so terribly touched, it's ridiculous.

"Sure. I mean, you had such a vision for *All's Well.*"

I recall my meeting with Hugo at a diner last summer to discuss my vision, to discuss the sets. I admit, I got drunk beforehand even though I was already deeply drugged. Still, I was in so much pain I was barely able to sit down, yet of course I did, my hands cupped around a tea I wasn't drinking. Unable to get over the fact that I was sitting across from him, from Hugo. Me and Hugo at the diner almost like we were on a date. He was wearing a T-shirt that read *Cornered by Zombies.* It was two in the afternoon. There was a crazy woman in a visor softly chattering to herself at the next table. I attempted to make small talk — *And how was your summer?* et cetera — which went terribly. He played along politely, told me he was building Adirondack chairs, going to a lot of metal shows. Some theater too, he added quickly, like I was his boss. And then, you know, lots of hikes and time outside. Good to just pack up and get out of town. Run around some mountains, you know?

Yeah, I said, like I totally knew. I pictured getting out of town with Hugo, running around mountains. Or sitting in his garden (probably he had a garden) on his home-made chairs. Standing beside Hugo at a metal show, the drums making my bones vibrate. It all sounded like ecstasy.

What about you? he said. *What have you been up to?*

I thought of myself lying on my living room floor in the semidarkness, weeping. Watching reality TV or the goat video. *This and that,* I said.

I recall how I wasn't able to look him in the eye. How I ended up talking to the table, going on and on. Telling the table about my vision for the play, telling the table all my hopes, my costume choices, my lighting thoughts. How I saw Helen as a woman in deep emotional pain that no one in the world of the play could understand. Except for the audience, of course. And all because Bertram didn't love her, didn't even see her, he was blind.

Sure, Hugo said.

How I conceived of the play as a kind of gothic fairy tale in which Helen endures many trials that transform unfeeling, unseeing Bertram's soul, that teach his eyes to open, to see her, finally. And when he does see her, how can he not fall in love? I finally looked up to meet Hugo's eyes, and I saw that he was looking above my head at something behind me. A passing waitress perhaps. A gaggle of girls. The clock on the wall. I didn't turn to look. *Sounds great, Miranda.*

"I'm sure it's wonderful, whatever you've done," I say now.

"Well, see what you think anyway." He pulls the drop cloth away, and I actually close my eyes. I envision a French court. I expect to see my soul. To look into a dark mirror and cry tears of joy, recognition. I open my eyes.

A tiny, bleak forest. Black, bare-branched trees of Plasticine. A low, full paper moon. Three little hags in shredded black in the corner. And in the center of the miniature stage stands a toy man with a sword looking surprised. A pained little O in the center of his face.

"What the fuck is this?" I whisper.

"Oh shit. You don't like it."

I stare at the hags. I shake my head. "I don't understand it. What is it?"

You know what it is.

"Oh. Well, you know it's in the first act? With the witches —"

"There are no witches in *All's Well.*"

"This isn't *All's Well,* Miranda. I mean it *was,* of course, but then I had to scrap it. This is . . . you know."

I glare at the three tiny crones cackling.

138

The tiny caped man with his sword. Swallowed by the black trees.

"*Macbeth*," I say.

Hugo winces. "Shit, Miranda, aren't you supposed to spin around three times and spit? Or pour salt over your shoulder or something?"

"Why?"

"To counter the bad luck, right?"

He means the Curse, of speaking the name *Macbeth* in the theater. I don't believe in such superstition anymore. I did once, of course. Would always avoid saying *Macbeth*. It was Mackers or the Scottish Play whether I was in the theater or out of it. Then I took my fall from grace, aka the stage, as Lady M herself. And I learned it doesn't matter, these verbal dance-arounds, these euphemisms, these word tricks. It hears you all the same.

The fires that had quieted are now ablaze again. I'm unable to stand on my right leg. I lift it off the ground. I turn to Hugo. Unseeing Hugo. Unfeeling Hugo. "I mean, why did you make this?"

"I'm sorry, Miranda, I thought you knew."

"Knew *what*?"

"About the change?"

"*Change?* What change?"

"Well, Fauve came in here this morning

and told me the play would be changing to Mackers and that you'd be in touch. She said the dean told her."

I picture her glossy mouth at Hugo's ear, red hair brushing against his neck. Loving her proximity to his wood-scented flesh as she leans in ever closer, her breath hot with the scandal of my dethronement.

I look back at the three tiny hags. One of them has red hair, I see. Eyes like little slits. Mouth a cruel black line, curving on one side.

"I'm sorry, Miranda. I'm really surprised that you don't know about this," Hugo says. "It's bullshit, if you ask me. Not that anyone would. But I figured you'd be the first to know. I mean you're the director, aren't you?"

"I'm the director," I whisper. And then I remember the empty theater. No one there except Ellie. Practicing Helen on the lip of the stage alone, under the lights.

"I have to go."

"Miranda, wait, are you okay?"

I walk hurriedly away, trying not to limp, trying to walk with grace. But I can't help but hobble. Probably he's not even watching anyway.

CHAPTER 7

When I enter the dean's office, I encounter not one but three. Three men. All in suits the same shade of gray. All sitting behind an executive desk. The dean in the middle. Flanked by the president on one side, the vice president on the other. Varying degrees of hair loss. Varying degrees of compensatory combing. Three pairs of watery eyes regarding me with neutral expressions. Three pairs of hairy hands clasped. A golden ring gleaming on each of their left hands.

Just a friendly chat, Miranda.

But I smell aftershave. I smell brine. I smell a witch hunt.

After my encounter with Hugo, I went back to the theater. It was empty, of course. My cell phone rang then. The dean again.

Come on by my office on your way out, Miranda.

"Come in, come in," the dean says to me

141

now with dogged sunniness.

The president and vice president smile coldly. I call them Bow Tie and Comb-over, respectively. Bow Tie is of course wearing a bow tie. Patterned today with little winged pigs. Comb-over's pate shines beneath the lights. Between them grins the dean. Who is the fool. Not even Shakespearean. A fool without the wit. Grace and I secretly call him Puffy Nips because of his propensity to wear a certain kind of thin turtleneck that leaves little to the imagination.

Puffy Nips smiles at me reassuringly. *This is not a trial, Miranda. You are not being burned at the stake, no no. Just a friendly chat is all, am I right?* He looks to the other two men, who glare at me.

"Come in, come in. Whoa! Got quite a bit of a limp there! What happened. Knee sprain?"

"My back. My hip and my back actually."

"Ouch." He smiles. "Well. Come in, come in. Have a seat."

I gaze at the flimsy plastic chair the dean is pointing to, which may as well be an iron maiden. If I sit in that ridiculous chair, I'll pay for it dearly. I may not be able to get back up. But I imagine asking these men if I can remain standing. I picture myself standing, casting my crooked shadow over

142

them. All of them gazing up at my body, lump of foul deformity. They'd think it was some dramatic strategy. The drama teacher's histrionics. My inherent need to make theater wherever I go.

"Miranda, everything okay?"

No. My body is a black sky filled with bright stars of pain.

"Fine." I sit. My leg cries out. Do they hear it? No. They're still gazing at me like all is well. *Just a chat, Miranda. Just a chat.*

The dean loves to remind me that he did some community theater in his time. Shakespeare, believe it or not. Oh yes, *The Tempest.* Have I read that one? He was Caliban! How he enjoyed being the monster. Best time of his life. And talk about a learning experience! *In other words, Miranda, I'm an ally. Here to help you.*

So why don't I trust Puffy Nips, his blue eyes twinkling with cataracts, his office full of photos of himself in the mundane throes of familial New England life? Because he always gives me this speech whenever he's about to propose a cut.

"Been trying to get a hold of you. You're not an easy one to reach."

"I was teaching. I am a teacher," I remind them. "I had a class. Then office hours. Then another class. Then rehearsal. But no one showed up."

Silence. I accuse him with my gaze.

The dean looks uncomfortable now.

"And how are your classes going?" he asks me.

After I respond, he says, "Good, good. That Shakespeare." He shakes his head. "Timeless stuff, am I right?"

"Absolutely," Comb-over says, unsmiling.

"Yes sir," Bow Tie says, knocking on the desk like a door.

"Makes you think, am I right?" the dean adds. "Maybe *too much.*" He grins like a fool. "Which is good! Thinking is good, don't get me wrong."

"The students like it," I say. I sound defensive. I sound useless.

"Sure, they must, they must," the dean agrees. "Of course, some plays are more exciting than others, aren't they? Wouldn't you agree, Miranda? That some plays are more exciting than others? For the students in particular?"

This is it. The trap. *Walk in, Miranda, go on.*

"I would say that all the plays are valuable, interesting, in their own unique ways," I counter.

The dean frowns. Bow Tie and Comb-over say nothing. Because the matter is not

144

a light one; I see that now.

"Well, that's what we wanted to talk to you about, Miranda."

"So talk," I say, smiling, though my lip is twitching wildly on one side. "I'd love to talk. I'd love to know why I found a maquette of another play in the scene shop."

I'm shocked at myself. Bow Tie and Comb-over look at each other, then at Puffy Nips, their idiotically smiling puppet. How is he going to handle me?

"Here's the thing, Miranda," he begins. "We know how committed you are as a teacher. How much you care about the theater program. How much you want to restore it to its former glory, am I right?"

I look at Bow Tie and Comb-over, mouths set in straight lines. By comparison, the dean's wide, imploring smile is obscene. He's sweating a little, I notice.

"We *all* want to see that happen, by the way," the dean adds. "But alas" — he sighs dramatically for my benefit — "for that to happen, Miranda . . . we need support, am I right? From the community, am I right?"

He looks helplessly at the two silent men on either side of him, his superiors.

"Bottom line," says Comb-over at last.

"Exactly, yes, bottom line," the dean adds,

nodding wildly. "Do you understand, Miranda?"

I stare at the framed photos of him and his boring wife and their boring brats on the Cape. In all the pictures, they're in various stages of sailing. In one of them, he's gripping a lobster fork, about to dive into the bowels of a boiled crustacean. He's practically leering at the creature.

"I understand," I say. "You need money." I picture the dean, Comb-over, and Bow Tie idling on a dark street corner, wearing spandex dresses full of holes. Thigh-high patent leather boots. Long blond wigs. Thumping the windshields of passing cars with the meaty heels of their hands.

They all frown now. I'm putting it so crudely.

"What we need, *Ms. Fitch,*" Bow Tie says, leaning forward, "are generous men and women in our community who are willing to support the program's initiatives. And we're so fortunate — y*ou're* so fortunate — that such men and women are already in our midst."

He's almost misty-eyed when he says this. *Such men and women. Already in our midst.* Why not just say the names of Briana's parents out loud? Why not just call the hideous thing by its name? I have a vision of a Waspy woman in capris, always capris she wears. Hair dyed to the former burnished glory that her daughter now enjoys. Beside her, an unsmiling man in a polo shirt, face reddened by a life of sailing and golf, gazing at me with the leaf-green eyes of his unholy spawn. Both of them seated in their reserved thrones in the front row on every opening night, looking like they own the theater, my soul. Which they do.

"Fortunate," I say. "Of course we are."

"In fact," Comb-over adds, "such is their commitment, their dedication to theater, that they've reached out to us with some concern of late."

The dean nods. *Concern. Yes. Such a good way of phrasing it.*

"Have they?" I say like I'm surprised. Like I'm not at all surprised. I'm gripping the armrests. I'm looking right into all of their eyes. *Fucking say it already.*

Comb-over and Bow Tie look at the dean. *Well?*

"Some complaints have been made, Miranda," he says airily. "About the choice of play this year. Apparently, it's not the one the students wanted to put on, is that right? They actually wanted to put on another play? And they were, in fact, quite excited

147

about it?" Like he doesn't already know the facts.

"Now remind me," he continues. As if he actually forgot. What a Caliban he must have been. "Which play was it again? The one they wanted?"

"Macbeth," Comb-over spits.

"Right. *Macbeth,*" Bow Tie says.

"Oops," the dean says, and winks at me, hideously. Falsely conspiratorial smile. "Not supposed to say that name aloud, I think, am I right? Curses things, doesn't it? Bad luck, isn't it?"

For a second, I see his true green reptilian skin shimmering beneath his thin white mask of a face. How many pills did I dry swallow before I came in here?

"Think that's just in the theater," Bow Tie says. His sour mouth curls upward.

The dean tsks. "Better safe than sorry, am I right? I know how much luck means to you theater people."

"Sure," Comb-over offers, giving me the sledgehammer of his smile. "Need all the help you can get."

"Absolutely." The dean beams. "Anyway, what we've heard is that you've insisted that they go in another direction."

"As their director," I interject.

Their smiling, jokey faces grow grave.

148

"Excuse me?"

"I'm the director. I led them in another direction. As their director."

They exchange looks. I'm making my little stand. It's lame. It's easily swatted away. My attempt to stand up for myself when I can't even physically stand.

"What we've heard is that you've insisted, despite their repeated misgivings, which they have communicated to you, on putting on another play. One they don't like at all. What is it called again? *As You Like It?*"

"Something like that," Comb-over says.

"*All's Well,*" I correct.

"Excuse me?"

"*All's. Well. That Ends. Well.* That's the name of the play."

"Never heard of it," Bow Tie says. As if that settles it.

"You sure that's a *play*?" Comb-over says.

"By *Shakespeare*?" the dean clarifies.

"Maybe it was one of those that was written by other people," Bow Tie offers. "Didn't he have other people writing for him?"

"Bacon, I think," Comb-over says.

"Francis Bacon, absolutely," the dean fills in, nodding.

"Marlowe too, wasn't it?" Bow Tie adds.

"Christopher Marlowe, oh yes," the dean

says, nodding vigorously now in the direction of Bow Tie.

"It's a play by Shakespeare," I say quietly, though I want to scream. "One of the problem plays."

"And we're sure it's *wonderful,*" the dean says. "But here's the thing, Miranda: the students don't agree. And here's the other thing: our donors feel the same way. Now, of course it's not up to us to tell you how to do your job, Miranda, am I right?"

"Course not," Comb-over says.

"No sir," says Bow Tie.

"I mean, we're not theater people by any means, are we?"

"Nope."

"And you *are* the director after all, aren't you?"

"Am I?" I ask them. I'm really asking.

They ignore this.

"But we also know that you, more than anyone, would want to see Theater Studies flourish again, am I right? Get a new stage. Get that platform you talked with me about once. The one that extends into the audience, remember? What was that called again?"

I stare at his desk. "A thrust," I whisper.

"Right, a thrust."

"We know too that you would hate to see

the program shrink," Bow Tie says.

"Dry up," Comb-over adds.

"Become obsolete," Bow Tie finishes.

They look at me meaningfully.

"Am I right?" Puffy Nips says to me softly. I seduced this man when I got the job. Not physically, psychically. It was easy, can I tell you how easy? How I fed off my audience, so long since I'd had an audience. How I shimmered with local glamour. Radiated a nonthreatening competence. It helped that I was replacing Professor Duncan, a withered, old Shelley scholar a decade past retirement and only tangentially qualified to direct. By contrast, and with the help of makeup and drugs, I appeared to be a shiny, pretty new coin fresh from the stage. Winking under the dean's bleakly flickering lights. Dropping one glittering theater anecdote after another. *We have such great theater right here in Massachusetts, don't you agree?*

Oh, definitely, Ms. Fitch.

My body in this room was seduction enough, promise enough, for him. I merely had to make my voice slightly pliable, a trick from my Helen or was it my Snow White days? Merely had to seem dumber, more helpless, more open to suggestion, than I actually was.

151

And why would someone like you be looking to teach at our little college? he asked me, his final question. Only then did I falter. Only then did my smile slip. Sweat broke on my brow briefly. I thought: *Because my dreams have been killed. Because this is the beginning of my end.*

But I gathered myself, attempted to look thoughtful. I gazed at the dean's waiting expression. The ugly concrete wall behind him, the grim clockface.

The theater has given me so much, I said, and smiled. *I'd just really love to give back now.*

He smiled at that. He bought it. I bought it myself. Believed my own lie even as the truth rankled within me. You would have thought I actually fucking wanted the job.

That interview was my best performance in years.

Now, of course, things have changed. Now he can see my actual helplessness, my interior deadness, my atrophied body shrouded in its tea-length dress. My gray hairs, which I do nothing to disguise. My lipstick that clashes with the misery on my face. My new despair-wrinkles, my pallor of lost hope. My forehead permanently furrowed from explaining myself to doctors, from trying to get a straight answer from

Mark, Luke, Todd, John. *Just fucking tell me. Is it structural? Is it mechanical? Is it neurological?*

It could be a number of things, Mark always says from behind his clasped hands.

"We're not telling you what to do, Miranda," the dean says now.

"We're telling you to consider," Combover says.

"To *deeply* consider —" Bow Tie adds.

"Switching to that other play."

"Macbeth."

The dean winces playfully for my benefit. *Whoopsie!* "Anyway. You think about it, okay, Miranda? Good luck!"

"They don't say *good luck* in theater," Bow Tie says, popping a mint into his mouth.

"Don't they?" the dean asks, eyes bright. *Look at us, learning even now, even here*!

"Nope," Bow Tie says, crunching, the white-green sparks flashing between his teeth like tiny lightning. "They say *break a leg.*"

"Oh, right! Right, right, right. Well! Break a leg, Miranda. Oh wait, maybe too late for that, huh? Ha ha ha ha ha ha. Ouch."

CHAPTER 8

"Thank you for seeing me on such short notice," I whisper to John in the dark. John of small mercies. John of the magic touch. John, my last resort, my shadow therapist. Unaccredited. Under the table. I stand before him in his dim, dust-filled garage, cash in my fist from the drive-through ATM, my head bowed low. A penitent returning.

I drove here straight from the meeting with the dean. I called John on the way. *I'm coming over*! I told him. *I hope you don't mind. I hope you don't have a conflict.*

Luckily, John never minds. John never has a conflict.

"No worries, Miranda," John says now. "I was just watching the game, but I'm recording it, so no worries."

I nod at the cracked garage floor, at the bright white of John's humongous running shoes, patiently pointed in my direction.

"Thank you," I whisper. "Thank you so much."

I'm leaning against his rickety massage table, unable to stand, unable to sit, unable to look directly at John, who probably looks very confused. Understandably. It's been a while since he last saw me. On the small table between us is an economy-size tub of lotion, which, if all goes well, John will soon be squirting into his large, hairy-knuckled hands, administering to my spasming flesh, while I weep quietly into the doughnut hole. But not yet. First, I must explain myself. My recent absence. Why did I disappear again? He doesn't get it. He thought we were making such progress — *We were really getting somewhere, weren't we, Miranda?*

"We were," I whisper to John, "of course we were." I lean more heavily against the massage table. Not quite bold enough to lie down on it yet. Waiting for John to give me permission. But he won't do that yet. He must attempt to diagnose me first. This is the painful part. The part I have to get through. Watching John think.

John observes me now, arms folded and legs spread like a coach. He is frowning deeply. I always make John frown deeply. John is not a licensed physical therapist. He might not even be a certified physical trainer. He might just be doing this as a hobby. He was recommended to me by a woman in the history department who has been wearing a neck brace for as long as I've known her. I don't ask her what happened because it feels like a private thing.

John is the best, she said to me. *He gets it. He'll get you there.*

Get me there?

She nodded as much as she could in the brace. *All under the table, of course. He doesn't believe in the system. He's been burned by it. Who hasn't?* she said to me. *He's a rebel. Totally antiestablishment.*

Is he? And I felt it. The terrible swell of hideous hope in my heart.

She slipped his phone number into my hand. *You'll see.*

And I did see. I stepped into the dark garage empty of all but the cheap table, saw John emerging from the shadows in his gym shorts with his lotion and his clipboard, and I saw immediately.

Still, I come to John's garage for comfort. I come to John because his hands can sometimes work a brief magic. And because he is kind. Kinder than Mark. Far kinder than cruel Luke.

Now I can hear John's wife upstairs banging kitchen cupboards. She's pissed that I'm here. That I'm back. She thought I was gone for good.

"I have to say, Miranda, you don't look good," John pronounces at last.

"I don't?" I'm shocked at the hope in my voice.

John shakes his head. Nope. "You're all out of whack," he observes.

"I am?"

John nods. "Oh yeah, you're off. Totally off. Wow. Have you looked in a mirror at all?"

"No."

"You're all . . ." And then with his hands, he makes a tower that is leaning wildly to the left.

"Really?"

"Way off," John says. "It's weird. Last time you were here your pelvis was in alignment." John is very concerned with things like pelvic alignment.

It's good, I tell myself. It's a sign of his expertise. Not everyone has to go to school to be an expert, do they?

John frowns now at my tilted pelvis, the right hip bone jutting aggressively forward. My right leg crooked and curled into itself like it wants to die. I'm veering off to the left like I am terrified of the right side of my body. He looks back up at me, but I'm avoiding John's gaze. His clear, fawn-like eyes that only want an answer to a simple question.

"What's happened since I last saw you? I don't understand," John says. Suspicious? No, not John. Merely curious. Merely genuinely mystified. I attempt to look mystified too.

"Me neither," I lie. "No idea."

"How long ago since I last saw you again?"

I gaze at the tub of lotion longingly. I pretend to think. "I'm not sure."

"Been like a whole month, hasn't it?" he says.

In which I tried Todd. In which I continued on uselessly with Mark. In which I tried the man with the pince-nez who stabbed my left boob with a long needle in an attempt to tap into my chi, then let me lie there for twenty minutes on his medical table like a corpse.

"Has it really been that long?" I ask John. I make a face like time is hard to follow. What with the pain.

I can't possibly tell him that I've allowed another physical therapist to strap me to a table with belts and then pull my leg out of its socket with quick, successive jerks. Instead I pretend to be confused like John.

I really don't understand what's going on either. My body is a mystery.

"Really no idea." I shake my head, leaning back farther on the table. Almost sitting. Almost there. But John refolds his arms. Frowns more deeply at my body. Widens his diagnostic stance.

"Maybe it's your quadratus lumborum," he offers. Normally I would enjoy the fact that John likes to refer to muscles by their proper names. It would comfort me. Rekindle my faith in his diagnostic capabilities.

"Maybe." I watch him write this down on his clipboard.

"Should we take some measurements?" he asks.

Measuring tape is John's primary tool. He doesn't do modalities like Mark. No ultrasound machine. No electric stimulator. No dry needles. He does have a set of Chinese suction cups that remind me of the suckers on octopus tentacles, which leave red welts all over my body. He brought them in from the house once like they were a plate of cookies — *Should we try them?*

I stare at John, who looks so confused, so well-meaning, the measuring tape hooked to his shorts like a gun. Genuinely wanting to solve the puzzle of me even though it's one hell of a puzzle, Miranda, he's not going to lie. Not just the picture but the pieces too. A million of them, and always changing shape, never fitting like they did before, the image keeps shifting. He wants to get to the bottom of it.

I feel for you, Miranda, he once said to me, *I do.*

And I cried. John handed me a Kleenex from a box patterned with smiling puffballs. He bowed his head respectfully as I blew.

But all I want tonight is the temporary fix of his magic hands. I want him to tell me to lie down. I want him to prod gently at my back, my thigh, my pelvis, until his wife calls his name from the top of the stairs.

John?

Yeah.

I've never seen her except as an ominously permed shadow on the wall.

"Maybe the best thing is to just dive right in," I say at last. "Feel around and see?" I lean all the way back onto the table. I turn onto my stomach, gasping at the pain, my legs like lead. I put my face into the dough-nut hole. I lie there waiting. I feel John standing beside me at a loss. I've never taken control like this before. If I did this with Mark, he'd tell me to get up. Luke would just walk out of the door. Through the hole, I stare down at the garage floor, at

John's shoes, still patient, still pointed toward me. A tear falls from my eye and splashes onto the floor between his feet. I hold my breath.

"All right, Miranda," John says. And I hear him at last lower the clipboard. "Sure."

"Thank you," I say. I close my eyes. I feel him lift up the back of my dress, gently, gently. Like I'm a human person. *John treats me like a human person,* I tell the other PTs in my mind.

Mark merely shrugs, looks indifferent. *You'll be back,* says his face. So sure of himself and his capabilities, his knowledge of modalities, his nerve expertise. *You want to be treated like a human person, go ahead.* He'll let me go walking into the dark with John; he'll let me go so easily.

I wait for John's touch. A touch I know won't save me, can't save me, but it will ease things for a while.

"Feel that?" John says now, pressing into my back with the pads of his fingers. But tonight I feel nothing. Nothing? Can't be. Surely something.

"Um, I think so," I lie. "Maybe go more deeply."

"How about that?" John asks now, pressing. "Feel that?"

Nothing. Nothing, nothing.

CHAPTER 9

Worse. Much, much worse now. More fucked-up than before — how is that possible? But it is. Broken. Truly this time. Even as John waves goodbye to me from his window, just before his wife draws the blinds, I know this. As I limp back to my car, parked behind John's and his wife's SUVs, I know this. As I pick uselessly at the ice on the windshield, my legs giving way beneath me, I know this. As I drive home in the dark cold, barely able to sit in the driver's seat, I know this. My bones tell me so. John John John, what have you done to me? Not John's fault. Mine. My own broken body that will not heal. That refuses to right itself. The drive home is excruciating, can I tell you this? New England never seemed so black, so friendless. Spindly trees shining with ice. Road slick and black, everything black and frozen. I think of the meeting with the dean. I think of Briana, triumphant. The

163

three plastic witches smiling around their toy cauldron with the paper flames. Home. Why go back to that dark place? Why lie on the cold, hard living room floor with my legs on the chair, listening to the couple fuck next door? Every other night, this happens. All night it goes on. And they don't just fuck, they talk between fucks. And not just talk, they fucking laugh. It's awful, awful. I never hear what they're saying or what they're laughing at, just the laughter itself, the fucking itself. I hiss at them through the wall, *I hate you.* I hiss, *Shut the fuck up.* I beg them, *Please. Both of you. Please die.* They don't hear me, of course. They keep laughing and fucking, talking and laughing, and she orgasms again and again and again, ocean waves crashing and crashing on the sharp rocks of me, refusing to stop, not caring if I scream, because this is nature, this is a force. The sounds coming out of her mouth make me feel like I'm dying. My body in this car right now, sitting in this seat right now, gripping this cold wheel right now, make me feel like I'm dying. Am I dying? Maybe I am. Finally. About time, really. Enough of this. God's way of telling me. Black sky. Starless. Can't face my apartment. Can't face my future. What is it even? Loveless. Cold. Black. Three toy witches. A low paper moon. Bare dark stage. One white light. And in it is Trevor mumbling at a toy dagger. Briana in a white dress with fake blood on her hands. Not fake blood, no. My blood. My blood on her hands. And she'll be happy. Ecstatic. No one will see the smile on her face but me. Grace will direct. No, Fauve. Fauve in my windshield now, triumphant, her chime earrings clinking softly as she stands in the wings, her palms pressed together before her curved lips, eyes on the stage as though she's watching God perform her will. Applauding herself, her patience. And I'll be forced to watch too if I'm not dead yet. I'll still have to teach for the health insurance. They'll wheel me into the theater like the ailing King. My body burning like a star, like a planet of mercury. Pull over. Just pull over now to this dark, cold shoulder of the earth, hit the brakes on the gravelly ice. Take the pills rattling in your pockets. Won't matter which pills from which pockets. Just swallow. Swallow them down. Swallow them all down, why not? Be done with it. Close my eyes. Stare at the dark behind my lids so heavy, just as starless. My breathing will slow. Everything will slow. The silence will sound like music. Forget my broken body once and for all. Cold won't feel cold anymore. Nothing. I'll feel nothing. Let the dark be the Dark. Enter the real Night. Not here though. Not here on this loveless New England road. Ice still on the windshield. Trucks roaring past like laughing devils. I think of that golden drink. What did they call it again? The golden remedy. How it made me glow from the inside, how it made a blue sky of my body. The three men at the bar. The middling man seeing my pain, seeing all. One more drink. One more drink for the road, why not?

"Ms. Fitch, Ms. Fitch. You're back."

"I'm back."

He claps as if to applaud me. They all do. All three. As if they know I limped back here from the abyss.

"Thank you," I whisper.

"Close Your Eyes" by Al Bowlly playing at full volume as I enter the bar. Empty for the most part. Except for them.

They're sitting just as they were before, more or less. Deep in drink. Suits the color of night. The middling man looking at me like I'm a puzzle, I'm a dream, but he's putting me together, piece by piece. It's all beginning to assemble into an image. He's starting to see. And what he sees delights him. There's a sheen to his salesman face tonight, a smile to his bloodshot eyes. I'm the best kind of theater. The fat man is still slumped into incomprehension. Head on the bar, yellow-gray Medusa locks falling across his eyes like a sick veil. The third man — tall, slender, beautiful as a dream, though I only ever see a sliver of his moon-shaped profile — has his suited back to me tonight. But he's listening, he's with us, he's smiling at me even, I feel this. I can tell by the back of his head, the shape of his skull, the nape of smooth neck flesh above his white shirt collar, that he's hearing me intently. Toasting me with his golden drink.

"Pour her one," the middling man says to the bartender. "We need it, am I right?"

Am I right?

I recall the dean. His small blue eyes shining idiotically. *Am I right? Am I right?* Do they know about the dean? How can they possibly know about Puffy Nips?

"We do, we do," the fat man whispers. "Am I right?"

They all chuckle.

And then it's there before me in a squat glass. I stare at the drink's golden-green color. Green like the leaf-green eyes of Briana. Golden as Hugo's hair. Glowing as if the liquid had a light of its own. As if it were a prop.

"Well, Ms. Fitch. What are we even waiting for?"

How do you know my name again?

"Ticktock, ticktock, Ms. Fitch."

" 'Tis time, 'tis time," whispers the fat man.

I drink. They all clap again. The fat man thumps and thumps his hand on the bar. Though the beautiful man has his back turned, I see him clapping too. It brings tears to my eyes, the sound of their tender applause. The music brightens my insides, I feel it brightening my blood. The fist of my body unfurls, opens its hands, fingers. I feel my nerves sigh. A candle in my heart relit, the flame growing tall again.

They applaud, so joyously now.

"Thank you," I say. "Thank you, all." And I bow my head a little. And suddenly it doesn't hurt to breathe, to sit, anymore. It feels like the golden peak of summer is inside of me. I'm smiling. Am I smiling? Yes. Wide. From ear to ear.

"There," the middling man says. "There, there. Better now. Aren't we better now, Ms. Fitch?"

I nod, yes. Better now. Much better now.

"All's well that ends well."

"I'm directing that play," I tell him.

"Are you?" he says, looking not at all

168

surprised.

And then I remember, I'm not. Not anymore.

"Trouble," says the middling man. "Trouble in the theater. Trouble with your back." He shakes his head.

" 'Double, double toil and trouble,' " The fat man laughs, wheezes, coughs.

The slender man makes a *tsk-tsk* sound.

"Trouble," I agree. "So much trouble."

"Tell us the trouble," the middling man says. "I'd love to lend an ear. I'm a listener. And we love theater, Ms. Fitch."

I smile at the middling man, my body like golden honey. He seems taller than before. Bigger. They all do.

I was going to kill myself tonight, I want to tell him. *I just didn't want to do it on the highway. It felt wrong plot-wise. What felt right was to come here. To stop in and have this lovely drink first. And say goodbye to you. Even though I hardly know you, sir, do I? Not even your name. What is your name again?*

The middling man smiles compassionately. Bloodshot eyes shining. I don't need to speak. He sees all already. Knows all already. All my misery. My humiliations. He sees the concrete that was once my flesh. He sees the red webs inside. Knows their intricate design. Knows the elusive spider.

169

Knows him by name. The red handkerchief in his suit pocket glows beneath the bar lights. I don't even need to speak at all.

"PTs will break you, Ms. Fitch," he says softly, so impossibly softly the words feel like hands stroking my hair. "They break whoever they touch. Your bank, your bones, your spirit."

"Bank, bones, spirit," the fat man whispers.

"Whoever they touch. And now this business about *Macbeth.*"

He shakes his head. "Trouble," he says.

"Double, double," whispers the fat man.

"A black play, Ms. Fitch."

How do you know about Macbeth? I want to ask. But the golden drink has made honey of my tongue.

"They're making me put it on," I tell them. "Instead of *All's Well.* They're telling me I have no choice." I talk as though I'm talking into a triptych mirror. In each reflection a man in a dark suit, nodding. *Go on, go on.*

He's still smiling at me, smiling at what the spider has spun.

"Can you even picture it? Toy dagger. Fake blood. *Witches.*"

Low laugh from the fat man.

"I haven't seen a scary witch in the longest

time, have you, Ms. Fitch? That truly frightened you?"

I look at the three of them. Shadows getting longer as they wait for my answer. Red
handkerchief blooming from the middling
man's pocket like a flower. The fat man
looks up at me through his yellowed locks
with the yellowed whites of his eyes. Even
the third man has turned his sharp profile
toward me. *Ticktock. Ticktock.*

"No," I say.

They laugh.

"Oh, the melodrama, Ms. Fitch. They'll
murder it. And Briana is no Lady M, is
she?"

"Never," I agree.

"She's no Helen either."

"How did —"

"No wonder, Ms. Fitch," he says, looking
like he's going to cry. "No wonder at all
about your back. No wonder you're all *out
of whack.*"

"Broken, broken," whines the fat man.
"Bank, bones, spirit." He covers his eyes.

"Bank, bones, spirit," I hear myself repeat.
"Broken, broken." I hear my voice crack. A
mirror shattered.

"It's a wonder you can stand at all."

"It's a wonder," I whisper, staring at the
shards. "It's a wonder."

"But pain can move, Ms. Fitch. It can switch. Easy. Easily. Do you know how easy? From house to house, from body to body. You can pass it along, you can give it away. Piece by piece."

"Give it away?" I repeat.

"To those who might need it," the middling man says.

"Even want it. Even thank you for it," the fat man says. He's looking right at me now.

"Exactly. Just like theater. It's all theater in the end."

"Here, here."

The middling man looks at me. "You know what I'd love? I'd love to show you a trick. Do you like tricks, Ms. Fitch?"

Shouldn't. Shouldn't like tricks. Up to something, these men. I should go. Now. Leave and never come back.

"I like tricks," I whisper.

"I think you'll enjoy this one a great deal. Being in theater. It's a theater trick."

The fat man starts to laugh so hard he begins to cough. He coughs and coughs, growing red in the face. The veins on his cheeks fatten, grow livid.

He's going to die, I think. Keel over any minute.

"May I show you?"

172

I look at the three men waiting for me to answer.

Run, I tell myself. *Drive home drunk. Die there alone in your dark room.*

"Show me."

And then the fat man reaches out his hand and grips my wrist. Blue skies in my blood blacken. Great weight on my chest. Spinal cord a column of fire. Can't breathe. Can't speak. On the floor. Cheek resting now on the cold floorboards. Three pairs of shiny black shoes pointed toward me, tapping. Tapping along to music. Music somewhere. Familiar. Old movie music. Making the floor shake beneath my temple. What's happening? What is this? I try to get up, but my body won't listen.

The pain is searing, immobilizing, an iron maiden, metal stakes holding me down. Through the fog of it, I see a stage lit before me. A mic wrapped in fake roses and fairy lights. One pair of suited legs, black pointed shoes walking toward it. Taking their time. I hear a voice from the speakers.

"First up tonight! The Weird Brethren!"

Who's that? I want to ask, but to even think the question hurts in a way I've never known. *You thought you knew pain,* says a voice inside. *Cryer of wolf. Wolf, wolf, wolf. Well, here is the wolf at last.* The teeth at my

173

throat, the claws sinking in.

Music suddenly swells. All around me.

Violins.

Horns.

A drum, a drum.

I know this song, I do. I've heard it before. Where?

The fat man is onstage, standing at the mic. My breath catches and this sends a fresh fire through my bones. Gone are his red veins, his pockmarks. His once yellowed eyes are white white, revealing bright blue irises. His stringy yellow and gray hair is golden now, leonine. His skin and eyes and teeth shine down on me. He smiles. He smiles at me lying immobile on the floor. And then I know. I know his tears are in my eyes. I know his black tarry blood flows through my body. His lungs of lead are in my chest, making my every breath burn. He opens his mouth and begins to sing. A show tune. A song my mother used to sing. Judy Garland. "Get Happy." His voice is rich and clear and deep. He knows the song well. He's an amazing performer. He glides around the stage, so light on his feet now, like the soles are slicked. The middling man and the third man clap along. Sing along. I don't see them, I hear them, feel them behind me. They know the song too, so well.

They raise their gold-green drinks. Tap their feet.

The fat man's voice soars. Black wings high above me. Circling and circling. Watching me inhabit his grief. Singing and singing.

Forget your troubles, c'mon get happy
Ya better chase all your cares away
Shout 'hallelujah,' c'mon get happy
Get ready for the judgment day

The stage lights die. All except for a single spotlight shining on his black pointed shoes. Descending from the stage. Walking toward me step by step. Gliding black leather feet with their heavy, slippery soles. Whistling. Skipping toward me. Every step hurts my skin. Every step brings a new tear of his to my eye. Makes his heart thrash its tail in my rib cage. He crouches down before me until we are nearly face-to-face. His eyes so bright — the whites so white, the blue so blue, where once all was yellow and murky red. Cocks his golden head to one side as though I'm such a curious thing, this woman who is riddled with his unbearable pain. He lies down on the floor next to me, facing me, pressing his rosy cheek, his temple, against the cold stone. Gazing at me dreamily as though the vibrating, cold bar floor is a pillowy velvet.

It's death. It's death at last, I think. He's somehow killed me with a mere touch of his hand to my wrist. Now he reaches a hand out again and I wince, but he just gently grazes my cheek. Caresses it softly. So softly.

There. There, there. There, there, there. Get happy, Ms. Fitch. All's well.

CHAPTER 10

Bright blue sky in the window. My window. Afternoon, I can tell by the light. Is this death? A crow goes flying by the window, shrieking. I watch it land on a snow-encrusted branch, shaking its black feathers, making the snow fall all around. I watch clouds drift pass, and I can smell the brine of the nearby sea. I hear cars driving by on the street outside. Not death, then. I'm alive still. I'm in my body, which is my body. Breathing my own breath with my own lungs. No longer filled with that terrible black heaviness. Just my own pain. Familiar aches. Familiar concrete limbs. Familiar fists already tightening. It's bearable for the moment. At least it's just mine.

I'd love to show you a trick. Do you like tricks, Ms. Fitch?

How did I get back last night? I can't remember anything after being on the floor, the fat man caressing my cheek. After that, black. But I'm in my bed, the blankets pulled up to just under my armpits. I'm not in my dress from the night before, but an old nightshirt of dark blue silk. I never sleep in my bed. I never sleep in this nightshirt. I'm always on the floor. Always lying in the sad dress and cardigan I'm too tired to change out of. Was I carried here by the fat man? Surely not. Surely I just found my way home alone, into this shirt, this bed. But I picture the three of them putting me to sleep. The fat man laying me down. The middling man pulling the covers up to my chin. The third man turning out the light. *Shhhh.*

I shudder.

Who the hell are you? I should have asked the fat man. *What did you do to me last night? How did I wind up on the floor full of your pain?*

I rise from the bed. Immediately feel the nerves in my legs seethe and hum. The muscles clench themselves into concrete. I recall John, gentle, sweet John, scratching his large head over the fact of my body. Prodding at it with a finger to "Nights in White Satin." *Feel that?*

They break whoever they touch, Ms. Fitch. Your bank, your bones, your spirit.

My phone buzzes on my nightstand.

Grace texting me from rehearsal. Fuck. I'm missing rehearsal as we speak.

Warming them up. Where are you?

Also, did you okay this???

Then Grace texts me a photo. A picture of a script she's holding in her hands. I look at the picture of the script, and I burn. The title of the play is center justified. In block letters. The Garamond font. Not the actual name of the play, of course, but the title that is used in superstitious stead, because the name is just too charged for the theater. *Bad luck,* as the dean said. The Scottish Play. The name relights the fires in me, tightens every muscle in my body.

I think of the middling man looking at me with his bloody eyes, smiling at what the spider has spun. *And now this business about* Macbeth.

I drive to campus cursing Briana, January, the afternoon, every red light. I curse her burnished hair, her smirking triumph. Her pushiness that she won't even bring to her portrayal of Lady M. No way. Not if I have anything to do with it. My hands grip the cold wheel. I am suddenly filled with a Helen-like resolve. *Our remedies oft in ourselves do lie which we ascribe to heaven.* Remember this, remember this.

No parking anywhere on campus. I circle and circle the student lots, spouting obscenities at the windshield. At last, I give up and park illegally in front of the theater. Fuck it. I slip up the icy, endless stairs. I nearly fall a thousand times. No one helps, no one sees. Every smoking student is on their phone, smirking at their small screens, in the throes of their own dramas, their own little theater making.

I run through the halls, and I never run, can't run, but somehow I'm running. I see Dr. Rainier smiling at me. *Ms. Fitch. If you can't walk, then tell me: How did you get here?* I burst through the double doors of the theater. Anticlimax. No one even looks up. I'm too late, of course. Briana is already there on the stage. Wreaking her havoc. Wearing one of her bell-sleeved tops, which she thinks makes her look more Elizabethan. Her gold cross glinting on her chest. Burnished hair ablaze beneath the lights, she stands at the helm of a semicircle of traitors, speaking low words, cradling her illicit script in her hands. She's smiling as she tells them there's been a change. She's enjoying this moment, I know. Being in charge. Having her way. Her hair gleams. Her skin glows. In many ways, Grace is right, she is a perfect Helen.

Grace is sitting up front in the audience, watching, looking a little helpless, a little lost, but ultimately indifferent. She looks at me as if to say, *Oh well. Why not let them do it? Why not?*

"No!" I shout.

They all turn around now and look at me. Standing there, lopsided before them and huffing from my run. My body a gnarled little fist. When has my voice ever been that desperate, that loud? Not in a long, long time. Like the howl of a pained animal that is about to die.

They look frightened. And young. Terribly, achingly young as they exchange *Uh-oh* glances. *What the fuck?*

But Briana's smile doesn't even break when she sees me hobbling to the stage toward her. Broken woman. Hag. Unsexed. No charms left. No fashion sense. Wildly unchristian. She can handle this. She can handle me. Her dancer-girl posture says this. The defiant upward tilt of her small, pointed chin. It's fine. It's already done. It's sealed. I've been told where things stand, haven't I? I've been put in my place. I've been scolded by the higher-ups. I've been informed of my rung in the universe, in the scheme of things, in the great chain of being. *None of this should be a surprise to you,*

Miranda, says her entitled chin, her folded arms, as I approach the stage. *At all.* In fact, I was asking for it. Wasn't I asking for it? Willfully ignoring their many requests? My drugged-out speeches, my absurd commands from the seats, pills rattling in my pockets like Tic Tacs. Making them, making *her,* put on a play that no one gives a shit about but me, that everyone agrees is lame, dated, problematic, she could go on. Making her portray "a poor unlearned virgin," a scheming orphan who is scorned by the only man she deigns to love like he's a star in her sad sky. When she could be Lady M, a sexy madwoman in a white dress, the blood on her hands bringing out the green in her eyes. I'm willfully destroying her college experience. I'm ruining her CV.

So here we are, Miranda. No going back now. Too late for that. I asked for this, her face says, as I join her now on the stage.

I face her, mere feet away from where she's standing now, surrounded by her little army.

I smile at them all. I try to. Play dumb. It's the only way.

"What's going on here?" I ask.

I look at Ellie standing a little distance away from the circle. She looks at me, then at the floor like she wants it to swallow her.

Trevor is embarrassed for me too. Won't look me in the eye at all. Just stands next to Briana with his shoulders hiked up to his ears, hands in his pockets, a reluctant groom, but he's at the altar; he'll say the scripted words when it's time.

Sorry, Miranda, but we all feel . . .

None of the students will look at me. The Ashley/Michelles are looking intently at their phones. Ditto all the other ones, my children, the ones who are but a blur of mediocrity. Only Briana looks at me. Right in the eye. Her smile doesn't break, I have to hand it to her. Her little chin stays lifted up. Her eyes don't blink. She is breathtakingly unafraid of me. So unafraid that I feel fear, queasy. Of course she is unafraid. Look at you. Withered and wavering on your feet in your Ann Taylor sack. Smelling of demonic pub wine. Looking at her blearily through your drug mist. Unable to say your words in one cohesive string. Your sentences breaking apart like brittle. Pauses that go on for minutes during which you just stare at dust, while they all cough pointedly. Hardly an inspiration. Authority? Forget authority. You have no authority here. You have lost.

Oh, but I refuse to lose.

This is a standoff. Have I had them

183

before? Yes, I've had them before.

"Can someone tell me what's going on, please?" I ask this kindly. Inquiring, merely inquiring. Like I'm curious.

You know what's going on, Miranda. You see the script in my hands that is not your script, that I'm holding in such a way that the title is visible to your eye. But Briana is also taken aback by my approach. I'm not throwing a fit. I'm playing dumb, confused, she didn't expect that. And I'm good at it. She forgets I was an actress once. On much bigger stages than this, oh yes. I played festivals. Critics raved about me in reviews. *A shining light. An impressive performance. Competently portrayed.*

Briana's smile wavers. I watch her white neck redden, her freckled chest flush, and it's delicious, the sight, it emboldens me. Even though a part of me feels shame. Because she's just a child, isn't she? The lip gloss, the absurd butterfly clip in her hair, the challenge in her green gaze. *Just a child, Miranda, remember.*

But then I hear chimes clinking. Fauve. Emerging from the shadowy wings with the softest steps. She places jangling white hands on Briana's shoulders as if she's her mother. She's going to make it all right.

"Everything okay here? I heard shouting."

Fauve looks at me. So concerned, so fake confused. But she's a hack. What did she do, community theater?

I look at Briana, who's looking away now. Smiling a little to herself. Biting her thickly glossed lower lip.

"Fine," I say. "All's well." I say it meaningfully.

Fauve smiles sorrowfully at me.

"Miranda." She pauses, like my name is its own sad thing. "Did the dean speak with you?" As if she didn't already know this. Help orchestrate it. Nudge Briana along. Perhaps she even walked Briana to the dean's office herself. *Come along, dear. You're doing the right thing. You're so very brave.* Bolstered her story of my steamrolling with evidence. Tapped a talon at the date/time in her silvery-blue book.

"Yes," I say, "he spoke with me."

"Oh, good." I watch her fingers encircling Briana's neck lightly. I think of the fat man caressing my face. She pats Briana's shoulder as if it's all sorted now. The hurly-burly done. The battle lost and won. *There, there.* Not because she loves Briana, no, no. Because she hates me that much. Doesn't believe this pain business. Thinks I'm faking. *Talk about theater, Miranda.* If only I'd put that kind of theater into my work here.

185

We shouldn't even be doing Shakespeare, anyway. We should be doing *Bye Bye Birdie.* *Meet Me in St. Louis. That's* theater. But if we're going to do Shakespeare we may as well go, you know, big. Some witches, for god's sake.

"How's your hip, Miranda? Or is it your back? I always forget," she says, "if it's your hip or your back."

"Both." *You know it's both!* I look at Briana's face. Cradled and beaming now between Fauve's jewel-suffocated hands. Suddenly I'm so tired. To the bone, the cell. Just standing on my concrete leg makes me sweat. I'm losing steam.

"You certainly are standing a little funny, Miranda. Perhaps you should sit down. Take it easy."

They both smile. They won. Fauve gets to see me in my directorial death throes. Her smile is the smile of the fat man looking at me when his body was a blue sky and I was pinned to the floor bearing the black tar of his pain.

"I'm fine," I lie.

"Well, if you need my help, you just call. I'm right across the hall, you know." *Watching you. Willing you to fail.* Fauve pats Briana on the back, walks away, clinking.

I look at Briana. Who feels protected now.

Happy. Relieved. I watch her exhale. Perhaps she was a little afraid of me after all. I look at her cradling the script in her hands, holding it close to her young body, so little and lithe. I look at her rib cage rising and falling, the prideful heart beating beneath.

"I'd love to see the script," I say. "If you don't mind. I'd love to take a look."

Briana looks at me. She hugs the script closer to her chest.

I'm just going to gently take the script from her, that's all. But Briana draws the pages even closer to herself, away from my reaching-out hand, which is ridiculous, humiliating. I reach out again gently, and she actually blocks me, absurdly, and I grab her wrist tight because this is really ridiculous now, how she won't let go, won't yield, can you believe this? How she's looking at me now like I'm some kind of monster, how she's pulling her arm away from my grip like I'm hurting her, which is utterly absurd, I'm only trying gently, very gently, to see the script. I squeeze her wrist slightly, looking deep into her leaf-green eyes with their little brown flecks. Her eyes widen. Her skin pales. Her breath catches. I watch the script drop from her hands. The pages fall, scattering loudly across the stage. She looks at me and her mouth makes a noise.

I look down at my hand, my grip on her wrist.

I let go. Or she pulls her arm away quickly. I'll never be able to remember which. If I let go first. If she pulled away quickly.

We stand there, silent. The felled pages of *Macbeth* all around us, scattered and fanning their way across the stage, to the farthest reach of all four corners.

I watch her rib cage rise and fall more quickly, her breath shallow.

"Trevor, would you mind picking those pages up, please?" I say, my gaze still on Briana's pale, shocked face.

Immediately, he picks up the few pages around his feet. Something in my voice. Which isn't so thin anymore.

She's looking at me, clutching her wrist where I touched it as though it burns. Her hands are trembling. She looks shorter somehow. Smaller.

"I just wanted to see the script." I say it softly. It's really true. It's all I wanted.

Briana just stares at me. Behind her, the students stare at me too. Absolutely expressionless. A sea of faces now turned to me. Mouths closed. Eyes wide open.

I hear a throat clear behind me. Grace. I forgot Grace was here. I turn to where she's sitting in the audience, bracing myself for her expression of judgment, or will it be commiseration? But she isn't looking at the stage at all. She's looking at the side entrance. I follow her gaze.

Puffy Nips. Standing between the open double doors. One hand in the pocket of his Dockers, the other stroking his tie. For a moment, I'm terrified. How long has he been standing there? Did he see? What did he see exactly? *I just wanted to see the script,* I'll say. *That's all. And she moved it away, what was I supposed to do?*

But he's smiling at me. He raps playfully on the doorframe. Three light knocks.

"Professor Fitch," he booms. *Professor Fitch?* When have I ever been Professor Fitch to this man? I am Miranda always. But I straighten up. I smile back, though I'm still shaking.

"So sorry to disturb rehearsal. Hope you don't mind my barging in like this."

"Of course not. Not at all. You're welcome to join us. We were just rehearsing, weren't we? We were just working out some kinks." I keep my eyes on the dean.

"Good, good." Because he's just had some *wonderful* news. He had to share it with us, with me, *Professor Fitch,* immediately.

Wonderful news? Really? I perform my surprise. I raise my eyebrows, try to smile.

189

"Wonderful," I say. "We love wonderful news, don't we?" I ask the students. They are still all mostly frozen in place, looking at me in quiet horror. They nod slowly. A couple have felt compelled to go over to Briana. An Ashley/Michelle is stroking her bell sleeve. *Are you okay?* she mouths. Briana doesn't respond, she just continues to stare at me, breathing hard.

I feel my heart thud in my chest.

The dean clears his throat, strokes his tie like a pet. "It is with great pleasure that I inform you all that we've just now received a very generous donation to the Theater Studies initiative."

"What?" says Grace.

"Yes. Very generous. Very, very generous." And then he laughs out loud. A wild bark. He clears his throat again, gathers himself. "The most generous donation we've ever received, in fact. To date."

I look at the dean beaming at me like I'm the love of his life. He's waiting for me to speak, but my mouth feels frozen.

"Have we?" I hear myself say at last. Beside me, I feel Briana bristle, her breath quicken.

"*To date.* Amazing. Am I right?" He laughs out loud again; he can't help it. Runs a hand through his nonexistent hair as if it were still flourishing thickly from his skull. "Wonderful, just wonderful."

I laugh too. I can't help it either. "Wonderful."

The dean and I laugh together a long time.

"What? What sort of donation? From whom?" Grace says. She's looking at me now, I can feel it. I keep staring at the dean, who is still chuckling, still grinning at me wickedly. Rocking on his heels now as though there's music playing instead of nothing, instead of stunned silence.

"An anonymous donation," he says. "Some local businessmen. They say they just love college theater."

We love theater, Ms. Fitch.

"We're obviously thrilled at their generosity, of course."

"Of course."

"Wow. That's unbelievable," Grace says. "Isn't it, Miranda?"

"Yes, unbelievable," I whisper. I see suits the color of night. Black leather feet tapping. A mic wrapped in roses and fairy lights. Something lashes its tail in my gut, but I'm not shaking, I'm not even sweating, I'm absolutely still. I'm standing up straight. I'm smiling. Nodding. Local businessmen. Patrons. Of course.

"*Business*men? Which business is this?"

another voice asks. I turn. Fauve standing backstage in a sea of pages. Trevor has quit picking up the script. Like Ashley/Michelle, he too has wandered over to Briana. He places a hand on her shoulder, which is trembling violently, unnecessarily violently. He whispers, "You okay?" and she doesn't answer.

She's fine! I want to scream. But I just smile at the dean, who appears to be oblivious to all of this. He's still rocking on his heels, chuckling to himself. Fauve's question about the source of the money is really irrelevant.

"They preferred to remain under the radar. You know how it is, am I right?"

I'm nodding wildly. I know how it is, absolutely.

"Anyway, they seemed to know Miranda, I mean Professor Fitch, quite well. The donors spoke very highly of our director here."

He smiles at me, and my soul shivers.

"Did they?" Fauve says. She's joined Grace in the audience. Standing beside her. Arms crossed.

"Oh yes. Said they were quite familiar with her onstage work. Real admirers. Big fans." He turns to my students. "Everyone, you've got a famous director here. Lucky, am I right?"

The students are still looking at me with eyes wide open. Frozen as though we are doing an acting exercise. Briana's trembling beside me, clutching her wrist. I feel her eyes boring into the side of my face.

"Well" — the dean claps his hands — "I'll let you get back to it. Just had to share the incredible news. Oh, there is *one* thing I forgot to mention." And here he looks at me and winks. Because he didn't forget, you see, he was just saving this bit for the end. For me. "The donors asked for us to put on a particular play . . . *All's Well That Ends Well?* Which I think is the play you were going to put on anyway, am I right, Professor?"

My thighs unclench. Beside me, I feel Briana pale, her mouth making a nonverbal noise.

"Yes."

"Wonderful. I bet it's going to be great. And you can go nuts with the production. Costumes. Sets. Effects. That thrust you've always wanted." He winks at me again. "Anything."

I see a cerulean-blue sky. My old outdoor production in Edinburgh. The starry cosmos above and an open human eye painted onto the stage floor. Helen in her red dress surrounded by cascading bubbles of light. The sun still high above the craggy landscape. The smell of wildflowers all around.

"Wonderful. Isn't it, everyone?" I look at them standing still, still watching me with horror. Or is it admiration?

"All's Well That Ends Well," the dean repeats, winking at me again. "Just great. That one of the comedies or tragedies, Professor Fitch?"

"Both," I say. And my own voice sounds richer, deeper, to my ear. "It's both."

CHAPTER 11

"Wow, congratulations, Miranda," Hugo says to me the next day.

"Thank you."

"You must be thrilled."

"I am, I am."

Friday afternoon before rehearsal. I stare at Hugo wondrously backlit by his own windows, grinning at me. I think surely this is a dream, it must be. We're in his scene shop. Hugo called me in here just now from the hall. Actually called me in here.

Miranda, he said, craning his head out the door, and I thought surely, surely, there was someone else in the hall he was referring to, someone else he was flagging down. Another Miranda. A student he was fucking, perhaps. But he was looking at me. He just heard about the dean's announcement yesterday. The donation. *All's Well.* We'll have a real Theater Studies program. An actual major. Maybe he'll even be able to do set work full-

195

time. Fucking amazing. He wanted to have a quick toast. With me? *With you, Miranda.*

And now I'm watching him pour whiskey into two small plastic cups. He's raising his glass to me. "Cheers, Miranda."

"Cheers," I say.

And we drink. And again, I think I'm dreaming, surely I must be. But no, I'm not dreaming. The scent of wood is too thick. The light too absurdly peach as it falls from the windows onto impossibly tall Hugo. Saying, "I'm really happy for you, Miranda."

All around us, catching the orange light of the sinking sun, are the flats that were the half-finished sets of *All's Well*. The maquette with the three plastic witches is nowhere in sight.

"Amazing about these donors," he says. "Almost cosmic, really."

"Cosmic," I agree. "Yes. Absolutely."

"Sort of weird too, of course."

"Weird? Why weird?"

He hesitates. Looks at me, almost apologetically. "I mean throwing that much money at college theater? Seems weird to me. Who would have thought people gave a shit about theater anymore, you know?"

We love theater, Ms. Fitch.

"Yeah," I say.

"Not that you don't deserve it," he adds

quickly. "And we could definitely use it. Take the money and run, right?"

"I guess theater still has its charms for some," I say. Am I flirting? I might be. Impossible. Haven't I forgotten how?

"Oh, you don't have to convince me, Miranda. I'm a convert, remember? I'm obsessed."

He grins. Hugo grinning. Grinning at me. My god. "I have to say, Miranda, I was rooting for you all along."

"You were?"

He laughs. "Of course, Miranda."

He's saying my name a lot. It's music. Better than the Edith Piaf I felt compelled to play on the drive to school. Normally I just drive in silence. Staring at the windshield. Picturing my dark future. But this morning, I thought, *Why not a little music for the road? Why not a little* life? As Edith sang, I thought, *This is so nice.* I forgot how nice music is on the road. How it always seems to go with the sky, the passing landscape. I sang along. When was the last time I sang along to anything?

"You're taking a risk," Hugo says now. "I admire that. Also, I've done *Macbeth* before, you know. A few times. It's a prison favorite. *All's Well* will be a new challenge for me. I'd never read it until this year, I'll admit. I've been reading through it again, and you're right. Helen *is* fascinating."

"She is?" Stop echoing him. "She really is."

"I still don't really understand why she loves Bertram though. He's such an ass."

"He didn't see her," I say. "He was blind for a long time. He was warped by certain diabolical influences." I'm talking quickly. Heatedly. With actual passion. When was there ever this much blood in my voice?

Hugo shrugs. Leans against the wood slabs. Pulls a joint from behind his ear. Lights it. It's poetry. There should be a play of just this.

"Still," he says. "I think she deserves much better than him."

"She changes him though. In the end," I say.

"Yeah, but is he worthy of it? I don't know."

"I think he is," I say quietly. "I do. I always have." I'm absolutely flirting now.

He looks at me. "Something's different about you, Miranda."

"Is it?" I say, flushing. I appear confused, unsure. I act like I don't know what he's talking about.

When I do.

Something *is* different. I feel it. Something. What? I felt it after they'd all left the theater yesterday, after the dean's announcement, after I sent them all home. Briana had already left. I didn't see her go. Didn't see how she left. Only that she left and left her coat and bag behind. Only that Ashley/Michelle and Trevor went with her. I gazed at the remaining students. I smiled like all was well. *Why don't we wrap up for tonight? You've all worked so hard,* I lied. *Let's pick it up tomorrow, shall we?* I said. *Let's start fresh.* I stood alone on the stage with the script scattered around my feet. I bent down to pick up the pages. Only when I had gathered all the pages in my hands, stood there on a stage cleared of Briana's overturned uprising, staring at her Garamond font, did I realize it. I had bent down to pick up the pages. I had bent down to the floor. I had picked up all these pages. Without my legs seizing. Without my back spasming. Without the webs sounding their blinking alarms. No fat man's chair on my foot. Nothing. Just me standing there with the pages in my hands. I gazed down at Briana's font.

A bark-like laugh escaped my lips.

A fluke, I thought, surely. Just a fluke. Definitely a fluke. I didn't realize I was picking up the pages, so I was able to pick up the pages. I was still in shock from all that happened, that's all. With Briana. With the announcement. Your body can do incredible things in times of shock, can't it? Lift up cars. Fight bears. Just the result of shock, then. No more.

I'd pay for it later, of course, I thought, as I drove home. When I got out of the car, I'd pay. Maybe on the way home, I'd pay. Surely I'd have to pay. Pay for running to the theater. Pay for the strain it took to face off with Briana. To pick up her foul script page by page.

All the way home I drove crouched low in my car as though waiting for an avenging god to smite me from above. I waited for the bottom to drop. For my legs to seize up. For my back to spasm violently. For my hip to swell with rage. Any minute now.

When I stood up to get out of the car, I thought surely my right leg would stay bent and locked, as it usually does, as it does whenever I have to go from sitting to standing. Mocking my attempt to stand.

Spasticity, Mark called it. The result of hypersensitization. My sympathetic nervous system being overactive. *Like your imagination,* he doesn't say but implies with the silence that comes after. But when I got out of the car, my leg straightened. I gasped as I

200

stood there, stood on straight legs, on the icy sidewalk, the breath leaving my mouth in dancing smoke. I haven't been able to straighten my leg since my first nerve-block injection, when I rose drugged from the hospital gurney and hugged my physiatrist in tearful thanks and felt his scrubbed body go rigid in my rank embrace. It lasted an hour, that release. But here it was happening again. A trick. Surely, a trick.

Do you like tricks, Ms. Fitch?

I was able to walk to the apartment door without limping, without dragging the dead weight of my leg behind. I still ate dinner standing up, peed standing up, drank my vat of wine standing up out of sheer fear, in case it was a fluke, because surely, surely, it was coming. The avenging rage of my body, the blinking webs, the crushing weight of the fat man. Yet I did not lie on the floor, like a dog playing dead, watching terrible television. Instead I stood there in my low-ceilinged living room, reading *All's Well* aloud, making new notes, my limbs buzzing, my heart thrumming wildly in my chest, a strange smile creeping across my lips. I gazed at my red couch longingly, more tempted to sit than I'd been in the longest time. The cushions gleamed bright red as cherries, as my former lipstick. Before every lipstick clashed with my grief.

Go on. Sit on me, Miranda.

But what if I can't get back up? I whispered to the couch. *There is no husband, remember? And I can't call the super again. Can't have her coming in here ripped out of her mind from a day of boxed wine and joints. Talking at me about her miserable life while I lie imprisoned on the floor. Pouring it all into me like emotional Drano. Forgetting she's supposed to help me.*

Try me.

So I walked over to the couch.

I sat down, I braced myself.

Nothing.

No scream of pain down my right leg. No slice of an invisible knife behind my knee.

I held my breath. I stood back up . . . and?

And nothing. No seizing of the leg. No clenching thigh muscles. No foot drop. No concrete. My back hurt still. Hip hurt still. But the leg was just . . . fine. I could bend it. I could straighten it. Bend, straighten.

I laughed. I sat down again: nothing. I stood up again: nothing. I sat down, I stood up, sat down stood up sat down stood up, nothing, nothing, nothing, nothing, nothing, and oh god I was really laughing now. I laughed and laughed as I sat down and stood up and sat down and stood up, jumping on and off the seat cushions like I was on a trampoline, like I was a child again, my mother watching, clapping, enjoying my performance, how I loved to be center stage, even then. I laughed until tears fell.

Then I saw the lonely man in the apartment across the way. Watching me through the window, in the middle of watering his plants. Plants that defy the laws of nature, of photosynthesis, with their ability to flourish in darkness.

He smiled and kept watering the green glowing leaves. I sat down. I stood up. I sat down. I picked up *All's Well*. I read again and again the scene in which the King is miraculously healed, which happens offstage. The lords discuss it as a miracle. It can happen onstage or it can happen off. Depends. Depends entirely on the production.

"Definitely, something's different," Hugo says now. "I can't quite put my finger on it, Miranda."

The way he says my name, the way he's looking at me. My body blooms under his gaze. My heart lifts. Alley shadows lightening, dead leaves brightening, whirling wildly now in the gutters.

"We should get together sometime," Hugo says. Speaking a line right out of my dreams, the ones I used to have drooling on the office floor. "To talk about the play. You know this play much better than I do. I'd love to hear more about your vision, Miranda."

"My vision," I say. "Yes." A bright blue sky shot through with a rainbow. Me and Hugo holding hands onstage. I've come back from the dead. He's gazing at me like I'm everything.

"Why don't we meet off campus sometime after rehearsal?" he says. "For a drink."

"A drink?" A drink with Hugo in the evening. Not weak tea in the afternoon. Not Hugo's eyes distracted by every moving object that passes through his field of vision. I picture Hugo's face in the bar. A candle between us. He's holding a glass of wine. No, probably Hugo doesn't drink wine. Fine, he's drinking a lager. Seeing only me, my vision.

"Why not?" Hugo says. "There's the Canny Man, that Irish pub nearby. Or is it Scottish?"

And then my bright blue sky darkens to pitchy night. I see a red-walled bar. A golden-green drink glowing with an unholy light. Three men gazing at me, tapping their black leathered feet. *There, there, Ms. Fitch. Get happy.*

"No," I say. "No, no, I don't think we

should go there."

"Well, you pick the place, then. I'm open. At your disposal. Completely."

Impossible that Hugo is saying these words to me. But he is. He's looking forward to it. He can't wait.

As I walk down the hall now, I feel my feet clicking along. Briskly, more briskly than usual. Dead leg isn't so dead, isn't so heavy today. Hip still hurts of course. Back still aches. But my leg. I'm not dragging it. It clops along. It keeps up. So that I'm walking straighter. Taller. Not so lopsided anymore.

Something's different about you, Miranda, Hugo said.

Is it? I said. I'm humming a little. Softly. Just to myself. A tune I heard somewhere, can't remember where from, but it's lovely. It comes easily to my lips, and I don't usually sing. My lips are usually pressed together, bearing the weight of myself.

Up ahead, I see a student in the hall. Slumped against the concrete wall, gazing at his phone. My student, I realize. Jacob Fox. He'll play Parolles, the villain, the vicelike courtier who leads Bertram astray in *All's Well.* Probably I would have cast him as King Duncan if we'd done *Macbeth.* But

205

we're not doing *Macbeth.*

Normally when I see a student in the hall, I go the other way, pretending I forgot something in my office. I make a real show of it. I do an *I forgot* face and then I shake my head angrily at my own decrepit memory. Or else I stay the course, my eyes fixed forward and faraway, professorial, like I see nothing ahead but Shakespeare, the stage. But today I look right at Jacob Fox. I smile.

"Hello, Jacob," I say. And I wave at Jacob, and he flinches. He says nothing. Maybe I've startled him. It's true that I've never until this moment remembered his name.

"How are you?"

Jacob just looks at me. Some students don't know how to talk to professors, it's true. But Jacob's never been intimidated by me before. He's always yawning in rehearsal. His fucking mouth wide open in my face. But he looks very awake now. Looks the way they all did yesterday as I reached my hand out to see Briana's script. Better not to mention yesterday. Better to act like all is well. Because all is well. Sure we had a rocky beginning, what with Briana attempting to overthrow me, what with my grasping hand clutching air and then seizing upon her wrist, but we ended on a high note, did we not?

"Cat got your tongue, Jacob?" I say. I try to sound playful. So he'll relax and stop looking at me this way. *I don't bite, Jacob. Promise.*

Jacob shakes his head. "No, Professor."

"Oh, good. Looking forward to rehearsal today?"

"Yes."

You're a bad actor, Jacob. We'll have to work on that.

"I'm so glad. Such wonderful news we received yesterday." Smile. Emphasize the high note. "I'm excited for us. Especially for you, Jacob," I lie.

Jacob just blinks. I'm excited for him? Really?

"Absolutely. Parolles is a very exciting role. Much better than Duncan, who dies so quickly."

I attempt to beam.

He stares at me.

"And villains are far more interesting, anyway," I continue. I'm babbling now. "Don't you think, Jacob?"

I look at Jacob as though I'm interested, truly, in what he has to say.

Jacob says nothing. Merely blinks again. Maybe I've put him on the spot. It's true I talk to no one outside of class or rehearsal. No one except Ellie, of course, and she's the one who comes to me. Seeks me out in my office hours. Her tremulous *knock, knock* on the doorframe. *Professor Fitch? I hope I'm not disturbing you.* And her voice is an immediate balm for my mangled nerves. Sometimes she'll just stand in the office doorway and wait for me to become aware of her presence. And I will. And I'll scream. And she'll look apologetic. And then I'll smile. *Oh, Ellie. It's you. Come in, come in.*

Perhaps it catches Jacob off guard, my sudden interest. Wanting to hear his, Jacob's, thoughts about the play when probably Jacob has no thoughts.

"Such an archetypal villain, Parolles," I continue. "A villain who outvillains *villainy.*" I smile. I'm quoting the play. Engaging him in a textual discussion. "Good for your CV, am I right?"

He looks at me like I'm a black funnel of wind, gathering force. Heading his way. "Yes, Professor."

"Well. See you in rehearsal, Jacob. I'm looking forward to seeing what you bring to the part." I'm trying to encourage him, but he doesn't look encouraged at all. *Fine. Have it your way, Jacob.*

I leave him, humming that tune I was humming before. And Jacob watches me go, and behind me, I hear him sigh with relief.

Strange. Was he afraid of me? Impossible. No one is afraid of me. How long since anyone has been afraid of me, really?

CHAPTER 12

Entering rehearsal, I had no idea what I would face. Would they refuse me still? Would they hold out? Would I come in to find a cauldron nailed to the stage? The Ashley/Michelles gathered around it, clad in shredded black dresses and witch hats, making abracadabra hands over paper flames? Trevor clutching a tinfoil dagger, ready to wave it in my face in protest? Briana still in her bell sleeves, chin tilted up, screwing her courage to the sticking place?

No. They're sitting in a silent circle on the stage. They're watching me walk toward them. They're watching me, rapt, as though I am a play all my own. They don't want to miss a beat. All eyes fixed on me, not their phones, not the floor, not one another. All mouths closed. No munching of food, no guzzling of drinks. No murmuring. No whispering. No giggling. No yawning in my face. They are absolutely still. I don't even hear them breathing, are they breathing? I hear every click of my shoes as I make my way toward them. Smiling as I approach.

"Hello, all," I say.

"Hello, Professor Fitch," they say in near unison. A rippling of my name. A first. It sends a shiver through me.

I see they have the scripts in their hands. The old scripts. My director's cut of *All's Well*. They're gripping them close. I exhale. I could laugh. I could weep. Ellie is looking at me, flushed, excited. She's smiling. Jacob is looking at me just like he did in the hallway. Even Trevor, his blue eyes wide open, appears enthralled. And then I see the empty space beside Trevor, where Briana should be sitting, in her bell sleeves, her gold cross dangling from her white neck, her burnished hair tumbling over one sharp shoulder. I stare at the air that should be Briana's body. She has never once missed rehearsal. No matter how many I schedule. No matter the weather. She is always there, always ready, always on time, like only the truly mediocre are. I look at the empty space, and I see refusal. Protest. So this is her way of fighting me. Her last gasp.

A lash of panic. A lick of fear.

I want to ask them, *Where is mine enemy? Speak up. Speak!*

211

Instead I say, "Well, shall we warm up?"

"They're already warmed up, Miranda." This from Grace. Also watching me like I'm the show. No laptop. No phone. She isn't even whittling something out of wood. I look back at my children. Still unmoving. Still not appearing to breathe. Like they're frozen from yesterday. Almost like they never left the theater. They were waiting for me this whole time.

I sit down in their circle — I'm actually able to sit down on the floor with only a little laboring. I sit between Ellie and Jacob, who make room for me. I smile at them.

"Wonderful. Well, let's have a read-through of the play, shall we? To reacquaint ourselves. To reconnect?"

And just like that, they gaze down at their scripts. And Ashley/Michelle reads the opening lines of the Countess. " 'In delivering my son from me, I bury a second husband.' "

And from there? From there it goes swimmingly. No discussion of yesterday. No hesitation. No complaint. No one raises a hand. No one pauses to ask a stupid question.

There's a brief moment of silence when Helen's first line comes. That's when the air where Briana should be sitting starts to crackle. The silence becomes loud then. The silence is a question mark. There is a cough. Now is the time I should ask them. *Where is the girl who is never absent? Who is always annoyingly here?*

I open my mouth. I take a breath. I look at Ellie seated beside me in her uniform of black, over which she's thrown some sort of vaguely glittering shawl. "Ellie," I say, "will you read Helen, please?"

A moment's pause, only a moment, before Ellie takes a breath and begins to read.

" 'I do affect a sorrow indeed, but I have it too,' " Ellie says, not reading from the script. Doesn't need to. She's been practicing. For this very moment perhaps.

I do affect a sorrow indeed, but I have it too. Can I tell you how exactly right she says it? Her voice is wavering on the surface, but deep and sure beneath. I hear her knowledge of her lowliness. Her pain and her aspirations both. Her love like an impossible star. I hear it all in her voice — deep, soft, fiery. Looking up at stars from the gutter. And then I see the play. I see it all. It comes wonderfully to me. In all its dark lightness, in all its strange fairy-tale splendor, with the sound of Ellie's voice.

When they're finished, I clap. I tell them bravo, well done. I clap and clap, they were so good! I tell them next time, we're going to plunge deeply into Act One. Get ready. I tell them I'm excited. Aren't they? They stay frozen on the floor. So I tell them they are dismissed. They gather their things, they leave quietly, so quietly. Saying goodbye to me, as they leave. Goodbye, Professor.

"Well, that went well, don't you think, Grace?" I ask her when the last student has gone. We're alone in the theater now. My voice echoes against the walls and back to me, rich, sure. I forgot the acoustics in this room are quite good.

Grace shrugs. "Sure. It did, I guess."

"I think it went very, very well." I turn to look at the empty stage, still lit. Grace wanted to turn the lights off, but I told her, *Don't yet. Please.* Because I can't stop staring at the empty stage, upon which the play is still unfolding. Revealing itself to me in bright colors. Black sky. Bright stars. Debussy's "Clair de Lune" playing in the background. "I think it went excellently."

Grace looks at me. *Excellently?* "They were well-behaved, I'll give you that. I've never seen them so compliant. It was a little weird actually."

"I don't think it was *weird.* I think they're just finally embracing *All's Well.*"

214

"Maybe."

"Wasn't Ellie just wonderful as Helen?"

"She was all right," Grace says, looking at her phone.

"She was brilliant. She was —"

"Too bad she's playing the King," Grace says.

"Yes. Yes, too bad."

She turns to me, and I immediately avert my gaze.

"I wonder what happened to Briana," she says.

I see my hand on Briana's wrist. Her looking at me with wide-open eyes.

"What do you mean 'what happened'?" I say.

Grace stares at me like what do I mean *what do you mean?* "I mean she was absent, Miranda. She's never absent."

I shrug at the floor. Hideous seventies carpet. Worn bare. We really should tear it out. Replace it with something red. Rich. Blood-colored.

"She seemed a little pale yesterday, when she left," Grace says. "Did you notice?"

I recall Briana standing defiantly before me, her face draining of color. Burnished hair suddenly dull. I shake my head vigorously. "No. I thought she seemed like her usual self."

I shrug again. I look at Grace, who's still staring at me, not smiling.

"I thought she looked unwell," Grace says.

"Well, it's flu season," I say in a singsong voice. Am I really singing? I am a little. "Things are going around. Can't be too careful, can you, Grace?"

Grace shakes her head. "Strange though. She's never sick."

"Well, it was bound to happen at some point," I snap. My voice sounds shrill now. "She's not *infallible,* is she?"

Grace has to concede this. She is, after all, a creature of reason. "I guess not."

"Anyway," I say, "it was good to hear the lines read from Helen like that — I mean from Ellie like that. Another perspective. A fresh *take*. It really opened up Helen for me and I'm sure for the cast too. I saw the play tonight, Grace, I did."

I realize I'm speaking quickly, and I never speak this quickly. Usually after rehearsal, Grace has to physically shake me from where I'm lying on the floor, drugged and drooling between the seats. *Miranda, wake up. Miranda, pub time. Atta girl.*

I think Grace is going to smile finally, rejoice with me, but she frowns. "What happened yesterday, Miranda? The dean barging in. Those donors. It was weird, didn't

216

you think?"

Yes. "No." The lie leaves my lips before I can think. "Not really. I didn't think so, no."

I look at the empty stage. Not at Grace. But I can feel her gaze burning my temple.

"I thought it was very weird," she says.

"I don't know why you have to keep saying *weird* like that. I don't know why you have to *keep* saying it."

"Because it *was* weird, Miranda, all right? It was really fucking weird."

"Maybe it was a little. I guess. But I also think it was cool, you know. Cosmic," I say, trying on Hugo's word.

"Cosmic?"

"Yes, exactly. Almost like a — a sign. A message from the universe."

"What sort of *message?*"

"I don't know. Maybe the universe wants us to put on *All's Well.*"

Grace lights a cigarette. Right there even though there's a NO SMOKING sign on the wall above her head. She doesn't give a fuck. She doesn't believe in *messages from the universe.* She believes in reality, the troubled earth spinning in a cold, black godless universe full of dead suns, in which there is no such thing as fairy dust, serendipity, heavenly design. She believes in the evidence of the senses, her own eyes and

217

ears that see things simply as they are. What happened yesterday seems a little too far-fetched to be coincidence. It reeks of interference from some all-too-human quarter.

"You seem different, Miranda," she says to me now. But she doesn't say it like Hugo. Not smiling. Not curious. She looks at me with narrowed eyes like little pinpricks.

"Do I?" I feel fear. Why do I feel fear?

"You seem a little more . . . I don't know. Alive. Peppy." She says the words accusingly.

Is she accusing me? I think of our first meeting, my job-interview day. When I was just a potential hire smiling nervously across from her at that terrible Tuscan restaurant — the dinner portion of that interminable day. Sweating fear bullets in my mall blazer. Trying and failing to charm a table of socially inept hags from the English department who all just blinked at me grimly — the Sisters Grimm, Grace and I would call them later. Grace was the only person there from Theater Studies. Silently, she watched me nod along, equivocate with the hags, my smile wavering. All day, I'd performed well-ness wonderfully, miraculously, before her and the dean, the hiring committee. I was withering now.

So, Miranda, I read that you worked at

Disney World as a princess? one of the hags said. *Is that true?*

Just for one summer, I said. And I laughed like it had been just an ironic, postfeminist exercise rather than a part to which I'd given my soul.

A demanding role, I'm sure. They smiled tightly, dipping their torn bits of bread into a saucer full of pungent oil. I wanted to throttle them all — *Fuck you, fuck this!* — and limp defiantly out the door.

Instead I surprised myself by saying, *Actually, it was very demanding. I learned many valuable lessons under that Snow White wig.*

They all looked at me, including Grace, a strange smile on her face now. *Such as?*

How to deal gracefully with pricks.

Silence from the hags. Then the sole laughter of Grace like a roar. She even clapped her hands. When she drove me back to the hotel after the dinner, she offered me a cigarette, the first of many we would share together over the years. Nearly five since that first night, which seems so long ago. *Long ago and far away,* as Snow White might say. The way she's looking at me now in the theater is definitely more Sisters Grimm.

"I had a lot of coffee today," I tell her. I realize I didn't take my palmful of pills before rehearsal. Just one instead of my usual three. Only one pill last night too, come to think of it. Grace gazes at me standing on both legs. Not so crooked. Not leaning so wildly to the left. No longer so terribly afraid of the right side of my body.

"How's your pain?"

I shrug. "I don't know. It's so hard to tell, isn't it? The pain comes from so many different places."

Grace blows smoke into the ceiling and says nothing.

"It's a cumulative effect," I continue, borrowing Mark's language. "From compensatory patterns. So it's very hard to compartmentalize."

Grace just stares at me. "You seem better," she says.

"I'm not, really. I mean I'm still in a lot pain," I try to say it softly, to reflect the pain that I'm in. And it's not a lie, I am.

"Like in my back. Right now." I touch it to show her. "And my hip. And my ribs." I hunch forward. *I do affect a sorrow indeed, but I have it too.* To show her the pain that's —

"You seem better," she repeats.

"Well, I'm not," I say, insisting. Why am I insisting like this?

"It's good to see," she says. She smiles at me sadly. She reaches out and touches my shoulder. I feel a surge of emotion, remembering the early days of our friendship. I hid my physical limitations from her at first. Prevaricated whenever she asked me to do something more strenuous than drinking. *How about we go hiking? How about we go sailing? Want to take the bus to New York to see the ballet?*

I was always busy.

Doing what? Grace would ask.

Getting divorced. Seeing another surgeon, another wellness charlatan. Gazing into the void of my life. *Busy with another production,* I'd tell Grace.

Oooh, what other production?

Oh, just this experimental thing, I'd lie.

Sounds exciting!

But at some point, a year in, I couldn't hide it from her anymore. She found me out, found me in tears one night in the theater after a particularly exhausting rehearsal of *As You Like It*. A student, aka "the prop master," had failed to put the props away. I was gazing helplessly out over the mess of forest paraphernalia onstage — the plastic shrubs, the stuffed sheep — weeping.

Miranda, are you okay?

She was sympathetic when I told her; of course she was. *Why the hell did you hide this from me?*

She quietly picked up the props that night, quietly took on the more physically demanding aspects of production. Later, she'd drive me to surgeon's appointments, to get steroid shots. Didn't invite me hiking or sailing anymore. Didn't ask me about other productions anymore. Knew there were none.

"Let's get a drink together?" she says to me now. "I'm dying for one."

I look at her with surprise. Another night out with me?

"I'm sure you want to tell me all about your *vision,*" she adds. I smile too now.

"Pub?" she says.

"Pub?" I repeat.

"The Canny Man? You know, the place we always go to."

I see the yellowed eyes of the fat man gone white. *Get happy, Ms. Fitch.*

"Oh, no. No, no, I think I'm good tonight."

She frowns now, raises an eyebrow. Good tonight? Me? The self-medicating queen? When have I ever been *good tonight*?

"Yes, I think I'll stay here," I say. "Make some notes. You know, while it's all still speaking to me. While I can hear and see it." I poke at my eye, I tug on my ear. I attempt to look mistily at Grace. I'm a director, remember? I'm whimsical. I'm swept up. Been a while since I've felt swept up.

The frown softens. Grace rolls her eyes. Pats me on the shoulder again. "All right. Enjoy."

I sit alone in the middle of the auditorium, before the empty stage. My legs hum, my hip throbs dully. Back aches. Ribs ache. But it's fine. Because on the stage, the play glimmers. Shimmers. Begins to take shape again. I hear its colors. I see its music. I see Helen on the stage. Poor unlearned virgin. Clever wench. A simple maid. Gazing at me with my own eyes. Bright, fiery, full of intention. Bewitching me. And look at me. I'm bewitched.

Midnight when I finally get up and leave the theater. Still able to stand up, still able to straighten that leg. I laugh a little, I can't help it, even as I limp to the door. I'm still limping, *You see, Grace? Look.* But Grace is long gone. Likely asleep in front of Netflix, her face covered in rose-petal clay. On the screen is a courtroom drama or perhaps one of her gruesome serial killer shows. The more blood, the more morgue scenes, the more forensic evidence, the better for Grace. I'm humming. Picking up that tune where I left it before rehearsal. And then outside the theater, in the foyer, cut against the red light of the EXIT sign, I see a shape. A human shape sitting in the dark. I scream.

"Professor Fitch."

I grope the wall for the light switch. Ellie. Sitting on the floor in her drab black. Hugging her knees, her back against the brick wall. Looking at me with a murderous intensity that I have come to learn is just her face.

"Ellie. Jesus Christ, you scared me."

"Sorry, Professor."

I see she's made a little camp for herself on the floor. Her glittering shawl fanned out. A take-out teacup from the library kiosk sits at her feet. In a small pile are the dried peels of what must once have been a sad tangerine. *All's Well* lies facedown beside her thigh, the book open and spiky with colored tabs.

"How long have you been sitting out here?" I ask her.

"Just since after rehearsal."

"After rehearsal? Ellie, that was hours ago."

Her pale face colors. "It wasn't a big deal. I had homework. I come here to work sometimes. I live in the dorm just there." She points at the dark window, at the black outside, at nothing at all.

"Oh," I say.

"I was memorizing the play."

I picture Ellie sitting out here in the dark, peeling her tangerine, reading the lines. I'm touched. Creeped out, but touched. She's looking at me like she wants to tell me something. But Ellie never just comes out and tells me. Even in my office, she'll just stand there in the doorframe, with her hands trembling at her sides. Waiting for me to draw her out.

"You were great in rehearsal today," I tell her.

"I was?"

"Yes. Really brilliant. You inspired me. You actually showed me the play."

"Thank you." She bows her head low. She can't show me her happiness at my praise. It's too indecent. "Well," she tells the floor, "I'm sure Briana will be great too."

I stare at the dull dark hair of Ellie, the blond roots peeking through. I notice there have been a few attempts at purple streaks, now faded.

"Sure," I say. "Sure she will be."

"I heard she was sick today," she whispers. She looks up, her gray eyes wide open.

"Sick?" Panic in my gut. No, not panic, why panic? Anger, more like. I should be

225

angry. She's obviously faking. Milking this moment as only she can.

"Trevor told me after rehearsal. Apparently, she's been in bed all day. She couldn't even get out of bed, he said. She told him through text. She said it hurt to move. It hurt to even text."

I don't say anything. My turn to lower my head. I feel a smile. Unholy. Twitching on my face.

"Maybe it's a flu," Ellie offers, so kindly filling in the silence.

"Maybe," I say.

"I've had one of those before once. Where it hurt to move. It hurt to text. It hurt to breathe even."

I nod at the floor. Such a hard floor. Did she really sit out here so long?

"It is flu season, Ellie. Better bundle up. Things are going around."

"I will."

"Good."

"Professor Fitch?"

"Miranda, please, Ellie. I've told you. Call me Miranda."

"Miranda. I just wanted to ask you a question. I would have asked earlier but I didn't want to bother you. When I looked in the theater, you just seemed so . . . rapt."

So you waited out here for four hours? Sit-

ting in the dark with your tangerine?

"What is it?"

"Well, I just wondered if you'd tried my bath."

"Bath? What bath?"

"I made you a bath, remember?"

And then I do remember. The pungent little baggie of dried herbs, oils, and salt I found tucked into my purse last night when I left the theater. Peppered here and there with the petals of dried flowers. Bearing a little purple note. *From Ellie.* It's currently funking up my glove compartment — making my whole car smell like a boreal forest crossed with a field of sage.

"Oh, your bath. Yes. Of course," I lie. "It was wonderful. Just the thing."

I look at her and smile. Does she believe it? Absolutely. She's positively beaming.

"Really? So it worked!"

"Worked?"

"Well, I cast a bit of a spell on it. To help you heal. It's a restorative bath, like I said." She looks away now. Embarrassed perhaps by her dabblings in the occult.

"Did you?"

She nods solemnly. "Yes. And I have to say, I think it's working. You seem better, Miranda."

"I do? Yes, I do. You know, I was wondering what it might be. But now you've solved it, Ellie. Thank you." I say it seriously, like I mean it.

Ellie beams again. Hideously. There is something loathsome about her intensity, her passion, I can't deny it. The depth and breadth of it — how fiercely it burns under her unassuming skin. For a second, I see what Grace sees, which is just a plain, grim-featured girl. A wanting girl. But then all of this is what makes her a great Helen.

"Good night, Ellie," I say. "And remember to bundle up."

I'm walking down the hall. Feeling her watching me go.

"Should I make you another one, Miranda?" she calls after me.

"Another?" I ask her, turning.

"Another bath." Her silhouette so hopeful. So full of faith in her own witchy powers. Can't burst that bubble.

"Oh, yes. Sure, why not?"

Chapter 13

"Better?" Mark repeats. His bro face is shocked. Did I really just speak this word here in the basement gym of Spine-Works?

I'm sitting on a medical table in a row of medical tables, gazing up at Mark, who is gazing down at my right leg, how it's swinging wildly. *Better?* Me? A word that I treat as verboten, a word that whenever anyone says it in my vicinity causes me to shake my head violently. No, no. Not better. Definitely not better. Not me. Never better, please. Worse, always worse. Always and forever.

"I think so," I whisper. "I think it is better." I say it softly, hesitantly. "Maybe it's just been a good couple of days." Days in which my pill bottles have remained rattling in my pockets, unopened. Still close at hand in case. "I mean, I don't know for sure."

I say this with my head down, looking at the carpet. The carpet is very similar to the one we have in the theater.

"Right," Mark says.

I look up to find Mark staring at my swinging leg.

"And I mean things still hurt, of course," I add quickly. "My back. My ribs. My hip."

Mark nods at my leg. We're on more familiar territory for him now. He appears to exhale for the first time. Of course things hurt.

"But it all feels more, I don't know. Bearable?" I laugh nervously. I realize I'm shaking, I'm afraid. I haven't dared to say the word *better* in a long time. I used to utter it so carelessly — declare it to my therapists so freely, hoping to get a reward, a dog begging for a biscuit — and whenever I uttered it, a fresh pain would seize me soon after. Almost as if God were mocking me and my hope. *Better. You think you're better, do you? Ha. Too funny. Well, let's see how you do with this. Still better?*

Mark's smiling at me now, his hands in his pockets. "Well, wow, Miranda. Look at you."

"And my leg. My leg, look." And I straighten and bend it for Mark. "I can sit down and stand up now without it seizing up, see?" To demonstrate, I stand up. And then I sit back down. And I stand up. Sit down. Stand up. Sit down. Stand —

"Okay, that's enough," Mark says. "Got it. Got the *gist*."

Beside me, on the next medical table, an elderly woman lies on her back, a Thera-Band wrapped around her knees, looking at me with something like fear. She's in the middle of doing a bridge exercise. Her legs are shaking wildly. All the patients in the gym are looking at me, I realize. They've stopped their band-walks, their sad clam-shell and bridge exercises. Stopped their slow pedaling on taped-up bikes. The PTs are all looking too. Every blue polo shirt branded with the SpineWorks logo turned toward me and Mark.

Stupidly, I think they're going to applaud us. At the very least, Mark will applaud me.

But Mark's hands stay in his pockets. He's just looking at me.

"Why don't we go into a treatment room? Little too crowded in the gym today, am I right? I think one just opened up."

A treatment room? Why? I thought surely Mark would want me to exercise today.

"Um, okay."

"Just go to the one at the end of the hall there. You go on ahead. I'll be right there. I'll catch up with you." He hands me a blue medical gown to change into.

■ ■ ■ ■

Alone in the treatment room, I put on the gown. It hurts my hip of course, my back too, but not like before, that's another thing I should remember to tell Mark. That it hurts less to dress. That it still hurts, but less. *Less, better,* these actual words on my actual lips, not so dry anymore, and Mark looking at me as if I've spoken gibberish. I sit down on the medical table. I stand back up, just to be sure. Leg straightens and I sigh with relief, yes, I can still do it. I smile. It still feels like a miracle, a fluke, a trick every time. Tears spring to my eyes. I sit back down. Stand up. I laugh at how easy.

Better. Maybe I really am. Not all the way better. Not even close. But who knows? Maybe I'll even be able to stop coming in a few months. Maybe I'll be able to tell Mark it's over, John too. Maybe I'll quit the pills altogether. Maybe I'll be able to quit this hideous job, go back to the stage. No, too old now. Well, maybe some community theater. Just being back on the stage again would be so nice. I'd do it for free. I cry when I think how I'd do it for free. In a run-down, drafty church, Grace alone in the pews clapping. *Thank you,* I'd say. *Thank you so much.* Maybe soon I'll be able to walk by my old house. I'll pick a spring day when it's sunny, when Paul might happen to be out in the garden. He'll see me walking along, how I'm smiling at the world around me — the grass, the sky, the street, the houses — not crying, not bracing myself as if the very air is something to be endured, not dead inside anymore. He'll see me walking and he'll gasp. *Princess, is that really you?*

I sit, with my leg swinging, it won't stop swinging wildly. Time passes. I hear it ticking somewhere, though there's no clock on the wall. Where is Mark anyway? *I'll catch up with you,* he said, didn't he say that? I feel it getting dark outside, even though I'm in the basement. No windows here. I stare at three-year-old magazines, magazines I've flipped through a hundred times already. But I can't read again about the anti-inflammatory properties of coffee or how the goji berry is a super fruit. Six ab exercises you can do at home that I could never do at all.

The tune I was humming has left my lips. The silence hums. I hear the creak of machines. The little gasps of pain beyond the door. The anxious voices complaining faintly, reporting their symptomology.

"Whenever I sit . . ."

"Worse when I stand up . . ."

"Here . . ."

"And here . . ."

"Should I put ice on it or heat?"

"Heat on it or ice?"

My bones are beginning to ache. I stand up just to check. Sit back down. Leg still swinging but more subdued now. I walk to the door. Open it. In the hallway, no sign of Mark. Just an old man with a TheraBand around his ankles walking sideways through an obstacle course of orange cones. At the other end of the hall, a therapist with hair out of a Heart video is watching, arms crossed. She's the one who put the orange cones in the man's path. Laid a ladder of rope on the floor. His job now to step between the ladder rungs, while also dodging the cones. He's shaky. Losing his balance. Taking the smallest steps. Mark made me do this very obstacle course once.

The old man looks at me. His eyes say, *We're stuck here, aren't we?*

I close the door. Stare at the ugly room. Mark's never made me wait like this before, has he? Only Dr. Rainier ever made me wait this long. I remember whenever he finally showed up it would always feel like a miracle. Like getting a visitation from God.

Silver hair gleaming. Smiling at me. Holding my medical history in his hand — divorced, mother and father deceased — like it was the key to me.

Your pain is your loss, Ms. Fitch, he would say. *The loss of your husband, your mother. Your pain is a vigil to all of this, don't you see that?* He wouldn't even look at my MRI. He just stared at my crooked body like it was proof. Proof of my grief, my inability to let go. I wanted to remind Dr. Rainier that I'd lost my mother a number of years ago, well before the accident. That I grieved her, of course I grieved her — I'd lost my one dark cheerleader, clapping violently in the wings. But her death had also freed me. Soon after, I left for Edinburgh. Found new solace in my craft, on a stage across the sea, playing Helen. I'd never connected with *All's Well* before, but Helen's orphan status, her drifting, lowly place in the world, her pain and longing for love, suddenly spoke to me, moved me beyond words. Grief, far from crushing me, had actually been a gift — it had given me Helen. And Helen had given me Paul. And Paul had given me back the family I'd lost. *You eclipsed them all,* he said to me that first night. And just like that, there were my mother's hands on my seven-year-old shoulders again. And we were

happy. So happy for a while. The theater —
my place on the stage, Paul's place in the
audience — brought us together, wedded
us. Only after I hurt myself were those
spheres disrupted. I wanted to remind Dr.
Rainier that the loss of my husband and
career had been casualties of the pain, not
its cause.

But I fell off the stage . . . , I began. *That's
how this all started. I fell, and then I injured —*

*We all fall, Ms. Fitch. We fall and we rise
again. Bones and tissue heal. But sometimes
we want to hold on to the pain. Sometimes
we have our reasons for not being able to let
go.*

I gazed at his thick black eyebrows. His
silvered hair cropped close to his scalp, the
haircut of all spine doctors, of all orthopedic
surgeons. The haircut of serial killers. His
dark alien eyes gazing at me with a thin attempt at humanity.

*Losing your mother, your husband. Must
have ripped your heart right out.*

What could I say? *Yes.* I nodded. Yes. My
heart. Ripped out. Ripped right out. I might
have even placed a hand on my chest like a
fool.

Now the door opens at last. Mark. Surely
he'll burst into applause. Surely he'll gasp
with me at my sudden improvement. But

236

Mark is dry-eyed. Hands still in his pockets. Expression neutral.

"Well, that was quite a display, Miranda," he says.

Suddenly I feel embarrassed. The way I stood up so gleefully in front of everyone.

"Sorry," I say.

I watch Mark walk over to the sink and wash his hands.

"Don't apologize. It's good to see. Really. Really something."

"That's sort of how I'm seeing it," I say quietly. "As just, I don't know, something."

"Right."

"I mean it might get bad again, right?"

"It might," Mark says. "Probably it will. But for now, let's see it as a little victory."

I look up at Mark, drying his hands.

"What does that mean?" I ask him.

"It's a step. It means what we're doing in here is working."

"What *we're* doing?"

And then I remember those ridiculous exercises Mark assigned. Which I was supposed to do at home. Which I haven't done since I left SpineWorks. Which all of these broken people are doing out there, in this basement gym out of the eighties, while their therapists look on, hair also out of the eighties. *Come on. Ten more, that's it.* Everybody faltering. Everybody scared that they are breaking themselves further. Voicing tremulous complaint/concern. *Is it normal for it to feel like this? Is it normal for it to hurt more?*

"Sure," Mark says, putting on latex gloves. *Why gloves?* I think. Why today? Doesn't he want to examine me first? Doesn't he want me to exercise?

"Pain is information. And your improvement here is telling us something. That we've hit upon the right method. So we just need to keep going. Stay the course, okay? Okay, so let's have you lie down and —"

"But I haven't been doing the exercises," I blurt out. "I honestly think not doing them is what's helped. Honestly, when I left last time, I hurt more. A lot more."

I don't look at Mark. I can't look at Mark. I look at my leg, which is only lightly swinging now.

"How much?" I hear Mark ask, his voice sounding utterly zen. "On a scale from one to ten?"

I shrug. "I don't know. Eight, nine, ten, I wanted to kill myself. Whatever number that is. That's how I felt when I left here."

Now I look at Mark. His face betrays no emotion. It's possible I stuck with Mark because of that face, eerily neutral, handsome in that yoga-bro way. I even texted Grace his profile pic back when we first started together.

New therapist?

Not bad! Grace said. And I fancied, in my drugged-out pathetic way, that Mark and I were dating for a time. That he was my boyfriend, sort of. I brushed my hair before appointments. Put on lipstick. Doused myself in perfume. Wore cleanish jogging pants, one of my comelier T-shirt sacks. And Mark would notice.

That an owl?

Oh, hey, I like the Doors too. You have some cool T-shirts, Miranda.

Thank you.

And now look at us, look at me. I'm challenging him. He knows it. He's looking at me in a way he's never looked at me before. His face looks set in stone.

"But then you got better, didn't you, Miranda?"

"I did, but I also didn't do the exercises."

"But you did them here, didn't you? Thirty reps if I recall, correct?"

"Yes, but —"

"Forty-eight hours. It takes forty-eight hours usually after a session. For things to calm down, to settle, you know that. So imagine if you'd done them at home, if you'd trusted. You might be all better now instead of just . . . your foot."

He looks at my foot, which isn't swinging anymore. It's near still. He smiles.

"Let's do a few tests, okay? Why don't you lie down for me." Not a question.

A thin slice of pain behind my knee like a red flash, like a hiss. *No,* says my leg. *No, no, no.*

But I lie down.

"On your stomach, please. Flip over, that's it. You know the drill. Careful."

I'm facedown in the doughnut hole. Gazing at the rubber floor. At Mark's black shoes. Shiny. Pointed. Tapping. Mark begins to prod my back with his gloved finger. I feel little shoots of fire going down my leg. My foot tingles lightly.

"Catch the game yesterday?" he asks me.

"No." *You know I've never caught the game.* "That hurts, by the way. Down my leg."

"Patriots won. You a Patriots fan, Miranda? I forget if I asked you."

"You've asked me. Did you hear what I said about my leg?"

But Mark isn't listening to me.

"Turn over, please."

"Why?"

Silence. I've never asked this question

240

before, not once.

"Because we're going to try some traction today."

No, I think. *No traction. It'll fuck up my leg. I know it. I feel it.*

I turn to look at Mark. "Won't that mess up my leg again?"

He smiles at me. A hard smile that leaves me cold. "Shouldn't."

I turn over. Mark straps me to the table with a belt. He wraps another belt around the top of one of my thighs and buckles it behind his lower back. He's standing between my parted legs now, propping my belted leg up on his shoulder, holding my other leg down on the table with a firm hand. I look up at Mark gripping my raised leg against his shoulder, getting ready to pull, and I feel the webs begin to flash, fear creeping through me.

I want to say, *Wait, maybe we should hold off.* I say nothing.

"Miranda, you're very stiff. Please relax."

"Okay."

He wraps both arms around my raised leg that's propped on his shoulder. He grips the flesh, his fingers pressing deep into my thigh. He tugs hard on the leg. I gasp. I gasp from the pain.

"What are you doing?"

Mark just looks at me, expressionless. *What am I doing? Really, Miranda?*

"Working on your hip. Helping it release. Now that your back has settled we can be a little more aggressive about this."

He gives my leg another sharp, jerking tug. Then another.

I wince. "That really hurts."

"It only hurts, Miranda, because you're so stiff. You need to relax your leg. I told you. *Relax.*"

"I'm trying."

"No, you're not," he says.

And he tugs again, harder now. And I gasp again. And he looks at me coldly. No mercy, no pity, only annoyance, anger now. It's simply going to hurt if I insist on being stiff like this. He jerks my leg again, pulls hard as if he's trying to pull the leg out of the hip socket. I cry out, and he shakes his head. Ridiculous. My refusal to relax. My insistence upon pain. My theatrics, he always forgets I'm an actress. I am the sad cartoon brain after all.

"It's great that you're better, Miranda. But you have to trust. You have to stick with the exercises. You can't neglect things. If you'd continued, if you'd stuck with the program, who knows? Who knows where you would be by now?"

242

He smiles at me in my straps. And suddenly I know. I'm exactly where I would be. I would be an old woman walking sideways down a basement hallway full of orange cones. Teetering across a ladder of rope, limbs flailing wildly. Sitting hunched on a medical table in a blue paper sack, letting Mark stick needles in me while I try not to scream. I'd be strapped to this table, to Mark, for eternity. To Mark, whose arms will keep gripping me, tugging me, pulling me until I've learned my lesson, until I fucking learn to relax.

I close my eyes, try not to cry out anymore.

After it's over, he unstraps me. Removes his gloves. Tosses them in the wastebasket.

"How do we feel?"

I try to stand up. But my right leg stays rigidly bent at the knee. The weight is on my foot again. Crushing it with a vengeance. I feel the concrete forming in my leg. I can feel the tears forming in my eyes as I sit back down on the medical table.

"Awful. My foot. It —"

"Might need to put some ice on it tonight."

"Ice? But you said —"

"Forty-eight hours, remember? Give it forty-eight hours to settle, Miranda. That's when I'll see you next. Let's try to stay on top of this thing, okay? We're making progress. Little victories."

"I can't stand up now. I can't stand up straight anymore." I hate the sound of my voice. Like a dog that's been kicked.

"Try again."

And I hate him. So much.

I stand up again and immediately go limp on my right side, my leg going rigid and caving in. I stumble forward.

"Whoopsie," Mark says, limply holding out his hand, which I have no choice but to take. "Steady now."

But Mark's limp hand isn't enough. I'm still unsteady.

I take a step forward with Mark holding me lightly by the hand. This time when I stumble, I fall down. I'm lying on the rubber floor.

"Miranda, you okay?" But my answer is irrelevant. These are just more of my theatrics. Why must I constantly undermine his attempts to make me well? I stare at his shoes, so close to my face. Black leather. Pointed. Tapping.

Do you like tricks, Ms. Fitch?

"Miranda."

I see the fat man on the stage, singing. Smiling at me while I lay collapsed on the

244

vibrating floor, collapsed and immobilized by his pain. My wrist throbbing where he touched it.

"Miranda."

Then it's Mark I see. Smiling at me fallen on the floor. He's reaching his hand out to me, limply. Presumably to help me up. I think of the fat man reaching his hand out to me, while the middling man smiled. *I'd love to show you a trick.*

I reach out a hand to Mark. I grasp him firmly on the wrist. I look him in the eye and grip, grip, grip as I slowly pull myself up.

CHAPTER 14

In my car, staring through the icy windshield at the dark parking lot of SpineWorks, engine on. Heart's beating fast. Ran out here in my medical gown and a windbreaker I stole off the rack on my way out the door. Did anyone follow me out? No. Parking lot's empty. Not a soul in sight. I gaze down at my hands gripping the wheel. Trembling. I'm trembling all over. I watch my shuddering breath leave my mouth in clouds of smoke. Foot on the gas pedal. I should go now. Fucking drive off, but I just stare out the windshield, grinning at the dark. I'm humming to myself. Why am I humming? I'm not happy. Not happy, no, I'm terrified, aren't I? I'm worried about Mark, how I left him, pale and crumpled on the chair in the treatment room. Mark's face when I grasped his arm to pull myself up off the floor. How his face suddenly drained of color. How his mouth fell open. How he tried to pull away from my grip and he lost his footing, stumbling backward. How I watched him hit the wall with the back of his head. Collapse onto the hard plastic chair where I'd put my clothes, my coat. There he sat. Slumped forward. Head down.

Mark?

No answer. I watched him breathe rapid, shallow breaths.

Panic fluttered in me like the wings of a great black bird as I stood there on straight legs. No pain anymore. Concrete gone. Foot light as a feather. Looking at Mark slumped in the very chair where I had sat so many times before, softly explaining my symptomology to the floor, to the dust.

Mark, I said again. *Are you okay?*

Nothing.

Mark? I sang, for my head was suddenly flooded with music. I watched his polo-shirted back rising and falling. Just like Briana's rib cage rising and falling. Shallow. Quick. Gripping his wrist where I'd touched him.

Fear filled me then. Bright fear. Golden as the golden remedy. *What have I done what have I done what have I done?* Yet I was smiling at Mark. Was I smiling? Yes. From ear to ear. I couldn't help it. Couldn't help the blue skies breaking in my blood. Neither leg screaming, for both legs were light as air. Mark was sitting on my coat, my sad dress, my tights, so I left them there.

Mark, I sang again.

Mark waved me away weakly. Not looking up. Not speaking.

So I slipped on my shoes. So I told Mark I'd see him in forty-eight hours. I agreed, we had to stay on top of this. I shut the door softly behind me.

And then I ran.

I jumped through the obstacle course of orange cones, I hopped through the ladder of rope still laid out on the floor for the old man, who was gone now. Easy it was. I could've done it a thousand times if I didn't want to get the hell out of there. No one in the gym anymore but one therapist with teased-out hair, hunched over a computer station, glaring at the monitor. Tapping her foot to Aerosmith playing staticky on the radio.

"Do you need to make another appointment?" she said to me, not even batting an eye at me in my medical gown. Not even looking.

"I'll call in," I said, grabbing the windbreaker from the rack by the door.

And now I'm here, in my car in the frozen lot, gazing at the empty dark, my humming hands on the wheel. Trembling, my whole body trembling still, though I feel my head nodding along now to a song on the radio, a smile wavering on my lips. Oh god, what do I do? I need a drink, I do. I need to talk to someone, who?

And then I know, of course I do. Black leather shoes tapping. Suits the color of night. Each pair of hands cupped around a drink that glows golden in the red bar. The three men. Drinking that gold drink right now at the Canny Man.

What have I done? I'll ask them. To Mark? To Briana? What is this humming in my hands? What is this tune on my lips? What is this smile on my face? What is this lightness?

At the Canny Man, no three men. I look around the nearly empty bar, the filthy air from which they seem to have vanished. No one at all at the bar apart from a few singles at the high tables against the red walls. Their heads bent low like Mark's in his chair. Is he still there in the treatment room? Don't think about that now. Get a drink. I walk up to the bar, lightly, quickly, I can't believe how lightly, how quickly. I walk a few circles around the bar just to check, just to be sure I haven't missed the three men, that they aren't hiding in a corner somewhere, not here or there or here. How easily I can walk these circles. No dead leg, no hip pain, no back twinge. No hobble, no hunch, no limp. I walk around the bar one more time for good measure. A few more times for good measure. Skipping a little? Yes, I'm skipping a little, I can't help it. I'm skipping, skipping —

"Everything okay there, lass?" says a voice now. Male, deep, lilting.

I freeze.

A bartender watching me from behind the bar. One I don't recognize. Tall. Black hair slicked back. Scottish, apparently. And handsome, I can't help but notice. Looking at me and grinning. When has a bartender ever noticed me in here before? When have I not had to flag one down again and again, *Hello, hello, sir, do you see me?* But here is this handsome Scottish bartender gazing at me intently with pale eyes. Me, I'm the lass.

Suddenly I become very aware that I'm in a medical gown and a stolen windbreaker. I draw the jacket more tightly around my body.

"Yes, fine, thank you. Just looking for someone." I'm about to try to smile, my attempt to convince, but then realize I'm already smiling.

"You didn't happen to see three men here tonight, did you?" I ask him.

He shakes his head slowly. He's wearing one of those black pirate shirts, shirtsleeves rolled, and a black kilt. He looks like he participates in Ren fairs. He's the one who roasts the pig, who cranks the spit.

"Three men? I've seen a lot of men here tonight. All professions. But three together? Don't think so, lass. Not tonight, anyway. What did they look like?"

But I find I can't describe them. "One's fat and sort of red in the face," I say at last. "One's middling with alcoholic eyes. He has a red handkerchief. He wears a suit the color of night."

"The color of night, does he?"

"Yes, and then one is tall and slender. He never looks you in the eye. He sits off to the side. You can only ever see a sliver."

"A sliver, is he?"

"Exactly."

He raises an eyebrow. "Not much to go on there, lass."

I feel myself flush. "They're usually sitting right here," I say, waving at the empty seats. "Just here at the bar. They drink the golden remedy."

"Do they now?"

"Yes, and they sing. On the stage. Well,

the fat man does, anyway."

I realize now that I sound insane. The bartender shakes his head slowly, but he's beaming at me, clearly entertained.

"I don't usually work karaoke nights, I'm afraid. The golden remedy. That a drink?" Why do I feel like he already knows this? Knows the three men. Knows everything. He's looking at me in a way that makes me feel like I'm vibrating.

"Yes, it's golden. It glows with its own light."

Why am I telling him this?

"Does it?" He leans forward, interested. Why is he so interested? Like he's an audience member. On the edge of his seat.

"Yes," I tell him. "In fact, I'd love a glass if you've got it."

He has a tattoo sleeve on his left arm. Floral. Some sort of shining black script like a winding path among the flowers. *What does it say?* I wonder, but just as I lean in to look closer, he steps back.

"Why don't you have a seat? Let me ask around."

He pours me a water and disappears. I sit on the barstool in my windbreaker. Like I belong here, absolutely. I've done nothing wrong, no. Just a drink after a long day. Long day, very long. I watch my legs swinging back and forth in front of me. Wildly, like I'm a child on a swing. I sip the iced water, which is sweet, like water from a well. My hands hum lightly against the glass. I stare at the empty stools where the three men should be. Explaining everything to me. About what I've done. What to do next. I think of Mark pale and slumped over, sitting on my clothes and coat, breathing quickly into his knees. *Do you like tricks, Ms. Fitch?*

Mark was breathing when I left him, wasn't he? I recall his rib cage rising and falling. Yes. Still alive. Not like I killed him, of course not. Since when do you kill someone by touching their wrist in a certain way, that's absurd. Laughable. I'm laughing now, because it is so funny. It's a strange trilling laugh that stops and starts. I wish the three men were here to laugh with me. We'd laugh and raise our glasses filled with the golden drink, wouldn't we? We'd laugh into the night. Laughable that I could hurt anyone. If anything, Mark was the one hurting me, wasn't he? He was breaking me, anyone could see that. The three men would agree, absolutely. *PTs will break you, Ms. Fitch. Bank, bones, spirit.*

"Surely you could see," I say to the stale air all around me. My audience of smoke and dust.

Above me on the ceiling, a headless statue of a woman hangs suspended from a web of rope. Was she always there?

As I look back down, I catch my reflection in the mirror behind the bar, between the bottles, before I can stop myself. I never look in the mirror when I'm here if I can help it. Because I'll look and find death. But what I find there takes my breath away. Hair gleaming. Eyes bright. Like actual stars are in them. The blue in the medical gown, the purple of the windbreaker, bring out roses in my skin. Roses I didn't even think were there. Roses I thought had long dried up, dried out. Nothing but a husk, this skin. But tonight, I'm luminous. I'm glowing. I'm the girl in the glossy Playbill photo, a girl I never thought I'd see again. There she is right there in the mirror. Breathing as I am breathing, right on the other side of the glass.

"I'm sorry, lass," says the bartender, back again. "No golden remedy tonight. Fresh out, I'm afraid."

"Oh."

He smiles. And now the way he's looking at me makes sense. How far he's leaning forward against the bar. How close he seems to want to be. I smell leather, sweet smoke, whiskey. That script tattooed down his bicep catches my eye again. He's close enough that I can read it easily now. *The primrose way to the everlasting bonfire.* Shining blackly under the bar light like a snake. Surrounded by golden flowers. He grins at me.

"No golden remedy," he says with affected sorrow. "No three men. Hope this doesn't mean you'll run off, Miranda."

Miranda, did he just call me Miranda? His pale eyes burn into me, and I suddenly feel vivid, like I've gone from black-and-white to crackling color. All my skin humming now, not just my hands. The pit of my stomach electric.

"No." I shake my head.

I notice he's wearing a necklace. A pendant of three silver skulls on a black leather cord. They catch the light, the silver gleams as he leans in, looks at me.

"So what'll you have instead?" he says. "Anything. On me."

I wake up to the smell of smoke, the smell of the sea. I brace myself for the pain, a reflex. But there is no pain, there's nothing.

Nothing?

Nothing.

I'm lying in my bed, naked, vibrating. Smiling, actually smiling, at the morning light pouring into the windows. Smiling at the melted-down candles, the twisted sheets, an empty bottle of Scotch on the floor beside a cord of black leather, a pendant of three silver skulls. What looks like pale blue confetti is scattered all over me, the bed, the floor. The medical gown, I realize. Ripped by hands and teeth into tiny shreds, was it me or the Scotsman who tore it up? Can't ask him. He left along with the dark.

On the ceiling, flashes of the night play for me. Me leading the Scotsman backward down the hallway of my building. Tugging on his skull necklace like a leash. And though he was a towering figure, he allowed himself to be led down the long, ugly hall to my front door.

You sure you're all right there, lass? he asked again and again.

I'm wonderful, I said, *wonderful.*

Dancing with him in my living room to some music he cranked on the turntable, a record I didn't even know I had. The drums, the swell of strings like a roar. The neighbors thumping on the walls while the Scotsman spun me round and round, and there was smoke, there were flashing lights, right here in the living room, and we were turning and laughing in the fog.

I smile at the memory of pushing him

onto the couch the color of my former lips. Straddling him, that can't be right, can it? Leaning forward to bite his pierced ear, his shoulder, my spine supple as a snake. Him lifting me, putting me under him. My legs wrapping tightly around his back, my ankles propped on his broad shoulders, easy, easily. The Scotsman's whiskey mouth on my neck, my ear, and how I shuddered and shuddered, my fists full of his long, dark hair. How he pulled the ice out of our shared whiskey glass with two fingers. Slipped the cube into my mouth, then his. Iced tongue of velvet on my jumping thigh, my hip, right where the surgical scar was. Still is. Three pale prong-like marks as though someone stabbed me with a pitch-fork. How he licked each mark, all three, while I moaned at the ceiling, spine arching, neck tilted back.

Impossible, I think, sheets snaked around my body, still light as air, light as the breeze in my hair, lifting it lightly off my shoulders. My window's open, but I'm not cold. I stare at the blue, blue sky through the window screen. A bright blue that reminds me spring is coming. *Right around the corner, Miranda.* Almost here. And for once, I feel no fear. No pain. Nothing. Nothing? No. Not nothing. Something. Something else is

■ ■ ■ ■

PART TWO

■ ■ ■ ■

CHAPTER 15

"Such a beautiful day today, isn't it, everyone?" I ask them, my voice reverberating richly through the theater. Afternoon rehearsal. They're seated in their usual semicircle on the stage, awaiting my instructions. Not a whisper among them. Not a yawning mouth or a phone in sight. All eyes on me as I stand absolutely straight before them, smiling.

"A beautiful day," I repeat. And it is. Outside the theater, the buds are beginning to bloom brightly on the wet black branches. Buds of the palest green. The sun isn't so weak anymore; the sky isn't so sick. No more deathly white for the sun or the sky. No more pale orb glowing tremulously through the gray mist, no no. The sun is bright today, golden.

"Lovely, isn't it. And we deserve it, don't we? After such a hideous winter. Don't we deserve it?"

I turn to them. They nod at me. They nod at whatever I say these days.

"Yes, Professor Fitch," they say. "We do, we do."

A month of rehearsals has gone by, flown by, it seems.

"Doesn't time seem like it's flying?"

"Yes, Professor."

"Doesn't time seem like it's flying, Grace?"

"Sure," Grace says, frowning. Always frowning these days. A real stick-in-the-mud of late.

"And now look, here we are. Spring. No point being in here," I say, I sing, waving my hand at the walls of the decrepit theater.

"Let's rehearse outside today for a change, shall we? Get some fresh air in our lungs, am I right? Sunshine on our skin. Get the blood flowing. Challenge ourselves diaphragmatically, how does that sound?"

"It's March, Miranda," Grace says. "It's still freezing outside."

I gaze at Grace, who sits on the stage with her arms folded, looking warily at me. Little furrow between her tiny brows. The furrow's been there for the past month. Ever since Briana left us and didn't come back. Still sick, apparently, so we hear. So sad. We are all terribly sad about it, truly. Truly, truly.

262

"Spring is in the air today, Grace. I felt it. I felt it myself on the way here. Let's experience it firsthand, shall we?"

"I don't know if that's —"

But I'm already out the door, leading them all down the hall, and they're following me as I sail down the stairs in my spiked heels, out of the building. I feel them all jogging behind me, breathing heavily, trying to keep up. My, my, am I really walking so quickly? I'm excited, I suppose. Aren't they excited? They should be.

"Quickly, quickly, everyone," I call as I march them across the campus green. Past the storybook little cluster of white Victorian-era homes that are the dormitories and lecture halls. Past the toy library, the glass dining hall where the children chew their food-shaped cud.

"Jesus, where's the fire, Miranda?" Grace hisses at my side, breathless.

"We have to get started, don't we, Grace? Ticktock. Ticktock."

I smile at Fauve, whom we pass just now on the green — she's in her winter coat, laden with canvas bags full of teaching materials, marching huffily to her class. What is she teaching this semester again? Oh yes, that's right. Music for Idiots.

"Hello, Fauve," I say, I sing.

263

But Fauve is silent, glaring, sick with suspicion as she watches us all clamor past, such a merry bunch of players, all the world a stage. I'm gloriously immune to her Dickensian plots, her sad schemes. I wave at Fauve wildly.

"Come along, everyone," I yell. "Follow, follow. Follow me across the green, along the snaking icy path, whoa, watch your step there. Bit slippery. Wouldn't want anyone to get hurt. Break anything. No more injuries or accidents or illnesses, am I right? Not with showtime just around the corner! Round the corner, can you believe it? Tick-tock, ticktock!"

I finally stop right in the middle of the rose garden, right before the great black goat statue. I used to hobble over here on my less inflamed days, in an attempt to experience some kind of beauty — *The natural world would do you some good,* Mark used to say to me. But the beauty of it all, far from soothing me, actually caused my legs to seize up in a kind of grief. And then the students in their beauty, who were sitting in the garden so carefree, in various yogic configurations, their limbs so pliable, their smiles so easy, just set off the red webs so violently that I was forced to limp away. But not today.

"What did I tell you? Doesn't it feel just like spring?" I sing, my breath a capering cloud.

I look at my circle of children. Huddled obediently on the green. Lightly shivering. Not so lightly shivering. Pink faces. No scripts, because I've forbidden them. And guess what? Now they've memorized the play. Now they know it by heart. They stare up at me, the tails of my black coat blowing behind me, standing straight in my heeled boots, taller than I have ever been, casting my shadow over them. Is it just them or have I grown taller in the past month?

Yes, Professor Fitch. They nod. *You told us. Just like spring.*

Wonderful. "Well," I say. "Let's warm up, shall we?"

Grace looks at me with panic. Oh no. Not another one of my "warm-ups." She thinks my warm-ups of late have been a little too —

"Wonderful," I say, clapping my hands. "Warm-ups are wonderful, aren't they? They get the blood going. Get the air flowing. Get the cobwebs swept away. Now let's all get in a circle, that's it. Closer, closer, don't be afraid. I don't bite, do I?" And I laugh. I'm always laughing these days.

"Good. Now let's all bend forward and touch our toes, very good. You too, Grace."

265

But Grace just stands there next to me, watching me fold forward, watching me reach down, watching me sigh with pleasure as my fingers touch the tips of my boots easily, so easy.

"Really reach down and touch those tips. Wow. Doesn't that feel amazing? So amazing, am I right? That stretch. Wow wow wow so good. Now let's reach up. Up, up, up and touch the sky, shall we? Touch the sun, that's it. Can you touch the sun? See if you can stretch up to the sky with your arms and touch the actual sun. Oh fuck yes. Feels fucking wonderful, am I right?"

"Miranda," Grace whispers.

"How your arms just love it. They want to stretch up, they want the sun. Which is not so weak anymore, is it? Not so pale and glimmering dully behind the clouds, but bright and bold and fierce, isn't it? So bright it'll burn your eyes out, am I right, Grace?"

Grace just looks at me. Her arms are still folded in front of her chest.

"Okay, drop your arms back down, arms back down," I tell them. "Now we're going to shake it out. Shake everything, that's it. Hands, arms, legs, head, hips. Really shake them, don't be afraid."

We all shake together. We shake and we shake and we shake. I shake with them. I'm with them every step of the way these days. I'm shaking and shaking and shaking. My limbs, my head, I really get into it with them. I'm jumping up and down, up and down, to show them how to shake. Hopping on one leg while shaking the other. And as I'm shaking, I'm laughing again because it's just so, so fun — "Isn't this so fun?" I ask them — as I shake and shake and shake.

"Yes, Professor," they huff.

I ask them is that all they have, really? *Really?* Oh, I don't believe it. I tell them to go faster, wilder! Really let loose! Lose yourself in it! Like you're trying to shake off your actual flesh. Arms, legs, head, hips, yes! Like you're possessed. Full of demons. The only way out is to shake, shake them out. Shake them free, you're free. Oh, it feels wonderful doesn't it? Exhilarating to move like this, am I right? Blood flowing. Air going. Cobwebs swept away. Blood air cobwebs, blood air cobwebs, blood air cobwebs flowing going away, flowing going away, flowing going away, away, away, away, away away, away, away away away away away away away away away away away away away away away away away away away away away away away away away away away away away away away away away away away away away

away away away away —

"Miranda!"

I stop shaking. All of them, I see, have long stopped shaking. They're all just looking at me in quiet awe. Out of breath. A sea of red, damp, panting faces. Gripping each other's shoulders, clutching their own chests. A few are doubled over, coughing.

"Wonderful," I whisper. "Now why don't we play a game?"

"A *game*?" Grace says.

"Just to round things off, shall we? A little Zip-Zap-Zop?"

Grace shakes her head.

"A *wonderful* game. An energy-exchange game. Which is what theater is all about, really. Energy exchange. Am I right? All right, let's begin. Why so hesitant, everyone? Come on now, you know the rules. You gather in a circle just like this, just like this, that's it. You look at someone in the circle, could be anyone, anyone. You reach your hand out toward them. You look them right in the eye. You say *zip*. Or you say *zap*. Or you say *zop*. And just like that, you're sending them energy. And they're receiving it, aren't they? And then once they have it, it's *their* turn, isn't it, to point? To zip or to zap or to zop someone else of their choosing. Sound fun? Oh it really is. I'll get us started, shall I?"

I look at them all in the circle. All watching me with wide eyes. My gaze alights upon Trevor. Looking cold and sullen, his arms crossed. Really the only one who hesitates in rehearsal. Who seems to question me with his eyes though he rarely questions out loud. It's more of a pause, really. More of a look he gives me before he does what I say. Like the other day, when I told him to kiss Ellie, go on. Ellie who is currently playing Helen. Just until Briana gets back, of course. Whenever that may be.

But it doesn't say to kiss her in the script, Trevor protested.

Up to us, Trevor, I said, *isn't it, to interpret the white spaces? The spaces between the lines?*

Now I point my finger right at Trevor's face and he flinches slightly.

"Zip," I say.

Trevor ducks. He actually ducks as if to dodge a thrown stone. Stumbles backward. Falls into the slush. I look at Trevor lying in the muddy snow and laugh. Clap my hands.

"Oh, Trevor! You're not supposed to duck. You're supposed to catch it, catch the energy! Have you never played this game? Why don't we —"

"Miranda," Grace says touching my shoulder, pulling me down to earth. "We want to get started on rehearsal, don't we? Before it gets dark out here."

Dark? I look around and realize the sun is already setting. A great ball of red, sinking fire. The sky is deep blue, the trees black. The students appear to be shivering violently now.

"Right. Right, of course. Of course we do. Grace, always keeping me grounded. Reminding me of the time, ticktock, ticktock! Am I right? Why don't we go back inside to finish up? Since we've taken what we can from the sun, hmm?"

Back in the theater, I make Ellie and Trevor do the final scene again and again. *Let's do it again, shall we?* Act Five, Scene Three. In which Helen returns from the dead. In which everyone who thought she was dead, killed off by grief, by the indignities she has thus far suffered at the hands of Bertram, at the hands of fate, is in for a very big fucking surprise. Because she was never dead, not really, of course not. "Were you, Helen?" I say gently, turning to Ellie.

Ellie shakes her head. "No, Professor."

"That's only what everyone thought, wasn't it? Including stupid Bertram," I say, waving a hand at Trevor. His pants are still

270

wet from the fall in the slush. I hear his inaudible sigh.

"But they were all fools, obviously. You, Helen," I say, placing my hand on her shoulder, "are far too resilient for death. Aren't you?"

Ellie smiles uncertainly. "Yes, Professor Fitch."

Grace ahems in the audience. "Resilient? *Try cunning.*"

I ignore Grace. I continue, my hand on Ellie's shoulder: "Helen reveals all she has endured to the French court, all the indignities she has suffered."

"All her schemes and tricks," Grace interjects loudly.

"All she has *withstood,*" I correct, "in order to survive. In order to navigate the cruel world in which she finds herself heartlessly thrown. She must reclaim what is merely, rightfully hers. Her husband. Her home. Her life! All she has suffered is laid before Bertram," I say, looking meaningfully at Trevor. "And he is mystified — Trevor, look mystified. He is enchanted. He is won over. He agrees to love her dearly, ever dearly. He kisses her — Trevor, kiss her."

"Kiss her?" Trevor repeats. He's still just standing there a few feet from Ellie. Look-

271

ing bewildered. Looking infuriating. Really, unintentionally a perfect Bertram.

"Yes, go on, please."

He hesitates but only slightly. I watch him reach forward and peck her pathetically on the cheek. Ellie goes red.

"Not a peck, Trevor, a *kiss*. On the lips. She's your *wife* back from the dead. She's wearing *your* ring. She's bearing *your* child." With my hand on her back, I steer Ellie closer to his face. She stands there, literally shivering at her physical proximity to this idiot. She lowers her gaze to the floor.

"The very least you could do is kiss her on the lips, am I right? Again, please."

I ask them to kiss again as I stand in the middle row center. As I stand in the back row. As I stand in the left and then the right wings. I want to see this moment from all angles. I want to see it from afar, I want to see it up close. I hop back onto the stage, to where Ellie and Trevor are crouched down, turned toward each other, their faces close as per my direction. His hands are gathered in her hands, her left hand bearing his ring (my old ring, which I lent them for the scene). I crouch down, the better to see their faces turned toward each other in this pivotal moment, in which all becomes well. *Fall to your knees with the knowledge of it, that's it, good.* I fall to my knees too. All this woman has endured. All her pain. Her many trials by fire.

"How can you not be charmed? How can you not be won? You are. Of course you are."

I place my hand on Trevor's shoulder, and he shivers at my touch. I look at Trevor shivering now. With desire of course.

"You desired her all along," I tell him. "You were blind up until this moment. You were a fool, an immature shit."

"Professor," Grace warns.

"But you look at her now," I say, pointing to Ellie, laying my hand once more on her shoulder, which is now still, now steady.

"You look at this steadfast young woman who has loved you all along, who has been forced to live in the shadow, cast out. Now you look at her and at last you see. You see how she glows with a light all her own. And you can only marvel. You can only be bewitched."

I'm inches from their faces now, still on my knees, which bear the weight of my body smilingly, lightly, like a feather. I'm gazing deeply into Trevor's dull blue eyes. Mine shine like stars in the dark. Does he understand what I mean by *bewitched*?

Trevor nods. Yes. He believes he does.

He turns to Ellie. He places his hands

gently on either side of her dumbstruck face. He tilts his lovely young head, he leans in toward her. Kisses her. Deeply. Gently. Wildly.

Ellie shudders, gasps, melts to the floor.

"Better," I say. "Much better."

And then a noise like a door creaking. I look up.

Hugo, standing in the side entrance. Smiling at me. Why can't Trevor smile at Ellie that way? He claps his hands silently. Mouths, *Bravo.*

CHAPTER 16

"Wow. Great rehearsal, Miranda," Hugo says after I've let them all go. Trevor and Ellie walked out together, I noticed. Not holding hands, but talking close together. Whispering. *Enjoy it, Ellie,* I think. Enjoy it as I enjoy the fact of Hugo standing here, grinning at me with his little white teeth. His wheat-colored hair catching the light, redder than I remember. Telling me I'm amazing.

"Amazing," I repeat. "I don't know about —"

"No, really," Hugo insists, walking in closer, closer to me, can you believe it? "You were so inspiring. I felt inspired just watching you, Miranda." There's my name again on his lips. My name on the lips of Hugo. "I mean that was some kiss."

And it's clear from his face that what he's saying is we'll kiss too. Very soon. And not just kiss, fuck. He's thinking about it right now, in fact.

I smile at Hugo. Heart brimming with light. Gone are its dead leaves and dark alleys. Full-on flowers blooming there now, rising openly toward the sun. "Wasn't it?"

Behind me, I can hear Grace gathering her things quickly, shaking her head. *Jesus Christ.*

"So what did you do to whip them into shape like that? What's your secret?" he asks me.

"Oh, a director never tells."

Oh for god's sake, I hear Grace say in her mind.

"Go on, your secret's safe with us." He's trying to include Grace with a wry look, but Grace won't be included. Her eyes are for her bag and coat alone.

"Well, if you must know, I cast a spell," I tell him.

He laughs. I'm so hilarious. Everything I say now is too funny or too clever. Everything makes him shake his head and stare at me with shining eyes. Marveling at the fact of me. "You cast a spell. That makes sense."

I hear a little cough. On the stage, I notice two Ashley/Michelles taking an awfully long time putting on their coats. Staring very hard at their phones, like they're not listening to us.

"Of course," I say, loud enough for them to hear, "it's the play that's casting the spell, not me."

"Of course. Well, it's got a hold on me too, I have to say," he says, looking right at me.

"Quite the hold." He says this last part softly. So softly I almost feel sorry for him. Sorry for Hugo? Impossible.

Grace snorts. Actually looks over at him, this man for whom she used to have a modicum of respect. *Are we kidding here?*

But Hugo is wonderfully oblivious. "So," he asks, walking even closer to me now, lowering his voice. He's about to put a hand on my shoulder, but he stops himself. "We still on for Thursday night?"

Thursday night. Our first date. He wanted to go out weeks ago. I've been the one putting him off, can you believe it? I've just been so wrapped up in the play. That time of year. Madness, am I right?

"Yes, of course, Thursday," I say to Hugo. "To talk about the play," I add, looking from him to Grace. Giving him the hint.

"Right, of course, yes. The play. I'm really looking forward to hearing your vision, Miranda."

I can feel Grace bristling beside me. She's

got her tote bag under her arm now, but she's not leaving. Clearly waiting to talk to me. *Alone, please, Miranda.*

But Hugo's still standing there in front of me like he's frozen, enchanted.

"See you then," I tell him like I'm giving him his exit cue.

He leans forward, seemingly about to kiss me, is he about to kiss me? I glance at the stage, the Ashley/Michelles still there, staring at us over their phones. Grace on the other side of us, watching too, her frown gathering force.

"See you then," he says, pulling back.

And then he walks away from me backward, actually walks backward. Until he hits his back against the double doors of the theater. We both laugh. It's awkward, but it's also so —

"Ridiculous," Grace mutters after he's gone.

I choose to ignore this. I turn to Grace. I look into her stony face that is full of questions, accusations. I smile wide. "Another great rehearsal, wasn't it?"

"It was long, Miranda," she says, looking right at me. "And cold. I'm exhausted."

"Exhausted? You, Grace?" And I laugh.

"I mean it, Miranda," she says. "These rehearsals are fucking killing me."

"Oh, Grace, come on. Nothing kills you, am I right? You're Puritan stock, you're Plymouth Rock, you're New England."

"New England or not, I can barely keep up with you these days."

"Ha ha. Very funny. You're *funny*," I say. But I'm not laughing, and neither is she.

I notice her dark coat is worn and weathered. Her left shoulder sags under her tote bag with the worn graphic of Degas ballerinas in mid-leap. Gray hairs I never saw before creeping through her brown pageboy cut. She does look pale. There are dark purple rings under her eyes. Clearly, she hasn't used her rose-petal mask in a while. Those living room nights with Grace come back to me, her face covered in cracking pink clay, gazing gravely at the TV while she poured me more wine. *I've got it,* she said. *Don't get up.*

"All right," I say. "Tell me."

Grace just stares at me. And suddenly I know what she wants to tell me. That it was fine for me to be a little better. Nice, in fact. Less of a strain on her, on us. For a moment there, she even saw the possibility of rekindling things. But now? Now Grace looks at me beaming as I stand before her on my high, high heels and she's at a loss. I'm no longer a faded Snow White lying on

279

her living room floor, complaining with her about the English department, drunkenly reminiscing about my days in the sun.

Who are you? her face says. *Who are you and what have you done with my wretched friend?*

"I don't know why you had to keep making them *kiss* like that," she says. She looks up at me, angry. Always angry these days. But her voice cracked on the word *kiss*. Because this is awkward for her too. When was the last time Grace kissed anyone besides her dragon?

"Why?" I say. "Because we have to get it right. It's one of the most important scenes in the play. It's pivotal."

"Pivotal?" Grace shakes her head. "It's not even in the script, Miranda."

I smile sadly at Grace. Of course she hates the kissing. Of course the idea that Helen might actually get some joy, some tongue after all she's been through, is revolting to Grace. In her view, Helen should get nothing. Should never have come back from the dead to begin with. Let her perish alone. Let her fade to black.

"You don't think Helen deserves one kiss after all she's been through? You're not going to let her have *one* moment — one! — of happiness?"

Grace just stares at the flowers on my silk dress, not like they're flowers at all but little forked tongues sticking out at her.

New dress? she said when I came into the theater.

Old, I told her. *Old favorite. Haven't I worn it before?*

Never, she said. *Bit thin for this weather, don't you think?*

But I just smiled at Grace. *I'm not really feeling the cold these days.*

Back when we were closer, I'd watch her swipe through Tinder occasionally. Always with a look on her face like she'd just taken a sip of very off beer. *Be fucking glad you're not out there,* she used to say to me. Because how could I be out there when I could barely walk? And I'd laugh like I was glad. But of course I wasn't glad, how could I be?

"The kiss isn't just for Helen, you know," I add, looking away.

"Isn't it?" she says, but I feel her staring at me intently.

"Not at all. The kiss is for the audience." I gesture at the empty seats all around.

"The *audience,*" Grace says. "Really?"

"Of course. The *kiss* brings the audience in. Lets them feel it too."

281

"Feel what exactly, Miranda?"

"Her joy."

Grace laughs joylessly. "Oh, we felt it, trust me," she says. "I'm still feeling it, as a matter of fact." I look at Grace, frowning at Helen's joy. I think she liked the fact that I was doomed to be single. A fellow spinster. I didn't even have a pet. Just some plant Grace bought me (*to cheer things up!*) that I always forgot to water. *You need to water it!* she'd tell me whenever she came into my office, running toward the sickly plant in the windowsill as if it were on fire. *And it shouldn't be in direct sunlight like this either; it's delicate.* I'd lie there on the office floor and watch her water it, whisper to it. A little annoyed, frankly, that she seemed to show it greater tenderness, concern, a softer touch, than she'd ever shown me.

"You want to deprive her *and* the audience" — I wave my hand again at the empty theater — "of resolution, of a happy ending — is that what you're saying, Grace? That's it, isn't it? You think she doesn't *deserve* a happy ending."

"I never said that," Grace says reasonably. "All I said is that the kiss isn't in the script."

Not all of us, I want to tell Grace, *are content with a running club and a domesticated reptile for company. Needing no other*

intimacy besides the darting tongue of a
dragon, a dirt trail, and in the evenings, a
television screen full of blood suspiciously
spilled in the Shetland Islands. Some of us,
Grace, are warm-blooded. Some of us need a
little more.

But I can't say that to her. Ever.

"Look" — and here I attempt to be the pragmatist like Grace — "you said yourself *All's Well* hardly compares to murder, madness, and witches. So you know, I'm doing what I can to spice it up."

"Have you heard from Briana at all?"

"No." Fear in my voice. "Have you?"

"No. But what I heard from Fauve is that she's still quite sick."

"Is she really? That's too bad." I look straight at Grace. I don't flinch. Keep my mouth a straight line of solemnity. I am grave in the face of this tragedy. Unforeseen. Utterly. "Well, no choice, then. No choice but to soldier on as best we can. I'm certainly doing my best to soldier on."

"I see that."

"What's that supposed to mean?"

"Nothing. Just that you're seeming very full of energy these days. Much better than you were."

"Better? Oh I don't know about better, really. My back," I say, touching it. "My back is still . . ."

Grace raises her eyebrows, waiting.

"It still has twinges and things. And my hip is still . . ." I shrug sadly. "My hip."

She looks at me. "Doesn't show."

"I guess I'm just not letting it *get* to me like I once was, you know? I guess that's the secret. Like you said to me. Sickness is really just psychological. Mind over matter. I guess I'm finally putting that philosophy into practice."

"Did I say that to you?" she asks me. But I know she's thinking of that time in the car after the steroid shots. When she pulled us over to the shoulder of the road. Told me maybe I should consider that this might be all in my head. Given how nothing had helped so far? Given how there was no real evidence in any of the tests? Maybe it was just psychosomatic. Stress. *Anxiety,* lots of people have that. Maybe I'm one of them. Something to, I don't know, think about. And then I felt sick with fear. I felt a blackness all around. *Miranda?* Grace said. *Are you hearing me?* But I could only stare at the road, my legs still clenched, my back on fire.

"Yes," I tell her now. "You used to say that to me."

My turn to look at Grace. Her turn to

284

look away. She readjusts the tote strap on her shoulder.

"All right, I need a fucking drink," she says. "Let's get one. Together, all right?" Her voice softens. "We should talk about the staging for the final scene anyway. And we really have to figure out this casting thing, don't we?"

"What casting thing?"

"Well, our lead is *missing,* Miranda."

"She's not *missing.* Don't make it sound so unnecessarily sinister. She's just under the weather is all. Anyway, we have a lead."

"*Ellie* is our lead now?"

"For now, yes. Why not?"

Grace looks at me. *Why not?* Am I insane? Surely I know exactly why not. Dethrone Queen Briana? Usurp the unspoken ruler of the program, our souls? Don't I understand that's essentially career suicide?

"And what about *Briana?*"

"Well, she's ill, poor thing."

"And what if she comes back?"

"She won't come back." I say it quickly, far too quickly. So I add, "Sounds like she's really down and out. Such a shame."

"Miranda, I really think we should talk about this more. I don't think you're considering —"

"Just leave it to me. You go rest. Recharge.

285

You said yourself that you're exhausted. And you look it. Why don't you go home? Do a face mask. Spend some time with Ernest, okay? Watch some Netflix. One of your murder shows maybe? Way more interesting than *All's Well,* am I right?"

CHAPTER 17

Afternoon the next day. Ellie stands in the doorway of my office, looking pale and afraid.

"You wanted to see me, Professor Fitch?" She looks at me sitting on top of my desk. Legs crossed, the top leg swinging. Smiling at her in such welcome.

"Ellie," I sing. I'm always singing these days. "There you are. Come in, come in. Shut the door behind you, please? Wonderful. Have a seat," I say, and I point to the empty chair with the toe of my new pointed boot.

Obediently, she takes the chair. I look at her sitting there, clutching her canvas bag, lank hair that I want to brush away from her face. I notice her hands are shaking. Has playing Helen all these weeks in rehearsal given her no confidence?

"And how are you finding rehearsal these days?" I ask her gently.

Ellie stares at my crossed legs in their spiked heels. "Good, Professor," she says.

"Ellie, it's Miranda. Call me Miranda, please."

"Miranda."

"You know, of course, why I wanted to see you today?" I say to her.

She shakes her head. "No, Prof — I mean, Miranda."

"No?" *Really, Ellie?* "Well, as you know, we're at that time of year again."

I gesture to the window and smile. Budding branches. Pale green leaves. Spring. Spring, does she see that? A time when everything is in bloom. Everything is having sex. Everything is so damp and fragrant and fuckable. Showtime, in other words. Right around the corner.

She nods nervously. Yes. Yes, she sees that. . . .

"Given that we're at this point in the production timeline, opening night not too far away, and our lead still . . ." I feel a smile creep across my face as I say this. I bite my lip, attempt to appear mournful. "Absent."

Ellie nods sadly. Yes.

"I've had to make some difficult decisions."

I stand up; I pace the floor to demonstrate the difficulty. My new boots click along the

288

floor. Haven't taken them off since I bought them. Drove to the mall one night. Skipped into the shop. Said to the shoe man, *I'd love a pair of leather boots. With a heel, please. High. Spiked.*

She looks at me, suddenly very alert. "Decisions?" Ellie says. "What sort of decisions?"

I spin around deliciously. Hop up onto my desk again. Easy. So very easy to hop and spin these days. I recross my legs of flesh. Not concrete anymore, flesh. I look at my Helen and smile.

"Casting decisions, Ellie."

I watch Ellie hold her breath. She knows. She's waiting for it.

"Ellie, I'd like for you to play Helen. For this year's production."

She closes her eyes. Lowers her head.

"Me," she whispers.

"You're perfect for the role, Ellie. You make Helen's pain, her love, her loss, her determination, your own."

Ellie says nothing. She's still looking at the floor. Her hands are still trembling.

"Ellie, surely you could see this was coming? It's your fault, really."

Suddenly she looks up at me, white with fear.

"*My* fault?"

"For being so wonderful. For being so luminous. Truly I've never seen Helen so luminously played. We're all riveted by it every afternoon. I know I am."

She looks back down at the floor. She begins to shake more violently now. I put my hand on Ellie's shuddering shoulder. I lift her head up, expecting to see tears. And there are tears. But what I see too is a flash of a smile on her face. A flash of glee. Obscene glee. Which she quickly conceals. I watch her bite her lip. Lower her head again.

"But what about Briana?" she says.

Oh, Ellie. So determined to take the honorable road. Even though she wants the part so bad she can taste it. I play along.

"What about her?" I say.

"It's her part," she says quietly. "I'd hate to steal it from her."

Standing at the precipice of her own desire. Shaking her head at the bottomless chasm.

"Of course you would," I lie. "But Briana's not here, is she? I don't see her here, do you?" I lean back, pretend to look for Briana behind my desk. I lift my desk calendar up. Nope. No Briana in sight, see?

Ellie looks around at the empty air, afraid.

"What if she comes back?" she says.

"She won't come back." Again, I say this

too quickly. "She's still not . . . *well* . . . as you know."

Ellie nods. "It's so sad."

She looks genuinely troubled now. All traces of that strange happiness gone. So I appear mournful once more. Pensive. Surprised by the turn of events that has led to this. Not at all ecstatic. Not at all dancing inside.

"It's very sad, of course," I say. "We are all in mourning. But we must soldier on. The show must go on, as they say." I smile sadly.

"Who's going to play the King?"

"Forget the King," I snap. "Do you really want to hobble around the stage playing an ailing, old wretch with a fistula? If I'm being honest, Ellie, I never wanted that for you. Never."

Suddenly I can't help but feel like my mother backstage. The way she'd look at me furiously whenever I used to get stage fright as a child, her painted smile tight. Why won't I simply go out there and shine like we talked about, huh? Like we'd practiced so many times in the living room? Me in my fourth-grade Dorothy Gale costume and red satin shoes, my mother nodding gravely from the couch in her kimono, goblet of wine in one hand, cigarette in the other, mouthing the words along with me. *There's no place like home. There's no place like home.*

Outside, the sun is going behind a cloud. I watch its shadow pass over Ellie's still-troubled face.

"Just leave all that to me, okay?" I tell her, gently now.

"Helen," I say, "is the most important thing right now. And I really can't think of an actress more suitable. Will you do it, Ellie?"

She's smiling again. That grin is creeping across her face in spite of herself. It reminds me of when I first tried pork belly, the curl of my lips at the first taste of the crackling.

"Yes," she says. "I'll do it. Thank you. Thank you so much, Miranda."

"You only have yourself to thank, Ellie. Really. You earned it."

"I mean, thank you for seeing something in me. Most people —"

"Most people are idiots."

She smiles at me gratefully.

I hop off my desk to signal the end of the meeting. Ellie takes her cue and rises from her chair. "Oh, I have something for you."

She reaches into her canvas bag. Pulls out a plastic baggie and hands it to me.

I look at the bag of salt, punctuated hither

292

and thither with dried pink and purple petals. Tiny green needles. Broken bits of twig. It exudes an overwhelmingly botanical scent, like I'm being punched in the face by a thousand flowers.

"What's this?"

"Another bath. Since the others worked so well. It seems to be working wonders for you."

I forgot I even had them. They're funking up a drawer somewhere. A few others are stuffed with the first, in the glove compartment of my car, making it smell like a rank forest.

"It really is working wonders, Ellie. You're a magician. You're healing me."

At the grocery store that evening, I weave the cart dancingly, lightly, between the aisles. Standing on my tiptoes. Standing on my heels. Sometimes jumping up on the cart, letting it sail with the forward momentum of my body. Letting one foot dangle off the edge. So fun. I say hello to all the shoppers I pass.

"Hello, hello. . . . How are you? . . . Oh, excuse me, ha ha. . . . Pardon. Pardon me." Beautiful, everything so beautiful. Raspberries so red. Blueberries so blue, like the dark part of the ocean. Apples, so many varieties.

I take my time thinking what'll I buy, what'll I have tonight? Because I'm going to cook again tonight. Something complicated and lovely, something that requires stirring, what do I feel like tasting? Last night, I made risotto. Mushroom. I stood there at the counter on legs that did not buckle, chopping the celery, the onion, the carrot. Finely, patiently, into little dice-size bites. The knife had grown dull sitting in the drawer for so long, so I sharpened it. Poured myself a glass of wine, sipped it slowly. Poured the last of my prescriptions — the benzos, the painkillers — down the sink. I hadn't taken one for weeks, but I'd held on to them all the same, still kept them in my pockets, then in the car, then in the bathroom cabinet, just in case. Until, finally, I felt safe enough to drop them down the drain. Didn't need them to kill anything, to numb anything anymore. Instead I could savor a single glass of wine. I could take my time. Admire the amber color, how it caught the light from the kitchen window. I soaked the dried porcini in hot water for ten minutes, witnessed the miracle of those little shriveled husks resuming their true shape. Stood at the stove stirring for twenty-five minutes, pouring the hot stock in, ladle by ladle. Watched it bubble away. Watched the pearls of rice fatten and swell. Everything transforming, coming into itself. It was beautiful. When it was all ready, I ate sitting down at the table. Sat down, stood up, sat down. Sat down. I lit a black candle. I raised my amber glass to the man in the window who was sitting at his own meal. He hesitated. But he smiled and raised his drink to me too.

Tonight, I'll have pasta primavera. Italian for "first spring." I picture myself at the sink, washing the spring peas, the asparagus. Humming as I snap the asparagus stalks between my hands like twigs. If you break them by hand like that, they always break at the right place, I find. I'll make my own pasta too, that sounds fun. I weave my way through the aisles, gathering the ingredients — eggs, flour, salt. Where's the salt? There. Still there on that bottom shelf in the baking aisle. On the bottom shelf, I used to think, to spite me. I remember how long I used to stand there crookedly, staring down at the salt canisters. So beyond my reach they might as well have been stars. Tears gathered behind my eyes.

Everything okay, ma'am? said a stock boy to me once.

How the *ma'am* stung. How the *ma'am* was a slap.

I'm sorry, but could you get me that kosher salt on the bottom shelf? I asked him.

I can't bend, I said. *I'm sorry.*

Sure, ma'am, he said. And then he reached down so easily and grabbed a smoked Celtic sea salt. And he presented it to me, the wrong salt, so pleased with himself, his good deed.

Here you go, ma'am, he said.

Couldn't tell him it was the wrong salt. Couldn't bring myself to say, *Can you bend down again and get the kosher salt?* So I bought the wrong salt.

For two months I shook the fat dark gray crystals over my plate, cursing him quietly, cursing myself. Everything tasted smoky, brined, unnecessarily witchy.

Now? Now I crouch down low before the canisters on the bottom shelf. I feel the wondrous stretch in the backs of my legs. I bounce a little on my heels, observing all the salt that is mine to plunder. They have far more salts than the last time I was able to bend down.

From there, I go to the butcher counter.

The butcher says, "What can I get you, miss?" *Miss.* It's always *miss* now.

"*Guanciale,* please," I tell him. Pig's cheek. That memory of pork crackling in the office with Ellie gave me a craving.

"*Guanciale*. Nice. What are you making?" They always want to know what I'm making these days. They're always so curious about me.

"Pasta primavera."

The butcher smiles. "Pig's cheek for pasta primavera? Never heard of that before."

"I'm mixing it up," I tell him.

And he looks delighted by this, by me, by my unconventional approach.

"Sounds wonderful," he says. "Sounds like my kind of spring."

At the checkout, I wait in line, admiring my pig's cheek in its butcher paper with the butcher's phone number written on it and a ☺, my cart brimming with salt, with spring greens, rosemary, sage. I'll tear the sage with my hands. I'll strip the rosemary of its spikes. I stand on both legs, and I do not lean, I do not crumble, I do not die a thousand deaths. I do not curse the line, the cashier, my body. Instead I take pleasure in contemplating the sideline merchandise. The echinacea pills, the chocolate truffles; I even take a few. I flip through the cooking magazines languorously. Read about dinners for two and heavenly desserts. A chocolate lava cake with a caramel sea-salt middle, how wonderful is that? Maybe something to make for Hugo and me, sometime, if all goes well. I grab a bottle of red wine from a pyramidal display, why not?

Then I hear a throat clear itself pointedly. The person in line behind me. I can feel them ticking like a bomb. Breathing impatiently into the back of my neck. Shifting their weight from foot to foot. Moving their basket from arm to arm. *Come on, now,* I can feel them thinking. *Let's move, please.* An old or ailing person, no doubt. I'll turn to them and smile. I'll say, *Go on. You go ahead, in front of me, please, I insist. I don't mind,* I'll tell them. *I'm not in a rush today.*

I turn, and the smile falls from my face. Fauve. Standing there in a worn black coat covered in cat hairs. Holding a shopping basket overloaded with cans and frozen dinners. Wrist tendons straining visibly under the weight. Looking dour and miserable but she dagger-smiles when she sees me.

"Miranda," she says to me. "Grocery shopping, I see?"

As if even this is a crime. But I'm immune.

"Just a little dinner," I sing.

She looks down at my cart.

"Pig's cheek?" she says, and sniffs. "Bit rich for my blood."

Always needs to remind everyone they're not paying her enough. It's sad, really. I pity her, if I'm honest. I look at her sad basket of cans and trays.

"You look like you've got a good haul," I say. "Always good to have something you can just heat up."

Fauve smiles, but oh how it stings. Everything an arrow to her thrashing little soul.

"Oh, this isn't for me. I was buying some soup for poor Briana. I'm going to drop it off on my way home."

I shudder at the name. Involuntary. Does Fauve notice? If she does, she doesn't let on.

"Briana?" I say casually. "Really."

"It's out of my way, of course," Fauve adds.

"Of course it is," I say.

"But her parents so appreciate it, you know. Those sorts of gestures. Such kind people, you know. So generous to the school."

"How kind of you," I say, smiling. "How utterly selfless."

Fauve looks at me like she wants to kill me. She's picked a method, even. Enjoys going over it in the nights.

"Well, we do what we can, don't we? Though I wonder if it's doing any good. Such a weird illness she has, poor thing."

She gazes at me now with blatant accusation. But it's a bluff. She knows nothing. Nothing to know, am I right? I look at Fauve right in her sickly eyes. That are boring into mine. Determined to find guilt there, sorrow. She'll find nothing. Nothing there but dancing, laughing light.

"Things *are* going around," I say tragically. "It is that season."

"Usually Briana is so hearty, so immune," Fauve insists.

"Like a weed," I agree.

"She just says everything hurts. So sinister."

Pathetic, this attempt to bait me. It's almost funny.

"Has she been tested for Lyme?" I ask like I really want to know. "Maybe she got bitten by a tick." I look so very concerned.

"The doctors are telling her there's nothing wrong with her at all. But what do doctors know, really? I told them she should see *my* doctor. He's holistic. Considers the whole picture, the energetics. A specialist when it comes to pain, especially. I would have recommended him to *you*, Miranda, but then, you don't seem like you need one anymore." She smiles at me. "You're seeming so remarkably well these days."

"Am I?" I smile right back at her. I shrug, unshaken. As if life is life is life. A mystery.

Sometimes we're down, sometimes we're up, aren't we? The wheel of fortune, always turning.

"I still have issues, of course," I say. "With my back. And my hip is . . . my hip."

"Her parents are worried sick, of course. They're saying Briana is murmuring things in her sleep."

"In her sleep?" Heart thrums in my chest now. But I continue to look unshaken. "Really?"

Fauve nods. "Your name came up, in fact."

"*My* name?" A flash of lightning in the small of my back. The wine bottle nearly falls from my hands, but I catch it just in time. I grip the bottle, collect myself. "Well, that makes sense. I'm her director after all."

I turn and smile at the moving conveyor belt. Still full of someone else's groceries. I will it forward. Fauve watches me.

"It doesn't surprise me either," she says, "especially given the conflict the two of you were having. The day she got sick. What was all that about again?"

I drop the wine bottle. It shatters, pooling redly at our feet.

I look up at Fauve. Triumph. Triumph on her face even though she's standing in broken glass, the wine flooding her salt-crusted boots. I turn to the cashier, who looks utterly gutted by the fact of me.

"I'm so sorry," I say to the cashier.

In answer, she picks up the receiver of her work phone. She's wearing a leopard-print tendonitis brace on her wrist. "Cleanup at register twelve," she says miserably.

"Oh, look," Fauve says, "they've opened up a line over there. I should run. I want to try and get there while Briana's still awake."

She crunches over the broken glass.

"Any words you'd like to pass along to Briana?" she calls over her shoulder.

In my mind's eye, I see a face full of hate framed by flaming hair. Eyes closed and fluttering. Pale, parched lips mouthing my name.

"Just that she should take all the time she needs to heal. That if anyone understands about that, it's me."

CHAPTER 18

Date night with Hugo. I sit before my triptych mirror, brushing my long, lush hair. The shine is really just incredible. The waves, like a Hollywood starlet's. Three women gaze back at me. Three Mirandas. Mirandas I hardly recognize. Mirandas from long ago. Before the misery lines. Before the forehead furrow cast its shadow. Before the pallor of death settled deep into our cheeks. I gaze at their faces like old friends. Smiling at me, smiling to themselves. Because we cannot believe this is how we look. Is this how we really look now?

I'm wearing a brand-new dress. White with red poppies. I've resurrected the lace from the back of the dead-lingerie drawer. I've plucked, waxed, exfoliated. Shaved all the prickly black hairs from my legs. Hairs that, formerly, I had to let grow. No choice. Couldn't bend to shave. Mark used to tell me not to be ashamed of them.

It's just the body, Miranda, isn't it? he'd say gently, rolling up my sweatpants leg, the disposable medical shorts. Tracing the incision scars on my hip with his fingers. Three incisions. Three raised white bumps, like three prongs.

I wonder how Mark is doing these days. SpineWorks called me the other day to let me know that he wouldn't be available for future appointments, sadly. He was on leave, they said. But another therapist, Brad, would be happy to take me on.

That's fine, I said. *I don't need an appointment actually. I'm feeling so much better these days. But please give Mark my best, won't you?*

In the mirror now, I see three Marks gazing back at me. Their faces pale. Breathing quickly, shallowly, with their mouths. Clutching their wrists. Eyes widening in fear, in horror. I take a sip of champagne. And then it's the Mirandas I see again. All seeming to glow from within. Like someone turned on a light right beneath their skins. Eyes literally sparkling. Lips bright as cherries. A smile that seems to smile on its own. I sigh with relief. Shaky, I'm just a little shaky. Nervous, I guess. Big date tonight, that's all. Haven't been on one of those in a while. A long, long time.

304

When was the last time?

I think of the Scotsman's whiskey mouth on my thigh. Well, that doesn't count as a date, does it? Not really a date. And then I remember Paul and me. All those heady first dates in Edinburgh after my shows. Sitting across from him in pubs, on the craggy grass of Arthur's Seat, on the green stretch of the meadows, and feeling electric, alive, lit up. And then later, back in New England, when he'd drive down from Portland to wherever I was working — a production in Boston if it was fall, a festival on the Cape or in the Berkshires if it was summer — and I'd sneak away with him for a night, an afternoon, a day.

And then, years later, there was the other kind of date. The ones we used to try to have after my fall, to reconnect. Sitting at our favorite sushi restaurant in Marblehead, not so very long ago. It was our tradition to go there to celebrate whenever I'd finish a production season. *Now I get to have you back for a bit,* he would say, smiling at me from across the booth, like he'd missed me so terribly. And I'd feel so happy to be home, to be back, to be his. The last time we went there was different. One of our final attempts to resurrect our romantic life. *You pick the place one week; I'll pick the place*

305

next week. It'll be fun. We have to try some-thing. I'm willing to try something, are you? Yes. Of course. Sitting across from each other at a tiny black table. People to our left and our right talking to each other, leaning in close, holding hands as if to show us how estranged from each other we'd become. Paul drinking his cold sake too quickly. Dead to the fact of me in front of him. Staring at me like his life was on fire. And me, I was the fire. With my colorless face bracing itself, always bracing itself against the threat of pain. With my dead legs and my hunch. With my benzo eyes always on the verge of tears I was too drugged-out to cry. Pretending to listen to him tell a work story when really I was just lost in the gray, twisting corridors of my own misery, my own fear. Staring at the waxy orchid in its thin vase. So unapologetically pink. Its pursed, vaginal mouth so flagrantly ecstatic that I remember I actually envied its life. I watched Paul eat miserably, cologne-spritzed, a shirt he knew I liked tucked into pants he'd ironed, though he knew he'd get no sex later. That I'd retreat to the pullout couch, which was already pulled out, always pulled out. He'd retreat to the bedroom. *Are you sure you won't come to bed?* he'd ask me, over his shoulder. Knowing already I'd say no.

I'm sure, Goldfish. I sleep better out here, actually. Though I didn't.

I close my eyes. Don't think of that now. Don't dredge that shit up. Think of Hugo. Hugo's not Paul, is he? And I'm not me anymore, am I? Just look in the mirror; look at that creature. Think of tonight. Think of the new lightness in your blood. Turn up the music, that's better. Where's that champagne, anyway? Is it already empty? So pour another glass. Totally understandable. Just nerves, the good kind. Nice to finally have the good kind. Anyway, this is sort of a celebration, isn't it? A resurrection. How long have I dreamed of this? Lying in my bed, listening to the neighbors fuck, to my super weep. Imagining Hugo and me sitting face-to-face. Hugo's face across a table, over the light of a bar candle. Not gazing through me. Not gazing to the right or to the left of my face. But at me, finally. His features fixed on me, drawn *in our heart's table,* as Helen says of Bertram. His crooked mouth with its smile-shaped scar saying my name. Saying *Miranda.* And then?

And then I have no idea. Can't imagine past that.

Past that, all I see are stars.

I run a brush through my hair, though really it needs no brushing. Went to the salon this afternoon and had my hair done for the first time in years. Got the gray out, got a cut, a conditioning treatment even.

And what would you like today? the hairdresser asked me.

Everything, I told her.

Sitting in the salon chair, I marveled at how I could sit without screaming. I laughed and laughed.

Someone's happy, the hairdresser said.

Me? No, no, just thinking of a joke I heard earlier.

I love jokes, the hairdresser said, and she waited for me to share.

You had to be there, I told her. *It's one of those.*

Now my phone chimes. Text from Hugo.

Meet me in the theater at 9 p.m.

Theater? My heart sinks. A work meeting? It's a work meeting, of course it is. He never wanted to date me, how could I be so absurd? *How could you ever think that, Miranda?*

I try to remember the way he was looking at me in the theater after rehearsal Tuesday. How he walked backward away from me, backward so he could still make eye contact, still smile at me with that smile that sent a current right down my spine. And Grace saw. Grace even observed that he was

308

ridiculous, didn't she? Didn't his fawning attention make Grace roll her eyes?

I text back, *No wine bar?* I put an emoji of stars beside two clinking champagnes. Then I feel like a fool. I watch the three dots in their gray bubble appear and disappear, holding my breath.

Theater. I have a surprise for you

When I reach the theater, the double doors are propped open. I step through them in my poppy dress. My S-shaped hair lightly grazing my shoulders. The light clip of my old heart-shaped heels on the wooden floors. Still dressed as though this is a date. He said he had a surprise, didn't he? And the smiley. Smileys are suggestive, flirtatious, aren't they?

But the theater's empty. Stage dark, red curtains drawn. My heart thrums lightly in my chest.

"Hugo?"

No answer. I walk through the aisles. Hop up onto the stage easily. It comforts me how easy. I look out at the sea of empty seats, the EXIT signs.

"Hugo, are you there?" I hear my voice reverberating in the auditorium. Rich, deep, but shot through with a thin thread of panic. Am I being stood up? Maybe he

309

changed his mind about the venue again.

Suddenly I feel ridiculous. Standing here on the empty stage in the dark in my poppy dress, in my perfume cloud. My waves and my painted lips. Clutching my lip-shaped purse with both hands. A smiling red mouth. I bought it in a moment of elation, sailing through a shop I used to hate, my hands literally itching to buy something.

I love this, I told the saleswoman, pushing the purse across the glass counter.

She smiled. *It's fun, isn't it?*

It is, I said. *So fun.*

Now the red mouth seems to smirk at me. I think of Hugo gazing through me at the diner last summer. A shot of electricity runs down my spine, flashing down my leg quick like lightning. I feel a hip twinge. Something in my back gives, buckles.

Oh god, I'm a fool. *I'm a fool, I'm a fool.*

I'm about to walk off when the lights come on. Behind me, the red curtains draw, revealing the stage. Music swells. And then I see it. All around me, a French court. Pillars and tapestry screens featuring black silhouettes of delicate-looking trees, vines, and flowers. Above my head, instead of a ceiling, there's a bright blue sky streaked with sinewy clouds. Like a dream. Helen's dream.

Tears fill my eyes.

The set of *All's Well.* Act One. Finished. Perfect. Just like I dreamed it. Just like I lived it that summer in Edinburgh. Those production photos from the Playbill sprung to life. It's the exact same set right down to the pillars on each side of me and the blue painted sky above. I look down and see the floor beneath me is a raised dark spiral, like the iris of an eye. The eye of Helen gazing upward at a fixed sky. And I'm Helen again. Alone on the stage with just the audience. An audience I can't see in the dark.

"Surprise," says a voice.

I look down into the auditorium. He's standing in the aisle, but I can't see his face because of the lights in my eyes. Familiar silhouette. Tall, broad, longish hair that curls at the neck, making my breath catch. Paul? *Paul, what are you doing here?* No, not Paul. Hugo. Of course Hugo.

"Well, Miranda," he says. "What do you think?"

I look around at the set, the impossible, perfect set that takes me back, god how it takes me right back to that moment when I was Helen looking out into the lights and I saw nothing beyond but the watching dark. I look at Hugo, who's beaming at my face, my tears. Why does he look so much like

311

Paul right now? Trick of the light, surely. Trick of the shadow. Has to be.

"Look familiar?"

"I can't believe it."

"I know we're a bit early," he says. "We can still make whatever changes you want. I just wanted to surprise you. Get everything ready so you could practice before tech week."

"How did you know? How did you do it?"

I'm shaking. Actually shaking as I watch Hugo hop up onto the stage. Walk up to me, right up to me so he's in close, so close I can smell the wood emanating from his body.

"What can I say, Miranda? You inspired me." He smiles at me. "Also, I saw the video."

I feel my face and chest catch fire. "The video?"

"Of your Edinburgh show. On YouTube? It seemed a lot like what you were describing. And the sets were just stunning, so I thought I'd give it a try. I really hope I didn't fuck it up."

I look at Hugo, backdropped by the French court, the painted blue sky.

"It's perfect. I can't even tell you how perfect."

He grins. So genuinely pleased with my

pleasure. "Probably a little rough though. I mean compared to what you had."

I shake my head. "It's better. Much better."

He laughs. He steps in closer. He puts both hands on my trembling shoulders. I'm dreaming. Surely I'm dreaming.

"You were incredible as Helen, by the way. Bertram's a fucking idiot." His voice so soft, like a hand stroking my face. I feel his voice in the back of my neck, in my gut, down my back, between my legs. Making me vibrate. Hugo's sea-colored eyes, which do not look to the left or the right of me but straight at me. Saying he wants to show me something else. Can he show me something more?

"There's more?"

"Just wait right here, okay?" he says.

I watch him hop off the stage and run up to the lighting booth. He looks at me from behind the glass and grins.

"Close your eyes," he says through the mic.

I close them. Smile at the red of my eyelids. My heart skips.

"Okay, open them, Miranda."

All around me, the lights have dimmed. Above me the blue sky has darkened to a black sky bright with twinkling little lights. Music swells. Debussy's "Clair de Lune."

Bubbles of light spin round and cascade down all around me like falling stars — a cheesy effect I love anyway. And I'm Helen. I'm Helen in my red dress. I'm on the stage under the fated sky, which gives me free scope, breathing a summer air perfumed with mountain flowers. Beyond the blinding lights, there's a sea of captivated faces breathing in the dark.

Hugo runs back down to join me on the stage, breathless.

"What do you think? For Helen's first soliloquy."

I look at Hugo under the sea of stars. Paul. He looks just like Paul again. I rub my eyes because it's a trick, it has to be. Just the light, surely. Just the shadow, surely. Still looks like Paul. Paul before he hated me. Paul before he was dead to the fact of me in front of him. Paul looking at me like he did that night we met in the Edinburgh theater. Later, he said he fell in love with me that night. During that first soliloquy, when I pined hopelessly for Bertram. *What power is it which mounts my love so high, that makes me see, and cannot feed mine eye?* And I heard something like a sigh from someone in the audience. The whole theater heard it. I remember I directed the rest of my speech toward the sound. During intermission, he sent a note to my dressing room, a note that simply read, *Bertram is fucking lame.* And then his number, the name of his hotel. But he was also waiting for me outside the theater, walking toward me when he saw me emerge from the doors. Paul walking toward me now. His golden hair. His grin that shifts now into an expression of concern. "Miranda, are you okay?"

"Yes," I whisper.

"I know this is kind of over the top, so listen, if you hate it, please —"

"I love it."

He smiles. He's looking at me with love, he still loved me then. No impatience yet, no anger yet, no coldness. Nothing but admiration in his green eyes. A little lighter than Paul's. Hair's the same. How long have I dreamed that he would look at me like this again?

"I'm so glad, Miranda. I —"

I kiss him. A charge in my lips when they touch his. He moans softly. It sends a charge through my body, lighting me up. All my cells electric and shimmering. His hands cup my face, stroke my neck. How does he know exactly how to stroke my neck? I feel his fingers grazing my flesh, and I shudder and shudder. I lick and tug at his ear with my teeth. I run my fingers through his golden-red hair. *Oh, Goldfish.*

"Goldfish?"

Hugo. I mean Hugo, I'm kissing Hugo. Hugo moans when I kiss him, he desires me that much; I'm not imagining this, I'm not dreaming this, am I dreaming this? Hugo's mouth on my mouth. His hands still stroking my face, my neck, my shoulders, my back. He wants to fuck me. He's hard. He's tugging on my straps now, gently unzipping the poppies, and I'm taking his shirt off. But not gently, not gently. I rip his shirt open, hear the buttons clattering around. My hands pushing Hugo down onto his back on the stage floor.

"Onstage?" he whispers.

Yes, says a voice. *Stage, stage.* My voice. My lips brushing against the hollow of Hugo's ear, making him shudder. My legs straddling him, unafraid. My thighs squeezing his ribs. My spine curving forward so we're face-to-face, mouth to mouth, breath to breath, under the falling stars.

CHAPTER 19

Glorious is the afternoon sun coming in through the theater windows. Bold. Golden. Friday rehearsal. We're gathered on the spiral stage, right along the dark iris of Helen's eye. Above us is the painted blue sky, under which Hugo and I fucked only hours ago. Made love? No, definitely we fucked. The sounds I was making. Hugo called them inhuman. *But hot,* he said. *So hot, Miranda. I'm getting hard again just thinking about it.* Oh god. Hugo's mouth saying the word *hard.* About his cock. That was hard. For me. *You, Miranda,* he said.

Here now on the stage, I shiver deliciously.

"Cold, Miranda?" Grace asks me.

"No, Grace. I'm wonderful, thank you."

I smile at them all, my gathered acolytes, and I can't help but feel a vibratory connection with them today. As though we're all one body. All of us have fucked beneath the falling stars. All of our cells are lit up like a million twinkling lights. They sit in a circle, still catching their breath after the admittedly exhilarating warm-up I just led them through. Gazing at me with their wide-open eyes as they are so wont to do these days. So riveted, so fixed is their attention. I'm still wearing the poppy dress from last night. Not because I was too tired, too soul-sad, to change, not like the old days. No, I wanted the smell of our sex on me. I wanted to exude his scent of wood. I wanted to find threads of his golden hair on the poppies all day and watch them turn fiery in the light. I wanted to feel the skirt that he pushed up around my thighs when he fucked me — for the second or was it the fourth time? — brushing against the backs of my legs as I walked the bleak school corridors, while I sat at my desk going over my rehearsal notes, skipped to the theater.

"Miranda?" Ellie says now. "I found these on the stage." She holds out her hand to me. I see three buttons winking in the bowl of her palm. Iridescent blue. Belonging to a man's pale blue shirt.

I look at the buttons under the hawk stare of Grace. Who sees all. Can see my hands tearing at his shirt. Letting the buttons scatter across the stage.

Careful, Hugo said. Which only spurred

on my hands. I snatch them from Ellie's open palm now.

"Thank you so much for catching these, Ellie. I'll let wardrobe know. Maybe someone's costume is coming apart." I smile sadly. The life of the theater, this.

"I don't know anyone who has a costume with these sorts of buttons," Grace offers behind me.

"Well, maybe the costume department is getting creative," I say, turning to her. "Maybe they're doing something we don't know about."

Grace stares at me. Darkly, very darkly. I remember that I couldn't find my underwear last night. They're here in the theater somewhere, and I can only pray the students or Grace won't find them first. Hugo and I looked everywhere, we really did. In the prop box. Behind the stage. On our hands and knees, looking. Stopping then and again to fuck.

"Anyway," I say, smiling, "why talk about costumes when there's so much else to discuss? The new set, for instance?"

And I wave a hand at the painted sky, at the pillars, the walls of the court all around us. I invite them to take in Hugo's set. I want their responses. This is not a fascist regime, after all, but a community.

"Well, what do we think?"

They nod as one body with many heads. They are clearly awed. They crane their necks to contemplate the details of Hugo's painted cosmos with their mouths open, their eyes wide.

"Incredible, isn't it? Show them the starry sky, Grace."

Grace looks at me a long time, her arms folded in front of her. *What?* I mouth at her. But she just turns and marches back to the lighting booth. Angrily flips a switch, and we're surrounded by the spinning stars I sighed under.

"Isn't it wonderful?" I ask.

"Yes, Professor," they murmur. "Wonderful."

"Isn't it wonderful, Ellie?" I say, turning to Ellie. She's showing a bit of cleavage today, I notice. Wearing lipstick too, a dark wine color.

"Yes, Professor," she says. "I love the constellations so much."

She smiles tremulously. Glowing as much as she humanly can. Trevor's sitting beside her, I see. And look, he's putting his hand on her shoulder. Are they dating now? They must be. He's smiling at her a little even, a secret smile. One that suggests intimacy. Not unlike the smile Hugo gave me earlier

320

when we passed each other in the hall and my insides immediately became fire. I look at Trevor, smiling at Ellie, patting her shoulder. Rubbing it, really. Did they fuck last night? I wonder. Was it Ellie's first time? Perhaps Ellie was fucking Trevor while I was fucking Hugo. How amazing would that be? Each of us flushed and grinning in the spinning dark of our own overturned world. Our backs arched, our heads tilted, making inhuman sounds at the stars. Perhaps we both walked home without underwear last night. Singing a tune to the spring night that the sweet black air carried. The whole town heard our joy. We didn't even feel our steps on the spongy earth so damp and green with growing things. We floated. We were so happy. We fell into our beds and we lay there grinning and grinning. Our faces hurt from happiness, and for once, we welcomed the pain.

"Isn't it a bit early for the set?" Grace says now.

"What do you mean 'a bit early'?"

"Tech week's not until next week."

Tech week. Aka the final week before the show. The week of madness. The week I always capitulate to the fact of Briana. The week I succumb to darkness, the floor of my office, death musings. The week I usually allow Grace to take over. But not this time, not this time.

"Around the corner, Grace. Around the corner. Plus this gives us a great advantage. Getting the set early, what an absolute gift. We have the set people to thank for their expediency, don't we?"

I hear Grace cough. *We have you to thank for fucking Hugo.*

"And sound and lighting not too far behind," I lie. "Luck," I continue, "appears to be on our side in all things. Ahead of schedule. All of us off book. Just excellent. We're in such excellent shape. We're in better shape than we ever have been, wouldn't you say so, Grace?"

I turn to look at Grace sitting in the audience seat in her hunting vest. Watching me now with an expression I can't fathom. "Yes," she says slowly. "I'd say so."

"So let's take a moment to congratulate ourselves a little, shall we?" I say. "I especially want to congratulate Ellie," I say, turning toward her again. She's turned predictably pink. *Confidence, Ellie, confidence.* "She stepped up to the lead so extraordinarily, wouldn't you all agree?"

They all gaze at me for a moment. Then they nod slowly. Ellie stares intently at the floor. I put my arm around her.

"Not only did she learn all those new lines, but she also lived and breathed them for us every afternoon, didn't she? It's been such a joy to watch her blossom. So I want to announce that Ellie will be officially taking over the role of Helen."

"What?" Grace says.

"Let's all give her a hand, shall we?"

I clap first. Then Trevor. Then they all begin to follow suit, clapping for Ellie. Even Grace comes around, clapping slowly, reluctantly, pointedly. *I wish you'd talked to me about this first, Miranda.* But I just smile at Grace. I keep clapping and clapping. Because it really is such a joyous occasion. It calls for applause. Ellie looks up from the floor at last. Looks at us all, applauding her. Finally giving her her due. She's overcome. Beaming now. She's positively glowing. Glowing as I am glowing. Finally allowing herself an actual moment of happiness. So deserved.

We clap and clap and clap for Ellie. And she nods, *thank you, thank you, thank you.* But then her smile fades. Her face falls. Goes white.

"Ellie, what is it? Are you okay?"

But she doesn't answer. She's looking at something behind me. Not something, someone. Someone behind me.

And I already know before I turn around who it will be. So that when I turn around, I turn smilingly. No dread in my gut. Just this grin on my face. Happy. So happy to see her standing there. Leaning crookedly against the side entrance like the literal undead. Breathing shallowly. Her once burnished hair dull as dust. Staring at me with daggers in her dead-leaf eyes.

"Briana," I say pleasantly. Is there a crack in my voice? Not at all. "Long time no see. Welcome."

She doesn't answer me. She continues to lean heavily against the doorway, regarding me with the dark pits that were once her eyes. She's grown smaller, paler, in these past weeks. Her little gold cross winks against her frighteningly pale skin. Not wearing her bell sleeves today. Just a drab sweatshirt that hangs on her. The sleeves swallow her small hands, but I see the little white fists bunched inside.

"We've missed you," I say.

Still nothing. Just those eyes. Staring and staring.

"Haven't we?" I turn to the cast. Ellie looks absolutely horrified. Trevor's looking away. Guilty, perhaps. Everyone else is just gazing at her in shock. I turn back to Briana and smile.

"Did you come to visit us today?" I ask her. Casual. Play it casual, not surprised. Not horrified in the least by the way she's still fucking staring at me.

"We're always happy to have you here, of course," I continue. "Our door is always open. We're actually about to start rehearsal so —"

She takes a step toward us then. Stumbles spectacularly. Trevor and Ellie both run to grab her hands, and she collapses into their arms on cue.

I watch them guide her as she limps hideously to the stage. Limps as I used to limp. Same limp. Dragging her right leg, which appears to be quite stiff, locked at the knee. Horror in my heart. Beats to the tune of a black pointed shoe tapping. Yet I'm still smiling, I'm patient, calm as you please as I watch her stumble to the stage. I think of Mark watching me fall. Not calling for help. Just rolling his eyes. Sighing. *Give me a break, Miranda.*

Everyone gives her a wide berth as she sits there hunched on the edge, still staring straight at me. Trevor and Ellie sit on either side of her, patting her sharp little shoulders. Asking if there is anything else they can get her, anything at all?

"Water," she whispers, eyes still on me.

325

Ellie runs to fetch her own bottle from the auditorium seats and runs back and presents it to Briana, practically bowing before her. Briana takes it without thanks. She sips. She smiles darkly at me now, clutching Ellie's water bottle to her bloodless lips.

"Briana," I say, "we're so happy to have you up and about, aren't we?"

No one says a word. I can feel Grace in shock behind me. All of them just stand there like slack-jawed idiots, looking at Briana hunched crookedly on the stage. Breathing like she's been for a run.

"So happy we are," I say. "But we are about to rehearse. Probably not the best place for you to sit and watch with your back to the stage like that. Why don't you sit in the audience, over by Grace?"

I gesture to Grace, who's sitting in the auditorium seats with a hand over her mouth. Briana doesn't move. She just stares with the voids of her eyes.

Thou hast no speculation in those eyes which thou dost glare with!

"I think sitting in the audience would be far more comfortable for you," I add softly.

"I'm not here to watch, Miranda," she says at last in a low voice. "I'm here to perform." Her voice is a husk of itself. Her breath is shallow.

Bolt of electricity down my leg. I feel it like a flash, and then it's gone.

"Perform?"

"In the play," she says. "I'm the lead, after all." Not a question.

Pain flashes brightly across my back. Two wings of fire. I pray for my face not to betray me. *Keep smiling, that's it.* "Well, we've had to make a few changes."

"I'm the lead!"

"Briana, do you really think that's a good idea given . . ." And here I trail off.

"Given *what*?" She looks at me. She waits.

"Given how long you've been away." I smile.

She looks at me in my new poppy dress, taking me in as only she can. The S waves in my hair, my legs in their spiked heels, which are not buckling before her for once. Perhaps she can even smell the sex on me, the new life. It hurts her, all of it. The sight of me standing straight smarts her eyes. She even appears to wince.

"Well, I'm back now," she says. "And I want to be in the play. And I will be in the play."

She's gripping the edge of the stage with her fists. A little hysteria in her voice. A pained wobble. A whine I know all too well.

It gives me courage.

"It's the week before tech week, Briana," I say sadly. "We can't have you play Helen. We've already made other arrangements for the lead, I'm afraid." *Don't look afraid, don't look afraid. You are not afraid of this dead-eyed child staring at you like she knows your soul, like you're guilty of something.* Is she going to insist? She can't insist; look at her. She can barely sit up on the stage. She's literally holding her body upright by white-knuckling the edge. Lopsided like she's afraid of the right side of her body, oh god —

"I'll be the King, then," she says. "I heard that part just opened up."

Beside her, Ellie's back to looking at the floor.

"And look at me, I'd be perfect for the role now, wouldn't I, Miranda."

Not a question. An accusation. A blatant accusation. But what is there to admit? Nothing. Absolutely nothing. *Thou canst not say I did it. Never shake thy gory locks at me.*

"Briana, do you think it's a good idea?" Grace says from the audience. "You really don't look well."

"Don't I look well, Grace?" She looks at me and grins, but it's twisted, like she's smiling through something. I know the

328

something. Her mouth begins to tremble. She looks about to cry, but she holds it together.

"The doctors say it could be good for me to get out. And who knows?" She turns to Ellie, who's shaking at this point, her eyes glassy. Looking at Briana as though she isn't sure whether to hug her or run away. Briana just smiles weakly at her.

"Maybe Helen here will heal me," she says. "The theater is a magical place. Am I right, Miranda?"

"The King has a lot of lines," Grace says.

"That's right," I say. "Very true, Grace. A lot of lines. There's that whole speech, isn't there? About soldiership?"

"I already memorized them," she says. "I've had so little to do for the past few weeks." Her gaze is a sword. Pointed right at me. "I've had a lot of time with the King. A lot of time. I feel like I have a new insight into his character now. I can show you."

"I don't think that's a good idea, Briana," Grace says. "Miranda?"

I look at this sickly creature, sitting crookedly on the stage. Withered. Pale. Lopsided. The once burnished glory of her auburn hair now falling darkly, flatly, in greasy locks around her gaunt face. Her lithe body a husk of itself, drowning in that black fleece sack. Her voice a shrill, faltering shadow of what it was. Looking at us both with the remnants of a countenance that used to make me tremble, cower. Now? She attempts threat, confrontation, but she can only manage so much through the veil of pain.

"Miranda?" Grace prompts.

"Show us," I hear myself say.

"Everyone," I say, keeping my eyes on Briana. "Act Two, Scene One. Helen and the King." I feel them all around us, frozen as though in tableau.

Ellie looks at me, terrified. *Don't make me do this, Miranda, please.*

But that's all the more reason to keep calm. All the more reason to look like all is well. Ha.

"Act Two, Scene One," I say again. "Helen and the King."

CHAPTER 20

Act Two, Scene One. In which Helen goes to Paris to visit the King, claiming to be able to cure his illness. In which the King refuses her help — who is she to come to *his* court? Who is she to claim she can heal him when all others have failed? *When our most learned doctors leave us,* says the King. We are truly past hope now. We have given up. Do not awaken our hope, strumpet. But Helen stands firm. She says to the King, Try me, trust me. The King says, Fine, if you're willing to die. I trust you, but if you fail, you die. Helen says absolutely she is willing to die by the rack if she fails, it's only fair. But if I succeed, Helen says, then let me win something for my success: the right to choose my husband from among your vassals (by which she means Bertram). The King agrees to this. He puts himself in her hands. He submits to this lowborn woman. And then we, as the audience, realize how truly desperate, how truly ill, how truly vulnerable and afraid, the King really is. We also realize how powerful Helen must be, to risk her life for this. And how much she must want Bertram. It's a scene in which everyone's desire is laid bare and the power dynamics — between king and subject, low- and highborn — are reversed. Helen will die at the King's hand if she fails to cure him. But the King will inevitably die if she fails too. His illness puts him at her mercy either way. It's a dialogue that never fails to remind me of the many I've had with Mark, with John, with Luke, with my surgeon. All of the times they told me to trust, have faith. All the times I submitted myself to their hands. All of the times they failed. None of them was ever put to death for this. They still asked me to pay them. I was no king.

I sit in the far corner of the auditorium, away from Grace, away from everyone, watching Briana and Ellie perform this scene. Briana as the King, Ellie as Helen. I ask for the lights to be lowered, please. So Grace and the students can't see my face as I watch Briana show me. With Briana as Helen, the first times we read this scene, it seemed it would never work. Its mediocrity, its soullessness, would keep me up nights.

Briana was never convincing as someone who could heal, let alone be trusted. Nor was her pining, her desire for Bertram, believable. But as the King today, on the stage, though she can barely stand, though she's deathly pale, she's luminous. She has gravitas. She plays shades of emotion I've never seen. She brings the crackle of death and vulnerability to the King's lines. She is distrustful of Helen. We feel she has given up hope, she dares not hope again, yet we know she has hope still. She's capable of letting that hideous flower bloom riotously in her soul once more. We want Helen to pay with her life if she fails to heal her, absolutely. Because it would only be fair for letting the King have hope again. The King will pay with her own life after all. We feel how desperately she wants to be well. We feel her giving herself over to Helen's will. *My deed shall match thy deed.* When Ellie touches Briana's wrist, Briana flinches. She appears to look at me, right at me in my seat in the dark, which is impossible, and I feel the hairs on the back of my neck stand on end.

I know. I know what you did to me, you bitch.

"Wow," Grace whispers into the back of my neck. "It works."

Yes. It does.

■ ■ ■ ■

"Well?" Briana says from the stage when the scene is ended. "Do I get it or not?"

I gaze up at her, sitting on her throne alone now, Ellie having run off the stage to join the other students in the wings. All of them looking at Briana, who looks even paler than when she first started. Breathing more quickly through her mouth. Everyone is watching us — my face and her face. Waiting. Will I yield? Will I submit to this sickly creature?

"Everyone," I say, smiling. "That's good for today. We'll see you back here Monday. Thanks."

They all scurry off. Mumbling their goodbyes to Briana as they pass, their *Glad you're backs*, to which she replies with a clipped *Thanks,* her ghostly face still fixed on me. Ellie tentatively tells her to take care, she hopes she's feeling better. Briana ignores her, even as she still holds her water bottle. Trevor offers her a limp goodbye, and I feel her pointed silence from here. Trevor feels it too, apparently.

"Do you want me to stay?" he whispers.

Suddenly she clutches his hand, still looking at me. "Wait outside for me," she says.

"Drive me home."

"Didn't you drive yourself here?" he deigns to ask her.

She looks at him, appalled. Dare he question her? Has the yes-man grown a spine in her absence? Impossible. Still. Best not to tighten the yoke, tug on the choke chain too quickly. Best to give him the illusion of free will.

She closes her eyes as if she's going through something.

"I don't think I can drive myself back," she whispers, shaking her head. As though she's afraid for herself. It's quite a performance. Is it a performance? I can't tell. Neither can Trevor.

He looks over at Ellie, who walks hurriedly out of the theater with her head down. She left without her coat.

"Okay, I'll wait for you in the hall," he whispers, and I think, *Spineless.*

Briana doesn't thank him, of course. He shuffles off, and Briana still sits there on her throne. Crooked. Unmovable. Looking at me, always looking at me. Her eyes shining with sickness and hate. And desperation, a naked longing I've never seen. She's actually unsure if the part will be hers. She will not leave until I tell her whether she will be King. Even though surely she is

King, isn't she? Her performance spoke for itself, didn't it?

"Well?" she says again.

"Very impressive, wasn't she, Miranda?" Grace says.

Is my leg seizing? What is this sudden hardness in my limbs? This flash of heaviness?

"Miranda?"

"Yes. Yes, very impressive. I even think your" — Don't say *illness*. Condition? No — "*absence* has really opened up some doors for you, as an actor."

"So I get to play him, then. So I'm the King."

I watch a sickly joy spread across her sickly face. Dread. In the pit of my stomach. Why? Why is she so fucking happy? To play a part she wouldn't have pissed on a month ago? An old, dying man with a malignant boil on his rectum. For Briana? Briana, who turned up her nose at the part of Helen? For whom nothing but Juliet and Lady M were good enough? And now here she is. Frothing at the chance to play a diseased invalid. Sabotage. She wants to sabotage me, of course.

She's about to rise from her throne and hobble out the double doors triumphant, far too triumphant for the crumbs she has won. Trevor will be waiting for her in the hall, of course, to drive her home. She'll tell him the news on the way. He'll pretend to be happy for her, but his heart will sink. He'll call Ellie later, after he's tucked Briana into bed, and she'll be crestfallen but understanding. She'll agree to give them both space during this awkward time. Perhaps she'll attempt to console herself. Take a restorative bath. Cast a sad spell. But she'll be miserable. And all of this will make her a better Helen, of course, for nothing will quell her love.

But what of her heart? What about Helen's heart?

And Briana will have won. Not only Trevor, a sad little game I know she cares nothing for, but at something bigger, something I can't guess. Something that is making her happy, far too happy at the moment. Something that is making my leg feel suddenly heavy, making the pain return to my back in small, bright flashes. She's clearly dreaming of whatever it is now as she sits crookedly on her throne.

"Miranda?" Grace prompts.

"I guess my only real concern is having you onstage when —"

"When *what*?" Briana says. Paler. She's getting paler suddenly.

"When you should really be at home." I smile. "Resting."

"Resting?" She spits the word.

"That's my concern too," Grace says.

"It is?" I turn to Grace.

"Of course it is. Theater is taxing. And I have to say you really don't seem well, Briana."

Doesn't seem well? Are you looking at her? The child can barely stand. The child is walking death.

"Grace is right. You just never know what might happen onstage. We'd hate for something to set you back."

We watch her blue lips tremble. She goes paler still, if that is humanly possible, and it makes my blood cold. *Set me back?* her face says. *We know all about setting me back, don't we, Miranda?* But does she know? Does she? She grips the armrests of her throne more fiercely.

"I'm playing the King," she says.

She looks at us both. Still attempting threat, but she's sitting more and more crookedly in her seat. Barely able to keep herself upright.

"Just let her do it, Miranda," Grace hisses into my ear.

"What? We can't have her onstage, just . . . *look* at her."

"At least she *wants* to do it. That's more than I can say for Dennis."

"Dennis?" I whisper.

"Dennis, the First Lord? Who's been playing the King? You were yelling at him for nearly an hour yesterday."

I recall a pear-shaped boy with a red face sweating profusely beneath a dubious crown, looking very frightened of me from where he was seated in his plastic chair/throne.

"Oh, Dennis, of course. Well, Dennis is wonderful. He's really stepped up. Do we want to alienate poor, dear Dennis?"

Grace looks at me. *Poor, dear Dennis?* Am I fucking kidding?

"Dennis *is* terrible, Miranda. There's a reason he was just a First Lord. He also doesn't want to be King. He told me so after you rushed away from the last rehearsal. He said he's having nightmares about — as he put it — 'fucking shit up,' and you yelling at him and never letting him be in the play again."

Grace is looking at me like, *Problem solved.* Why won't I let the problem be solved when there is such a simple, tidy solution before us in the form of a girl whiter than a sheet who is all too happy to take this meager morsel and call it cake?

Exactly what she ordered, believe it or not.

I look at Briana, watching all of this from her throne, taking sips from Ellie's water bottle. Looking smug but sick. Anxious to see what she's won.

"Well, Briana, you've given us a lot to think about. And we're going to think about it, aren't we, Grace? We'll let you know very soon. In the meantime, we're so happy you decided to visit."

Her smug face falls. Her lips tremble. She's so obviously crushed, she can't hide it from us. But she says nothing. Just glares at me as she rises from her throne with a wince. We watch her begin the burdensome walk to the door. Limping as I used to limp. Same limp. Can't be the same limp. Can't be. She's performing. Mocking me, my old pain. Has to be. No way this could be real. *Bravo, Briana. You've done it.*

Except.

Except that she was never this good. I watch her drag her right leg, so heavy. Like it's actually made of stone. And I remember the stone. The heaviness I couldn't shake, how I would dream each night of lightness. I look at Briana hobbling away. Horror, horror, in my heart. I look at her face wincing, seething, and underneath that, frightened. Pity breaks a dam in me. I reach out my

340

hand toward her.

"Get some rest," I say gently. "We'll let you —"

"If you ever fucking touch me again," she hisses, "I'll scream. I'll scream and the whole school will hear me."

My face stings like it's been slapped.

"Briana, what's going on?" Grace says.

But Briana just looks at me. Her face raw with emotion, her eyes dark with hissing and spitting rage. No cloak of coolness, no semblance of control anymore.

"You did something to me," she says.

"What?" And then I laugh weirdly. A weird, trilling laugh.

But Briana keeps her daggery gaze on me, pointed and shaking.

"That day," she says quietly. "Here in the theater. I felt it."

Bolt of lightning down my leg. Bluffing. Surely she's bluffing.

"What is this about?" Grace says. "What is she talking about, Miranda?"

"I *felt* it!" Briana screams, hysterical now.

"Briana," I say calmly, as calmly as I possibly can. "I think surely you must be confused. You haven't been well. Pain does that; I should know."

"Oh, I'm not confused, Miranda. I'm very clear."

She leans forward, toward me, wavering on her feet. I think she's going to fall, but she grabs hold of the stage beside her for support. She looks at me with wild eyes, her body still leaning to the left like a wind-warped tree. Her breath is getting shallower, quicker. I can see what I think is her heart drumming wildly beneath her ribs. Suddenly she smiles.

"And I'm going to tell everyone. The dean. The VP. And you'll get fired! You'll get sued! You'll go to jail maybe!"

She looks thrilled. And sick. Terribly sick. There's a shine to her eyes that I recognize. Drugs. *Take one for muscle stiffness. Take one for pain.*

"Tell everyone what?" Grace says.

"I have witnesses!" she screams. "Grace, you were there, weren't you?"

She turns now pathetically to Grace, pleading. Her eyes suddenly full of hideous hope.

"You saw! You *saw* what she did to me, didn't you? Or does she have you under her power too? Are you both in on it together?"

"In on *what*?"

Then Briana begins to cry pitifully. It's a loud, keening wail that reverberates through the theater.

Fauve comes running in as if on cue, from

stage left. She gathers Briana's frail body to her velvet drapery. "Oh my poor, poor dear," she murmurs, or some such nonsense like that, meanwhile casting a threatening look at me, her eyes full of triumph. *I've got you now.*

"This is my fault. *I* suggested she come in today. Oh, let's get the poor thing home, shall we? Poor dear."

I watch Briana limp pathetically away, scowling at me from under Fauve's dark velvet wing as she hobbles toward the hall, my whole body ringing with fear. *What have I done? What have I done? What have I done?*

Chapter 21

Driving to the pub. Sun a bloodred light over the blackening trees. Not even thinking. Not even seeing the road. Only seeing Briana's pale face. Her white hands gripping the throne. Her shaking voice, her shining eyes. Faking, she had to be. Still. Convinced me. Convinced everyone. Grace looking at me. All of them looking at me. Like what? Like I did something. Ridiculous. Sun burns my eyes through the windshield. I think of my hand on Mark's wrist. The way he fell backward into that patient chair, onto my sad coat, my musty clothes. My suddenly singing lips, my swinging limbs.

Pain can move, Ms. Fitch. It can switch. From house to house, from body to body.

I think of myself on the floor, full of the fat man's pain, while he smiled and sang.

I'm going to tell everyone, Briana said. She will too. She'll point her frail, shaking finger at me, scream my name from the heights, no gag could stop that hissing mouth. But tell them what exactly, Briana? Nothing to tell. Nothing at all. No proof of anything. You're going to accuse me of what? Of *magic*? Ridiculous. Who'll even believe you? "Who?" I ask the windshield. Not the dean. Not Grace. For sure not Grace.

Grace looking at me, looking at me after Briana left the theater.

Well, that was fucking crazy, I said, *wasn't it? Can you even believe that?*

And Grace said nothing. And I said, *I told you, didn't I? I told you we shouldn't trust her on the stage, didn't I? And she proved my point, didn't she?*

And she said, *Are you all right, Miranda? You're shaking.*

Do you think she meant it? I asked her. *About telling the dean?*

And Grace looked at me funny. *Funny* is what I would call the look.

What is there to tell? she said. *I mean, it's crazy. Isn't it?*

And she kept looking at me with that funny look.

I have to go, I said.

What? Where do you have to go?

Out, I said. *Somewhere.*

Miranda, don't you think we need to talk about this? About all of this?

Of course we do. Of course we will. Just not tonight, because I have to go, I'm afraid.

Miranda, wait —

But I was already out the door. Bypassed Hugo in the hall too. Looking so amorous. Looking so like Paul it almost took my breath away.

Goldfish, I said.

Goldfish? he said. *Who's Goldfish?*

You, I lied. *Your hair, the color. Sort of reminds me of a goldfish.* And just like that, his hair appeared pale, the color of wheat. He smiled.

Miranda, he said. *Where are you running off to?* And I could tell he wanted to take me into the scene shop and fuck me.

I have to go, I said, and I left him there in the hallway.

Darker the sky is getting now. Pale sliver of moon above the red sinking sun. It's a twisting drive through woods, all these pale green leaves fiery in the dying light. Turn down the music. Turn it down or turn it up? Turn it up, that's better. Ridiculous. All of it. But I need to know for sure. Need to ask the three men, *Did you give me something?* If something, what? A power? I laugh to even think of the word. Here I am in the

346

car, laughing. I'll ask them, *Really? Have I really done what I think I've done?* And if I've done it, then what? What now?

I park outside the entrance to the Canny Man. There's a spot right in front of the door, fit just for me and my black bug. Never a spot right in front of the door, even though inside it's always dead. I gaze at the door like it's the mouth of hell. Maybe it is. There's the carved wooden figure of a suited man hanging just above. The Canny Man himself, I guess, swinging in the wind from his metal hook. I never noticed him before. My head was always bent too low, I suppose. I was too eager to go inside, too bowed down with pain, too desperate for wine. How many skies and suns did I miss that way?

Inside, it's dark and dead as usual. Some nothing music playing. The usual couple of tables occupied by the usual lone souls. Gazing at their drinks like they're sunsets, they're seas, they're whole worlds — they appear to be lost in the colors even though there are no colors to speak of besides shades of amber. No three men at the bar. No one at the bar at all. Why did Grace and I ever start coming here? Who discovered this place, was it me or was it her? We were looking for a bar near the theater, I remember. *Oh look, a bar,* someone said, and pointed.

Little divey. What do you think? Should we give it a go?

I walk up to the bar now. Long walk. Farther away than it seems tonight. I walk and I walk and it feels like I'll never reach the bar. It feels like I walk miles down the dark red room to get to the end. The floor beneath my feet sloping downhill, then uphill. I'm sweating. My clothes are damp, my poppy dress clinging to my skin. Am I beginning to limp? I pass a sign written on the blackboard with white chalk.

PERFORMING TONIGHT:
THE WEIRD BRETHREN!!!

The music switches from sad nothing to a song I know. That tune I've been humming. Can never remember the name, but it's too familiar. The bartender is one I've seen before. I remember him from that January night I came here with Grace. Pushed Grace out the door with the hands of my voice. Met the three men. Are they here? No. Bartender only. He's polishing that same dirty glass that will remain dirty for time eternal. Still spotted and streaked. Lipstick still caked on the rim like a kiss. My lipstick, I think.

"I'll have the golden remedy," I tell him.

And just like that he pours it. Right into that dirty glass, where it glows like a prop, and I drink. To the last drop. The gold does its trick.

Do you like tricks, Ms. Fitch?

I like tricks. And just like that, my foot stops screaming. Spinal column settles. Fire everywhere dies right down to a pale blue flame. I'm smiling into the shining eyes of a goat's head mounted on the dark red wall.

"Where are they?" I ask the bartender, the words on my lips before I can think.

Who? he should say.

Instead he points to a staircase in the corner. On the wall, a lit sign that reads GAMES, MORE. A lit arrow pointing down.

Since when did this place have a game room? Or a down, for that matter?

"There's a downstairs?" I ask him.

But the bartender's turned away from me. He has another dirty glass in his hands that he's polishing to no end with his dirty rag. There'll be another glass after that. And another, and another. All these glasses that will never be clean. All these spots that will never out. All these lips on the rim. All this work to be done. *What have I done, what have I done? What happens now? What happens next?*

Down, down, down. How many stories? How far do I descend? Stopped counting flights, even with the gold glittering in my blood. Should turn back but the golden remedy keeps my feet marching down. Keeps the upstairs tune on my lips, though it trips, it falters now. Keeps my hand on the rail. Which is starting to curve into a spiral. A tight spiral. So that I'm turning around and around on the winding stone stairs. Almost spinning. How far down to the bottom now? Too far down to turn back, to ask the bartender, *Is this a trick?* Has to be a trick. No way a pub basement could go this deep beneath the earth. What sort of pub would that be, am I right? I hear the sound of music up ahead. A soft red light up ahead too in the dark. Up ahead or farther down? But light, sound, that's something. The clip of footsteps ahead of me. I'm not alone, thank god. There's someone else ahead of me on the dark, winding stair. I see them in the soft red light coming from somewhere below. A man, it looks like. One of the three men? No. No, but he looks familiar. Golden-red hair. Tall. I know the back of this body in my bones.

Paul. How could Paul be here? But there he is, just ahead on the winding stair, walking the spiral that never ends.

"Paul," I say, "what are you doing here?"

But Paul doesn't turn around. Doesn't answer. Just keeps going down the stairs. Like I'm not even here. Not even behind him, can you believe this? I'm limping now, stumbling down the stairs trying to catch up to him. "Paul, Paul, Paul. Wait. Please!" No answer. Typical. Toward the end it was always like this. Me no longer traipsing ahead of him in my heart-shaped heels. It was him ahead of me, always ahead of me. And me always behind. Trying to catch up, keep up. Didn't matter where we were going. The grocery store, the park, a restaurant when we could manage those last-gasp dates. Always he'd be walking ahead. Never looking back. *Paul, wait,* I'd say feebly, hating the simper in my voice. But he didn't hear me. Didn't hear me or didn't care. Doesn't hear me now. Even as I'm stumbling down the steep steps to catch up.

Careful. Wouldn't want to fall again. Wouldn't want to take a nasty tumble, would we, Ms. Fitch? Not another one. We know how that ended last time. The beginning of so many ends. I look at Paul, now drifting away from me down the stairs. Tired of waiting, I guess. Tired of my limp, my leg of stone, my pained face.

"Paul," I shout. And I think: *If you just look back now, you'll see. How I've changed. How I'm better now. Just look back. Just turn around. Look behind you and see.* But he's gone so far ahead of me now he's practically blended into the dark. I hear a door slam farther down in the distance. I feel the slam in my chest, reverberating through my bones. And then I see an EXIT sign farther down. Paul! I try to quicken my pace to catch up. And just like that I trip on a stair. Fall. Falling down forever. Hard, sharp stones hitting my flesh, my bones. Neck. Back. Arms. Legs. I'm screaming as I fall, fall, fall. Hit the hard ground at last with an awful crack, my body tumbling through an open door.

I'm facedown on a carpeted floor. Cheek pressed into the soft carpet, one eye open. Red carpet. Red walls. A crooked electric chandelier hanging from the low ceiling. Dead? Not dead. But bones ache. Back gives. Soft music somewhere. I hear the crackle of a fireplace in the corner, feel the warmth of flames. The quiet click of a pool cue hitting a snooker ball. Darts, it sounds like, being thrown at a board. I hear the needles sinking in. Where am I? The GAMES, MORE sign comes flashing back to me.

"Paul," I whisper. But I know Paul isn't here. A trick.

Do you like tricks, Ms. Fitch?

I hear laughter. The soft sound of applause. Three pairs of hands clapping. Three pairs of leather shoes tapping in time. All around me.

"Ouch," says a soft voice. "Am I right?" Male. Low. Singing. The hairs on the back of my neck stand up. I look around, but I can't see them — all I see are red walls, empty tables, a pool table. But I feel the fact of their suited bodies close. Close and looking down at me. All three. Smiling at my body crumpled on the red floor.

"Careful, careful," says another voice softly. Deeper, broken, muffled, as if being spoken through hands. "Better watch those steps, Ms. Fitch."

"Wouldn't want to have another fall." Low laughter.

"We know how that ends."

"So many ends."

Tears fill my eyes. I hear laughter all around me. Soft. Knowing. Knowing my beginnings and ends.

"Here," says another. "Here, how about a hand?"

And then there's a hand in front of my face. Gloved. Bright white. Fingers wriggling. *Try me, try me.*

I take the hand and it grips me, lifts me, gets me to my feet easily. I'm about to say, *Thank you.* But then I see they're on the other side of the room, all three. The fat man stands in the far corner, his back against the dartboard, covering his face with his cupped hands. He appears to be shaking with fear. Shaking so violently it seems theatrical. He's whimpering as he waits to be struck. It's a bit much. Like he could be laughing, not crying behind his hands. Meanwhile, the tall, slender man is standing before him, his suited back turned away from me so that as usual I see only a sliver of his pale, perfect face, so sharply cut. He's grinning at the fat man, I see an upward curl to his lip. There are darts in both his gloved, clenched fists.

The middling man's sitting right on the pool table. Pool stick laid across his thighs. Polishing the tip. A soft, scraping sound. Looking at me with his red-rimmed eyes.

"Ms. Fitch, Ms. Fitch. Welcome back. How is that back, by the way?"

The other two turn and smile. Three smiles. My patrons.

A black-and-white television suspended

from the ceiling plays above their heads. There's an actress on a stage in a long white nightgown. Me. Me playing Lady M in Maine however many years ago. I recognize the footage. How could I not? My final festival. My last show, though I didn't know it then. I've never seen it on-screen before, didn't know it had even been taped — who taped this? I'm pacing the stage on my bare feet. Cold stage, I remember. White-hot light on my face. My nightgown floating ghostlike around my body. My hands are covered in blood that only I can see. Behind me, a man dressed as a doctor and a dubious nurse discuss my case, my doom. I don't see them, of course. I'm too haunted by my own demons. I'm too busy trying to get the blood no one else can see off my hands. No idea that I'm about to fall off the stage, that my life as I know it is about to end. I'm having a ball performing my horror, pacing the very edge like a madwoman. And then my bare foot meets the air. I crash spectacularly to the ground. It makes my whole skeleton thrum now to see it. My body lying brokenly on the auditorium floor. Then the recording loops back, and miraculously, I'm pacing the stage in my white nightgown again. Staring rapturously at the blood on my hands. Performing my horror once more. I knew nothing of horror then.

I look away from the screen, back at the middling man. Standing beside the pool table now. Holding the cue stick in his fist. He seems larger than last time. Jacket off, revealing red suspenders, shirtsleeves rolled. Smiling. This supposed stranger who knows my name.

Who are you? I want to say. *What do you want from me? What have you done to me?*

"Sorry, could you speak up? The acoustics in this room are so terrible. It plagues mine ears."

"Project," shrieks the fat man through his hands. "Breathe diaphragmatically."

"Maybe step a little to the left," says the middling man. "More. Right. Little more left. There. Right there."

Now I'm standing under a bright light. Their faces are shrouded in shadow, but I feel them looking at me. Waiting. Wanting to hear. *Go on. Tell us. Why you're really here.*

"Briana's back," I say.

They gasp softly. *Back?*

"She came to rehearsal today. And she wants to be King," I say.

"King, you say?"

Behind his hands, the fat man starts to chuckle.

"I think she's trying to sabotage the play. Why else would she want to be King?"

Laughter now from the fat man.

"And she's sick. Really sick," I continue. "She has a limp."

They all begin to laugh now. The middling man looks rapt.

"She's accusing me. She accused me today in the theater."

They break out into applause. "Oh, that's good, really good. Love it. Bravo. Wonderful."

"Encore," shouts the fat man. The third man brings his fingers to his lips and whistles.

A rose is thrown at my feet. I gaze down at it lying on the floor, the sharp thorns, the riotous red petals. I smile in spite of myself. How long has it been since anyone threw me a rose?

When I look up, the spotlight above my head is out. They've turned back to their games. The third man has a dart in his raised hand. He's taken aim at the fat man, who whimpers, perhaps in earnest now. The middling man is hunched over the pool table about to make a shot.

"Wait!"

They look back at me.

"You have to tell me what to do, what I've

done. What you did to me."

They're smiling, why are they smiling?

"Do, did, done," says the fat man.

"What's done is done," says the middling man.

"Is done, is done," says the slender man.

"But she's really accusing me. She's going to tell the dean. It's very serious."

"It sounds very, very serious." They all look about to laugh. I can feel them brimming with it. The fat man is chuckling again.

"Just tell me," I whisper. "Please. Did I make her sick?"

The middling man looks at me, mistily. "Oh, how could you do anything like that, Ms. Fitch? You're so, so good."

The fat man laughs uproariously now behind his hands.

I look down at the rose in my hands.

"It was an accident," I say to the rose softly.

"Of course it was."

"I didn't know what I was doing," I insist. "I really didn't."

"How *could* you know, Ms. Fitch?"

"Maybe it was just a coincidence. Her getting sick like that." I look back up at him, at them all, hopefully.

He just looks at me. "How's that back now, by the way?" he says.

"Limp's gone, Ms. Fitch," the fat man says.

"Where did it go? I wonder," says the third man. Not wondering. Knowing. Knowing exactly. I think of Briana dragging my dead leg today in the theater. Her bloodless face slicked with sweat. Her once bright eyes dark as death.

They smile at me. "Or maybe that physical therapy finally paid off in the end."

Mark falling forward in his chair. His pale face. My face twitching with a smile as I stood over him on suddenly straight legs.

"He was hurting me," I shout. "It was self-defense."

They appear to look solemn now. The fat man cries for me. The middling man looks at me with watery eyes.

"Absolutely it was. And Briana needed to learn how to act, didn't she?"

"You could say you gave her a gift."

"Your gift."

I look down at the rose again. The pads of my fingers pressed into the thorns. Bleeding, but I feel nothing, nothing.

"Look at you back on your feet. Doing all this good. Making people feel. That's the work of the theater. All's well that ends well, am I right?"

They look at me. Bloodless faces smiling,

smiling, beneath the red lights. Eyes shining with mirth. My patrons. I feel fear. Bright fear.

"Why are you helping me like this? What do you want?"

They go back to their games. The thin man is about to strike the fat man, who braces himself. The middling man takes a shot. I watch all the balls go sinking into the holes.

"What do you want?" I ask again. "From me. What's the cost?"

They turn to me now. The fat man and the third man stop. The middling man looks at me casually.

"We just want to see a good show, Ms. Fitch. Just put on a good show."

"A good show. That's all?" My turn to laugh now. Can't be. Can't be all. "There must be something else. You must want something else."

"What else could there possibly be, Ms. Fitch?"

My soul? My life? I look down at the rose. It's rotted. Turned the color gray in my hands. The red petals are black, dried up, the stem shriveled. I look up, horror in my heart, ready to accuse them, ready to cry —

And then I see her. Standing at the foot of the staircase, her hand gripping the rail.

Behind her just one flight of stairs. An open door that leads right to the bar. I can see the bartender who directed me down here. Still standing behind the bar, polishing his dirty glass that will remain dirty for time eternal.

"Grace?"

She stares at me, still holding the rotted rose in my hand. Like she's never seen me before.

"Grace. How long have you been standing there?"

She turns around and runs up the staircase and out of the bar.

"Grace, wait!"

I'm running to catch up with her on the dark street. Barely lit with streetlamps. A joke of a street. Lined with shops full of fake witchery. How many times have Grace and I walked these streets together? She's walking so quickly now. Ahead of me, as far ahead as her legs can carry her. I feel a twinge in my hip as I jog to catch up. A little lash of pain down my leg. Oh god oh god oh god.

"Grace! Please, wait. Where are you going?"

"Where does it look like? To my car."

"But don't you want to talk?"

"Not anymore."

"Grace, wait. You're walking so fast. Please don't walk so fast."

"Leave me alone, Miranda."

She's reached the parking lot. Her car is the only one in it at this hour. A sensible RAV4 shining in the dark. Silver, of course. Four-wheel drive. Spotless despite all the hiking day trips she takes into the mountains, all the drives on dirt roads. How many times have I sat in that car, in the passenger seat, in the back seat on my worst days, my legs propped on her dead dog's pillow, the top of my head pressing into the door, while she drove me to the outpatient surgery? Waited in the waiting room, flipping shitty magazines. When they wheeled me out, she sat in the chair beside my gurney, checking her phone.

Sorry, I kept saying through the fog of Valium.

Don't be, she said.

I remember the first time she came with me, we drove past a Jamba Juice on the way home. I thought how wonderful it would be to have an icy drink. Something brightly colored and cold and sweet, though I didn't dare say so. And she stopped the car right in front of it. And she turned to me and said, *What do you want?* And I cried. It was

362

one of the few times I ever really wept in front of Grace. She didn't know what to do. At last, she put her hand on my thigh. *I'll choose for you, all right? How about that?* She began to get out of the car.

Pumpkin delight! I shouted through my tears. And I could hear her smile as she shut the door and ran toward the store entrance. I watched her through the windshield. Running so easily, so lightly on her legs. And I loved her and hated her and loved her.

Now I look at Grace jogging lightly to her car, her ballet slipper key chain jangling in her fist. The back seat where I sat seems like another country. If she gets in her car now, she'll drive away. She'll never look back.

I run ahead of her. It's suddenly easy for me. Can I tell you how easy it is? For me to sprint ahead and beat Grace to her car? She stops in front of me. Is she afraid? If she is, she doesn't show it. And why would she be afraid of me, anyway? I'm her friend, aren't I?

"Let me get in my car, please, Miranda," she's saying. Not even looking at me. She can't. I'm reprehensible in her eyes now. I'm a horror show. Monstrous. How I'm standing before her in my red poppy dress. The way the skirt billows up in the breeze. I

363

keep pushing it back down like I think I'm Marilyn Monroe.

"Grace." I reach a hand out.

She backs away. Almost instinctually.

I lower my hand slowly, calmly. Okay. Okay, be rational. Stay in the world of reason. Be a creature of reason, a creature like Grace.

"Look, I just want to talk to you. Please. For just a second."

Grace is shaking her head. "I don't want to talk, Miranda."

"But didn't you come here wanting to talk to me? Isn't that why you followed me here?"

"Yes, but now I feel differently. Now there's nothing to talk about." Even in the dark, I can see her face is not revealing anything. Now she's staring at me like I'm someone else. Like she's seeing me for the first time. Her eyes are a wall. Briana. Did she hear us talking about Briana? Did I admit something?

"How long were you standing there?" I ask her.

She looks down at the rotting rose I'm still clutching between my fingers. Why am I still clutching it like this? But I don't dare drop it now.

"Long enough."

"Look, Grace, I can explain. Please just let me explain."

"All right, Miranda, explain. Who were those men?"

"Honestly?"

She stares at me.

"Honestly, I don't know."

She starts walking past me toward the car. I'm a waste of time. I'm a waste. But I block her with my body. I'm standing right in front of the driver's side door.

"Grace, please don't walk away like this. Look, you don't know what you saw."

"No, Miranda, you're right. I don't know what I saw. You tell me. What did I see?"

Think, think. Be a creature of reason like Grace. What would Grace want to hear?

"Look, it's just a bit of theater. Just a bit of theater I do on the side." Perfect. "We were rehearsing for this other play I'm putting on."

"Another play?"

"Yes! That's why I've been so strange. So distant. So distracted. That's why I've been so unavailable these days. It's this other play. You see, Grace, how it all makes sense?"

She looks suspicious. I've lied to her about other plays in the past, after all.

"What other play? What's it called?"

365

"Untitled," I say coolly, waving the rose around now like it's a prop, just a prop in this other play. "Sort of an updated *Macbeth.*"

I watch Grace shudder in the dark at my casual use of the blighted name.

"Maybe a little *Doctor Faustus* in there too," I add. "I wish I hadn't taken it on, Grace. It's a problematic production. I mean it has some real kinks. These actors I'm working with." Here I shake my head like it's all been too much. "I wasn't lying when I said I don't know them. I really don't. They work in a different tradition. Very Method. But we're working it out. We're working late. That's all you saw. That's all."

I'm nodding, nodding. This all sounds so good to me. It all makes sense now. It's such a great performance.

Grace says nothing. And then I remember Briana again. Did she hear us talking about Briana? But surely she can't believe I made Briana sick with a touch. Grace is far too sensible for that.

"Grace, I don't know what you heard back there but you can't possibly believe" — and here I start laughing, to show her how funny it is, how absurd — "that I'm actually responsible. That I did something to her."

"I have to go home," she says.

"Grace, look, please, please. You don't know what it's like to be in pain! You've never been in pain. You have no idea. You really don't. To wake up and feel dead to the day. Just another day with your back on the floor. Limping through your life. Dragging your concrete leg behind you. Not being able to shop at the supermarket." I start to cry, but it rings so false. My words sound hollow on my red, shining lips. I'm murdering them just like Briana used to murder anguish with her unmitigated glee, her rampant, smug happiness. Grace hears it.

She tries to push past me toward the driver's side door, but I slam back against it.

"Look," I tell her, my back against her door, "you're tired. You've been working such long days. I have too. Please, we're both so, so tired. Our minds play tricks on us. We can't necessarily trust what we hear or see. Especially at this time of year." I wave a hand around at the thick night. "So close to opening night. And it's shaping up to be a great production. We've done so well. In fact, let me buy you a drink to celebrate. I owe you one, don't I? And then I can explain a little more."

I'm talking fast. But everything I'm saying

makes sense. Everything I'm saying is reasonable. So why is Grace's face like that? Why is Grace backing away from me?

"Grace, are you afraid of me?" I laugh to show her how ridiculous that is, how utterly unreasonable. Being afraid of me. Her friend for how long. Sure we've had our ups and downs, but come on, am I right? But she doesn't laugh. Doesn't even smile.

"Grace, you can't be afraid of me." I smile. "Please. Please, don't be. It's just me. It's just Miranda. How long have we known each other? I'm your friend. We're friends, aren't we?"

I'm walking toward her now, slowly, calmly, to console her, to reassure her really, to remind her that we're friends, that it's just me, Miranda, and she's backing away, still backing away, which is ridiculous, crazy. She's being crazy. I reach out my hand and she falls backward. Falls down in her effort to get away.

She's on the ground now. Lying on the wet, gravelly pavement. She fell down trying to get away from me, her friend. Just me in my red poppy dress that's swaying lightly in the breeze. Emanating the scent of angels. My red mouth purse that's smiling at her, as I'm smiling at her. Saying, "Grace, Grace, are you okay?" It's all so ridiculous.

It's absurd. Grace trying to get away from me even as I step toward her in complete kindness. Offering to help her up. Reaching out a hand even. Saying, "Here, Grace, let me help you up. My turn to help you up. You've helped me so much." But she's scrambling backward on her hands away from me. I imagine the palms raw, scabbed with glass and gravel. "Careful, Grace, please, I say. Don't hurt yourself." But Grace is so dexterous. Even crawling on the ground like a dying dog, you can see that. Utterly unkillable. *I don't do colds,* she told me when we first met. Like colds were a kind of cocktail she didn't care for.

I reach out a hand again for her to take, to help her back up. She'll get back up. Won't thank me. She'll just run away. Run away from me as fast as her well-stretched limbs will carry her. Bearing the message of what she witnessed on her lips. Which she can hardly believe. Which I can hardly believe myself. But who is she to question the testimony of her own eyes and ears? Who is she to turn away from the evidence of the senses? Her job as a stage manager just to deliver it. First thing in the morning she'll run all the way to the school. What will she say about me? Whom will she tell? Everyone. The dean. Fauve. *My dear, you*

369

were right about her. That's what she and Fauve call each other, *my dear.* They'll both back up Briana.

I picture them nodding at my inevitable trial by fire. Pointing at me.

Yes. She.

I crouch down beside Grace, who's cowering from me, won't look me in the eye. Her ballet slipper key chain lies on the pavement beside her, all muddy now, but don't worry, I picked it up for her. Her head is bent low like a wretch, never seen her so low. It's strange. Usually I'm the one on the ground and it's Grace looking down at me. Rolling her eyes at my body on the floor. With exasperation. Impatience. Kindness too, I remind myself. Wasn't there kindness? Grace wanted to help me. And that's all I want to do right now. Help Grace. I'm looking kindly at her. Kindly as I reach out my hand. Kindly as I touch her limp wrist. "Are you all right?" I say.

"Please, Grace," I say. "Believe me. Trust me. I'm sorry. I'm so sorry. For all of this. Let me at least help you up. It's the least I can do."

PART THREE

CHAPTER 22

Bright blue afternoon. The day of my trial by fire. The sun shines in the windows of the dean's office. Shines down on me where I recline upon the chair where once I could barely sit. My legs crossed daintily at the ankle, swinging. My hair sitting lightly on my shoulders in the shape of an S. My heart drumming steadily behind my ribs. Panicked? Maybe a little panicked. But my face is serene. I gaze serenely at the three empty chairs soon to be occupied by Briana and her parents. Who will surely point their fingers, accuse me. But I am the picture of reason.

Puffy Nips sits behind his desk, smiling idiotically, twiddling his thumbs. "Should be here any minute now." He taps his watch with a hairy-knuckled finger.

"Please," I say, my crossed legs swinging to and fro under my seat. "I'm happy to wait." And I realize it's true. I am happy.

My heart is filled this afternoon with a kind of impossible lightness.

"We're so glad you could meet on such short notice like this, Miranda. On a Saturday too," the dean says. Referring to his hasty email. Which I received this morning, just hours after I left Grace. He needed to meet with me in his office today regarding a somewhat concerning accusation from a student. A Ms. Briana Valentine? *An accusation concerning you, Ms. Fitch, I'm afraid.*

His email tone was firm but apologetic. He knows it's my busiest time of year. But Ms. Valentine, he continued, was being quite insistent, as were her parents. And the nature of Ms. Valentine's accusations was um . . . troubling, to say the least. Her parents would also be present at this meeting, the dean informed me in the email. If Grace and I could attend this afternoon, it would be much appreciated by all.

I wrote back: *Of course! Count me in!* Like he'd asked me to join a picnic. Then I added: *I'm so sorry to hear about the concern* ☹ *. I'm sure we can sort it all out* ☺ *.*
Xoxo Miranda.

Now the dean makes light, stupid chatter. The weather. So warm today. "Unseasonably, am I right?"

"I like it."

Did I catch the game?

"I never catch the game."

"I should apologize," the dean says in a low voice now. To his credit, he is embarrassed for me that I even have to endure this. "It's a crazy accusation, of course. Troubling, very troubling, but crazy, am I right?" He can't quite make sense of it, truth be told. Throwing up of his hands. Helpless laughter. But Briana's kicked up quite a fuss, apparently. Making quite the scene. And her parents have been so supportive.

"Such good people," Fauve adds. Fauve's here, did I mention that? I look at her sitting in the corner like a caftaned spider. Dressed like a knockoff Stevie Nicks. Hair freshly feathered. Tears hover in her silver-lined eyes at the goodness of Briana's parents. Of course she managed to snag a front-row seat to this. She's claiming to be a witness.

Witness to what exactly? I asked her.

I think it's better to discuss it when all the parties involved arrive, she said gravely, face positively shining with the drama of it all. The blue felt notebook sits in her lap. Thick with her detailed accounts of my many sins. She can't wait to open it up. She could turn to any page, really, and point to such damning evidence, all documented in her tight, tilted script. Her silver pen necklace is gleaming around her throat along with her usual jangle of pendants. It's served her so well.

"How is the play going, by the way?" the dean asks me now.

"All's well," I say. "We're in great shape."

"Oh, good. Well, we really do appreciate you taking the time today, Miranda."

"Of course. I'm happy to address any concern."

And I am happy. I'm so, so happy. My lips smile so wide they stretch my face. They don't even need lipstick today, they're a natural rose color. The color transfixed me in the mirror this morning. As did the sight of my black hair, which seemed to shine all by itself, shine with an interior light, the lick of red highlights from my youth back with a vengeance. Face lines gone. My skin looked literally dipped in dew. Like I'd gone out into the early morning, pushed my hands into the damp grass, gathered dew into the bowl of my palms, and pressed it into my cheeks. I'm still wearing my poppy dress. Probably should have changed, but poppies are just so cheering. I smell of sex. I smell of the sea. I smell of the starry sky I skipped under all the way home. There's that tune on my lips. I really should figure out its name.

"A lovely tune," says the dean now. "What is that tune?"

"I can never remember the name," I say. "I heard it on the radio last night."

It's true I did. When I drove Grace home. *I'll drive you home, shall I?* I sang to Grace. After I reached out my hand, after I helped her to her feet. And she sort of caved into herself. She was in no shape at all to drive. The whole ride home, she sat slumped in the passenger seat, her face pressed into the passenger window, and how I could blame her? It was such a beautiful night. *You can smell the ocean from here, can't you, Grace? And look. Look at all those stars. Oh, I love this song. I heard it in the pub earlier. Do you know the name of this song, Grace? Do you mind if I turn up the radio?*

Grace didn't mind. Or didn't seem to. It was one great hit after another all the way home. I sang along to all of them, my hands humming on the wheel.

Suddenly I seemed to know all the words. I could sing every song. Maybe I'd always known all the words. Maybe it was just a question of remembering. I looked over at Grace every now and then, in the passenger seat.

All right there? I said. Grace said nothing. Just tired probably. That time of year. *It always nearly kills us, doesn't it? But it never kills you. You're unkillable, aren't you? Not like me. You've seen me die a thousand deaths, haven't you?* Grace said nothing still. So very tired, perhaps.

So I said, *Nearly home.*

When we arrived at Grace's house, I helped her to the front door. *Grace,* I said, *let me help you.* No resisting this time, no backing away. She was limp in my arms, her body so heavy. *One step at a time, that's it, Grace,* I said, and I was patient. I said, *We have all the time in the world.* I led her through the tidy but drab living room to her weirdly frothy bedroom. I laid her gently on her bed of stone. I sat in the ornamental chair at her bedside. Just like Grace used to sit at my bedside when she visited after my shots. But unlike Grace, I didn't check my phone. I didn't flip through a magazine or grade essays, or pretend to read a script. I didn't tap my foot like I had somewhere else to be. No, I sat with my elbows propped on the bed's edge, with my chin in my palms, just watching Grace lie there on her side with her eyes half-open. Mouth-breathing. I gave her my absolute full attention. In case she needed anything. I even

378

anticipated needs. Got her water, which she didn't drink.

Are you sure, Grace? All right, well. I'll leave it here just in case. All right?

Grace didn't answer. Just looked at me.

You're just tired, I said to Grace.

I'm tired too, I lied. I pretended to yawn so Grace wouldn't feel alone in her fatigue. But the truth was I was brimming with oxygen, I was terribly awake. My eyes were wide open. I had a spring wind rushing through me, singing through me. Like I was the spring air itself. I felt my hair shining on my shoulders. I felt the whiteness of my teeth in the dark. I felt myself rising out of the chair. Levitating from the seat.

Can I get you anything else before I go? I asked, smiling, singing. *Tea? How about a Throat Comfort? Or a Cozy Chamomile?*

Grace didn't want anything else. So I just sat there beside her a little longer. I looked deep down into the dark wells of her eyes, the irises the color of fox fur surrounding two ever-growing black pupils. I saw Grace peering up at me from the very bottom of that blackness. A blackness where I myself have languished, a blackness from which I have looked up at her how many times. Trying to speak. Trying to make myself understood.

I asked her if she was sure she didn't need anything.

I asked again because sometimes, when you're ill, you need things and you're afraid to ask. Like I used to be. When Grace used to drop me off after a medical procedure or paid a visit, she'd call *Need anything?* from the front door she was already going out of, jangling her slipper key chain in her hand. I always said, *Nothing, thanks.* So when I asked Grace if she wanted anything, I didn't jangle my keys, I wasn't going out the door. When I asked her, I was inches from her face. My voice was a hand stroking her cheek. Just so she knew that she could ask me for anything. That I was happy to wait on her for once. I could wait on her all night.

Grace wanted me to go home. She didn't say that. She didn't say anything. She just lay there on her side, breathing through her mouth with her eyes still open, still gazing at me from that black place, the very bottom of a place I know so well, I know every nook and shadow. I looked at Grace deep down in that place and I said, *Sleep is all you need.* And I tucked her in. I went into the living room and got Ernest, her bearded dragon, out of his tank. I was surprised again by the drab sight of Grace's living room. Her hiking paraphernalia everywhere.

Recipes for post-workout recovery snacks pinned to a corkboard. The smell of takeout and beer and cigarette smoke. The dragon, Ernest, wriggled in my arms as I carried him back to the bed, put him in there with Grace. I watched his scaly body scamper toward her. The creature curled himself on the pillow right beside her face. He closed his eyes as if to demonstrate sleep. Grace immediately shut her eyes.

Good night, Grace. And I left quietly. I walked home. Singing those songs from the radio. It was a beautiful night. My feet barely touched the spring earth.

I texted Grace, *Hope all's well.* And then I texted Hugo, *Cum over.* We fucked furiously until sunrise. I saw the dawn break beautifully from my window as I rode him like a horse.

Now the door of the dean's office opens. Enter Briana. Fauve draws a breath. So does the dean. But I am the picture of fortitude as I watch Briana enter, hobbling even more than yesterday, leaning heavily on her mother. Her father trails soberly behind, hands in his pockets. I see the hospital bracelet around her wrist. Her hair, still lank and unwashed, the color of mud, hangs around her bloodless face. No panic inside

381

me as I watch her traverse the room, dragging that dead leg behind her.

Fauve rushes to help her — of course — even though she's already being assisted by her parents. I watch Briana pause many times to cry. Meanwhile, her mother and Fauve whisper, "Be brave, be strong." Briana shakes her head, then nods. She will be. We watch her rally, gather herself. Hobble bravely to her chair, which she then falls into. She sits there crookedly, glaring at me. It's truly a spectacular performance, the whole thing. I nearly applaud.

I look over at the dean, who's attempting to look discreetly at his watch.

"Sorry to be late like this," Briana's father offers. "Bit of a rough morning, huh, kiddo?"

She doesn't answer him. Just glares into the middle distance.

"We went to the emergency room," her mother offers gravely.

"Uh-oh," the dean says. "Everything okay?"

"No," spits Briana just as her father says, "Yes. Just a panic attack. Nothing to worry about."

He wears a corporate plaid today. A pale blue that only accentuates the redness of his face. I think of golf courses, rare steaks eaten in restaurants like dark, glimmering caves, a pitcher of ice-cold lemonade that's mostly gin. He smiles mirthlessly at his daughter, at all of us, puts his phone in his inside breast pocket with a sigh. He should be in his office, his face says, upturning the global economy, setting the Amazon on fire. Not here. A shame he can't throw a credit card at this.

Briana glares up at him. Her face contorts with a cry she holds in.

"Oh, well," he says, looking down at her like she's an alien. "We could have rescheduled."

"She wanted to come today," her mother says, clasping her hand. "Didn't you, dear?" The mother is clearly day-drunk. Wearing dark-tinted Jackie O glasses. Her dyed burnished hair tucked behind tiny ears studded with diamonds. Capris (of course) and a boatneck sweater (of course). Pearls always. She reminds me of my mother in her inebriated state, except with far more money and less style. Even with her waitress salary, my mother always dressed to the nines. *All the world's a stage, Bunny,* she'd say, painting her lips with a shaking hand. *Remember that.* I think of her in a vintage dress, her dyed red hair like a fountain of fire, reeking of alcohol and Chanel N°5, staggering toward my high school, ripped out of her mind, to see me in the play. To clap loudly for her daughter. To stand up and clap. *Why are you all still fucking sitting?* she'd mutter at the audience of frightened parents. To complain to anyone who would listen — my drama teachers, the administration — that I didn't have enough lines, why were they giving me such minor roles? When it was clear to anyone with eyes that I was a star. And she should know — she worked in a hotel dining room after all, *Talk about theater!* Banging her fist on the desks.

Ridiculous, she'd hiss. *Fools. All of you.*

Thank you so much for your feedback, Ms. Fitch.

Briana nods now at the floor. I take the sight of her in as she used to take me in. Briana hunched in a dark sweatshirt. Hospital bracelet hanging from her wrist. Gold cross on her neck. Good job with the props, as always. Flanked by her parents — the mother glaring too, but softly, drunkenly, uncertainly. The father looking away. Of course she wanted to come today. I'm not panicking at all. Because it's absurd that I did this, that I'm culpable. Did I mouthbreathe like this? Were my lips ever this bloodless?

Now the dean ahems. "Well, let's get this

started, shall we? Now, Briana, you've raised some very concerning accusations."

Fauve reaches across and grips Briana's hand fiercely. "Go on, dear," she says gently.

Laughter begins to rise in my throat. I almost crack up. "Briana, do you want to tell us what's brought you here today?" the dean urges.

Briana nods. She stares at me with her dead-leaf eyes. She raises a hand. It shakes, can you believe this? It trembles as she points her little white finger at me. "She," she says.

"Professor Fitch," the dean offers.

"She made me sick."

Everyone is silent.

Her father is still looking away. Her mother is looking at me like I'm a siren from hell. But I'm not a siren from hell. The sun is still shining down on me. I feel it warming my bare arms and my hair. I sit lightly in my chair with my legs crossed at the ankle. I say nothing. I smile. I look at the dean like, *What? What can I possibly say to this?*

"How did she make you sick, dear?" her mother urges gently.

"I don't know!" Briana wails. "She just *did,* all right! I *felt* it."

"You felt it," the dean repeats.

"She touched me! She touched me, and then I got like this!" She looks down now at her husk of a body. Tears fall from her eyes.

"*Touched* you!" Fauve repeats. Practically salivating. *Oh, now this is interesting.* She looks at me like she's got me now, but I stay smiling, still smiling at Briana. Beside me, I feel the dean suddenly grow grave. Alert in his chair.

"*Where* did she touch you?" he asks.

Briana draws in a breath. This is her big reveal. But it's not much of a moment — it can't be, she realizes that now. She looks away from us all. Breathing more quickly. She's frustrated. We're all fucking fools. But she already knows she's lost.

"On the wrist," she says at last, limply.

"On the wrist," the dean repeats.

Even Fauve looks confused.

Briana cries. "It was so horrible."

We watch her crumple into herself and weep.

I look at the dean, helpless. I look at Briana's father, who's got his arms folded in front of him, looking up at the ceiling. He's embarrassed for his daughter now, embarrassed for me that I have to sit through this. But what is he supposed to do? She's ill and she's throwing a fit. He's indulged her all his life. He can't not indulge her now.

"So let me get this straight," the dean says now. "You're claiming that Professor Fitch touched you on the wrist. And then somehow, by virtue of doing that, she hurt your . . . is it your leg? Or your back?"

"BOTH!" Briana screams through her tears.

"And that she also gave you some kind of . . . flu?"

Briana looks down at the floor. She nods.

Silence now. I feel the energy in the room shift. The sunlight pouring down on me is the light of reason. I sit bathing in this light. I recross my legs at the knee this time. My top leg swinging. I lean back in my chair. I have to press my lips together to keep from singing.

"Can you explain to me a little about how that works?" the dean asks.

"No," Briana spits.

"No?" the dean repeats.

"How can I? *I'm* not the witch."

The dean coughs. Her father clears his throat.

"Briana," chides her mother softly. And I hear the booze, the Valium, in her gravelly voice. She's humoring her too, I realize. They both are.

Briana ignores her. Instead she looks at me, sickly and triumphant. "I'm not the witch!" she says again, as if she's just getting started. "Ask the witch!"

The dean is embarrassed for her too now. Her father is red in the face. Only Fauve and her mother look at me like perhaps, just perhaps, I have something to hide.

I turn to the dean. I smile. "Am I supposed to respond to this?" I ask him gently. In my gentlest voice. I'm a creature of reason in my poppy dress. *Really? I'm supposed to respond to this? Surely now you see what I'm dealing with.*

The dean looks thoughtfully into space. "When you say *witch*," he begins, "what do you mean exactly?"

Briana frowns. "What do you mean what do I mean? I mean *witch*. As in she did witchcraft on me. Black magic. Satanism. She *made* me sick!"

"Well, now, witchcraft isn't necessarily synonymous with black magic, am I right?" the dean says.

"And Wicca is also very different from Satanism," her father offers. "Whole different kettle of fish there."

"Oh, you bet," the dean says seriously.

"Do you see my leg?" Briana shrieks. "I'm limping! She touched me on the wrist and now I'm limping how *she used to limp*."

The dean frowns. "Let me get this straight:

388

you *felt* Satanism?"

"HOW SHOULD I FUCKING KNOW? I just know what she fucking *did.* I know what I *felt*! I know and she fucking knows she did this to me, don't you, you *BITCH*?"

"Briana!" shouts her mother.

Briana's panting, out of breath now. Shaking with rage. Her pale little hands gripping the armrests like she's trying to keep from collapsing.

"She needs to be fucking FIRED," she seethes. "She needs to go to JAIL! She needs . . ." But she's exhausted herself. I watch her upper body cave into itself a little. She grips the armrests tighter, her white knuckles pointed in my direction like sad little swords.

"Briana, that's enough, you're making a scene," her father says.

"It's all right," I say calmly. And beneath my rib cage, my heart continues its slow, rhythmic thud. Voice smooth as a lake. Body light as a feather. My smile serene. "I'm used to scenes."

"Apologize," he orders.

But Briana will not apologize. She clamps her trembling lips tight like a child in protest. She looks down at the floor. I gaze at her greasy scalp full of dark, unwashed locks. She is going to cry again.

"It's really okay," I say gently, generously. My voice full of forgiveness and understanding, full of empathy, really. Totally unruffled. Still smooth as the surface of water on a windless day. "I forgive Briana. She's obviously upset. Anxious. Under a great deal of stress, who wouldn't be?"

Anxious. Stress. I've said the magic words. I've rung the bell.

Briana looks up at me like I'm a nightmare she's trapped inside of. I'm the thick, dark forest. I'm the lightless sky. I'm the hunter dogging her every step. I'm the heavy air and the sucking mud beneath her feet that make it impossible for her to run.

"Stress!" the dean says eagerly. "Yes. *Stress* is a terrible thing."

"Yes," her father says immediately, "stress. She has been. Under a lot of stress."

"She has been working herself up a lot, haven't you dear?" her mother adds. "She hasn't been able to sleep."

"BECAUSE I'M SICK! And I've never been unwell before! I've never been sick!"

"Apparently, she's not sick now either," her father adds.

"Jim," Briana's mother hisses.

Briana looks at him, eyes flashing with betrayal. She could kill him, strangle him, her own father. Right here, right now, with

390

her small, frail hands.

"Well, it's true, isn't it?" her father continues, unfazed. "How many doctors has she seen now. Six?"

"Seven," her mother says, patting Briana's greasy hair, but Briana shakes her off.

"Seven." He looks at me. "We've had all kinds of tests done. They all say there's nothing wrong with her. That she's healthy as a horse."

"No one's said that!" Briana protests.

"They say that *maybe* she had some kind of virus," he continues, talking to me and the dean now, "but that stress is what's keeping her immune system out of whack."

"What about my leg, then?" Briana demands. "What about my back?"

She's looking right at her father, pleading, but he's a wall. He continues to address me and the dean.

"They say her back is probably just messed up because she's been in bed for so long. That her leg is messed up because her back is messed up."

"Only *one* doctor said that! And he was an idiot. He didn't even *listen* to me!"

"But it makes sense, doesn't it?" her father presses, looking at us.

"A domino effect," the dean says happily. "Absolutely. One time, I hurt my ankle.

Next thing it was my shoulder. Next thing I knew I had a headache. That's your domino effect."

My phone buzzes in my lap. I look down. Hugo, sending me texts.

Last night my god
Can't stop thinking about it
Jesus ur fucking hot. my god.
Meet me in wkshp now?

I hide my phone under Briana's sick glare.

"All compensatory," the dean is saying. "Weakness begets weakness. And stress can play terrible tricks on us."

"Sure it can," says her father. "That's what we've been telling her."

"Don't talk about me like I'm not here! I hate when you do that! I'm right here! Right here in this room!" Her voice is wavering wildly. She looks less angry, more desperate. Her sweaty white face punched in with self-pity and fear, real fear. *Fucking look at me! Am I invisible?*

How many surgeons, physiatrists, doctors, have I looked at like this? Only to have them address themselves instead to Paul sitting beside me? Paul would nod along solemnly with the doctor and then look over at me, at a loss. *Did you see how he just talked to you again? Did you see?!* I'd ask in the car after we left.

392

I saw, Paul said.

Am I invisible? What the fuck was that about?

I don't know, Miranda, okay? he sighed. *Calm down.*

And then after our split, when I went to the doctor alone, they still wouldn't look at me. They would direct their questions, their diagnoses, to the corners of the room or to the medical table or to the diagram of the skinned body on the wall. As if these objects were somehow more trustworthy, more reasonable.

"I'm here," Briana says again. "Right here."

"Of course you are," the dean says.

"And I'm *not* stressed, I'm sick! SHE made me sick."

"No one's *saying* your pain isn't real, sweetheart," her mother begins. "But remember that video they showed us? About pain and the brain?"

Briana looks at her mother like she could smack her. Then tears fill her eyes again. I recall Mark's face in the SpineWorks basement. Looking at me like he understood me, like someone finally understood me. *I have a video for you to watch, Miranda. I think it would help you. That it would be a great place for us to start.* The sense of betrayal that welled up in me later as I stood crook-edly in my apartment, watching the anthro-pomorphic brain wander a sad gray world of its own design.

I wonder where Mark is, if he's watching that video now. If it's helping him.

"The brain is so powerful, remember, my love?" Briana's mother says now. "Some-times we just get so upset we can literally *keep* ourselves sick, can't we?"

"Absolutely," the dean and her father say at the same time.

"Well, Miranda should know all about this," Fauve says, looking at me and smil-ing. Little snake in the grass. Slithering, slithering.

"After all, she was unwell just like Briana here, weren't you? For a while there, Mi-randa, I wasn't sure if you would be fit to continue. I was actually prepared to step up and fill in. Not that I'm a Shakespeare person by any means — I prefer musicals, so much lighter and uplifting and accessible — but anything for the students."

Slither, slither. All for the sake of her sad career, her sorry survival.

"So noble of you, Fauve," I say, smiling too, still smiling through all of this. "So self-less."

"But now look at you, Miranda. You've

recovered so spectacularly. Just in the past month. Just after Briana came down with this condition, as a matter of fact."

So here it is at last. Her little accusation. She smiles more widely now. Caftan shimmering with petty triumph. *That's right. I've put two and two together, Miranda. Even though it's an impossible two. An unthinkable two.* But it's not an unthinkable two for someone who burns sage in an abalone shell, puts rocks of amethyst in her bra (according to Grace), and wears vision oil like perfume.

She's ready to open her silvery-blue book. To fatten/substantiate this admittedly thin charge with my litany of transgressions: chronic lateness, flagrant substance abuse, tyrannical incompetence. I gaze at the notebook, open now. Fauve's hand on the first page, dense with her shimmering blue script.

"I really don't want to take up more of Professor Fitch's time with this," the dean cuts in, looking warily from the notebook to his own watch. "What's your point, Fauve?"

Fauve's face tightens with anger. She closes the book. *For now,* her face says, glaring darkly at me before her eyes brighten again with mere innocuous curiosity.

"Just that maybe Miranda has some tips

for Briana."

They all look at me. And it's right then that it happens. It happened a couple of times the night before too, on my long, lifting walk home, but I thought nothing of it. I thought I was simply high on life. It's this: I feel my body begin to rise from my chair. Literally rise. Levitate so that I'm hovering in the air, about a half inch above the seat. Impossible, it's impossible. Defies how many natural laws. Gravity, for one. I grip the armrests. And just like that, I sink back down. It's over in the blink of an eye. But did they notice? Did they see?

No. They're all still looking at me, waiting for tips.

I clear my throat.

"Well, the one thing I'd say is to be very, very kind to yourself. Anxiety is a tricky beast. It can manifest in weird ways. Psychosomatic iterations are the worst. Once the sympathetic nervous system is alarmed, it can be very tricky to put it back to bed."

Do you like tricks, Ms. Fitch?

"Perhaps try breathing diaphragmatically. Some meditation, acupuncture. Aromatherapy is always good, I find. Biofeedback. Physical therapy is a given, of course. It's done wonders for me. I'd be happy to send Briana some videos. Some podcasts."

"That's kind of you," her mother says warily.

Briana looks at me darkly, hopelessly. "She doesn't want to fucking help me. She hates me."

"Briana," I say. "That simply isn't true. I think you're wonderful."

The dean and her mother look so touched by my kind words. But Briana's shaking her head. *No. No, no, no.*

"She's lying! She doesn't want me to be in the play! She said so yesterday!"

I look at her so pitifully, like the crazed wretch she is. Like I'm so very sorry for her. All that stress she must be under. How profoundly it's clouding her understanding.

"It was never a question of what *we* wanted, Briana," I speak so softly, so reasonably, to emphasize her loudness, her crassness. "We only raised concerns — very understandable concerns — about your health. We only wanted to give you an opportunity to heal. If we didn't do that, what sort of monsters would we be, am I right?"

The dean and her father are nodding like this is all so reasonable. It makes such sense.

"But we'd love to have you back, of course," I add.

"But —"

"In fact," I tell them all, like I've really

been considering, really giving it some thought. "I think absolutely she should be in the play. She obviously can't return to the position as the lead, of course. That would be far too much of a strain. And we both know Briana was never a fan of Helen anyway."

Briana glares at me.

"But the role of the aged King is serendipitously open. And I think she'd be perfect for it. And what would the play be without Briana, after all? I'm not sure if she'd want to work with me again, given her current feelings. But I'm absolutely willing to take her back. In fact, I'd love it."

I can feel her looking at me now, shocked. Suspicious. Not a little afraid.

"She's lying," Briana says. I'm lying, I must be.

I only smile at her sadly. How sad that she sees such darkness, such subterfuge, when there is only light, a smile, a hand reaching out to her. A symptom of her condition.

But I can see there's a small, sick part of her that's pleased with my offer too. Her dull eyes flicker with it. Really? I'd really love it?

"Of course," I add, "there are some risks, you understand. Given how you're feeling these days. I just want to make sure those risks are understood by everyone, that the school won't be responsible. Theater is very taxing, after all." I look at her father and the dean, both of whom nod sensibly. I'm so sensible. "But if you're willing to take the risk, then, of course" — I smile at Briana — "I'd love to have you."

"Would you like that, dear? To be back in the play?" her mother asks her. She places a hand on her daughter's shoulder, and for the first time, Briana doesn't shrug it away. Her mother exchanges a pleased look with Mr. Valentine, who's smiling now.

"A very, very generous offer, I think, Professor," the dean says, still nodding at me approvingly.

Briana looks at me. I think she's going to spit in my face. Scream, *Fuck off. I wouldn't go near you.*

But she just nods sadly at the floor. "I'd like that," she says at last, quietly, and then weeps.

"Wonderful!" The dean raps on his desk with his knuckles. Gold ring gleams on his finger like the ring of a king. He smiles at the swirling motes of dust. "It's all settled, then, isn't it?"

We watch Briana and her parents leave. I'm about to get up with them, but the dean makes a silent gesture at me to hang back, wait.

Wait? I think. *Why? Isn't it all settled?*

"All right, Fauve, what's this about?" the dean says. Impatient now. He looks openly at his watch. Jangles it on his wrist. It's Saturday, for god's sake. He should be miles away from us all on his boat, skirting the gray sea. But Fauve looks too happy. "There is one more thing I think we should discuss," she intones. And then she pulls a plastic baggie from her pocket.

She holds it up gravely. Inside is what looks like a silky red handkerchief.

"What are we looking at?" the dean says.

But Fauve just stares at me. "Maybe Miranda can tell us."

Looking at the red silk, I flash to the three men. The red handkerchief blooming in the middling man's pocket like a rose. Was Fauve in the pub last night? Did she see us? *What do you know?* I want to scream.

"Tell you what?" I say. Calm as you please.

"I imagine, Miranda, that you've been looking for these?"

These? Then I see what it really is. A thong of red lace. My thong. Balled up in the baggie like evidence. "I found *these* unmentionables on the stage floor," Fauve presses.

The dean looks at my thong and immediately colors. He gazes down at his desk.

But Fauve is just getting started. "Miranda, do you happen to know who these belong to?" And I know she happens to know exactly.

I stare at Fauve. I smile. "No idea. Could be anyone's. Any of the students'. We change in and out of clothes backstage all the time," I say to the dean. He nods quickly at his desk. Eager to grasp on to this, to anything.

"There you are," he says. "Now —"

"Oh, I don't think these belong to a *student*, Miranda." Fauve smiles. "No, I can't really picture a student shopping at Agent Provocateur, can you? It's a pretty high-end lingerie shop. I doubt our students would be familiar with it."

She turns to the dean for validation, but he's staring at the thong now like he wishes he could make it disappear. Or turn it into a boat and sail away. Sail away from here.

"I thought I should bring it to your attention, Miranda. Though I'm sure that as a faculty member, you know far better than I that *sex*" — she pauses here, letting the weight of the word, of my crime, fall — "between faculty, or between faculty and *staff*" — another meaningful pause — "is absolutely prohibited on school grounds.

And clearly these" — she holds up the thong-filled baggie now between her thumb and forefinger — "are evidence of illicit activity between adults in the theater. Which *is* school grounds. Where I know you and Hugo have been spending so much time lately."

She smiles sweetly. Hideously. Willing me to crack, to break. But I won't be broken. Jealous of me and Hugo. Her every cell seething with it.

"Fauve, what are you implying?" the dean cuts in. "Are you saying that you *saw* something . . . illicit . . . between Professor Fitch and Mr. Griffin?"

Fauve looks at me and flushes. And then I know. She absolutely fucking saw something. Skulked around the theater after her ridiculous music class. Lurked in the wing. Her periwinkle eyes widening at the unholy arch of my naked back as I straddled him among the falling stars. But she can't admit it. The dean is practically purple with prudery at having been forced into this thong conversation to begin with. Fucking New England. She can't bring this home without implicating herself, a Peeping Tom in the wings.

"Have you *seen* the two of them in the halls together lately?" she spits. "It's *ob-*

scene. It's —"

"I don't make it a point of going around following my faculty. Or my staff, for that matter," the dean says.

Now she becomes aware of how terrible she looks clutching a bag full of my underwear between her fingers.

"If that's all, Fauve? I really think Professor Fitch has had enough for one day. Quite enough now."

CHAPTER 23

In the bathroom, I'm gripping the sink, gazing into the cracked mirror. Cells glittering inside me. Literally giddy with health. This lightness in my heart like a balloon that's lifting, lifting my feet off the ground. I'm levitating again. Biting on my grin. Biting down so hard, I taste blood. The vital warmth on my tongue brings me back to myself. Three men in the mirror, I see, biting on their grins too. *All settled, then. Isn't it?* The blood drips a little from our lips. We can fix that, can't we? I pull a lipstick from my smiling-mouth purse. Fumble a little with the tube. Okay, so my hands are shaking. But we got away with it. We got away with it, didn't we?

Just then the bathroom door opens with a creak. Stop smiling. Apply lipstick with an even hand. There you go. Russet Moon by Chanel. *Such a gorgeous color. Such a rich red,* the lady at the counter told me. *Goes so well with your hair and your eyes.*

Fauve appears in the mirror. She's beside me at another sink. Fussing with her absurd hair cloud. Pulling some sort of tube of gloss from her cloth purse.

"Well that was some meeting, wasn't it?" she says. Congenial now like a true coward. Like we were only just spectators to the same show. She never waved my own underwear in my face. The red silk is now nowhere in sight.

"Poor Briana," she insists.

"Yes," I agree, playing along. "Poor, poor Briana."

"Oh, Miranda, I meant to ask . . . where's Grace, by the way?"

Grace flashes in the blink of my mind's eye. Lying on her side, on her bedroom froth. Eyes like black pits, staring. But I'm still applying the lipstick. Good to put it on thick.

"Oh, Grace couldn't make it today, sadly," I say easily. "She's come down with something."

"What?" She turns to face me, but I don't look at her. I keep my eyes on my red mouth, on my face, in the rusty mirror. I try to shrug, coolly.

"Yes, isn't it terrible? That time of year, I guess."

"Better not be that thing Briana has," Fauve says, bringing a hand to her chest, brimming with all those quasi-mystical pendants. A silver hand with an open blue eye in the palm. A feather, a scarab, a small bronze skull. And, of course, the ornate silver pen. All of them clinking lightly under her fingers. "Is it?" A note of real fear I hear in that voice. It gives me courage.

I look Fauve right in her flashing eyes, which are gazing at me like I'm what? Some kind of monster? I smile at her with my freshly painted lips.

"Just might be," I say. "Better be careful. Might be going around."

"I suppose I should call on Grace," Fauve says. "If she's under the weather."

"Oh, Grace doesn't want to be disturbed," I say quickly. "She told me. Rest is really what she needs," I say. "Not visitors."

"Well. Maybe I'll call on her all the same."

Call on her. Are we in the Victorian era or in the 1960s? Decide, Fauve. Please.

She looks at me, testing me.

"Call on her," I say to Fauve. "Of course. Go ahead. Maybe even bring her some soup. But I'd protect myself, if I were you. Like I said, might be going around. Oh, and enjoy those underwear, by the way. I have

406

to say, they were a real hit. As I'm sure you know."

I watch her turn and clip-clop hurriedly away on her Danish sandals, shimmering with moral certitude, leaving the scent of sage and treachery in her wake.

The minute she's left the bathroom, I quickly pull out my phone. I text Grace.

Hey! We missed you this morning. All's well?

I watch dots form. My heart soars. Then they disappear. Then nothing.

Need anything??? I text again.

I wait. Nothing. Not even dots this time.

All right. All right, I'll just call her, then. I listen to the phone ring and ring, a smile hovering on my lips. Ready to say, *Grace! How are you? Feeling okay today? God, what a night we had, am I right? Crazy. Both of us always so crazy at this time of year, aren't we?*

No answer. "The mailbox belonging to *Grace Pines* is full." Grace's voice saying her name. No-nonsense. No suffering of fools. Saying her name like it's a root planted deeply into the earth.

Don't panic, why are you panicking? What did you do wrong? Nothing. She's the one who treated you like you were a criminal. Backing away from you like that, ridiculous. Falling to the pavement. All you did was reach out and help her up. Drive her home. Put her in bed. She should be thanking you, if anything.

Maybe she's just getting rest. Everybody gets worn out, even Grace can't be immune. Maybe she just needs TLC. The thing to do is be there for her in whatever way I can. Show her I'm here. I care.

Quickly, I pull up the Instacart app on my phone. My cart is still half-full from the last time I attempted to shop. Back when I was still on the floor after a failed acupuncture appointment. Didn't even have the energy to order in the end. Now I change the delivery address from mine to Grace's. I add some items to the half-filled cart. Things I know Grace loves: A rotisserie chicken. Mashed potatoes. Fish sticks. Grape-Nuts. Green apples. Grace likes crunch. Every species of citrus fruit. And then some fun things, things Grace would never think to get herself. Things I never thought to get myself. Pink peppercorn passion fruit dark chocolate bark. Dried acai berries. Walnut oil. Some frankincense. A little spa atomizer. Sage and lavender oils. A rock-salt lamp.

I pay extra for quick delivery. I give the delivery person a huge tip.

Then I look up local flower shops. Call a

random one that sounds nice.

"Hello!" I say. "I'd like to send some flowers to someone. . . . Occasion? No occasion. Friendship is the occasion. Since when do we need an occasion to send flowers to our friends, am I right? Ha ha ha. . . . What do I have in mind? Oh, just a wonderful arrangement of spring flowers, please. Something revitalizing. Restorative. Tulips. Freesia. In every color, please. Red, white, every color, every. Oh, and baby's breath. And plants, why not throw in a plant too? Do you have a cactus? . . . Perhaps throw in a cactus. Oh, and a fern. And do you have those balloons with the smiling faces? . . . Get Well balloons, right. Send those too, please. How many balloons? All you have. . . . A card? No card. She'll know who it's from, I think. Ha ha. . . . Monday delivery? . . . Yes, that's fine. Thanks so much."

Then I call the liquor store and I order a twelve-pack of IPAs to be delivered to her apartment. The kind Grace loves. The kind that tastes like soap. The kind she's always trying to get me to drink, waving the neck of the bottle under my nose. *Fucking try it, Miranda, who knows? Maybe it will cure you. Maybe it will help.*

But nothing helps me, right, Grace?

409

And then because I can't resist, I add a bottle of pink champagne. Veuve Clicquot. *Veuve,* French for "widow." Grace and I drink a bottle of it together every year, after the last wretched performance of the season. *God, it's wonderful, isn't it?* I always ask Grace as I pour it for us into paper cups.

For not-beer, she always concedes.

See, Grace? We've had some good times.

When I hang up, I feel happy. Flowers. Balloons. Booze. Groceries. She'll know I care now. She'll remember how long we've been friends. How much we've been through together.

After I hang up, I see some texts have come through. *Grace!* I think. Oh, Grace, thank god, thank god.

I look down at my phone.

Not Grace. Hugo.

I want to see you. I'm on campus right now, tying up some loose ends. Come visit me?

Another one from Paul.

Miranda, all okay? Haven't heard from you in a long time. Getting worried.

It surprises me to hear from him. Paul almost never texts or calls. But then I remember how frequently I used to text and call him in my darker days. Not so very long ago, those darker days. The days before *All's Well.*

410

To my ex-husband, I type, *All's well* ☺
To Hugo, *Coming now.*

CHAPTER 24

A day and a night and a day fucking in Hugo's basement. Then sleep. Sleep for Hugo, that is. Not sleep for me so much. My eyes are still wide open in the dark, in the smoke of his bedroom. They won't close tonight. Or is it tomorrow already? It might already be tomorrow. Can't tell by the light. His windows are high and small, very close to the ceiling. It's a nice basement place. He's set it up nice. *Fixed it up,* as my mother would say. All white and shining, not at all like I imagined. The wooden furniture gleaming in the dark. Has a woman's touch, but it's Hugo's touch, I guess. Earth-toned rugs here and there that warm up the cold floor. Candles everywhere, plants that don't need much light at all. More books and records than I would have thought. A framed poster of Johnny Cash wearing black on the wall. The house is owned by a widow who lives on the ground floor. Mrs. Lee.

She lets Hugo pay rent in pot and landscaping, some handiwork around the house. Her own little handyman for free. Hugo's nothing but grateful.

She really helped me get back on my feet, Hugo said of her. *I honestly don't know what I'd do without Mrs. Lee. I owe her so much.*

She sounds wonderful, I said, knowing already we would be enemies.

I was right. Mrs. Lee didn't like the look of me at all when she saw us approaching her house, all over each other already. My mouth was a red smear from making out with Hugo in his truck, my mascara bleeding black tears down my cheeks, and my hair was wild. I saw her sitting on the front steps, a crouched silhouette and a plume of cigarette smoke in the black of the evening. Beside her was a large, very white dog who glowed in the dark. *Miranda, this is Hester and Tulip,* Hugo said. Tulip was the dog, I guess. Tulip growled at me. And Mrs. Lee said nothing at all.

Hello, I said cheerfully. Too cheerfully perhaps. The dog began to bark.

And she and the dog went into the house, letting the door shut pointedly behind them.

Don't mind her, he said. *She's been through a lot.*

Oh, it's all right, I said.

413

I was extra loud during our fucking, for the benefit of Mrs. Lee. I moaned at the ceiling.

Now I hear the dog scampering around up there as I watch the light change through the windows, go from blue to pink to peach to flaming red to blue again. Eyes still won't close. Eyes still wide open. It's all right, I'm wonderfully rested. I wonder if Grace is resting like this in her own bedroom of rose froth, her dragon dreaming beside her. I hope so.

I look at Hugo lying beside me, eyes shut tight and fluttering, his eyes roving beneath the lids, mouth open. Dead to the world, wide awake and wandering in another. His blond hair haloed by the dawn or is it the dusk? The shadows in his face cavernous. Making him look so much like Paul in this light and in the next light and in the next and the next that comes through the windows. Just tricks of the light, I know. Casting these shadows over his face, over the room. Telling me that I'm back in my old house. Back in my old red bed. Paul lying beside me, my arm around him, I'm breathing in the honeyed scent of his neck. I never fell off the stage. I never walked out the door. Soon he'll wake up and we'll have a lazy day together like we used to, won't we,

Goldfish? Morning sex and then maybe Dutch pancakes, Paul's specialty. After, we'll curl up on the couch in the bright living room, each reading a book. Maybe he'll play the piano and maybe I'll work on that garden that I never let go to shit. Maybe I'll rehearse because I've got work again; I'm in a show. I'm Cleopatra or Lady Anne; maybe I'm Helen again. Paul will run lines with me, read Antony, Richard, Bertram.

It's fun for me, he'll say. *I like it. I like you.* Sex again, this time on the couch. His mouth on my neck, my hands in his hair. We'll go for one of our drives up the coast in the afternoon, maybe a walk on Singing Beach. In Manchester-by-the-Sea, remember? Just like the Singing Sands in Scotland. *Our own Scotland right here,* we said. And I won't limp behind, and he won't charge ahead. I won't have to ask for us to stop, can we please stop and just sit here, here on this bench for a second and rest? I won't sit there while he stands over me, trying not to be impatient while I try not to cry. We'll walk the shoreline together like we used to, we used to do it all the time. He'll hold my hand the way he did then. Later, we'll go out for dinner, that sushi place we both love in Marblehead. *I'm starving, are you?* Yes. I'm starving too.

We'll order everything, Paul says, *how's that?*

Smiling at me. Squeezing my hand. He hasn't let go of it all day.

Oh, I love that idea, I say. *Yes, let's! That's perfect, perfect.* "What's perfect?" he says. And just like that, his features shift, dissolve into another face. I'm not in the golden light of an afternoon in another life, I'm in a dark basement. It's Hugo lying beside me, awake now. Hugo who looks only like himself in the soft blue morning or is it night? Looks concerned at me. Maybe even a little frightened. Did I doze off finally?

"You okay?" he asks me.

"Fine. I'm fine, why?"

"Just you were really having a fit in your sleep."

"I was?" I laugh. "I didn't even know I'd fallen asleep."

"You screamed something," he says. "A word."

"A word?" My heart drums in my ears. "What word?"

He shakes his head slowly.

"I couldn't make it out. It sounded like another language almost. You screamed it over and over."

"Huh. Probably just production anxiety," I say. "I have the weirdest anxiety dreams

416

around this time of year. Always. Always, always. If I manage to sleep at all, that is." I smile.

But Hugo still looks troubled. He reaches a hand out and strokes my hair.

"Are you sure you're okay? Last night was a little . . ."

"What?"

"I don't know. I mean I loved it, of course, but —"

"But?"

"Nothing. Never mind. I'm hungry, are you?"

"Starving," I say.

"How about I take you out," Hugo says. "Might be nice for us to have a real dinner together, you know? A date. Before the craziness of production really kicks in this week. Get to know each other a little. Talk."

"Dinner. Talk," I say. "Sure, why not? Let's talk."

"Great. You pick the place," he says.

"Okay. I'll pick the place. I'd love to."

"Quite a drive for sushi," Hugo says when we finally arrive.

"I thought something light might be nice. Since it's so late. Don't you like sushi?"

"Sure, yeah. Just Marblehead's a little out of the way. You must really like this place."

"Oh, I've only been a couple of times," I lie. "But I remember it being great."

We enter the place, Paul and I. I mean Hugo and I, I'm with Hugo. He's holding my hand. We still smell of the incense sticks he burned in his bedroom, his basement flowers. All the sex we had in the fragrant smoke. Sex on crisp white sheets with tiny red petals like little tongues — sheets I twisted and gripped while I screamed, *Oh, Paul, Paul. Fuck me.*

What did you say? Hugo said. And then he turned on the light.

Nothing, nothing.

And now he's taking my hand. Paul never did that. Maybe he did in the early days. The early, early days. How long ago was that? God, don't remember. Live here, be in the here and now with Hugo. The sushi place is lovely, isn't it? It hasn't changed at all since the last time I was here. Same bamboo trees still in their heavy pots. Same paintings of warrior women on the walls in black frames. Same barefaced hostess in willowy black. Balmy lips, soft smattering of freckles. Does she recognize me? Hard to say, I look so different from the miserable wretch I was when she last saw me come hobbling in. I'm glowing with life now, glowing from hours of basement sex. Wordlessly, she leads us to a table. Same tiny black tables gleaming like mirrors. On each table, the same slim-throated vases out of which a bright orchid emerges, the same orchid whose boisterous color and life used to mock my death, my grayness. And the way he sat across from me then. Looking like he'd been sentenced to something. His life was a cage, and my hunched body, my drugged face, were the bars. But not tonight.

Tonight he's looking at me like he'll never get enough of me. Tonight, the sight of me is wine and all he wants to do is drink of the cup. Tonight, I no longer envy the orchid. Tonight, I'm the one blooming. Paul hasn't looked at me like this since the beginning. But this is another beginning, remember? With him, this man who looks like Paul in certain lights. A lot of lights, frankly. Light of the theater but those are tricky. Light of his basement, but again that's off — not a lot of natural light in a basement. Light in this restaurant, frankly. But he isn't Paul, I checked his driver's license while he was showering to remind myself. Even looked up his crimes on the internet. They were more serious than I thought. I thought maybe marijuana possession or trafficking. Maybe some dabblings in cocaine. And there were drugs, yes, but there was also a count of assault. Aggravated. With a weapon, no less. I imagined the knife, imagined him gripping it. I stared at his mug shot on my laptop screen, his young face washed out by that grim light, the deep, dark hollows under his eyes, which looked not green at all but gray and drugged. His blond hair dark and hanging lank around his face like Briana's does now.

An accident, I thought. Or self-defense. Or maybe that person just deserved it, you never know. I wanted to tell him that no matter what he'd done, I'd understand. That sometimes these things happen, of course they do, I know that now. It didn't even scare me, seeing his mug shot. If anything it made me feel closer to him, closer to Hugo himself. In that picture he didn't look like Paul at all.

Everything okay? he said to me when he came out of the steaming bathroom. I snapped the laptop shut. Gazed at his long, wet hair slicked back from his face.

And what could I do but fuck him again?

The restaurant's track lighting shines down on him now like a spotlight. Doing something weird to his hair, to his eyes, the cut of his jawline. So that he really truly looks like —

"What? What's wrong?" Hugo says.

"Nothing. Why?"

"Just you're looking at me funny again."

"Am I?" I say.

"Yeah. Almost like you've seen a ghost."

"Just the light," I tell him. "Just in this light, you look like someone."

At first he frowns, but then he smiles. "Someone good I hope," he replies.

"Yes," I say. "Someone very good."

He's smiling at me over his menu. That grin-shaped scar on his lip. Paul didn't have a scar like that but everything else is uncannily the same. Clothes are a bit off though. Paul wouldn't wear a Motörhead shirt or lumberjack plaid. But apart from that. He reaches out and takes my hand. All I had to do was hold it out, palm up, and he took the cue.

"What do you think you'll have?" Paul says.

"The eel, like always," I say. "And you'll have the sunshine roll, of course."

"I will?" He laughs. "How do you know? I haven't even really looked at the menu yet."

"Because it's the best. Because I know your taste."

He raises an eyebrow. "Should I trust you?"

"You should absolutely trust me."

"All right," he tells the waiter when he arrives, "the sunshine roll. And a Sapporo, please."

"The cold sake is really good." I take his hand and squeeze.

"Okay. Sake, then." I order my usual.

The waiter leaves, and I look at Hugo. Perfect. Perfect, except the clothes.

"Did you get those shirts I left in your mailbox?" I ask him.

"Shirts? Oh yeah. The shirts. Yeah, I got them."

"I just felt so bad about the one that got torn," I say.

"Just a few buttons missing, really. Still a good shirt." He grins.

"Well, these new ones I got you have snaps. So you don't even have to worry about —"

"They're cool. Just not really my style, Miranda. I mean I like them, don't get me wrong, but I'm all about this combo right here." He tugs on the plaid shirt, then on the T-shirt beneath. "Much better for my kind of work. Wearing those fancy shirts, I'd feel afraid to do anything, you know."

"Well, those shirts wouldn't be for working. They'd be for going out." With me.

"Still. They're just . . . I don't know. Not me."

"Oh. I'm sorry."

"Don't be sorry. Please. It was really thoughtful of you. I'll still hang on to them."

The food arrives, and he switches the subject to production. Asks how rehearsal's going, and I say going so well. He tells me more about the sets, how the new budget has been a dream come true thanks to me. And lighting and sound are all ready to go for tech week too. We're in great shape.

We feed each other smoked eel. Gorgeous. "God, isn't it great to be back here?" I ask him.

"I've never eaten here, remember?"

"Right, of course."

Every now and then I look down into the mirror of the table and smile. And then he says, "Hey, I heard there was some kind of weirdness yesterday with Briana, is that true?"

I'm holding a piece of smoked eel between my chopsticks. And I drop it. But I pick it right back up. I look confusedly at Hugo, who is definitely Hugo now.

"Weirdness? What did you hear exactly?" But I'm already picturing it. Fauve wandering into the scene shop after my trial by fire, whispering hotly into his ear, her hand gripping his shoulder. Failing to mention how she implicated him, of course.

"Just that Briana came to the dean's office with her parents and that you all had a . . . was it a meeting?"

I shrug and smile. "It was fine. She just accused me of making her sick, that's all." I eat the eel. Chewy, this piece.

"What?"

"I know, can you believe it?" I shake my head. Roll my eyes.

"What did she say you did to her exactly?"

"Take your pick, really. Witchcraft. Black magic. Satanism." I laugh out loud at that last one. Can't help it.

But Hugo's looking at me strangely now, not laughing at all.

"Oh, come on, it's funny," I say.

"I don't think it's funny, Miranda. I think it's fucked-up."

"It's that too. And sad. Frankly, I feel sorry for her. I mean it's a ridiculous accusation. What century are we in, am I right?" I shake my head.

"Right." He shakes his head too. But he's still looking at me funny. "I guess I just don't get why she would accuse you of something like that," he says.

I shrug. "Grasping at straws, I guess. Trying desperately to find a reason for her illness, a cause. Easier to point the finger at someone else than at yourself, I suppose."

"I'm sorry," he says quietly.

"It's fine. I don't mind being the bad guy. And we sorted it out in the end. But the fact that we even had a meeting about it. That we even entertained her grievances in any official capacity." I shake my head again. "New England's puritanical streak is clearly alive and well. Sorry, I know you're from here — Maine, right? And don't get me wrong, I'm from here too, but —"

"I'm not from Maine, Miranda."

"Aren't you?"

"I'm from Oregon. Eugene. I've told you. I've told you a few times now."

"Oh, right. Of course. Well, then the puritanical streak probably seems even crazier to you, am I right? Oh, look, you haven't even touched your sunshine roll."

But Hugo's just staring at me now, a serious expression on his face.

"Miranda, I think we should talk about last night."

"Last night? Last night was wonderful, wasn't it?"

He takes a sip of cold sake. Winces. "It was. It just . . . got a little intense, don't you think?"

"Intense? What do you mean 'intense'?"

"Asking me to go harder," he says quietly. "Asking me to hit you and stuff."

He doesn't look like anyone to me now.

425

He doesn't look like anyone but an awkward, sheepish boy.

"So I could feel it." I smile. "I just wanted to feel it. That's all."

"You closed your eyes a lot too. You turned your head away, a few times. You wouldn't look at me."

He's looking at me now. Hurt, I realize.

"That's how I feel it. That's just so I can concentrate on how it feels."

"And then afterward you started crying —"

"I was just happy. Aren't I allowed to be happy?"

"It's just . . . look. I almost felt like you weren't really with me. Like you were but you weren't. You wanted someone else. You wanted me to be someone else."

"What? No. That's crazy," I tell him. "Totally crazy."

"Maybe. But that's sort of how I felt."

"I don't want that. Who else could I possibly want you to be but you?"

He's thinking about me calling him Paul. Is he going to mention it? No.

"Look, Hugo, I wanted you from the moment I first saw you." *Back before you even knew I existed,* I think. "You and no one else, okay? Really."

"And then this morning —"

426

"What about this morning?"

"Well, I woke up because I heard screams. I thought for sure it was someone outside being attacked. That maybe Mrs. Lee was hurt or something." I'm careful not to look annoyed at the mention of Mrs. Lee. "But it was you. You were screaming right beside me. Your eyes were wide open but you were asleep. You were screaming something."

He looks frightened now.

I think of the little statue of Mary I saw on his dresser. *Didn't know you were religious,* I said to him.

I'm not. Not really. I stole her from the jail library. I know it's stupid, but she comforted me. So I keep her. She's sort of a talisman.

"We talked about this, and I told you. It's just production anxiety," I say. "I have weird anxiety dreams around this time of year. You know how it is."

He nods. He knows how it is, of course he does.

"It just reminded me of jail. People having nightmares all around me. Screaming in their sleep. You sure there's nothing you want to tell me?"

"I'm fine. Really. Really, really."

"I'm just hoping you're happy with me is all. I'm hoping I'm what you want. Because you're what I want, Miranda. You are."

"Are you kidding? *Of course* I'm happy with you. I'm so happy my mouth literally hurts from smiling. Seriously. Ask my students. Grace can barely stand me these days."

He smiles. Relaxes now. "How is Grace, by the way? Didn't see her on campus yesterday. We were supposed to go over some set changes but she never showed."

"Oh, she's ill, sadly. Must have caught that thing Briana got."

"You're kidding." Hugo shakes his head. "Jesus, when those things come, they really sweep, don't they?"

"They really do."

"God, I hope I don't get it."

"You? Not you. Never. I promise you."

CHAPTER 25

On my way to school from Hugo's, I decide
to stop by Grace's place. Not to disturb her
or anything, I wouldn't dream of disturbing
Grace. I don't ring the bell or knock on the
door, no, no. Just sit in my parked car and
stare at her shuttered house from across the
street. Just to make sure the flowers and Get
Well balloons get delivered all right. Just to
make sure she receives all the gifts I've given
her. Through the windshield, I watch the
delivery boy amble up to her front door, his
gangly arms encumbered with all my
thoughtful arrangements for Grace: the
tulips, the irises, the freesia — can't we all
agree that spring flowers are just the pretti-
est flowers? — and the cactus, of course, of
course. I hold my breath as he rings the
doorbell with his nose. I'm excited. Any
minute now, she'll open the door. She'll be
wearing her gray silk kimono patterned with
cherry blossoms that she loves. I bought that

robe for her. It was a gift just like these flowers are gifts. It's a kimono just like mine, like the one she admired so much when she saw it hanging on the back of my bedroom door. She even stroked a silk sleeve.

This is pretty, she said darkly.

I smile in my car now, remembering how she lifted the new robe up out of the sea of pink tissue paper I'd wrapped it in. Her blushing surprise at the sight of all that silk.

You didn't have to, Miranda, she said, putting it on right away. Now she almost never takes it off, do you, Grace? When you're at home?

She'll be wearing it now when she comes to the door, I'm sure. She'll look a little pale, a little tired maybe, but otherwise still hearty. Still Grace. I can't wait to see her face, I'll admit it. Her hard, possibly confused expression — *What is all this?* — puddling into delight, understanding, at the sight of all those bright spring flowers, all those grinning yellow balloons beaming at her. Small smile. Shake of the head. *Oh, Miranda.*

The flower boy rings the bell again and again.

So she's a little slow-moving, that's all. Obviously, I understand about that. I watch him set down my flowers and balloons on

430

the front step and begin to knock. Nothing. Another knock. Still nothing. Grace's windows stay dark, her frilly curtains drawn tight. I'm not worried at all. I'm still smiling behind the wheel as I watch the boy knock and knock at the door. One more long ring of the doorbell. And then he leaves it all there on her front steps.

I watch him drive away in his truck.

Probably just sleeping. I forgot how deep Grace can sleep. She just goes out. *Like a light,* she always used to say, snapping her fingers. I envy her that. No rest for me these days, not with showtime right around the corner, am I right? But it's fine. Really it's a welcome change. A nice break for Grace. And when she wakes, all my gifts will be waiting for her at the door.

You rest for now, Grace, while I get on with the show. Speaking of which, I'd better get a move on, hadn't I?

Tech week flies by. And I get caught up. I get lost. I work round the clock, and I don't even feel the time. Without my stage manager, I need to be in five places at once. And I am, I manage this. For days on end, my feet barely touch the ground. I'm here, I'm there. There, here, here, there. Stage left. Stage right. Lighting and sound booth. In front of the curtain, behind the curtain, watching with my arms folded, my feet rising a little off the floor from time to time. It happens within the blink of an eye, and thankfully, no one notices. I coordinate all the components, like a conductor does their orchestra. I'm with lighting, I'm with sound, I'm in the costume shop with a pincushion between my teeth driving a needle right into a ripped-up seam. I'm crawling around on the stage on my hands and knees, coaxing out the most brilliant performances. I'm inches from their faces, I'm gazing deeply into their eyes. My hands are on their shoulders, which jump only a little at my touch. I'm speaking soft, low words of encouragement, my lips very close to their pierced, fuzzy ears. They hear; they nod; they take direction. They are well-tuned instruments, and I am the player of them all.

I thought you were the conductor, Grace would say if she were here.

I'm both, all right, Grace? I'm both.

"Who are you talking to, Professor?"

"Me? Nothing. No one. Can we take it from the top, please?"

"Professor Fitch," they say, "it's one in the morning."

"Professor Fitch," they say, "I don't know,

432

but I think it's dawn."

"Professor," they whisper, "I have an eight thirty class in ten minutes."

"Let's run it one more time, shall we?" I say.

In short, it's going well, Grace. All's well. Ha.

All right, not all, Grace, not all.

Two hiccups. Minor, I'm sure you would say. We're working through them, absolutely. The first hiccup is Briana, who is back with us now. Every afternoon she hobbles silently, spectacularly, into the theater, helped by one of her girl underlings or Trevor. Back together with Trevor, I think. I'm not sure, very hard to say. She clutches Ellie's water bottle, from which she takes slow, performative sips. Ellie has never asked for it back. Instead she just stares at Briana like she's seen a ghost. And she does look like a ghost, Grace. Pale as anything. Mouth-breathing always.

"Anything I can get you, Briana?" I ask her pleasantly, always pleasantly.

"No," she whispers, then takes her seat on the lip of the stage, looking on the brink of collapse. Burns a hole in the side of my face with her glare while I lead the rest of them through a vigorous warm-up.

"Let's really push ourselves today, shall

we? Briana, would you care to join us? Or you can sit this one out. Up to you, totally," I always say. "Listen to your body, of course."

Briana doesn't answer me, just sits slumped in the corner staring at me through a veil of hate and pain, her parched lips half-open, her dark hair falling in greasy locks she's no longer bothering to wash or even brush. Her arms hang lifeless at her sides, palms up.

"Probably best if you just sit there and watch," I say.

And she does watch, too drugged to disguise her sorrow and her rage at the sight of our bodies stretching and moving before her eyes.

"Really stretch yourselves, that's it. Feels wonderful, doesn't it?"

Every rehearsal, I half expect her to point her finger at me and scream. But she doesn't say anything to me at all. There is no more talk of witch. No more pointing fingers.

On day two of tech week someone asks, "Where's Grace?" I shrug. I tell them how you're sick, sadly. And Ellie says, "Oh no, something must be going around." And I say, "Yes, Ellie, something must be." And I wait for Briana to say something. To accuse me. But she says nothing. She just sits there quietly in her corner, breathing raspily.

During rehearsal, she learns her blocking with no fuss. She takes direction with a nod, and she needs almost no direction. As the ailing King, she is everything I could have dreamed. Wonderfully wretched and desperate. Believably without hope. She limps regally across the stage, her face beautifully punched in by sorrow, her breath perfectly ragged. Everything about her face says, *I was a giant once, I was. Now look. Look at the husk I've become.*

It's brilliant. So very believable. Bravo.

The problem? The problem is the King is magically healed in Act Two by Helen. The problem is that for the rest of the play, His Majesty is positively brimming with miraculous health. The post-healing scene — where the King is so euphoric and giddy from his recovery that he is supposed to dance through the halls of the court with Helen — is particularly difficult for Briana.

Day three of tech week, I decide we really need to tackle the matter head-on.

"King of France," I tell her, "you've just been cured, remember? It's a miracle. You're well now. Show us how well you are by rejoicing." I smile encouragingly at Briana. Hunched and drowning in her kingly robes. One hand clutching her scepter like a cane.

The other gripping Ellie's shoulder like she's a human crutch.

Briana looks at me like, *How dare you. How dare you say the word* well *to me.* But then her face falls pitifully. "I can't," she says.

"Try," I say gently. And it's like I struck her. Her face becomes even more warped with self-pity. She shakes her head.

"Imagine," I say, walking up to the stage, toward her trembling body, "coming back to yourself at last. Who is this person," I ask her softly, "who can suddenly walk? Who can suddenly bend? Who can stand on two feet without a cane or a crutch? Whose feet suddenly seem to float as if on air? Who isn't afraid of staircases or chairs anymore?"

She looks at me standing before her, and I feel her cower slightly. The other students have moved off the stage. All except Ellie, who's still standing there beside Briana, sagging beneath the weight of her grip. I take a step closer.

"Only a moment ago, you were so, so heavy. What a heavy, hopeless world you lived in for so long. Limbs heavy. Heart heavy. Head muddy with useless drugs. Useless doctors. Sadistic therapists. So many white rooms. So many doctor heads shaking at you. People keeping themselves at a distance. Thinking you're lying. Thinking you're contagious. Thinking you're just unpleasant to be around now. Your tears bore people. All that sadness and fear's getting old. You're getting old. There's your life. One long gray corridor, twisting ever downward. You would do anything, anything, to go back. Go back to who you were. And then? And then along comes this stranger with a miracle in their hands. They know your pain. They know its name."

I smile. "And now, Your Majesty? Now you're suddenly filled with this impossible lightness. You want to cry, but how can you cry when you literally can't stop smiling? You'd like to, but you can't. The smile is always there now, stretching your lips. Now you laugh for no reason at all."

And I laugh to show her. I laugh and I laugh and I laugh.

"You're free," I say, still laughing. "And the freedom is exhilarating. The freedom makes you drunk. It's like the streets are suddenly perfumed. It's like you can look directly into the sun. You feel so light, like you can literally lift off the ground. You want to run, you want to dance."

Briana looks at me like I'm on fire before her very eyes. My glowing, laughing, supple self. How is it possible? It can't be possible.

437

She shakes her head. "No."

"Yes."

"I *can't.*"

"It's in the script, I'm afraid, Your Majesty," I tell her. "Following his miraculous cure, Lafeu remarks that the King is able to lead Helen in a *coranto.*"

"What's a coranto again?" Ellie says.

"Ellie, we've gone over this. It's a sort of dance. A running, jumping dance."

"A *jumping dance*?" Trevor says from the corner of the stage. "But Grace said it was more like a glide. . . ."

See? How they do miss you, Grace. You are missed.

"Well, Grace isn't here, is she? Different sources, different interpretations, am I right? I think Shakespeare would have wanted the King to do a jumping, running dance. Far more celebratory than a glide. You'll have to jump a little to do it. See? Like I'm doing, look. It's really fun."

But Briana just stands there watching me jump up and down. All the students watch. I get lost in the dance, I have to admit. Because it's such an exalting moment. Vindicating. Joyous. That taste of the air beneath your feet. That impossible lightness after such heaviness. It brings tears to your eyes, laughter to your mouth, to move like

438

that. Mark was right, movement heals, movement is king. Which is why the King must dance.

"And after you dance alone, you're supposed to dance with Helen!" I say, waving a hand at Ellie. I take Ellie's hand, leading her away from Briana, who immediately falters without her crutch. I dance with Ellie while Briana watches, while the students watch, everyone riveted. We turn ecstatic circles. Fast. Like you did as a child, remember that game? Where you turned and turned and turned with someone? Faster and faster and faster. How the laughter just fell from your mouth? Oh, it's so joyous, you wouldn't believe how joyous. The whole court is supposed to applaud, so applaud, everyone! We spin faster and faster and —

"Professor Fitch," Ellie whispers, "I'm so sorry, but I think I'm going to be sick."

I let Ellie go, and she stumbles a little, nearly falls backward on the stage, but she catches herself. All the students stop clapping. They stare at me, standing perfectly still in the center of the stage. Not even breathless. Smiling at Her Majesty the King, who gazes at me now with exhaustion.

"You see, Briana," I say. "A *display* of wellness. *That's* what's called for in this moment. A performance of health so that the audience understands. The audience will only know how deeply you have been in pain when they see how hard you dance afterward."

I turn to Ellie, sitting on the floor now, her red dress fanning around her beautifully. "Ellie, you'll have to learn to land on your feet."

"Yes, Professor."

"You both will."

"Professor," she says, "you're bleeding."

"Am I?"

She points to my lower leg. And I see that all the students are staring, looking horrified. I look down at my leg. Oh my, look at that. A gash. A gash, how did that happen? In all the running around this week, I must have hurt myself and not noticed it. I gaze at the grin-shaped gash on my shin, oozing bright red blood. Smiling at me as I smile at it. The two of us smiling at each other. Smiling because I feel absolutely nothing. Not a burn, not a sting, not a pinch. But then I remember the students are watching. So I make a show of looking disturbed. I excuse myself, go to the bathroom, and try to wash away the blood. I raise my leg onto the counter. I hold up the wound to the mirror and the light. The blood really is bright red. Thin streams of it pouring down my leg and onto my hands. *Ouch* is the word in my head, am I right? *Ouch, ouch. Ouch,* I tell my leg, but it's a lie, Grace. I feel nothing. I can only smile when I see how truly deep the gash is. Can only smile at the bright red gushing blood. *Panic,* I command myself. But my heart continues to beat steadily behind my ribs, my body a calm blue sky. I look in the mirror. I see a woman in a white dress patterned with red poppies. The blood on her hands brings out the rose color of her lips, which are still curved serenely.

I tell myself I'll go visit you again after tonight's rehearsal, Grace. Right after rehearsal, I'll check in. Instead my feet walk me backstage, where I fuck Hugo in the scene shop. He's resistant at first — "I don't think we should do this, Miranda," he says. "I really don't. Not here." But he succumbs to me in the end; he can't help it. He melts under my touch in spite of his better judgment, even as I lead him to the stage. "Let me take you back to my place."

But I don't want to go back to that sorry place with the suspicious widow and the glowing dog. "I want to be here," I say, under the starry sky of the theater.

"Let's stay here, under this sky, in this

light," I tell Hugo. Hugo, whom I keep calling Goldfish, who looks more and more like Paul every time he turns on the light to say, "Goldfish?" Whom I keep commanding to bite my shoulder, I'm curious, will I feel it? When will I feel it? Not when the teeth break skin. Not even when they hit bone, probably. But Hugo barely leaves a mark there or anywhere.

"I told you I don't want to hurt you," he says. And I laugh at the idea. That Hugo could hurt me. That anything could hurt me.

He keeps pointing to the cut on my leg, which admittedly is disturbing to see. Getting wider, darker. He wants to address it with something, alcohol, gauze. I let him bandage it up in the workshop. Watch him wrap the gauze around and around the wound.

Behind him, on a worktable, there's the maquette of *Macbeth*. The three little plastic witches are gone because one night after rehearsal I buried them in the dirt. Got on my knees on the damp campus green. Dug a hole in the earth with my bare hands. Deep, deep into the earth, I dug. I didn't have to dig so deep. The dirt just felt so wonderful between my fingers. Now there's nothing left of the maquette but its husk.

Just an empty black box. Black painted sky streaked with silver. That low red paper moon. The world of *Macbeth* in which he is trapped for the whole of the play. *A black play, Ms. Fitch.* A far cry from the rainbows and the starry cosmos of Helen.

"Why haven't you thrown that away?" I ask him now.

He looks at me like, *What a question.*

"Because I can always paint over it. Use it again. I like to salvage things where I can," he says. Not smiling. Because he's bandaging my leg. Trying to salvage me.

"I think you should burn it," I tell him.

"And I really think you should get stitches for this," he says.

Second hiccup: Ellie. Don't get me wrong, Grace. She's wonderful, she's luminous. More luminous perhaps than ever before, thanks to being presumably dumped by Trevor. He appears to have switched allegiances again — a Bertram to the core. Each day he and Briana enter and leave the theater together, walking slowly to accommodate her dragging gait. Briana leans heavily on his arm like he's a crutch. And Trevor bears her weight like a stoic Englishman at a country dance who has no choice but to take the debutante for a spin. He

443

doesn't dare look at Ellie, and neither does Briana, who still holds on to Ellie's water bottle. The pain on Ellie's face as she watches them is palpable. Her eyes are always red. Her face is gaunt and pale. She looks fantastically thin in her red dress with matching cloak, which is the costume we decided on for Helen's return from the dead. *I want the audience to see her beauty immediately,* I explained to the costume designer, a senior in the fashion department. *I want it to blaze like the sun.*

But Grace said she should look like a wretch.

There again, Grace, I had to smile at your intrusion, our little collisions of interpretation around Helen. I missed you in that moment, I did. But you need your rest, of course.

Well, Grace isn't here, is she? Besides, Grace and I discussed it again, at length. A lie to the students, Grace, is probably easier in this case than the muddy truth, I'm sure you'll agree.

And happily, now we all agree. Helen needs to look hot. And formidable.

When Helen — I mean Ellie — first tried on the dress, she took my breath away. And nothing these days takes my breath away. She would have taken your breath away too, Grace.

Oh, Helen, I said. *You look beautiful.*

And Helen looked at herself in the mirror, and she burst into tears. Overcome, I suppose. How could she not be? She's lived so long in the shadows. She cried and cried and cried. A little too intensely. I wanted to tell her to calm down, really.

All of this emotion should only help Ellie's performance, of course. Should work so wonderfully for her Helen. When she's onstage, delivering the lines *All's well that ends well yet, though time seems so adverse, and means unfit,* I shiver, Grace. And I tell her this, I tell her, "Ellie, you're making me shiver."

The problem, Grace? The problem is it's incapacitating her. She's running to the bathroom a lot, presumably to cry. She stops in the middle of her lines like she's lost.

The final day of tech week: I call the line and Ellie doesn't speak it. She just looks at me like I've spoken gobbledygook.

"Do you want the line again, Ellie?"

And she just continues to stare at me like she isn't sure who I am.

"Is something wrong?" I ask her.

Then her expression shifts. "Miranda," she says quietly, "can I talk to you, please?"

And can I tell you that when she says that

445

I know exactly what's coming? Because how many ledges have I talked them off over the years? How many tears have I wiped away from their cheeks? How many hyperventilating bodies have I told to breathe, *just breathe, my dear.* Watched their small chests heave as they tried to just breathe. *Now,* I'd say, *talk to me.* And then they'd tell me their stories. Depression stories, anxiety stories, misfit stories, bullying stories, parents-who-don't-understand-me stories, so many dead grandmothers, so many dearly departed dogs. Stories that make them stammer, that make them look at the floor, that make their eyes well up again to tell. Hyperventilate anew. Wash. Rinse. Repeat. Always the same ending: *Ms. Fitch, I just don't know if I can be in the play after all. I just don't know if I can go up there.*

Stories that tighten my chest, that make me heavy with panic, that make my heart go like a drum. That have kept my spine a different shape. Made it bow like a branch. That used to light up the red webs. Grace, it's no wonder, really, that I had a dead leg for so long.

I look at Ellie now. Standing there like she's about to faint. Her fingers twitching of their own accord at her sides. It's so perfect, her anguish. So scene-appropriate.

If only she would speak her line. *All's well that ends well yet, though time seems so adverse, and means unfit.*

"Here is your line, Helen," I say encouragingly. "Speak."

But Ellie runs offstage, her red dress billowing behind her.

"All right, everyone," I say. "Take five."

I float out into the hall, where I find her sitting on the floor against the brick wall. Clutching her knees to her chest. Head in her hands. Weeping, presumably. This is the moment when normally I would crouch down to the floor. I'd say, *What's wrong? What can I do?* But these words, even though I mean to speak them, I want to speak them, don't leave my lips.

Instead I just stare down at her hunched pathetically on the floor.

She becomes aware of my shadow falling over her. Looks up.

"Miranda," she says at last through her tears. "I'm so sorry."

It's all right, Ellie. Of course it's all right, I should say. But I say nothing. My lips stay closed, smiling. My silence has the effect of making her gather herself.

She stops crying abruptly. She shakes her head. "I'm sorry, Professor," she says again. "I just don't know if I can do this."

447

"Do what?" I say. And I'm surprised to hear that my voice sounds cold, threatening, impatient. She looks at me like I've slapped her. Then she looks back down at her knees. Shakes her head sorrowfully. "This is all my fault. All of it."

"All your fault? I don't understand."

"I shouldn't be in the play anymore."

I crouch down low before her. I lift her chin up to meet my eye. Her face looks punched. Her colorless eyes are swollen. Snot is trickling from her nose down to her lips, which are crackled and trembling.

"Please don't make me play Helen, Miranda. It's too much."

"Ellie, of course you're going to play Helen. You are Helen."

"I don't know if I can."

I reach out my hand and trace her face with my finger. She doesn't flinch. She closes her eyes at my touch. This is what she wanted. All she wanted in the first place. My consolation. My understanding. Fresh tears stream down her cheeks. Oh, the pain of loving this idiotic boy.

"Ellie, sometimes pain is a gift for an actor. And we can use it to deepen our performances. Pain can make us better. It's actually made you a better Helen, it really has."

"I just feel terrible. Taking this part away

from Briana," she whispers.

Oh god, really? How her offstage anguish about this bores me now. But I attempt sympathy.

"You didn't take the part away, Ellie. That's absurd. She got *sick*. People just get sick, sadly."

She laughs, a little miserably. "Do they?" She shakes her head. "I don't know about that."

"What are you saying, Ellie?"

Then she looks at me seriously. "I wanted something like this to happen, Ms. Fitch," she whispers.

"What do you mean?"

She shakes her head at her knees. "I just wanted this role so badly." And then she bursts into tears again. I picture Ellie lying in her dorm room — probably painted purple or black — surrounded by waxy red candles, tears leaking out of her cat-lined eyes, wishing Briana ill.

"Ellie, wanting something isn't a crime."

"What if you want a terrible thing?"

"Sometimes we wish for terrible things, things we deserve. How could we not wish for them when we deserve them? And sometimes the heavens hear us. Something hears us. And our wishes come true. Should we feel guilty? Of course we shouldn't feel guilty, why guilty? Why guilty when we deserve it, when maybe, just maybe, it's a question of justice?" I smile. "Anyway, it all worked out in the end, didn't it? Briana's back."

"She looks awful."

"She looks wonderful. Doing better than ever before, really, as an actress. You could almost say she's been given a gift." I smile encouragingly, but Ellie looks miserable.

"She's getting worse, Miranda."

"She's not getting worse! She's just playing it up for the role."

"I just feel —"

"Ellie, listen to me: this is a ridiculous conversation. You are Helen. You will play Helen. It's what you wanted, and, miracle of miracles, you got it. We're one day from opening night and you are not going to back out now, do you understand me? It's too late now. Too late for guilt, too late for tears. And as your director, as your teacher, as your *friend* — and I do like to think I'm your friend, Ellie — I will *not* allow your guilt to stand in the way of what you so completely deserve. I will not allow guilt to dog you like this. People get sick and people get better and it's nothing to do with us. The wheel of fortune, Ellie. The wheel, the wheel, always turning. Look at me."

She does look at me. She looks at me a long time, how I'm glowing. My impossible lightness, so light my feet barely seem to touch the earth. How I'm always on the verge of laughter, even now. How even now, my lips are close to smiling though I know this is so serious. Can't help it. Too happy. Blood happy, bones happy, cells always singing.

She reaches into her pocket and pulls out a ziplock baggie full of craggy pink salt spiked with prickly-looking twigs. Small dried flowers of all colors. Immediately a pungent forest scent rises up.

"I made some adjustments to the recipe this week," she says gravely.

She hands me the bag, heavy with putrid essential oils and god knows what herbs she grows in some secret campus shade. Dutifully, I slip it into the pocket of my dress and smile.

"Thank you, Ellie," I say. "Thank you so much."

So a couple of hiccups. Just a couple of hiccups, Grace. In short though? In short, we really are doing wonderfully, don't you think? Another great rehearsal, am I right?

But Grace isn't here, I remember. I'm by myself in the theater again. Standing on the stage alone after they've all shuffled off into the predawn dark. The space beside me where Grace usually stands, holding a giant mug of coffee and smoking an illicit cigarette, is empty, just motes of swirling dust in the light. I recall how I left her, lying on her side in her bedroom with her mouth open, looking up at me from the deep dark wells of her eyes. But then I think of all those lovely flowers waiting on her doorstep, those grinning balloons. It makes me smile to remember that. She'll have picked them up by now, surely? She hasn't reached out just yet to say thank you. No answer to the text I sent days ago, a tulip emoji plus a balloon emoji followed by a question mark followed by a winky face. Probably just conserving her energy for healing. Probably my gifts are helping with that, of course they are. I'll bet they're cheering her up as we speak.

Now I text her, ☺?? When she doesn't respond, I don't panic at all. Nothing beats its black wings in me. My heart doesn't pound. Indeed, the place where my heart is is deliriously open as a field, light as air. I'll text her again, I think. No, I'll call, that's much better, isn't it? A voice is better than a text, am I right? When you're not well? Remember not being well? I can hardly remember at all. But instead of calling her, I send her another Instacart delivery. I add more restorative items to the cart. Rainier cherries. Dragon fruit. Ginger chews. Steaks for the iron in the blood. Elderflower water. In the morning, I'll call the flower shop and I'll ask them to send more balloons. Another cactus, please. I'll call the liquor store for more champagne.

Really hope you're getting rest, I text. *I've got everything covered here.* ☺

I've got everything covered, Grace. Really, I do. "Miranda, who are you talking to?"

I look up from my phone. Paul. Standing there in the doorway of the theater. Dressed strangely. Hair longer. Looking slightly afraid of me.

"What are you doing here, Goldfish? Have you come to see the show? You're early. We don't open until tomorrow."

"Miranda, are you all right?"

Hugo. Just Hugo standing there with a coffee in hand. Black Sabbath T-shirt under a weathered plaid shirt. Over that, a worn biker jacket studded with pins.

"Fine," I say. "Long night. Eyes playing tricks on me."

"You should go home. Get some rest before tomorrow night. Tonight, I guess, now," he says, looking at his phone.

453

"I need to be here. Grace isn't here, sadly, so I need to be."

"You need sleep, Miranda."

"I don't need *sleep;* Grace needs sleep. I don't need anything at all. All's well and we're doing wonderfully."

"You're bleeding again," he says.

"Am I?"

He comes over to me and kneels down. Looks at my leg, which is indeed bleeding again. He traces the wound with his finger, tenderly. So tenderly I can't help but close my eyes. So much tenderness now. Over what? A little cut. A cut that doesn't even hurt at all. I could drown in this tenderness, suffocate under all these soft words, these soft touches and looks. Where was it all before? Where was all this tenderness when I needed it most, when I was lying on the floor dreaming of a touch like this, of a voice that would say something, anything, kind? Nowhere. Then his face was a shut door. His heart was closed like a fist. His hands stayed at his sides and his eyes observed my weeping like unfortunate weather. Something to be borne until it passed.

"Does that hurt?" he asks me now, touching my leg like I'm such a delicate, wounded thing.

"No," I say. "Not even a little bit."

I run my fingers over the fine blond hairs at the back of his neck. Golden in the light. "Just a little blood, Paul. Just a little blood, for fuck's sake, that's all." I smile.

Underneath my hand, his neck stiffens. Suddenly all the tenderness in his face goes out like a light. He brushes my hand away, gets up, and walks away from me.

"Where are you going?" I ask.

"Work," he mutters over his shoulder.

"Wait! What's wrong? Tell me."

He stops. Turns to me again, shaking his head. "I just don't understand it."

"Don't understand what?"

"I don't understand why you're not feeling it."

"Not feeling what?"

He looks at me. *You know what. This. You and I.* But he says, "That cut."

He looks down at my leg and frowns. Pouts, really. I can't help but laugh, but Hugo doesn't laugh with me. He just looks at me dead serious. Offended.

"God, what is it with you and this cut?" I say. "Do you *want* me to feel it? Is that it?"

"No, I don't *want* you to feel it, I just don't understand how you can't."

"It's just a little fucking cut."

"It's an open *wound,* Miranda."

I shrug. "People have different degrees of pain tolerance. It's all relative." I smile to show him how it's relative. But he's still frowning at my leg, at the cut that goes on grinning.

"Are you on drugs, is that it?" he says. So serious.

"*What?* No. No, no, no." I shake my head.

"Do you have that condition where people don't feel pain? I saw this whole thing about it on *60 Minutes.*"

"Did you?"

He nods. He looks at me so earnestly, so hopeful even. Wanting me to tell him, yes, that's it. Absolutely. That's me. I'm this thing he saw on *60 Minutes.* That's all this is, this happiness, this health, this immunity. Waiting for me to explain my smile as an affliction.

"You really want me to feel pain, don't you? You want me to hurt. That's a bit sick, don't you think?"

"I don't want you to *hurt.* But if something is supposed to hurt, then yes, I want you to hurt. You're human."

He reaches out and touches my cheek. So fucking tenderly. A tenderness that says, *Go on. Break for me. I'll pick up every piece of you, promise.*

"You wanted those people you assaulted

to hurt, didn't you?" I say to him. "You wanted them to be in pain."

Silence now. He drops his hand from my cheek. His expression shifts, darkens. A shimmer of violence, of who he used to be, flashes across his face like lightning. For a second, he looks like someone who would have held a knife. Pointed its blade at a pulsating throat. I can see those hands on a neck, wringing. Those eyes watching the breath leave a face, watching it turn blue above his grip. No remorse in those eyes. Those eyes looking at me now. Then he looks away.

"Yes, I did," he says quietly, shaking his head like he could shake it all away. "But I was a different person then. And that was a different time in my life. And I can tell you I suffered a hell of a lot more than they did. In the end."

I watch him stare remorsefully at the floor. I have a flash of Hugo in jail. His redemption through Shakespeare and a cheap little Mary statue he stole from the library. Hugo kneeling before it in his orange jumpsuit, a broken, repentant man whispering his paltry sins into her little bump of an ear. Feeling so atoned by this. Forgiven. Reading Shakespeare plays in his cell under her lidless gaze. Discovering a world of complicated monsters. Building his first sets, making that world come alive without a hammer. Learning life skills through *The Tempest, Macbeth, Richard III.* Performing stories of men who cross line after line after line. Thinking, *Not me anymore.* Thinking, *Never again.* The Mary statue sits on his bedroom dresser now beside a dog-eared *Collected Works of Shakespeare.* She watches him with her painted smile while he sleeps. He dreams so peacefully. I've seen him sleep like this, with my eyes wide open. Always wide open now. I think of Grace's open eyes. Staring at me as I glowed with stolen health before her.

"What, am I supposed to feel guilty?" I say.

He looks confused. "Guilty?"

"That I feel fine for once? That I'm not limping and moaning around? Dragging my leg like Briana? Lying on the floor, crying into my ears while everyone else around me rolls their eyes? I'm supposed to feel bad that I'm better now? I'm supposed to cry over a little cut. To what? To make you feel like I'm not a monster. I need to perform my little bit of pain for you so you'll know I'm *human?*"

"Miranda, I didn't mean —"

"But not too much pain, am I right? Not too much, never too much. If it was too much, you wouldn't know what to do with me, would you? Too much would make you uncomfortable. Bored. My crying would leave a bad taste. That would just be bad theater, wouldn't it? A bad show. You want a good show. They all do. A few pretty tears on my cheeks that you can brush away. Just a delicate little bit of ouch so you know there's someone in there. So you don't get too scared of me, am I right? So you know I'm still a vulnerable thing. That I can be brought down if need be."

He looks at me. "Miranda, that's really not what I —"

"Why don't we try it? Why don't you try hurting me right now and see? See if I can feel it. See if you can make me feel it. Make me cry out. You probably like a little of that, don't you?"

A flicker of recognition in his eyes. *Yes.* He likes a little of that. Of course he does. But he plays shocked, confused. Looks at me like I'm fucking crazy.

"What? No. Of course not," he says. Shakes his head again and again as I move in closer to him. Asking him to pull my hair, to punch me in the gut, go on. To strangle me if it turns him on. Does it turn him on? *Yes.*

"*No.* Miranda, look, stop this, okay? I'm

leaving. I'm —"

But I've already grabbed his hands and put them around my neck. He tries to resist but my grip is surprisingly strong, my strength surprises both of us. He looks at me in horror as he tries to pry his hands away, but he can't now. I'm holding his hands down. Holding them down around my neck. His hands encircling my throat.

"Miranda, what the fuck are you doing?"

"Go on," I tell him. "Hurt me."

He shakes his head, horrified. So appalled by the fact of his own hands around my throat. The drumming of my pulse under his thumbs. He tries to pull away again but I hold him there.

"Is this what you did?" I ask him quietly. "Was it like this?"

He shakes his head again. I press his hands deeper into my neck.

"It's all right, you didn't mean to. We never mean to, do we? Or maybe we do. Maybe we fucking do mean to, don't we? Anyway, it's done, isn't it? No going back now. Too late, am I right? So do it. You know you want to. I feel it. I feel it from you."

I drop my hands. Now he's the one gripping my neck all by himself. His hands, resting hot on either side, holding tight. Each thumb poised above the clavicle. Ready to

460

press. I know he's tempted to press into my flesh and see. Will he leave a bruise? Will he leave a mark like Mark used to? All of Mark's little marks. All those soft black, purple, and yellow spots blooming down my legs and flanks, the strangest watercolors. John's welts on my thigh. The surgeon's scars on my hip. Three prongs like a pitchfork under the Scotsman's tongue. And Paul? The hurts Paul inflicted, his marks, are on the inside. Does Hugo want to leave his mark too? Here on the neck where the skin is so thin, shot through with blue veins, right here in the little hollow where my pulse jumps. See what I'm made of? See if he can make me cry, make me scream?

"You want to. I know you do. They all do."

He wrenches his hands away from my neck. Wrenches his hands away like I'm the one still holding them there. He drops his hands like he's awakened from a terrible dream. He hasn't had one like this in a long, long time. He looks at me. Wide-eyed. Afraid.

Then he walks away. He doesn't look back once as he pushes through the exit doors. Gold hair glowing in the dark morning. Red-gold like a fish.

"Probably just as well," I call after him. "You couldn't handle my pain. Couldn't

CHAPTER 26

I drive home in the predawn dark, singing. I'm really my own radio these days. I tell myself I'll stop at Grace's on the way home again. Just to check in on her. Definitely. Make sure she's all right. *All's well?* I'll ask her.

But I don't stop at Grace's on the way home this time. I keep driving. Keep my hands on the wheel, my foot on the pedal. I turn up the music. Up, up, up. The song is so lovely, isn't it? It really transports you. I float above my seat. Literally. Surely because the music is so uplifting. Judy singing about being happy. Poor Judy who was mostly so sad. Who wouldn't levitate to hear Judy sing? What did Paul once say to me about Beethoven's "Ode to Joy"? That it sounded like the happiness that can only come after great sorrow, great pain. Judy is my "Ode to Joy." "Zing! Went the Strings of My Heart" is a happy roar all around me now. I turn it

463

up higher. Not only because I love it but because lately there's been this other sound I've been hearing. Scares me a little, if I'm honest, but I've really been too busy, far too busy, to deal with it. At first, I wasn't even sure, was it even a sound? Was I even hearing something? It was so very slight. Far away and close at the same time. Underneath everything, like a hum. Could you call it music? You could call it an underneath music. I wasn't even sure if it was outside or if it was inside. Could it be inside? Surely it was outside, I told myself, and I forgot all about it, there was so much to do. But no, no it was inside. Definitely inside. Inside me somewhere. Something like a drone. A drone? No, that doesn't even make sense but, yes, a drone. In my skull. Surely my head doesn't have a skull anymore. My head feels far too light for a skull. I'm hearing it now. Just under this song like a bass, but it's not a bass sound. More like the music has a lower floor, a basement that Judy's "Zing!" doesn't know about. Dark and unfinished. Full of boilers. *Dread* is the word that comes to mind. *Dread, dread, dread.* I see the word in my mind as black stones. But I don't fill with dread. At all, at all. I put my fingers on the dial and turn up the volume. I drown it out with Judy's joy, which really can't be any louder.

I think of the toe tapping of the three men. And I look into my rearview mirror, just to check. Just to see if anyone's behind me, back there on the road, following me. I'm doing that lately. Just checking, just looking behind me. Nothing ever back there. Nothing back there now. Just some dark dawn. That's good. Because lately there's been this feeling, along with the noise, along with the hum inside, I feel it on the back of my neck, raising the small hairs there. Of eyes. Of watching. Being watched. Who's watching me? Never anyone when I turn my head. Never anyone even when I turn all the way round. Again and again and again.

Professor Fitch, did you lose something? they ask me when I do this in rehearsal.

Lose? I say. I haven't lost.

Professor Fitch, are you looking for something?

Nothing. No one.

The only problem with this feeling, the feeling of eyes watching me, following me, dogging me, is that no sound can drown it out. Not even Judy cranked all the way up. It's always there. On the nape of my neck. Making the hairs stand on end, the skin prickle. Making me drive a little faster now. My foot pressing down on the pedal. My car door, that the hum would be gone. But the hum is now a roar. *Just the waves,* I tell myself. *The black waves.* And no eyes on me here, though I feel them still. On the back of my neck. Although where could there be eyes here? I turn around and around and around to be sure. No eyes.

And then something fizzes and bubbles around me like champagne. A shimmer of brightly colored lights like a flash on the water. By the light of the moon, I see what looks like pine needles, twigs, flowers, floating around me in the white hissing foam. A sweet, earthy scent rises up from the waves. Botanical. Familiar. Thick. Like a million essential oils mixed. Like suddenly there's a boreal forest in the ocean. In the ocean? How could that be?

I look at the tiny needles and petals floating around me under the bright moon, my eyes beginning to close. Close on the flashing waves, close on the black sky. Like I might actually sleep here. Sleep hasn't come easily these days. Hasn't come at all, really. What comes is the night, then the day, then the night again. And my eyes always wide open. Taking in all the light, all the dark, never closing.

But here, now, with my hands in the cold, rocking sea, these flowers blooming all around me, my eyes close at last. Black sky. Bright stars . . .

And then blue. Blue so bright it hurts my eyes.

I'm lying on the rocks in a heap like I fell from the sky. My body on black sharp stones fuzzed with green. But I feel no pain at all. Sorry, Goldfish. No tears for you. I feel gorgeous. My open hands are full of sand. My hair is filled with seaweed and small flowers. My poppy dress, I see, is dripping, crusted with salt. I've lost a shoe, it seems. Judy's still playing from the open car door. Still "Zing! Went the Strings of My Heart."

The caw of crows and the caw of gulls circling above me in the blue, blue sky. One crow perched on a rock nearby. Not three. See? No one's watching me.

Then two more fly down to join the one. Each black crow on his own black rock.

Something is ringing in the sand. My phone somewhere, must be.

Opening night tonight, I remember. And look, I'm all dressed. I'm ready.

CHAPTER 27

Opening night. Usually it's a shit show. Usually I'm drunk on the floor in my office smoking and staring at the ceiling until the ceiling becomes a stage upon which I replay certain former glories. I'm Perdita in pastoral exile singing prettily to my flowers. I'm Lady M ablaze with dark ambition, pleading for the night to fall thick, *That my keen knife see not the wound it makes.* I'm Helen in my long red dress, lamenting my love for Bertram under a bright Scottish sky. The sweet smell of spring wafts in through my open office window. Making me so full of life, so aware of my living death, I could weep. The window carries their inane conversations up to me. About lighting. About sound. About *Places, everyone, places.* Grace's managerial voice. Fauve's shrill laughter. Briana's whine. The floor trembles with their boundless animal energy. Usually I can't go down there, won't go down there.

Can't watch them run. Can't watch the excitement, the jittery energy I used to live for. Can't watch Briana's glee nor Ellie's quiet death. It will all literally kill me. *Do it without me this year, please,* I always think. I'm good up here. I'm Helen on my imagined ceiling stage. I haven't fallen off the stage yet. My life is still ahead of me, not behind. The sun is still in its zenith. My hip still in its socket, labrum untorn, my spine a supple S. And look, there's Paul at the edge of the stage with flowers. He doesn't love or hate me yet. Hasn't even met me yet. He's just a handsome man without a name, holding a bouquet of spring flowers. *For you. I so enjoyed your performance.*

Until Grace shows up.

Showtime, Miranda, she'll say.

Is it? I'll say.

She'll help me down the stairs. But I never want to go. *Do I have to go?* I'll ask her.

Yes.

Oh god, I'll whisper. *Oh god oh god oh god.* All the way down the stairs.

Then? Then I'm in a nightmare for four hours. Standing crookedly in the far corner of a series of disasters that harden my limbs, that make my heart drum. I attempt to close my eyes, and it's no good. My shoulder is tapped. My cardigan sleeve is tugged. High-pitched voices disturb the air very close to my face. *Ms. Fitch! Ms. Fitch! Ms. Fitch?!*

I drown in their questions.

Ms. Fitch, where's my hat?

Ms. Fitch, where do I come in again?

Ms. Fitch, where do I exit again?

Ms. Fitch, what's my cue again?

Ms. Fitch, what do we do at the end again? Do we bow? How do we bow again?

I never know the answer. They bear legitimate witness to my incompetence, my inebriation, until the curtains part for showtime. And at last, I'm able to retreat. Shake off the pretense that I'm actually doing something. Melt into the backstage dark, a ghost spying on the living.

Tonight? Tonight's different. Look at me, I'm here. Right here behind the curtain. In the eye of the storm. I'm standing on my legs. Standing straight. Standing tall. I'm a shining tower of calm behind the curtain. My body emanating two words: *All's Well.* And all is well. Not dying at all for once. Not a ghost for once. Not even pale. So I'm trickling a little blood from my shin. It's fine. I'm roses. They gasped a little when I entered the theater. Because I looked so wonderful. Didn't even need to shower or change. Why shower, after all, when I washed myself in the sea? Why change when my poppy dress looks so good on me?

Professor Fitch, are you all right? they said when they saw me. They stared at my dripping hair and dress streaked with seaweed and salt. Looking so concerned I almost laughed. Oh, children.

I'm wonderful. All's well. All's well here. You're the ones with the scrunched-up faces.

Professor Fitch, we need to get into the dressing rooms, they're locked. Do you have the key? They pointed to the closed dressing room door.

Of course, I have the key, I said. I looked down at my hands, which were empty of all but glittering sand grains. I felt the pockets of my poppy dress. Nothing in there but seaweed and some herbal mulch. A few shells I collected at the water's edge all morning and afternoon. The colors were so entrancing, the iridescence so shimmering.

Professor?

Must have lost it, I said. *In the waves.* And I tried to sound sad about this, but it was hard when there was this grin sliding around my face.

Where's Grace? one of them said. *She must have the key.*

Grace? I said. *Grace isn't here. Grace had to go.*

Where did she go?

Home, I said. *She went home. I took her there. I helped her up the stairs. I tucked her in. Now about this door,* I said, and then I kicked it hard, and just like that, the door opened right up. *There you are children,* I said. *What are we waiting for? In you go.*

And they just stared at me. You should have seen their faces.

Go on in, I told them. *We just need to put on a good show. They just want to see a good show. That's all they want. All they said they wanted.*

Who's "they," Professor?

The three men, of course.

The three men?

They gave me a gift. I'm not tired at all. Grace is tired, that's why I let her sleep. Let her rest. I didn't want to wake her. But me, I'm not ever tired. I slept a little last night in the sea.

In the sea?

Oh it was lovely. Have you ever slept there? The waves are just like a blanket. The black waves give you dark green dreams.

Professor, you're bleeding.

So awake all the time. Eyes wide open. Taking in all the light. They came to see a good show. We have to give them a good show. So

473

let's get a move on, shall we? Chop, chop. Ticktock.

Now I look out into the theater from behind the curtain. Full house tonight. When did we ever have a full house? Not ever. Not even for one of Fauve's hideous musicals. Full house except three. Three vacant seats in the front row, dead center. RESERVED written ominously in block letters on a sheet of paper taped to each. No sign of them. No sign of those suits, those tapping leather feet. Those eyes that know me.

We just want to see a good show, Ms. Fitch.

The auditorium keeps filling. Can you believe this turnout, Grace? Grace isn't here, I have to remember. Grace is resting. She needs her rest. Better she isn't here tonight. People pouring in from every open door. Some parents. Some students. Some . . . are they locals? People I've never seen before. Not from the school. People who appear to be, are they pushing open the theater doors?

"Professor Fitch, I think Peter might need your help," Dennis says, pointing to the double doors, where a chubby boy in a bow tie looks frightened.

I run to the doors, to Peter, who is standing there clutching his last program like a

474

sad shield.

"What's going on here?" I ask Peter.

Peter, I recall now, played a tree two years ago in my highly conceptual and somewhat unorthodox production of *As You Like It*. Human trees were crucial to my vision. And yet his was a valiant but ultimately wanting performance. Moved too much. I took him aside. Quietly, I told him, *Peter, the role of usher is highly underrated. Perhaps this is your niche. In the theater, we all have our roles to play.* Peter, poor wretch, believed me.

"Professor Fitch," Peter says to me now, "these people want to come in, and they don't have tickets."

"Don't have tickets?" I gaze at the crowd. A sea of bodies cloaked in semiformal wear. Faces I don't recognize. All gazing at me and Peter, at the doors to the theater. Angry, impatient, murmuring to one another. Holding cups of wine. How did they get wine? And then I see an open bar by the foyer doors. A man in a black shirt pouring drinks. People in long lines, ordering. Who the hell are all these people? A woman in a fur coat appears to be their ambassador. She stands at the helm with a glass of champagne, staring at me. Her eyebrows are drawn in thickly with brown pencil. Her lips are bright red. Beside her is a funny little man who looks like an elf. He's wearing a hat with a feather in it and leering at me.

"We want to see a good show," he says.

"We were told it was going to be a good show," the woman says to me.

"That's all we want to see, Ms. Fitch. A good show." Did she just call me Ms. Fitch?

Peter looks at me.

"Of course. It is going to be a good show," I tell them. "A very good show. May I ask if you have a ticket?"

"Of course we have tickets," the woman says. "What are we, animals?" She holds up two tickets I've never seen before. Red as the poppies on my dress. ADMIT ONE.

Then I notice everyone in the crowd, their hands. Each hand clutching a red ticket like this. Panic rising like black waves. I let them carry me. I smile more widely at the crowd.

"All right, Peter, let them in."

"But, Professor, those aren't even our tickets," Peter says.

"Sure they are," I lie.

Peter looks perturbed by this betrayal. Then he narrows his eyes. He has embodied the role of usher so completely. "Professor, I'm sorry, but I think you're lying to me."

I look at Peter, my inept former tree.

476

"Peter, listen to me. Let these people in, all right? They have tickets. You don't turn anyone away with tickets."

"But there's no room. The theater's full!"

"So get chairs from the props room and line them up along the aisles."

Peter looks appalled. "But, Professor, that's a fire hazard!"

"Peter, theater is about *risk,* all right? Whoever said theater was safe? No one. This is your moment to shine. These people came to see a good show and we can't let them down, okay? You can't let them down. I believe in you, Peter. So much. All right?"

"Professor Fitch!"

I turn. Ashley/Michelle, half-dressed as Diana the virgin. Face flushed with some sort of drama. "You have to come backstage now, Professor. It's Briana."

Of course it is, I think. *Absolutely it is.*

"Briana," I say. "What about Briana?"

"She's sick. I think she's getting worse," Ashley/Michelle says with unconcealed glee. "I don't think she'll be able to go onstage!"

I run to the back. There is Briana, her body draped dramatically across two plastic chairs. Looking frail yet regal in her fake beard and glittering robe. Leaning on her scepter. Face quite pale. She's mouth-breathing quickly. Fauve's kneeling at her

477

side, of course she is. A small cluster of the cast is gathered around them, looking on helplessly. Trevor stands nearby, dressed in his Bertram costume, which suits him well. Making little fists at his sides that keep opening and closing. He looks sheepish, culpable. Like Briana's body is a bike he crashed into a tree.

"I found her like this, just collapsed backstage," Ashley/Michelle says, pointing at Briana.

"I wasn't *collapsed*. I'm *fine*."

"You're *not* fine," Fauve says, turning to look pointedly at me. And then her face changes. She takes in my dripping dress, my hair of seaweed. Horror, then happiness. My ruin, she thinks wrongly. So wrongly. I've never been better.

"Miranda," she gasps. "Are you —"

"Wonderful. I'm wonderful."

I gaze down at Briana's pale body. Small and broken-looking. A sheen of sweat on her face.

"How are we feeling tonight, Briana?" I ask, the picture of professionalism, politeness. Briana looks up at me from her reclined position on the two chairs. Inscrutable, her expression. Too dark to fully see her eyes. Suddenly I can't help but feel like Mark. The way he looked down at my hunched, fallen body in the treatment room. Impatient. Bored. Annoyed. Is she truly sick? Or is this her revenge? Her true performance? Impossible to say, really. She's improved so much as an actress.

"Fine," she says quietly. "Ready."

She looks at me. A small, sickly smile across her deathly-pale face.

"I feel wonderful," she says. "All's well."

"You're not well," Fauve insists, shaking her head. "Miranda, please do something. She's really ill."

I look at Ashley/Michelle and Fauve, kneeling at Briana's side. Ashley/Michelle is stroking Briana's forehead, taking Briana's hand like she saw perhaps in a painting of a martyr. Fauve is crouched down beside her like her Prince Charming. Trying to ask her questions. Would she like to go home? *No!* A nurse? *No.* Can she please at least bring her parents backstage? *NO!*

Now Briana pulls her hand away from Fauve's grasp. She bats Ashley/Michelle's fingers off her forehead. "I said I was fine." She's staring dead at me.

Fear flutters in my heart. I feel myself rising off the ground, an inch, maybe two. Briana observes this from where she lies mouth-breathing on the chairs and says nothing. Just observes it dully, unfazed. Her teacher levitating off the ground. Everyone else is too focused on Briana to notice me.

"I'm going on," she repeats to me.

"Miranda," Fauve says, "you can't possibly let her go on like this. Who's her understudy?"

"Dennis," Ashley/Michelle says. She points at a boy in the corner, dressed like First Lord.

Dennis pales. He shakes his head. "Oh god, Professor. Please don't make me."

"Dennis should go on instead," Fauve says.

"No!" Briana croaks.

Dennis looks at me pleadingly. "Professor, do I have to go on?"

"I'm going on," Briana insists quietly.

"See she wants to go on," Dennis says.

"She can't go on!" Fauve screams at Dennis.

"I'm going on," Briana says, staring at me. It sounds like a threat.

"Professor Fitch!" Peter's round face appears in the curtain. "We're filled to beyond capacity now. I put the chairs in the fire exits and now there are no more chairs and there are still people coming in! What do I do? Can I tell them to go now?"

"No, Peter. Find a way."

I can feel him still hovering there between

the curtains. Silent. *A way?* I can feel him thinking. *How can I find a way if there is no way?*

I look back at Briana. So sickly and intent. *What do you have in store for me? Are you going to kill my play? Are you going to have your revenge? Show everyone what I did to you?* What will that even look like? I picture the various outcomes. Briana in her kingly beard. Breaking the fourth wall in the midst of her soldiership speech. Pointing her trembling finger. Accusing me of sorcery. Or will she just sabotage her performance? Mess up her lines? Faint spectacularly beneath the bright lights? Will she purposely fall off the stage? Smiling as the crowd gasps and leaps to its feet. All those cameras flashing in her eyes and she'll welcome the blindness.

"How are you going to play the part where the King is magically healed by Helen? You're supposed to do a dance, remember?"

She could barely do it in the run-throughs this week. Just sat there watching me demonstrate the dance again and again, spinning and jumping with Ellie.

"I'm going on," Briana says, shaking her head. "I'm going on, I'm going on, and there isn't a goddamned thing any of you can do about it!" Tears fill her eyes.

481

The black waves of panic rise. The drum of my heart beating wildly.

"Professor Fitch," Dennis whispers. "Should I go on?"

"Five minutes to curtain, Miranda," Fauve says smilingly. I look through the curtain. Peter is turning circles in a sea of chairs. All fire exits filled. Every chair filled with a body. Only those three reserved seats in front row center are still empty. On one side of them sits the dean and his wife. On the other, Briana's parents staring right at me through a crack in the curtain, holding cups of foyer wine. My stomach flips.

"A good show! We're here to see a good show," I hear in the murmuring crowd.

Peter sees me looking through the curtain and mouths my name. *Professor Fitch, help!*

I close the curtain.

"What the hell is going on out there? I've never seen it like that," Fauve says.

"Well, you know *All's Well That Ends Well.* It's a hit."

Fauve looks at me strangely, suspiciously. "Where's Grace? I called and called and couldn't get an answer. I even drove by her place yesterday and knocked on the door. Nothing."

"Resting. She's resting."

"*Resting* on opening night?"

"I told her I'd take care of things."

Fauve stares at me. I stare right back.

"Right after the play I'm going to go and see her again," she says. "I think we should both go. And if she doesn't answer, I think we should call the police."

"Absolutely," I say. I don't even fucking hesitate a second.

She keeps staring at me. Waiting for me to break, repent, confess. Confess what? She knows nothing. And yet I see her dreams of my capitulation right there in the hungry brightness of her eyes. Something is fucking afoot, she knows it. Doesn't know what exactly. Doesn't care. Because whatever it is is delicious. Whatever it is spells my end. Her beginning and my end.

"Absolutely, we should," I say to Fauve. "You and I together. Hand in hand."

I smile and reach out my hand to her.

"Miranda!" says a voice. A hot grip on my arm. Pulling me away from Fauve into the wings. "Miranda, please. I need to talk to you."

Ellie in her Act One dress. A dress exactly like the one I wore how many years ago. Dark hair pulled back. Clutching Kleenex, which is slightly anachronistic. Already crying beautifully. Helen. My Helen. It's like looking into a mirror.

"Helen," I breathe, "you look so perfect."

She starts to cry again.

"Helen, please," I tell her. "Please, save your tears for Act One. Let them fall then, all right?"

"Miranda, I just want you to know I didn't mean for it to go this far. I swear I didn't."

"For what to go this far?"

She looks at the floor. "Briana," she whispers.

Oh Jesus Christ, not this again. "Ellie, what did I tell you only yesterday? Remember? About the wheel? Wishing for something won't make —"

"I didn't just wish for it, Miranda," she says now.

"What?"

"I didn't just wish for it," she repeats. "I did more than just wish for it." She lowers her eyes. "A lot more."

Oh god. "Ellie —"

"I know you don't want to believe that I'm capable of such a thing, Miranda. Good little Ellie." She shakes and shakes her head as if it's all too much. "But I am capable. I am."

"What did you do to her?" I ask her. But she just begins to cry again. So overcome by her notion of her own dark will. I picture her eyes shut tight in her dorm room as she

484

calls upon the Harpies. Casting her hex by tealights.

"Look, Ellie, this is absurd, do you hear me? It's just not possible. None of it is. It's coincidence is all, all right?"

She looks up at me. "I healed you, didn't I?"

"Healed me?"

"With my baths, remember?"

She gazes at me with such hope. I should just say I never used the fucking baths. Forgot they even existed. I should tell her about Briana, about Mark, about Grace. The three men. How they gave me a gift. But she's looking at me so seriously now. With such mesmerizing intention. So aware of her own low place in the scheme of things, yet weighted by what she believes to be her awful powers. Putting two and two together. Her powers, her place. Taking the remedy into her own hands, just like Helen. She is so absolutely Helen. Through the curtain, I see the three seats up front are still empty.

"Of course you did," I lie.

"You took the new bath last night," she says, suddenly smiling. "I can smell it."

She reaches out her hand and pulls something from my hair. A white flower petal. She smiles at it sitting there in the small

485

bowl of her palm.

And then I remember those petals and twigs floating around me in the sea, that musky, woodsy scent that suddenly rose up from the waves. The herbal mulch I found in my dress pocket. Ellie's little ziplock bag was in my pocket. Must have opened in the water.

"Yes. Yes, of course, I took the bath." At least it's not a lie.

"I'm going to fix it all tonight, Ms. Fitch," Ellie says to me, looking up at me now with new purpose. "That's what I wanted to tell you."

"What? How are you going to fix it, Ellie?"

Ellie looks at me, like, *Isn't that obvious?* "Just like I broke it, I'm going to fix it. On-stage."

"On*stage*? What —"

"One minute to curtain, Miranda," someone cries.

"Ellie, listen to me —"

But then music suddenly swells all around us.

"Oh god, the music already."

"Music?" Ellie says. "What music?" She looks at me confused. "I don't hear any music."

How can she not hear it? The swelling of

the strings, the dreamy violins. Dreamy violins? Is that the opening I chose?

"Ellie, how can you not hear that music? Are they putting on a show tonight in the black box theater? Is Fauve putting something on? Did she go behind my back and put on a musical?"

"Miranda, are you okay? Oh god, I hope it isn't the recipe. Maybe I should stop putting so much —"

"Speaking of stops, I have to go put a stop to this music. Otherwise, how will you be able to perform, am I right? How could anyone be expected to perform in this *din*?"

"I really don't hear any —"

But I'm already off toward backstage, running toward the source of the sound.

CHAPTER 28

I float through the dark corridor from the main stage to the black box. Don't even feel my feet, that's how light and quick I am. I hear the first lines of the play being delivered by Ashley/Michelle on the main stage. How can she even hear herself over this music? Getting louder and louder now. Pretty. Very pretty at least. I'm moved in spite of myself. *What production is this?* I wonder. Familiar anyway. I've heard this music before. Do I know this play?

When I enter the black box, I see a single spotlight shining down onto the stage. The rest is black. The music is so loud here. So there is another show! Unbelievable. On opening night of all nights. Feels like a plot. Why did no one tell me? Grace, did you know about this? Grace isn't here, that's right. I float toward the single spotlight, toward the swelling sound. My feet seem to lead me there, barely touching the floor now, right to center stage. There's an *X* marked with red tape in the dead center, and that's where I stop. And just like that, the music stops. The spotlight falls hot on my face. Blinding my eyes. I can't see the audience. But I can feel them out there in the dark, watching. Oh god, have they already started?

"I'm sorry," I say to them. "I'm so very sorry."

They all applaud lightly. Then they fall silent as if waiting for me to continue. I should get off the stage, but I can't seem to move from where I'm standing. I'm the only one here, how come? Isn't there a production? Where are the actors? No one else onstage but me. And they seem to be watching me. Waiting for me to say something else. Almost like I'm the one they came to see. I feel them rapt in their seats.

I look around the stage. I see I'm on a set. A living room. What play is this? *The Glass Menagerie? Long Day's Journey into Night?* Furniture looks too contemporary. And familiar, why familiar? I gaze at the walls lined with bookcases, at the floor lamp shaped like a dragon, a television in the corner where a crime show is playing on mute. My heart begins to beat a little faster. I know these bookcases, I know this lamp, this television. I know these framed posters on the wall. One of a *Romeo and Juliet* ballet we saw together once, the one time I managed the New York trip, surprised her with tickets. The other of a production of *Salome* she must have gone to alone. A window with a drawn shade of rose froth. The flowery couch where I once sat weeping while she watched helplessly from an ornamental chaise. I know the half-finished puzzle of the Venetian piazza on the coffee table. She was working on the sky the last time I was here. Still is.

"I know this living room," I say aloud, accidentally.

The audience laughs lightly.

"This is Grace's living room. I'm in Grace's living room." My heart starts to pound now. The audience applauds. Why are they applauding?

"What am I doing in Grace's living room? What play is this?"

A smell hits me then. Pungent and thick. A sick sweetness. The sweetness of rot.

"What is that smell?"

The audience laughs again. Now more stage lights come on. I see a woman lying on the floor surrounded by wilted Get Well balloons, their smiley faces warped by deflation. All around the woman are dead flowers in vases full of murky water. I know the flowers. *Oh, just a wonderful arrangement of spring flowers, please. Something revitalizing. Restorative.* Torn bags of Instacart groceries are scattered around the floor, flies buzzing over the packages of meat and the rotting dragon fruit. The champagne bottle is a heap of broken glass. I stare at the woman lying there in the middle of all this shattered rot, her eyes wide open.

"Grace!"

I run to her. Fall to my knees amid the torn bags, the shattered glass.

Relief washes over me at the sight of her. Grace, Grace, thank god. Lying here so peacefully on the stage floor. Getting a good rest just like I told her to. It's true that Grace can sleep anywhere. I've always envied that. Look at how peacefully she dreams even now. On the stage with all these lights shining down on her face. With the clapping and everything else. With her eyes wide open.

"Grace, I'm so glad you're here," I say. "I was worried."

The audience laughs softly. My heart thrums darkly in my chest.

"I *was* worried," I tell them. "I was calling and calling, wasn't I, Grace? Or at least I wanted to call. I didn't call only because I

491

didn't mean to disturb you."

The audience laughs again. I look out into the theater, but I can't see their faces because of the light. I look back at Grace. She hasn't moved. Still staring straight ahead. Sort of smiling.

"Grace?" I shake her.

Nothing. Still that smile. Those open eyes.

"Grace, say something, please. Are you asleep? Please wake up, is this a joke?"

The audience laughs uproariously at this. I touch her forehead. Cold skin. It's not real, I tell myself. Can't be real. I stare at her face, so pale. Her eyes unblinking.

"Someone please get help," I shout. "Please!"

I look out in the dark. No one seems to stir.

"Hello? Did you hear me? I said someone please get help!"

Still no movement. A throat cleared. I feel their eyes staring at me in the dark.

"What are you all doing? Why are you just sitting there?"

Run, I tell myself. *Get help.* But I don't move either. I'm frozen in place, in this kneeling position by Grace's side. Like the spotlight itself, the light itself, is holding me down, pinning me here on the floor by Grace's body, my knees right on another taped X.

My heart starts drumming now, knocking against my ribs like a fist on a door.

"Please," I say. "Please, help. I think she's . . ."

No. I shake my head. Not dead. Not even dying. Just unwell, under the weather. Very under the weather. Ambulance. She needs an ambulance. I reach for my phone in my pocket, but all I pull out is seaweed. I look at the wet, mulchy web in my fingers while everyone claps.

"Stop clapping! Someone call for help now!"

I feel someone shaking their head in the dark. A mouth grinning behind a fist. Pain shoots down my leg. A bolt of bright fire. For a moment, I think I glimpse them in the back row. All three. Sitting back comfortably. Enjoying the show.

"Oh god," I whisper. "What have you done to her?"

Silence. I feel them smiling sadly at me beyond the lights. I flash back to me and Grace in the dark parking lot of the Canny Man. Grace crawling backward on her hands and feet. Backward to get away from me. Me taking slow steps toward her. Reaching out my hand.

"I just helped her up," I say, shaking my

head. "I just helped her up, that's all. I would never hurt Grace. Never."

I take her hand. Cold like her forehead. Suddenly I can't breathe. Tears flood my eyes. I feel them hot on my skin, sizzling under the lights.

"I thought she could take it! I thought she was hardy! She's from Plymouth, for fuck's sake, aren't you, Grace? Tell them how you're from Plymouth!"

I grab her shoulder, which is so very cold, and I shake it. "Come on, Grace, please. Puritan stock. The Pilgrims, remember? So strong the Pilgrims are. Resilient. Unkillable, remember? Please remember you're supposed to be unkillable!"

The audience laughs and laughs. *Doesn't look like it now.* And I shake and shake Grace, who just lies there like nothing.

"Grace, listen to me, please. I take it back, okay? I take it back! I would if I could, I would, I would. I wish I could. If I'd known this was going to happen, I would have never done it." More tears fall, making Grace blur around the edges, making her body mix with the laughing dark beyond the lights. I shake my head at the dark. "I'm not going to just let you die like this."

I try to rise, and this time the light doesn't hold me down. Now the light is just light.

The audience gasps as I run down the aisle toward the exit door. They're watching me. Smiling. All those teeth and eyes on me, I feel them. And then I see them, the three men. Sitting toward the back. Taking up a whole row. Their large silhouettes leaning back in their chairs. Their feet propped up on the seats in front of them. Smiling at me running in the dark, smiling at Grace dying on the stage — making my heart drum and drum. Oh god, don't look, just run, go, go, go, get help for Grace. Keep your eyes on the EXIT sign. Keep your eyes on —

The lights go black again. I'm in complete darkness.

Oh god.

What is this?

Music again. Everywhere. All around me like the dark. That same swell of strings.

The light is back. Faint. Red now. Coming from the stage behind me.

I turn around to find the set's changed. Gone is Grace's living room. Gone is Grace.

Now under the dim red light there's a group of men on the stage. Men in blue hospital scrubs. Men in white lab coats. Men in polo shirts. The men are gathered around a long medical table.

"What's this?" I say. The men onstage

ignore me. So busy they are with whatever's on the medical table.

There's a man standing at a distance away from the huddled mass, watching with arms crossed. A crew cut frames his sensible face, sharp under the red light. A yin-yang pendant glows in the open collar of his polo shirt. He's nodding slowly. As if it's all part of the journey. Mark.

Mark, what are you doing here?

He turns and looks at me then. Standing there, swaying there in the aisle of a theater so dark I can't see the seats around me. His face is grave and pale. *What have you done, what have you done, what have you done?* He holds up his arm. There's a bandage on his wrist — right where I touched him in the treatment room. I can see a blotch of blood seeping through the gauze.

The audience gasps at the sight, horrified.

I shake my head. Ridiculous. It's a lie. I didn't draw blood, I just touched him. He never bled. "It's a lie," I tell the audience all around me that I can't see, the three men behind me now. "This man hurt me. *He* hurt *me*! Again and again and again."

And then I point at him. "He hurt me, and I had to defend myself!"

They don't listen to me. They go on gasping and shaking their heads at Mark's wrist.

Mark looks at me standing there in the audience, and then he turns away. He looks back at the huddle of men on the stage, gathered closer around the medical table. More red lights on these men. Brighter now. They're working on something together, working at whatever's on the table. What are they working on? Whom, I realize. Whom, not what.

And then I see her. I can see her unshaven legs trembling between their huddled bodies. Her bare feet poking stiffly out from among the khaki thighs of the men. She's squirming, and I know she's strapped to the bed with belts. I feel the weight and tightness of the straps bearing her down. I can feel her heart jumping under her ribs. I can feel her breath broken and raspy in her throat.

"Who is that?" I mean to scream, but my voice is suddenly very thin. Because I know who it is. I feel their every touch and pull on my skin. A sudden soreness in my muscles. A stiffness beginning to spread across my limbs. A sudden cramp that curls my foot into a claw. Inner webs lighting up red, red, red. "Stop it!" No one answers me. Not the men on the red-lit stage, not the audience in the dark who are rapt. Watching.

Onstage, Mark just continues to watch

too. Watches the men huddle closer and closer around the table, pulling and prodding at the woman's body. Mark is sorrowful but smiling. As if whoever that woman is, well, she asked for this, didn't she? She's trouble. We have to shut her up. She just won't quit complaining. About how much it all hurts. Well. Well, what if we give her something to cry about, shall we?

"No." I shake my head. "Please."

But the men don't hear me. They're talking among themselves. Now one of them — Dr. Rainier? Dr. Harper? — readies the needle. Larger than any needle I've ever seen. I watch the needle squirt liquid into the air.

"No. No, what are you doing to her? Stop! Someone stop him."

No one stops him. I run toward the stage as he injects the woman on the table.

"Never," he says. "I would never. Never, I would never."

"If I had known," chimes in another doctor. "I would never."

"Wish I could take it back," says another. "If I could, I would."

"I would, I would."

"Would have never done it."

"Never, I would never."

And then I feel it. For the first time in

how long. That bright hot fire. Running right down my thigh. All the nerves there screaming. Onstage, I hear a muffled scream coming from the woman on the bed just as a scream escapes my own lips.

The audience applauds. Dr. Rainier bows a little.

I fall down in the aisle. Down to the black floor. I'm staring at a black leather shoe that is tapping, tapping on the floor. I can't bring myself to look up, to see which face, which of the three. Weren't they just in the back, behind me? Now they're sitting up here near the front. Clapping. Laughing.

We just want to see a good show, Ms. Fitch.

No.

I drag myself back up to my feet. The audience gasps. I'm standing in the aisle, crookedly now. I start to walk toward the stage, toward the circle of men, who are gathered more tightly around the woman, around me.

"Never, I would never," they're chanting. "Never, I would never."

They're going to kill her. Though I want to run to the stage, my walk is slow. I'm limping so heavily. I have to make it to the stage, where two men are about to slice up my leg. Another pitchfork into the thigh. Three marks. I feel the bones in my hip instantly scream, stretching open my mouth. "Wish I could take it back," they sing. "Would if I could."

"I would, I would."

The breath is knocked out of my lungs. My leg instantly turns to concrete. I fall down to the floor again. This time I can't get back up. If I can just reach the stage. If I can just save her from them. I drag my body along the floor with my arms. Drag myself toward the red lights of the stage, toward the ring of men, still chanting, all working upon the woman at once. I want to speak, to scream, but my throat feels strangled. My head is throbbing with blood.

The audience is clapping fiercely now.

"Help," I whisper to them. But no one helps. They only applaud. The woman on the table is limp. She's given up. Surrendered. Her leg is just hanging there. Dead. I can feel its deadness. The men clap one another on the back, applauding themselves. Job well done.

The audience just laughs at me on the floor. Stamps their feet. Black leather and pointed. I feel them pummeling my body with their stamping and clapping as all the lights go out again.

I stare out at the black. So dark and quiet

now. No pain now. Nothing at all now. Black as pitch all around. No, not black as pitch. Some soft glimmer of light coming from somewhere. Pale blue like early morning or evening. *Pretty,* I think, but I'm afraid. Why am I afraid? The stage underneath me is soft like the softest grass. My fingers clutch what feels like little blades. I smell flowers somewhere. Sweet like spring. Hyacinths. Lilacs. That's better too. Much better. Flowers. Soft stage. Blue light. Where am I? Still here. I can sense the audience out there in the dark. Still watching me. Fear sharpens. What's next? Run. Maybe I'll try to run again. Get out of here. Call someone. Get help. Find Grace. But can I even run? Did the men break me? Now I try to wriggle my toes, easy. Then I try to move my legs, easy. I get up off the floor, and it's so very easy I nearly cry with relief, with joy. I'm all right! Thank god, thank god, thank god! I'm surprised there is no applause. The audience is dead silent. Waiting.

Run. Run out of this theater and never come back.

But something in the sweetness of the flowers, in the soft blue light, holds me there. I can run, but I'm not running. I'm standing still. Standing there on the soft dark stage, breathing in the flowers. I could breathe them in forever.

And that's when I hear the sound of a baby crying. Of nursery music. What? Where is that coming from? There's a bassinet in the center of the stage, under a single blue spotlight. All by itself. I have to go up there. I have to make sure she's all right. I can't just leave her alone, not with these animals. I walk to the center of the stage, to the bassinet. I gaze down at the baby shrieking inside. Kicking and batting the air with her tiny hands and feet.

"This is a real baby," I say.

The audience applauds softly.

"Whose baby is this?" I ask them. "Where did this baby come from?"

They laugh. The baby cries more loudly.

I pick up the baby. She immediately stops crying. I gaze at her face gazing at me. Fat cheeks. Bright eyes. Something familiar about her eyes. Some kind of deep knowledge in my hands that are holding her warm, small body. That seem to know how to hold her. That maybe have held her before. When? In a dream maybe. I stare into her small face still gazing at me, curiously. *Who are you? Who left you here by yourself? Is your mother in the audience? Why does my body seem to know who you are?*

502

More lights come back on. I'm in another living room. A living room like any other except for the grass floor. Blue-and-white floral couch. Two red chairs. A piano. Bookcases. Coffee table fanned with baby books, picture books. Flowers everywhere. Flowers growing all around me in the grass floor, fresh cut flowers in vases on the end tables. A family lives here. A happy family.

Where am I? I want to ask. But I feel in my bones that I know this place. Know it just like I knew Grace's. Better than Grace's. Why do I know this place? I feel a prickle of fear.

The baby begins to cry again in my arms. She begins to kick at the air with her impossibly small socked feet. I bring her closer to me. A rush of something courses through me. A warm wave. She immediately quiets down.

The audience claps lightly.

"Oh, good. You got her," says a voice. I turn. Paul. Not Hugo. Paul. Actually Paul. His goldfish hair gleaming under the lights. Coming onto the stage. Coming toward me. Smiling. He's holding more freshly cut flowers in his hands. He's looking at me like I still belong to him, like I never hurt him, I never limped out the door. Never wandered past this life into a darkness that swallowed me whole. I still live here. Here in this house I don't even recognize anymore — it's been so long. Our house. Outside is a garden where I planted roses, lilacs, irises, my own gothic garden where dogwood and cherry trees grow. Their shade keeps us cool in the evening. Each night, we sit out in the garden holding hands, watching everything we planted bloom.

"Goldfish," I say. There's no way it could be Paul, but it is Paul. His smell of baked bread. His smell of home.

Paul smiles. "Sorry, Princess, I was out in the garden," he says. "She doesn't usually cry like that, do you, Ellie?"

Ellie. I look at the child kicking and crying in my hands. Which are beginning to tremble. Grow damp with sweat.

He smiles at both of us. The love radiating from his face. He makes a funny face at her that I've never seen, and she cackles with laughter. He laughs, and I laugh too, even though I feel tears sliding down my cheeks. Oh god. Oh god, what's happening?

He touches my back. A dream, a dream. Has to be. But his hand feels so incredibly warm and familiar and real on my skin. I feel the shadows and the weight that I didn't even know were holding me down lift now. My soul filled. My heart whole again. My feet planted firmly in the soft earth like flowers.

"Probably just knows tonight is her mother's big opening night, don't you?" he asks the crying baby I'm holding in my hands. Her eyes somehow my eyes and his eyes. My mouth shape and his mouth shape.

Her mother's big night. Her mother.

The audience gasps.

Paul smiles. A swell of something rising in my heart. I feel the stage beneath me begin to get softer, softer. The blue lights grow hot on my face. The baby in my arms is suddenly so heavy. She cries harder as she begins to slip from my shaking hands. He takes her from me just as she's about to fall. She immediately stops crying.

"Don't worry, Ellie," he tells her. "Your mother is a born actress. She's going to light up the stage. Eclipse them all. Like she always does." He smiles at me warmly, so warmly, and I know that the shadows of our past life never happened in this one, never dogged this life, never darkened this door.

"She knows this role like the back of her hand, doesn't she?" he tells Ellie. "That's how I met her. I saw her play Helen in Edinburgh. I didn't even want to go to a show that night. Talk about kismet, am I right? And she enchanted everyone. She won me over. I've been bewitched ever since."

He looks at me and smiles. Then he frowns suddenly. "Oh, wait, you're not dressed. We have to get you ready, Princess. This is your big opening night, after all."

He hands Ellie back to me. She nuzzles herself against my shoulder. He takes the red tablecloth folded on the arm of one of the red chairs and wraps it around my body like a cloak. Then he ties the corners on my free shoulder so that it drapes across me like a toga. I used to do this with my mother's tablecloth as a child playing dress-up. Did I ever tell Paul that?

Now he takes a step back and considers me in the tablecloth. Still holding my shoulders. Paul's warm hands on my shoulders. Considering me with kindness.

The audience is holding its breath.

"It's missing something," he says at last. He pulls a rose from the basket of flowers on the coffee table. "Your roses are all in bloom, Princess," he says. "Your gothic garden. Look." He points to a fake window, through which there appears to be a fake blue outside light. A crude painting of a backyard — green swirls full of red, purple, and dark blue dots.

"See?" he says.

"Yes, I see."

"Beautiful, isn't it?"

"It is."

He places the rose in my hair. There. "Perfect. You're going to be an amazing Helen." He smiles. Takes my hand and kisses it. The feel of his lips on my skin. I thought I'd never feel it again.

Then a spotlight shines on the back of the stage. I see Grace standing behind Paul. Standing in the far corner of the living room. She's standing barefoot among the flowers.

"Grace!" I say. "Oh my god, Grace, is that you? Grace, you're alive! You're awake!"

Grace doesn't answer. She just stands there on the grass, staring at me. She's wearing a blue medical gown. Her skin is terribly pale. She looks frail. Her hands hang at her sides. Her eyes are dark and sunken. Watching.

In my arms, Ellie stirs slightly. I look back at Paul, who's still smiling like he didn't hear or see a thing. Doesn't see or hear Grace. Still smiling at me like we're alone in the room. I, he, and Ellie are the only three on the grass, among these flowers.

"Are you all right, Princess?" He moves in closer to me. Puts a hand on my face. As his hand strokes my cheek, Grace's breath

507

quickens. Out of the corner of my eye, I watch her chest rise and fall, more rapidly now. As if my closeness to Paul and Ellie makes whatever is happening to her worse.

I close my eyes. *No. Can't be. Can't be.* When I open my eyes, there's Paul smiling at me, there's Ellie in my arms. But there's Grace too. Still standing there in the corner, still gazing at me. Her body trembling now, her breath quickening.

"Oh, look at you," Paul says to me, "you're nervous, Princess. You're shaking. Should we practice once? For the road?"

The audience claps, making *aww* sounds.

"Why don't we practice that very last scene? The one where Helen comes back from the dead? The one where Bertram falls in love with her. I know you love that scene," Paul says. "I love it too."

I look at Grace, who is going paler, her breath catching as Paul takes my hand and kisses it. The feel of his lips again on my skin. The feel of Ellie's cheek against my shoulder. Her little arm gripped around me.

I turn away from Grace and look up at Paul. "I do love it."

The audience applauds wildly.

Paul smiles. "I'll play Bertram and the King," he says. "I've just discovered that you're not dead after all, are you?"

I shake my head. "No."

"That you've been alive all this time. In fact, you're pregnant with my child. You're wearing my ring. And I'm about to fall in love with you. Like I should have done from the beginning. They're transformative lines. They reverse the cosmos. They reverse everything. And then we're free. We're free to start again."

Behind Paul, Grace's breath catches more and more quickly now.

"I'll bet those are probably the lines you're the most nervous about, am I right?"

He smiles at me encouragingly, sweetly. In this world, I can do no wrong. In my arms, Ellie has gone to sleep. Her honey-colored hair impossibly soft against my cheek, my neck.

"Yes," I say.

The audience murmurs approval.

"How about I get you started? I'll say the King's lines." He clears his throat. " 'Is there no exorcist beguiles the truer office of mine eyes? Is't real that I see?' " Paul says with a gruff old-man voice. He looks at me with the eyes of a king. The audience laughs, utterly charmed. Paul bows a little.

I look over at Grace. She's hunched forward. Her breath coming in gasps.

"Grace!" I shout. And in my arms, Ellie

stirs again. Paul just smiles at me, hearing nothing, seeing nothing, seeing only me, this scene of him and me, of Helen and the King/Bertram. He reaches out and squeezes my hand.

"Your line now, Princess," he whispers.

" 'N-no, no, my good lord,' " I say to him. " ' 'Tis . . .' " But the line falls away from me as I watch Grace clasping her chest.

" ' 'Tis but the shadow of a wife you see,' " he whispers, prompting me gently, turning my face toward his.

" ' 'Tis but the shadow of a wife you see,' " I repeat, closing my eyes to feel the warmth of his hands. " 'The name and not the thing.' "

I open my eyes and will myself not to look at the corner. To keep my eyes on Paul. Paul, who is looking right back. With love. Such love. He's no longer the King, he's playing Bertram now. His face softens into a young courtier's. Unseasoned, but now, as a result of moving through the arc of this story, wise. Prepared to love and cherish the thing he cast aside. Me. The wife he spurned, back from the dead. My ring on his finger. Our child in my arms. So heavy and soft and warm in my arms.

" 'Both, both. O pardon!' " he cries.

He strokes my face and kisses me. We both

drop to our knees onto the soft stage. The scent of the flowers all around us is getting thicker. We're bathed in blue light. Paul's hands are still cupping my face. I'm still holding Ellie close. I keep looking at Paul. Not Grace. Who is bringing her hands to her throat. Her eyes, fixed on me, are full of sorrow and pleading and panic. I know in my soul that if I move in any closer to him, if I hold Ellie any tighter, if I complete this scene with Paul, Grace will die.

" 'Will you be mine now . . . ?' " Paul whispers, prompting me again. My line. Helen's line.

Ellie stirs in my arms. I look down at her. She's awake and gazing up at me with her large, bright eyes. His eyes and my eyes. His mouth shape and my mouth shape. She reaches out as if to touch me with her impossibly small hand. Instead she grabs at a lock of my hair and tugs. And now in her hand is a tiny dried purple flower. She smiles. Holds out the flower to me. A gift. A gift from my own hair. I take the flower from her. She looks so pleased with me. Her mother. I can do no wrong.

" 'Will you be mine, now you are doubly won?' " Paul says, cuing me one more time. *Go on, Princess.*

I look at Grace, who is on her knees now.

511

Doubled over. Choking. Holding herself close.

"I can't," I say to Paul. "I have to go."

I pull my face away from his hand and feel a rip in my chest. A chasm in the core of me opening wide.

"Grace! Grace!" But I can't run to her with Ellie in my arms. I set her down on a small blanket on the grassy floor beside us. To set her down on the grass, to leave her warmth, to empty my arms of her, feels like drowning. The chasm is opening wider and wider inside.

"I'll be right back," I tell her. She smiles, looks at me with such love and trust. I wrench myself away from her and rise and turn toward Grace. "Grace!"

But now the corner where Grace stood is empty. The corner is just darkness. No Grace. No one but Paul standing there in the blue light of the living room. Ellie's gone. The blanket and bassinet are gone. The grass beneath our feet has turned gray. Around us, all the flowers have dried up, wilted. Paul stands there in this ruin, looking at me.

"What's happened, Paul? Where's Ellie?" I ask him.

But Paul doesn't answer. He just stands there on the gray grass. His eyes are sunken

512

and hollow now. His face half-shrouded in shadow.

"Paul, where's Ellie?"

"You're right," he says. "You do have to go."

"What do you mean? What's happening?"

"They're waiting for you out there, Miranda. Can't you hear them?"

And then I do hear them. A roar of wild, distant applause. Too big for the black box. Too far away. It's coming from outside, coming from the main stage.

"You better go out there," Paul says.

Suddenly I'm afraid. I run to Paul. I take his hands. But now they feel slack in mine. Resigned. Ready to let me go. I press my face against his neck, breathe his honey-and-bread scent. I run my fingers through his hair, catching the light. Red-gold like a fish.

"I don't want to go," I tell him. "I want to stay here with you and Ellie. Can't I stay here with you and Ellie? Where's Ellie, Paul? Where's Ellie?"

"You have to go. It's your show, Miranda."

I look down at Paul's hands in my hands. No longer holding mine tightly. I'm the one holding on tightly, fiercely now. "Let's rehearse again," I say. "Please, Paul, I'm ready now. I'll say my line now: 'Will you

513

be mine, now you are doubly won?' "

I wait for him to speak Bertram's next line, the line where he admits his love, etched in my soul. *If she, my liege, can make me know this clearly, I'll love her dearly, ever, ever dearly.*

Paul smiles sadly. His face begins to blur before my eyes. " 'And all our yesterdays have lighted fools the way to dusty death,' " he says.

"What?"

But he just looks at me, so tenderly. " 'Out, out, brief candle. Life's but a walking shadow. A poor player that struts and frets his hour upon the stage and then is heard no more.' "

He smiles. For a second, I think I see his skull flash under his skin. I shake my head, and it's gone. Just Paul standing on the gray grass, his eyes dark.

I feel the chasm in me opening wider. Black as pitch. "That's not the line," I tell Paul. It's a line from *Macbeth*. His final speech. Before he's killed.

Paul kisses me on the forehead. I feel his lips, dry and hot on my skin.

"Paul, did you hear me? I said that's not the line."

Paul just looks at me. He knows that's not the line. The spotlight on him begins to dim.

"Paul, what's happening?" I grasp his hand more tightly still but he's slipping from me. The stage lights are dimming. Suddenly my chest feels very tight. Suddenly I can't breathe. I can see Paul retreating before my eyes. Fading before my eyes.

"You can't leave your audience waiting, Miranda." His hands are slipping out of my hands, though I cling and cling to them. He's getting swallowed by the dark. "Can't you hear them?"

"I can hear them. I don't care. Please don't leave me, Goldfish."

The stage lights go out. I feel something inside me rip apart. My heart. Ripped out. A pain so sharp and swift it brings me to my knees, it takes my breath away.

"Paul?" I call. "Paul!"

Paul's gone. The audience is gone. I'm alone in the dark. Alone in the black box. Hearing the distant cheers and screams coming from the main stage theater. Waiting for me.

CHAPTER 29

Tears in my eyes that make the dark swim. I follow the sound of applause to the back of the stage, through the dark corridor, toward the red velvet curtain of the main stage. The roar of the audience is getting louder and louder. At the sound, my sadness lifts a little. My goodness, they sound so excited. I hope I don't disappoint them. How does the play even begin again? Oh yes, that's right, I'm supposed to cry. I'm crying with the secret pain of my heartbreak over Bertram. People think I'm crying over my dead father, but I'm really crying over Bertram. Lucky I'm already crying. *I'll use this,* I think, as I approach the red curtain. *Pain is a gift.*

The applause is so wild I can't help but smile. What's my first line again? *I do affect a sorrow indeed, but I have it too.* That's right. Don't forget, don't forget.

I pull back the curtain. I see they're all

onstage in a line holding hands. Have they started without me? Am I late? *Late for your comeback, Miranda.* Unprofessional. But they can't start without Helen. Suddenly I feel dizzy, as if I'm about to fall. I look down and see blood on the floor. My leg. Still bleeding, I see.

"Ms. Fitch!" someone says to me. A young boy dressed as a lord. "Ms. Fitch, we did it!"

"Ms. Fitch? I'm *Helen,* my lord." I wink at the boy. "Where is the Countess of Roussillon?"

He looks at me, confused. "What?"

"Am I late?" I whisper. "I don't want to miss my cue."

"Your cue? Ms. Fitch, the play's already —"

"Wow, they're really applauding, can't you hear them? God, what a rush, isn't it?"

"Ms. Fitch, wait! What are you —"

I walk out onto the stage, smiling even as tears are still streaming from my eyes. Laughing and crying. It's a problem play, remember? Neither a tragedy nor a comedy. Both, always both.

Onstage, I'm immediately blinded by a light brighter than the sun. It warms me to the bone. Everyone is still standing in a line. I watch them take a bow together. What's this? Are we already taking bows? How can that be?

"Ms. Fitch," they cry, "congratulations. We did it!"

"I'm Helen," I whisper.

"Ms. Fitch, are you okay?" they say. "Ms. Fitch, where are you going? Ms. Fitch . . ."

The stage is so soft beneath my feet. Like the softest carpet in the world, the gentlest earth. It tilts slightly to one side. It spins slowly. Strange. Perhaps that's some kind of newfangled effect they added? This play is the cosmos reversed, after all. Still, I wish someone had told me about this. The tilting and spinning makes it hard to walk a straight line toward the front of the stage where I belong, where it seems like a young girl and boy are already standing, holding hands. Bowing together. Everyone in the audience is applauding so wildly for me. Whistling and whooping and stomping their feet. I've only just stepped onto the stage and look, they're already on their feet.

"Thank you," I tell them. "Thank you so much."

The young man and woman have turned to look at me as I approach. They're waving me up to the front of the stage. Is this how the play starts? Where am I supposed to stand in mourning for my broken heart?

Probably the director told me once, but now I can't seem to remember. I'll have to ask someone onstage, that's awkward. I'll have to whisper it. I'll ask that boy and girl waving me over. The boy is dressed like a young courtier. He must be Bertram, my costar. He'll know. Or that girl beside him. Who is she supposed to be? She's wearing a red dress like I am. She's holding a bouquet of wildflowers. Helen? It can't be, I'm Helen. She must be my understudy. They asked her to step in because I'm late, because I got stuck talking to that lord backstage. Well, I'm here now. I walk over to the young woman dressed as Helen, who is taking her bows, who is holding my flowers. *I'm Helen,* I'll have to explain. *I'm the one.*

She looks at me and smiles. "Professor Fitch," she says.

"Helen," I say. I think I'll have to fight her for the role on the stage, and I'm ready to do that. My hands are curled into fists. But she just hands me the flowers.

"For you," she says. Face flushed and shining. Beneath me, the stage continues to turn like the earth. The theater seems to be turning too.

"Where do I start?" I whisper to the other Helen. "Did I miss my cue?"

She frowns like she doesn't understand

519

me. "Professor, the play is over." She looks at my toga dress. "Are you okay?"

I better say my first line before it's too late, before she takes it from me. What's the line again? Oh yes. I look at the audience and smile.

" 'I have supped full with horrors,' " I say.

The audience quiets. Clapping peters out. Wait, is that the first line? Definitely not that. I turn to the other Helen, who's looking at me, afraid now. Oh no, I've said the wrong first line. Shit. Better try again.

" 'I will not be afraid of death and bane till Birnam Forest come to Dunsinane,' " I shout.

The audience is still now.

"Professor Fitch," hisses the other Helen, tugging on my arm. Her face begins to spin just like the stage, just like the walls, just like the clapping bodies in the dark. Everything spins and tilts. No wonder Helen appears to be panicking. She takes my hand.

"Take a bow with me, Professor," she pleads.

I bow and the audience cheers again. They applaud wildly, so sideways. Then out of the corner of my eye, I see someone approaching. A young woman dressed as an old man. She's got a fake beard and scepter. A rhinestone crown sits on her burnished curls. The King coming toward me. To ask me to heal her, of course. She' so very ill.

"Miranda," the other Helen whispers, "come with me."

"Wait," I tell her, "it's the King. I have to heal her. She's in so much pain."

But the King doesn't look in pain at all. Her face is glowing. Her cheeks are flushed with health. She's positively beaming as she bounds toward me, calling, "Ms. Fitch, Ms. Fitch!" Completely unbothered by the tilting, spinning stage. Tilting and spinning more quickly, more fiercely now.

I stare at the King running toward me. Her bright leaf-green eyes fixed on me. Not the King, I realize. Mine enemy. Mine enemy reaching out her hands to kill me. To take her revenge for everything I have done. Right here on the stage in front of my wildly cheering audience.

"Ms. Fitch," she screams as she lunges for me.

I back away, away, out of her grasp, and when I do, I fall. Right off the stage. It's a long way down to the theater floor. For several minutes or hours, I feel like I'm floating, floating down. Sailing through the bright, spotlighted air, screaming. I hit the floor with a loud crunch. Feel my whole skeleton rattle. My bones vibrate and ex-

CHAPTER 30

A light. Soft on my face. Is this death? The light of God or the devil? No. Earthly light. Theater light. I'm alive. Sitting in a bright little room. Concrete walls lined with vanity tables, lighted mirrors. And children. Children in shoddy Elizabethan costumes are gathered all around me. Sweaty faces bleeding bad makeup, looking at me with concern and fear.

"She's awake, she's awake," they murmur to one another. Then they walk away from me.

I feel a cold, damp cloth on my forehead. There's a soft hand holding mine. Paul.

"Oh, Paul," I whisper. "You're here, thank god. Where's Ellie?"

"I'm right here, Miranda," says a nearby voice. Young and soft like the hand that's holding mine. The voice belongs to the hand, I realize.

I turn. Ellie. Not baby Ellie. Not my Ellie.

Ellie full-grown. Dressed in her red Helen costume. She looks worried. "Who's Paul?" she says.

And I see his face swallowed by the dark. A cold dark creeping at the edge of my consciousness.

"Ellie," I whisper, "what happened?"

"Don't you remember? You fell off the stage, Miranda."

"I did?"

"Yes. It looked like a pretty bad fall too. At least I thought it was. We were all so worried. For a minute, we all thought we'd lost you. Luckily, there were some doctors in the audience."

"Doctors?"

"Yes, three of them. Sitting front row center, right where you fell, can you believe that? They examined you and said you were just fine. Nothing at all broken." She smiles. "Isn't that lucky?"

The cold dark grips me. "Yes. So lucky."

"Oh, Miranda, what's wrong? You're pale. Are you all right? Are you in any pain?"

I recall the crunch of my bones when I hit the theater floor. The rattle of my skeleton. I search my body, bracing myself. Nothing. Just a heaviness in my chest. A dull hum in my limbs that wasn't there before.

"Pain," I say. "I'm not sure."

"You're probably still in shock. I mean, considering what you just went through."

A flash of Paul on the gray grass. The baby that never was, so soft and warm in my arms. And Grace. Oh god, Grace.

"The doctors said you would be in a lot of pain for a while, especially after the initial shock wears off. They said that's to be expected."

"They did?" And I realize there's no singing in my voice anymore. No shimmer in my cells, no lightness in my blood. My voice sounds heavy, like a felled thing.

"I'm sorry, Miranda. I think it could have been so much worse. Even the doctors were shocked that you weren't more hurt. Almost annoyed that they couldn't doctor you more or something." She smiles. "It's such a good thing you took that bath. I think maybe it saved you."

I look in the vanity mirror beside me. There's a fork in my hair. I'm wearing the red tablecloth Paul tied over my shoulder like a toga. I'm covered in seaweed, twigs, and tiny white and purple flowers. I recall baby Ellie pulling one from my hair. Handing it to me like a gift.

I look back at Ellie, still smiling at me so hopefully, still gripping my hand. It hurts a little, I notice. The bones, the flesh. My heart. Everything.

"You still need to take it easy, of course," she adds quickly. "Probably weak from that cut on your leg too. It was bleeding pretty badly. But they bandaged you right back up. One of the doctors had a medical bag with him, can you believe it? I've never even seen one of those except in the movies. It looked like a prop. I told him it looked like a prop, and he laughed. He said he liked that idea. He said he loved theater so much."

I look down at my leg, which has indeed been freshly bandaged. The blood is finally not bleeding through. Someone has drawn a frowning face in the center of the bandage like a bull's-eye. And then I feel it, a dull ache pulsing behind the gauze. Like a dark bruise is blooming there.

"What else did the doctors tell you, Ellie? Did they tell you anything else? Anything about the show?"

Ellie flushes now. "No, nothing."

"They said something. What did they say, Ellie?"

Ellie just shakes her head. "Miranda, what does it even matter? They're just doctors. What do they know about theater? Besides, art is subjective."

"Ellie, please. Please tell me what they said." I feel the ache in my arm, in my hand as it grips hers.

Ellie looks away from me now. "They said . . . to tell you that they didn't really care for it."

"What did they say *exactly*?"

"They said it was very . . . anticlimactic," she says, still looking away. "Not cathartic enough. Not . . ." She shakes her head again.

I see myself crying beside Grace's body in the black box. A circle of men torturing me. How I dragged myself across the stage floor toward the medical table like a snake. The bond I felt holding Ellie in my arms. Before I turned away from her. Before I tried to save Grace. And then there was no Grace. Just an empty corner of gray grass. The agony of my heart ripping apart on the stage, taking my breath away.

"Not a good show," I finish.

She says nothing.

I feel the wound in my chest again. A sadness that rises and falls like a wave. Only a matter of time, then. Only a matter of time, and it will all come screaming back. The concrete, the webs, the chair, the fat man. *After the initial shock wears off. To be expected.* Surely no bath or tiny purple flowers can save me.

"I'm sorry, Miranda. I wasn't going to tell you, even though they said to pass it along.

That it was very important that you know. I thought, *Why? Why would you* need *to know that?* They were a little weird, honestly. They even said they wanted a refund. That they'd be in touch."

"In touch." I close my eyes. The cold darkness fills me. "Of course they will be."

"If it's any consolation," Ellie says, "I thought the show was wonderful. Everyone did. And . . ." She pauses. Takes a breath. "I'm just so grateful to you. For giving me a chance; for giving me Helen. I really can't thank you enough for . . . everything." She squeezes my hand, and it hurts. Hurts everything. But I don't pull away. I let it hurt. My whole heart. To my surprise, I even smile at her. "You're welcome, Ellie. You deserved it."

"And anyway," she whispers, "I fixed everything."

"Fixed everything?"

"Didn't you see? I fixed everything, Miranda, just like I said I would before the show. It worked. Just like the baths, like when I healed you."

"What do you mean 'it worked'?"

Just then there's a playful knock on the door.

"Ellie?" a voice calls in a song.

And I know the voice. Of course I do. The

528

voice whose former shrillness used to make fire of my nerves, concrete of my leg. The voice whose impossible lightness used to mock my authority, my pain. The voice that of late has sounded like a husk of itself, now back to its former full-bodied pitch. Except there's a new gravity to it. A new richness that I don't recognize. I turn to look at her there in the doorway, her face no longer sickly but rosy and smiling and framed by her burnished hair. No longer dressed as the King but as herself. But it's a different self. Not the shrill girl in bell sleeves. Nor the shrunken shell in hospital-gown blue who hissed *witch* and dragged her dead leg, my dead leg, across the stage while sipping Ellie's water bottle. This glowing girl, standing straight in the doorway, not breathing through her mouth, smiling at Ellie like they're actual friends, is someone else.

"Ellie," Briana says, "there you are."

She crosses the room toward Ellie like Ellie is her lighthouse, her beacon, her best friend. She doesn't limp, nor does she move with the thoughtless lightness that would have made my eyes smart to behold in former times. Instead she crosses the room with a new heavy grace. Like she understands what a true gift it is to walk without pain, to walk at all. *It is a gift,* that's what her steps say. *I must tread carefully, gratefully, I must tread from hereafter with deep thanks.*

I watch her come up to Ellie and kiss her on her pallid cheek. She places a hand on Ellie's shoulder.

"Ellie," she says, with her new rich voice, "I've been looking for you everywhere."

Ellie looks at her like this news does not surprise her. Of course Briana, a girl who never once in three years acknowledged her existence, would be looking for her everywhere.

"Oh," Ellie says, "I've just been sitting with Miranda."

At last Briana turns to look at me. Her leaf-green eyes have returned to their former brightness but there are shadows among the leaves now. They've glimpsed death, the dark precipice. They gaze at my tablecloth toga, the fork in my hair.

"Ms. Fitch," she says, "that was quite a fall."

"Yes," I say.

"I thought for sure you'd die. But you're alive. I'm glad," she says hesitantly.

"Thank you," I say. I look at her standing straight before me. "You look well."

"Yes." She looks at Ellie and smiles at her like she is the sun. She puts her arm around Ellie's pale shoulder, which immediately

530

goes red at her touch.

"Maybe the stage was what I needed after all," she says to Ellie, who is biting on her grin, who is looking at me like, *You see, Miranda? Didn't I tell you that I would right things? That I would fix things just like I broke them?*

"Theater heals, I guess."

"Yes. Isn't that what you always say, Miranda?" Ellie prompts. "That theater heals?"

"I do," I say. I've never said that.

I watch Briana tug on Ellie's hand. "We're taking off to celebrate. Are you coming with?"

"Oh, I should stay with Miranda. At least until Grace gets back. But I'll catch up with you, all right?" Briana kisses Ellie again, says an awkward goodbye to me, then leaves. But I don't hear her words to me or Ellie's words to her because all I can hear is the word *Grace*. Echoing in the void of my body. *Grace, Grace, Grace.*

"Grace," I whisper. I look at Ellie smiling at me and steel myself. Deep breath. "Ellie," I say, "Grace is dead."

"What? No, Miranda, Grace is here. She gave us all notes after the show. She was so helpful. She's —"

"I killed her. Did you hear me, Ellie? I

killed Grace. I tried to undo it, to take it back, but I couldn't, it was too late." When I say these words, the dam breaks. Tears flood my eyes as I gaze at Ellie, who is looking at me not with horror, but with pity.

"Oh, Miranda," she says, "you really have had quite a fall, haven't you?"

"Well, look who's back from the dead," Grace says from the door. Grace standing at the door in her hunting vest. Grace half smiling at me like I never left her for dead. Grace holding the champagne I had delivered to her home and two plastic cups. Grace looking at me with kindness, saying, "It looks like someone could use a drink."

CHAPTER 31

I tell myself it's a dream, surely, that Grace and I are sitting here together. That I'm still in the black box, I never left. Or perhaps I'm dead. I'm in a coma and these are my last minutes of consciousness, and in my last minutes of consciousness, my mind decided to play this palliative trick. Because surely Grace is dead or deathly ill or else she's calling the police. Surely we are not sitting together in the Canny Man of all places with the red walls all around us and the black animal eyes gazing at us in welcome, welcome. She wanted us to come here.

Why not go to our old haunt? Grace said as we left the theater, walking leisurely, easily, in the parking lot, like nothing bad had ever happened between us in a parking lot or anywhere else. And I kept taking her hand, Grace's hand, in disbelief, in gratitude, a hand that was not cold anymore, and though she looked surprised, she didn't pull away. She let me take it. Took mine right back.

Pub? she said again. *I'm dying for solid food, and those fish and chips are just what the doctor ordered.*

A fog had come rolling in. And I thought, *Don't go back there, don't ever go back there.* But I looked at the miracle of Grace holding my hand in the dark, impossibly alive and smiling and wanting to celebrate in our old haunt, and I said, *Of course, sure, whatever you like, Grace.*

By the time we reached the Canny Man, the fog was so thick you could barely see the wooden man swinging from his hook above the door.

Thought it was supposed to be a clear night, Grace laughed as she groped for the door. *I felt a drop. Did you feel a drop?*

I felt a drop, I told Grace. Felt their anger in the filthy air. Felt the sword above my head. Felt my doom in the thickening night as we drove here. Three silhouettes looming in my side mirror, loping along the shoulder like wolves. But the dread had strangely left me in the dressing room. I even smiled at the fog all around as I parked the car and walked toward Grace. Walked, not limped. Not yet. I held up my aching hands to the drizzle. *Go ahead,* I whispered to the black clouds gathering. *Come for me.*

What was that, Miranda? Grace asked, smiling at me through the fog.

Nothing.

And I went through the door with Grace.

I thought any minute surely something would give, the seams around this scene would split, revealing the black, starry void of death or else the lip of a stage, an audience watching in the dark.

Nothing. Just us smiling at each other over the thin orange flame of this bar candle, smiling at each other by its red, mottled light and the fog outside thickening and the rain starting to gently fall. She's playing a song on the jukebox just for me. "Me and My Shadow" by Judy Garland. I've been humming it so much lately, she says. All season. Such a strange season it was, she says. And I agree. It was. Such madness this time of year, we both agree. Always madness.

"Tonight especially," Grace says now. "Lots of curve balls, wouldn't you say?"

"Lots."

She tells me that she got to the theater late. Didn't think she was feeling up to it at first, but then she suddenly felt better. Almost like something had lifted, she says, looking through the window at the fog outside. When she got there, they'd already started the show, and she couldn't find me anywhere, it was madness, a full house, did I see that?

"Yes."

So she just watched from the back. Standing room only. And then at the end, there I was on the stage suddenly. She saw me fall. Heard the terrible crunch of my bones when my body hit the floor. She heard it from all the way at the back of the theater. It was so loud it almost sounded fake, like a sound effect. She thought that surely I was dead, that she heard my soul leaving my body. Grace doesn't believe in souls but what else to call that awful, anguished gasp that seemed to escape not through my mouth but from my whole body, making my chest cave into itself, like all the air and flesh and blood was leaving all at once? Quite a spectacular fall, it was. Quite the scene, it was. Quite the scene stealer, I was. She smiles. Doesn't say anything about me crashing the stage in a tablecloth, reciting those lines from *Macbeth.* Maybe she's chalked it up to production madness. Me being alone on opening night.

"And then those doctors," she says.

"You saw them?" I ask. And my pulse quickens. Did she recognize them from that

536

awful night here, in the basement?

"Nice men," Grace says, "but a little intense. Weird-looking. One was incredibly fat and sick-looking for a doctor. Another was thin and tall and sort of beautiful. And then the other one, he looked a little like a sleazy salesman. The salesman did most of the talking." She couldn't believe their diagnosis, but then who is she to question the authority of not one but three doctors, right?

"Right."

"And look at you," she says, "you seem fine, don't you? I mean, considering?"

A shimmer of lightning in the window.

"Considering," I say quietly. Again, I brace myself. Brace myself for the pain to spread back through me with a vengeance, like a wildfire. For the chair to return to my foot. For the fat man to return to the chair. For concrete to replace flesh once more. For the fists to return to my back, clenched tighter than ever before. For my heart to break. For my throat to catch. For a surge of tears to blind me, to fall and never get done falling. Nothing. A throb beneath the bandage on my shin. A new weight in my body, my limbs, my chest. A swell of something in my heart — sadness or is it happiness? — that rises then falls, rises then falls, like an ocean wave. Rises and falls at the sight of Grace, alive and across the table from me. She clinks her glass against mine. Smiles at me.

"Miranda," she says, "you're staring at me again."

I tell Grace I'm sorry to stare. I don't mean to make her uncomfortable. I'm just so glad that she's . . .

"What?" Grace says. "That I'm okay? Of course I'm okay, Miranda. Pilgrim stock, remember?"

I look at her face, not at all angry, but perhaps she's still just in shock. I wait for her to call the police. Wait for her to punch me.

Grace laughs in the red light. "Miranda, I'm fine. *All's* well," she says to me.

She puts her hand on mine. "Thank you for all the cacti and dragon fruit, by the way," she says. "You kind of went a bit overboard with the Instacart deliveries. But I do appreciate the thought."

"I was worried about you. I meant to visit. I just —"

"But you did visit me, didn't you? Didn't you sit by my bedside?"

I remember sitting beside her in the dark, staring into the voids of her eyes. Surely she can't mean that first night. But maybe she hallucinated me in her fever.

"I could have visited you more," I say.

"You just had to go on with the show, Miranda," says Grace. "I know how it goes. Anyway, I wasn't very good company. I haven't been ill in years. But it was bound to catch up with me at some point, wasn't it? All that good health."

I watch her light a cigarette with the candle, the cherry spark from the thin orange flame.

"Grace," I say, "that night here, in the basement, in the —"

"Forget it. I'm embarrassed that I was so . . . I don't even know what I was. Suspicious, I guess? Of you."

I tell Grace she was right to be suspicious. "I've done some terrible things, Grace. I wish I could say I didn't mean to do them. But I don't know. Maybe I did. I'm sorry. I know that."

Grace shakes her head. She says she is the one who is sorry actually. She says that lying around all day sick, it gave her some time to think. And actually, Grace thought a lot. About me, in fact. About what I must have gone through. With my hip. And my back.

"What?"

"With your hip and your back. Both, right? Miranda, what's wrong?"

"Nothing. Go on."

"I realize I wasn't always the most — I don't know. I could have been kinder. More patient." She's looking down at her glass.

I recall my coldness, my impatience with Ellie the night before opening night, her weeping about Briana. How heartlessly I watched Briana drag her leg of stone into the theater. How quickly I assumed she was faking.

"It's really okay, Grace," I say.

"No, it's not. I'm sorry, Miranda. I am."

She's actually sorry. I know this. I know this because Grace can't bring herself to look at me.

"Anyway, I'm just so glad you're better now."

A rumble of thunder overhead. A hiss of rain. The skin at the back of my neck prickles. I look at Grace's hand on mine, and I want to tell her everything. The truth about the three men, who might appear any second, demanding their refund. The truth about where my pain went all those weeks. Into which bodies. Into her body. That in the black box, I almost didn't save her. That the feel of the baby in my arms, of Paul's hands on my face, of my own body light as air, free of concrete, webs, fists, was almost too much to turn away from. Was excruciating to turn away from. That I'm waiting for it to all come screaming back. For what was reversed to be righted again. *After the initial shock wears off. To be expected.*

"Am I better now?" I ask her. "I don't know. I don't know that I am."

"You are better, Miranda," Grace repeats. "You were scaring me for a while there, I can't lie. But now, you seem . . . I don't know. More like you. More like the Miranda I know and love." She smiles. "I'm happy for you. And I hope you can forgive me for whatever I did to make things harder."

The warmth of Grace's hand on mine. Asking me, impossibly, for forgiveness.

"Only if you forgive me, Grace," I say to her.

She squeezes my hand, and I'm reminded of Ellie in her red Helen costume, holding my hand just like this. How it hurt just like this. And I held on anyway. Like I'm holding on now.

"How was the show, by the way?" I ask her.

Grace looks at me, shocked. "You didn't see it?"

I have a flash of kneeling over her dead body in the black box.

"I missed some parts," I say.

"Oh, it was great. Briana was brilliant. As

541

the dying King she was unbelievable, obviously. I did worry she was going too far. She played the frailty up so much, you know. It was almost *too* real. I was convinced she was going to die up there. But then that transformation." She shakes her head. "I didn't realize you were going to have them do the healing on the stage like that."

"They did the healing onstage?" I see Ellie's tear-streaked face before the show, her low voice saying to me, *I'm going to fix it all tonight, Ms. Fitch.*

"I thought you knew," Grace says to me.

"Oh, of course, I knew. Yes."

"Well, it was incredible. People were crying. Me too, if you can believe it. It was really the most amazing onstage transformation I've ever seen."

I think of Briana striding into the dressing room, aglow with sudden health, high on miracles. Her face the picture of cautious glee. Her hand on Ellie's shoulder in the dressing room. *Theater heals,* she said, smiling at Ellie, who smiled at me. *You see, Miranda?*

"The kiss really surprised me," Grace says. "I thought it was quite daring of you."

"Ellie and Trevor have always kissed at the end," I say. "It's actually quite common

542

for Helen and Bertram to kiss."

"No. Ellie and Briana. They kissed, and then they danced insanely across the stage. This weird jumping dance. Briana really got into it. She was screaming her head off with joy. I actually thought it was getting a bit out of control, I have to say."

I picture Ellie and Briana dancing and laughing together. Briana's great pain suddenly taken away. I remember how that felt. Like a roaring in your head turned off. The beauty of the sudden silence. The miracle of lightness when you have lived so heavy.

The pub door blows open just then, making me jump in my seat. I turn, expecting to see their suited shadows crossing the threshold. Nothing there. Just the door creaking on its hinges. The windblown night like a blank face.

"Miranda, are you okay?"

"Fine. Sorry. What were you saying?"

"Just that Briana's become quite the actress."

"Yes," I say, "quite the actress."

"Maybe that terrible virus did her some good after all. Gave her some depth."

"Maybe." But I don't know about good, I want to tell Grace. And I don't know about depth either. What's down there. If it does us any good. I look out the window at the impossible night. "Maybe we should have done *Macbeth* after all."

"I don't know, Miranda. I actually think *All's Well* was a success. The audience ate it up. My god, Hugo especially."

I turn away from the window to look at Grace, who's grinning at me now.

"Hugo?" My heart lifts even as my face flushes with embarrassment and shame, thinking of the last time we saw each other.

Grace tells me how when she got to the theater, he was standing in the back, his gaze glued to the stage. Totally transfixed for the whole show. He even cried at the end during the scene when Bertram and Helen reunite, the scene I made Trevor and Ellie rehearse to death, the one where he improbably declares his improbable love and they kiss. Right then, Hugo turned to Grace with tears in his eyes, tears if I can believe it. *Where's Miranda?* he said. And Grace says I should have seen his face. The poor man looked like he was under some kind of spell. "When I told him I had no idea, he took off to go looking for you."

"He did?" A surge of lightness in my body. That blooming feeling that used to brighten my heart. Before his wheat-colored hair turned to red-gold. Before his face turned strangely, terribly, into Paul's face.

"He actually texted me earlier and said he'd been trying to reach you. You should really let him know you're okay," Grace says. "Let him know you're a walking miracle."

Peal of thunder now like a warning. Like a sheet of shaking tin. My shin throbs, and the blooming lightness fades to black. I remember I lost my phone in the sea.

"Must have left my phone in the theater or something," I tell Grace.

"I'll let him know we're at the Canny Man but that you're heading back soon," she says, pulling out her phone and typing away before I can tell her to stop, that I'm doomed anyway. The instant she sends the text, her phone buzzes in her hand. She smiles at her screen, then hands the phone to me.

A selfie of Hugo. Sitting on my front steps in the dark. Beside him is what looks like a bottle of champagne, a bouquet of stargazers. He looks tired, worried. He looks beautiful and nothing at all like Paul.

Tell her I'll be here when she's ready.

I feel my face break out into a smile in spite of myself. A sharp pang of longing that's all for him. Back when he was just himself, in his cathedral of wood and light, smiling at me with no tricks.

"I guess he must have missed you back-stage," Grace says. "Where the hell were you anyway? During the show?"

"I thought I heard a noise," I tell her. "In the black box."

"What was it?"

Just my worst nightmares come to life. Just three demons trying to win my soul. The coming storm is a vengeful triumvirate howl.

"Just some people fooling around in the dark," I tell Grace. I smile at her. "You know."

After I say goodbye to Grace, I walk over to the bar. A drink while I wait, why not? Might as well wait. Not like I can run, *am I right?* Not from this, not from them. *'Tis time,* as they say. *'Tis time, 'tis time.* I feel them coming. In the crackle of the air. In the static around the music. In the wind that keeps blowing the door open, then shut. Grace said I should leave with her, go home, get Hugo to take me to the hospital. She even offered to come along. She said I can't be too careful. It was quite a fall, after all. She doesn't know about those doctors who said I hadn't broken anything. I mean really, how do they know? *Well, they* are *doctors,* I told Grace. I told her I feel fine. I told her not to worry. I told her go home, get rest. She shouldn't push it, what with her recent illness. These things have a way of rebounding, I said. They have a way of coming back around. I hugged her then. Breathed her in one last time. *Goodbye, Grace.* Hard to let go of her. I held on for a long time.

But what about the storm coming? she said. *You should get home before it really hits.*

I should, I said. But I sat back down in my seat, eyes fixed on the table, ears tuned to the storm. I could feel her hesitating before she turned away. I looked up, managed a smile. *Soon.*

At the bar, there's almost no one. Just another woman sitting alone. The songs Grace selected are still playing on the speaker. What song is it now? "Me and My Shadow" again, sounds like. Or maybe it never stopped playing. Perhaps it's a long version. Maybe there's a long version of this song that I don't know about. There's a roar of rain overhead now. A wind blowing all around. The windows flash white with lightning, lighting up the bar as I take a seat. The bartender's back there. I've seen him here before. Middle-aged. Thinning hair. Somber eyes. He was the one who was here the night I first met the three men, and then again the night I learned there was a down-stairs to this place. And I went down and down and down.

Tonight, he's wiping down the bar with that same dirty rag. Shelves of amber bottles gleam dully behind him. Just as I'm about to order, he turns away from me toward the woman sitting a couple of seats over.

She's around my age probably. Long, dark hair. Some bone-white hairs among the black. Faded red lipstick. Pale face etched with misery lines. Looking at her, I feel a sudden tingle of recognition at the base of my spine. Do I know her? No, of course not, she's a stranger. And yet she's familiar to me. Something in her grim gaze. The downward turn of her red lips. I smile at her. She doesn't see me. She's staring straight ahead, into the middle distance. Eyes glassy and sad and faraway. Unwell, I think. Definitely. Her eyes are glassy from drugs. I know what kinds.

The bartender smiles at her. I watch her come back to herself. Feign a smile through the pain. She orders her drink quietly. I can't hear her over the sound of Judy's singing and the roaring rain and the now shrieking wind. The storm and the singing are like a singular music. The bartender sets a single napkin down before her that reads THE

548

CANNY MAN. He pulls up a bottle from under the counter and pours her a glass. Places it on the napkin with great ceremony, then bows a little at her like she's a king. The drink is a golden color, I see. It glows with its own light. The golden remedy. She thanks him with a nod of her head, and he bows again.

I watch her reach out for the drink, bring it to her lips. She's got a bandage on her forearm, quite like the bandage on my shin. When she takes a sip of the drink, she closes her eyes. And I can almost feel the gold of it from here. The brightness of its blue, blue skies.

She smiles to herself.

A cough. I turn to find the bartender standing over me, waiting. No bow. No ceremony. Drumming his hands on the bar. Performing his impatience with his eyebrows. *Well? What'll it be?*

I look back at the woman hunched over the golden drink, glowing between her cupped hands. She's smiling brightly now.

"The golden remedy," I hear myself say.

Why not, right? Might help. Might delay whatever is about to descend.

For a moment, he stares at me. "We took that off the menu," he says. "Limited supply. Limited time only."

"What? But didn't you just give her —"

"Limited supply," he interrupts. "Limited time only."

I stare at him. He stares right back at me, not even flinching.

"A Scotch, then," I say. He pours it quick, then slides the squat, sloshing glass in my direction. I have to catch it with both hands before it slides right off the bar.

I stare down at the spotty glass filled with the dull amber drink. He's filled it to the very brim, I see. A generous pour at least. Perhaps he thinks I'm celebrating. What am I celebrating?

The wind howls again outside. It sounds like a man's scream. Not just one man. Three.

A spectacular crack of thunder that makes the whole bar shudder. I whip my head toward the door. Nothing. Yet. A small purple flower tumbles from my hair into the glass. How many flowers were in that bath anyway, Ellie?

Maybe it saved you, Miranda.

I look at it floating limply in my Scotch like a fly. I'm about to fish it out, but something in the look of those tiny petals stops me. The memory of baby Ellie holding it out to me like a gift. I take a long drink, leaving the flower in there. A blunt warmth runs through me. A sharpness dulled. A sense of things inside dimming, dimming. Like a light being turned very slowly out. I can see the hand on the dial, turning, turning. There now. That's better, isn't it?

I glance back at the woman beside me. Her eyes appear misty now, fluttering closed and then open. She looks completely lost in reverie. Lost in the blue skies in her blood. Wandering down some sunny, happy road in her mind. Each sip a footstep down the road. A dark road, I remember now. No matter how sunny it may seem in the mind's eye. No matter the brightness of the flowers that grow on either side. Impossible colors that hypnotize. She's oblivious to the storm raging all around. Doesn't seem to feel the floor shuddering beneath us. The glasses rattling in their racks. The amber bottles trembling on the shelves. The headless woman above us swinging wildly from her ropes. Wish I could leave here. Drive to Hugo sitting on my front steps, waiting for me like a dream on the other side of this. *But there is no other side of this, Ms. Fitch.*

Suddenly the jukebox music dissolves to a drone. Another song starts to play. Still Judy. But not "Me and My Shadow" anymore. She's singing that other song. About

551

getting happy. About the sun shining. About getting ready for judgment day.

The storm begins to bang its fists on the walls, on the doors. *Knock, knock, knock.* A pounding and a pounding and a pounding. I grip the bar for dear life, bracing myself. I look at the bartender, but he also seems untroubled. Keeps polishing his glass like all the glasses and bottles aren't now crashing to the floor. Like the tables and chairs haven't all turned over and the bar itself isn't shaking to the foundation. Or if it is, he's seen this before. Seen it all, all before. He'll stand there until the end of time in a sea of shattered glass, polishing spots that will never out. And the woman beside me keeps smiling at her reflection in the now cracked mirror behind the bar. She's still under her blue skies, on the sun-dappled road.

Beside us, the glass window breaks. I want to take cover, but I'm paralyzed. My whole body freezes as the screaming wind comes tearing through the pub like a tentacle of mist. Lifting my hair up all around me. Blasting my bare back like a blow. I look in the cracked mirror and see it surrounding me, the shrieking wind circling me like smoke. This is it. My whole body. Filling with cold dark. Ears, eyes, mouth that's apparently screaming though I can't hear the sound. I can only hear their three-pronged voice in my skull. Low and steady as fire under Judy's happy roar and the storm, which are one song. *The wheel, the wheel, Ms. Fitch. Always turning. Coming back around.* In the mirror, I see the smoke wrap itself around and around my throat. I see the flowers in my hair light up like tiny embers. Blooming flames encircle my head. I close my eyes and I'm nothing. Everything screaming. Every cell a roaring black.

And then.

Wind stills.

Thunder quiets.

Rain stops.

I hear the music switch. Judy isn't roaring about getting happy anymore. She's singing softly again about shadows. Like she never stopped. Just the sad, familiar swell of strings filling the air. It's gone. Gone from me, gone from the bar. Taking the cold dark with it. And I'm still here. I open my eyes, where there are tears now. There I am in the cracked mirror, sitting in the shattered bar. No blooms of flame around my head or rope of smoke at my throat. Just my sea-straggly hair shimmering with small flowers. Just my hands around my miraculously un-spilled Scotch. And my tear-streaked face impossibly smiling. Not the brightly beaming face of the young woman from the old Playbill photo, not anymore. No more eyes like stars, no more blinding eclipse. This face shines another light. This face says I have lived, I'm alive. This face says I've known joy and pain, known them both. I'll know them both again.

The woman beside me is looking at me now. She smiles like she saw nothing at all, like she's only just now seeing me for the first time.

Something sparks at the base of my spine. A small, familiar fire. I smile at her.

She raises her golden drink to me.

I raise my Scotch with its dead flower. Only the flower doesn't look so dead anymore. Seems to be blooming now. The whole drink seems aglow with its own rosy light, a dancing shimmer of green. I recall the waves flashing around me when I stood in the sea. Those strange colors shimmering in the black water. Shimmering with god knows what. Maybe actual magic. Maybe something that saved me. Maybe just a trick of the light.

ACKNOWLEDGMENTS

To my parents, James Awad and Nina Milosevic, and to my dearest friends and readers, Rex Baker, Alexandra Dimou, Laura Sims, Chris Boucher, Emily Culliton, Teresa Carmody, Ursula Villarreal-Moura, and McCormick Templeman, for their support. Special thanks to Jess Riley, without whose friendship, faith, and genius, I would be lost.

To my brilliant editor, Marysue Rucci, for making this book better with her insights and artful suggestions. Also to my wonderful Canadian editor and publisher, the one and only Nicole Winstanley at Penguin Canada. So grateful to you both for your excellent feedback, dedication, and support of my work. To Chris White at Scribner UK, for giving *All's Well* a dream home across the pond.

To the amazing teams at Simon & Schuster and Penguin Canada: Anne Tate Pearce, Elizabeth Breeden, Zack Knoll, Brittany

Adames, Hana Park, Steve Myers, and Meredith Pal.

To my new Syracuse University colleagues, students, and friends. So much thanks to George Saunders, Mary Karr, Dana Spiotta, Jon Dee, and the amazing Dympna Callaghan for reading and for their early and generous support of me and this book. To Jeff Parker and my former MFA students at UMass Amherst for giving me a job I loved while I was writing, and a weekly drive from Boston that helped me dream.

To Julie Slavinsky at Warwick's (and to Warwick's) for keeping me in great books while I drafted this novel in La Jolla. And to Angela Sterling for the beautiful space in which to work.

To the wonderful Shakespeare productions and innovators from which I drew inspiration: Punchdrunk's *Sleep No More* in New York; Rupert Gold's 2010 film production of *Macbeth;* Alan Cumming's brilliant audio performance of his one-man *Macbeth,* and the Royal Shakespeare Company's production of *All's Well That Ends Well* directed by John Dove.

To the pubs that helped me conjure the demonic Canny Man: Canny Man's and Bennets Bar in Edinburgh, Scotland; Rockafellas in Salem, Massachusetts; and the Irish

Snug in Denver, Colorado.

To everyone at the Clegg Agency — Simon Toop, David Kambhu, and Marion Duvert — and to Brooke Ehrlich at Anonymous Content for their hard work and commitment to my books.

Endless gratitude as always to my infinitely wise agent, Bill Clegg, for being the absolute best reader and champion I could hope for.

And last but never least, thanks most of all to Ken Calhoun, to whom this book is dedicated, and without whom there would be no book.

ABOUT THE AUTHOR

Mona Awad is the author of *Bunny*, named a Best Book of 2019 by *Time, Vogue,* and the New York Public Library. It was a finalist for the New England Book Award and for a Goodreads Choice Award. Her first novel, *13 Ways of Looking at a Fat Girl,* was a finalist for the Scotiabank Giller Prize and winner of the Colorado Book Award and the Amazon.ca First Novel Award. Her writing has appeared in *Time,* the *New York Times Magazine, McSweeney's, Ploughshares,* and elsewhere. She teaches fiction in the MFA program at Syracuse University and lives in Boston.

The employees of Thorndike Press hope you have enjoyed this Large Print book. All our Thorndike, Wheeler, and Kennebec Large Print titles are designed for easy reading, and all our books are made to last. Other Thorndike Press Large Print books are available at your library, through selected bookstores, or directly from us.

For information about titles, please call:
  (800) 223-1244

or visit our website at:
  gale.com/thorndike

To share your comments, please write:
Publisher
Thorndike Press
10 Water St., Suite 310
Waterville, ME 04901